DAMNED BY DEATH
THE VAMPIRE'S HAMMER
J. K. GRUEBER

Mystic Ridge Publishing, LLC

Mysticridgepublishing.com

ISBN: 978-1-965796-08-5 (Ebook)

ISBN: 978-1-965796-09-2 (Paperback)

ISBN: 978-1-965796-10-8 (Hardcover)

Cover design by: J. K. Grueber, Bruce Sanderson, Anne Graff, Andrew Grueber, and William Grueber.

Contributing cover photo and editor: Bruce Sanderson, Sanderson-Decello Design, LLC. reproduced with permission of the curators of Chateau LaRoche, aka Loveland Castle Museum, 12025 Shore Dr., Loveland, Ohio.

Printed in the United States of America.

ANDREW

Thank you for all the support you've given me throughout this journey,
from the first PB & J sandwich you delivered to my office door to your
latest contributions to my endeavors.
You continue to inspire me with everything you do!

And...
To every adventurous spirit who has traveled beyond the boundaries of
reality through the joy of reading! Whether sprawled on a beach towel or
lounging in your favorite recliner, have a safe and wondrous journey!

ALSO BY J. K. GRUEBER

The Envy Series:
COLORS OF ENVY: A Paranormal Romance Mystery
FACES OF ENVY: A Paranormal Romance Mystery
ECHOES OF ENVY: A Paranormal Romance Mystery

The MacDade Brothers Mysteries:
EXPOSED IN SHADOWS: He Who Plays.
A Paranormal Mystery Rekindling Lost Love
EXPOSED In The CROSSHAIRS: He Who Rides
A MacDade Brothers Paranormal Mystery
EXPOSED By The RIVERSIDE: He Who Lives
A MacDade Brothers Paranormal Mystery

The Vampire Tales:
Cursed At Conception: The Vampire's Henchman

PART ONE

CHAPTER 1

Even in daylight, the castle wore a pall of shadows, the narrow windows holding the light at bay as effectively as the winter winds that swept across the Carpathian Mountains. In darkness, the immense weathered black stone melded into the forest and purple sky; the arched slots offered little more than candle glow despite the capacity for electric within. As forbidding now as eight years earlier, Darius Brock suffered a chill inside and out, refusing to acknowledge the torrent of emotions threatening the edges of his mind. He'd lost his life, his son, his ignorance and his innocence within these black walls, and he had no more choice now than then.

Behind his cousin, Teddy Brock, who followed the Baron Amadeus von Hendricks, Darius strode up the spiral stairs to the cathedral entrance, refusing to consider the likeness to the hotel where he'd glimpsed and gasped his last clear breath of life. Wide awake, akin to the darkness as never before, he continued through the door that one of a half dozen butlers held while bowing. Old school, by no will of their own, the castle staff adhered to the subordinate status, several of them hurrying to collect the Baron's long coat, assisting Teddy and offering Darius the same courtesy. Slipping from the wool, though he might have preferred keeping it wrapped around him a tad longer, Darius handed the coat to an elder steward, who bowed smoothly and ducked away. Already, the chauffeur and two stewards hustled in their wake, delivering their bags.

Before Darius could fully grasp the musty scents and familiar sights of the great hall, he spun and glimpsed the blurry image racing into the

Baron's outstretched arms. As the child settled on the Baron's hip, he became clearly visible. A split second passed before the wide blue eyes, as livid as a summer sky, pivoted from the embrace and shot over the Baron's wide shoulder, lancing Darius in a quick silver shine.

If not at that instant, the lad knew a second later when landing smoothly on Darius's hip. "Darius!" Raphael heaved, but something in his handsome round face carried more wisdom than joy. His full, soft lips quivered; his brow furrowed beneath a scruff of thick black curls. "I dinnae 'spect to see you so soon!"

"Nor I you, lad," Darius admitted and despite his every effort, he breathed the child's scent, the faint musty odor that never seemed clearer, more familiar. Looking into the stark blue eyes, Darius quivered a smile, an uncertainty in his mind. The scent . . . a scent of corruption, but an odd mix. The child reminded him suddenly of the sunlight he had glimpsed in the streets of Pittsburgh, the scent reflective of the snow melting on the walks and posts . . . and meadows . . . and sea air beneath a rich blue sky as brilliant as the immense eyes. Innocence! By all that was real, the scent professed innocence . . . as if it emanated from within the musty odor, escaping through a crack of the fetid armor. How was it even possible? How could a child of so many years, a damned soul, offer such a scent as this? Far more stunned, Darius drew warmth from the small arm linked over his shoulder, the hand clasping his neck for balance. Beautiful, the boy truly was beautiful and, as if to enhance the essence of his innocence, he lifted his free hand, a delicate ivory hand, and nibbled his index fingernail under his quivering lips. A nervous habit which Darius had seen dozens of times in the past. The dark lashes dipped shyly, but the eyes held firm, speculating and calculating.

In every instant, Darius gleaned the Baron watching this exchange inside and out, and there was no point in attempting to deceive this night child. "Lad, we'll need to talk," Darius said quietly.

"No," the boy stated. In a single motion, he withdrew his hand and slid from Darius's arms, hitting the floor without a sound. Neck wrenched to lift his too perceptive, piercing eyes, Raphael decided, "I dinnae want to speak with you, Darius." Arrogantly, despite his slight size, he spun and tilted his gaze to his father. Pools of water swam over the blue eyes, the lips quivered more on the verge of tears. "You, Pappa? You've done this to him? Boot I doon't know why. Why did you dooo sooch a thing?"

"Mind, lad," Amad said smoothly. "You'll note, he's no worse for the wear. Alive, too, I should think you'd notice."

"How loong, Pappa? How long before you take what's left of him and leave his carcass to the wolves in the hills?"

"Raphael," Darius said and reached, touching the boy's shoulder. The child danced away and spun his angry gaze skyward as Darius continued, "I don't think there was a choice, lad. There are things you don't understand. Things I couldn't explain—"

"Aye, and if ye believe that you're a damned fool, Darius," the boy said gravely. "Oh, and I see it clearly, so I do. Tis more than a bit of me father in me, you'll notice if you're not tae blind already to notice."

"Oh, I notice, lad. Especially with your temper showing," Darius commented, if only to prove that he still held something of himself inside.

"Darius, m'friend," Raphael spoke in a descending tone, the sadness spilling across his youthful face like clouds pouring over a clear sky. "You know the loss, m'friend, but ye'll never know the lie. Oh, ye'll wrestle with it, as you are now, believing there was nae choice besides this end, but let me ask you, lad . . . are ye safe here, now? In the keep. With not a scratch to show for the hell ye've endured?"

In a heartbeat flash, Darius knew what the child meant to show him—what he'd feared to realize for himself. The Baron could have spared him the change and dealt with the madness in Pittsburgh with no help from him. In slow motion, Darius lifted his gaze and found the dark glitter in the far more menacing blue eyes. "What mistake did I make to pay this price?" he asked simply and suffered the amusement at the edges of his mind. "Why?"

"Do you expect an answer, truly, son?" Amad asked in a beguiling tone.

Raphael sidled closer to Darius then, clasping his hand and tugging. His free hand lifted again to nip his index fingernail between his teeth. "Dinnae be mad a me, Darius," he uttered. "Perhaps, I don't know—joost what my pappa wants me tae know. Tis moore the lie I fed you. C'mon then."

Darius held firm against the gentle tug, more intent on the Baron's gaze. Jenna. If nothing else at this moment, he knew he'd paid the ultimate price for loving Jenna Windrow . . . and even that was a lie. No choice and none needed. This end had hovered at the fringe of his existence for the past eight hellish years.

Whether he heard the footsteps or merely reacted to an accumulation of senses, Darius listed his gaze. The Baroness and another young cousin strode from an arch across the great hall. Dark and brooding, the entire manse composed of narrow passages and high arches, pillars and cur-tained walls or entries. Bronze sconces, some still sporting the original oil lamp fixtures, stood at opposing points in the room. Overhead, a gas chandelier offered an economy of light with an even mix of ruby and clear-colored crystals to disorient the natural eye. He suffered no distor-tion now, if he ever had. Brian still appeared as fierce and headstrong, as hot-tempered as ever, with his pale blue eyes darting and lips lined in a curve to suggest a wry sense of humor. Bookends, the Baron had called Brian and Teddy, and Darius had recognized the concept even then. Nearly the same age, born of different fathers and different mothers, the pair complimented each other more like brothers than second or third cousins. Where Teddy wore the softness and effeminacy of his nature, Brian boasted the hardy physique and macho arrogance of his preferences.

From the onset, Darius had failed to warm to this hot-blooded cousin. The lad had struck him as a bully at the onset, a condition which set his arrogance on the rise, and nothing had changed with the years. To Brian, Darius nodded cordially.

The Baroness ignored Darius entirely, other than to glance at Raphael with a gray, undoubtedly disapproving glance. Gray, an odd crystalline gray. Her eyes evoked less life than either of the anomalies to nature in their midst, and on her heavily lined face that hadn't changed in the past eight years, the lips seemed never to move. Upon a time, she might have been regal, even beautiful, but whether time or attitude had transformed her, she evoked only a shrew's persona now.

Almost in comic tolerance, the Baron accepted her proffered, spindly hand, and bowed as he brushed a kiss on the mottled taut flesh. "My dear, so good of you to make such a trek to welcome my return."

"For you, dear, anything," she said with a twisted smile. Almost as smoothly as the Baron rose, the old woman lowered her gaze and lanced Raphael. "Have you welcomed your father properly, child?"

"Aye, and it widnae be your business if I dinnae!" Raphael snapped.

Darius stifled a smile at the shrew's annoyance and, by no surprise, landed under her dead glare. "Madame Baroness," he offered and tipped his head in acknowledgment, not entirely stifling the smile until he caught the scent . . . a rotten scent. Rather like raw meat festering under a midday sun. Stifling a cough, he tilted his head further as she started toward him, and far more warily, recognized the stench emanating from her.

"Darius, I've never known you to be shy. It's good to see you, child. Come here now, let me get a good look at you—"

"Not on your life," he stated, and nearly bit his tongue with the force of the slash inside his head. Uttering a breath, he shook his head and flashed his gaze toward the Baron, who studied him indifferently. In front of him, the Baroness stopped cold. Her glare turned granite. "I uhm . . . do apologize, madame," Darius managed.

A few paces away, Brian studied him avidly. Teddy just appeared more depressed, which had changed very little over the past twenty-four hours.

If the boy's condition declined much further, he'd be dripping tears by the barrel.

Again, looking at the Baron, Darius's gaze heated. *What the hell do you expect of me here? Should I bow to this wretched hag? Or strip and bed her now in my cousin's stead? Name it! My wish is your command! I've nothing left. Why consider my moral outrage or the vulgarities of life?*

Temper, son. I've warned you once and not again, you may reap what you sow.

In a frozen instant, Darius studied the cold blue orbs and realized suddenly, he truly didn't give a damn what he reaped or sowed. Perhaps his morality had ebbed with his mortality. Of his own free will, he turned his gaze to the hag, flashed a glance at the worried child spying on him, and slipped his hand free of the soft grip. In two steps, Darius moved forward, caught the startled old shrew's bony shoulder before she recoiled, and drew her into a lover's embrace. Dropping his mouth over her parted lips, he snatched her breath in a kiss that threatened to pitch stomach acids into his throat. Her spindly fingers ceased to struggle, crawled into his hair above his shoulders and clawed him with an unnatural strength and lust for a woman of her years. If evil possessed the power to endure, this elder crone would endure for a hundred years. Before she attempted to climb his trunk, he withdrew and stepped back, leaving her breathless and stunned with lusty light ignited in the depths of her platinum eyes. Suffering to appear only amused with the anger burning behind his eyes, Darius commented, "A proper greeting for a proper lady, Madame Baroness. Do hope I haven't offended you."

Both Teddy and Brian stared from opposite sides—bookends—lips parted in disbelief.

The Baron rumbled a low idling chuckle, drawing the old woman's startled gaze. "Apparently, my lad's feeling his oats, Rebecca. I apologize if he's taken you by surprise."

Nothing left for him, nothing left but to endure and cling to every breath. His smile lingered in perfect contrast to his thoughts. Unwavering, he met the old woman's returned gaze. If the Baron forced him to endure this hag's carnal ministrations, he would oblige without a doubt . . . and likely retch daily. He retained only one recourse. To accept and survive whatever injustice or outrage the Baron commanded, and it didn't matter one way or another in his mind. His body, his mind, nothing remained at his disposal. Nothing left of him. To believe otherwise was as much a deception in his mind as to believe the Baron had changed him, destroyed him, enslaved him . . . to protect him.

Perhaps, though, perhaps, something remained inside of him . . . something festering and rising all too swiftly, like a coiled snake unfurling for a strike, and he was no stranger to this sensation. Hatred. In all its wicked essence. A bitterness lingering in the depths of his tarnished soul, collecting and boiling from these eight years of service, if not all the years of his life. He could bed this harpy, could tumble her in total degeneracy, and he would revel in his hatred and decadence. Humanity. Humanity bedamned! He was no more human than the little beast at his side or the monster holding his leash.

Under his heated shine, the old woman recoiled another step, and Darius turned his gaze to find the Baron studying him still. Inside and out. "If you'd like me to bed the bitch for your entertainment, I will, master," he offered the latter word with a sarcastic edge, less concerned than ever before at what recourse he could pay for his defiance. Life. Death. What did it matter? Human suffering, he could endure. In a half-waking sleep, he'd spent the past twenty-four hours considering his future and the lack thereof.

"Decide to defy, have you, lad?"

"Darius," Raphael intruded hesitantly, coming forward and again clasping his hand.

Darius slipped his hand free, sidling from the child, looking down at him. "You were right, and you were wrong, lad. I am not the man I was. For your safety, for your own sake, stay the fuck away from me now. I can't love you any more than your grandfather could, lad. I'd only hurt you and have no sense to feel shame or remorse, nor any regrets."

Tears gathered in the deep blue eyes, pooling and swimming on the surface, clotting the thick black lashes. "Dinnae say sooch, Darius. You are human—"

"Then you are the fool to believe that, lad. I've not been human since I first passed through these doors, only less so now. Take your tears and turn to my cousins for compassion. What remained of that wretched condition has expired."

Turning his flooding eyes to his father, the boy uttered, "Papppa . . . whyyy? Why did ye dooo this tooo himmm?"

"Come here, lad," the Baron coaxed in a soothing tone, a comforting tone the child could never ignore. Opening his arms, Amad welcomed the boy who flew to him, scampering to rest on his hip. With a hurt cry, the child buried his face at the Baron's collar and gave way to a wrenching sob.

Nothing. Darius felt nothing watching the Baron comforting the child, felt nothing as he heard the sobs. The chill had settled in his bones, wrapped through his mind, and around his heart a night past. Only indifference remained on the surface and hatred at his core. His dark eyes lifted. He met the Baron's studied gaze, feeling the eyes inside his mind. "Do you like what you see? I have the sense to wonder and yet, I don't give a damn. Is that what you wanted from me? My total submission and disregard? Fuck you, fuck your child, and fuck me. I don't give a damn. Is that the inheritance you've invested in me? The privilege, father?" he asked with a new hatred and sarcasm inflected on that wretched address.

"Kissing the harpy certainly had a wretched effect on you, son," the Baron said in mocked sympathy. "We may need to take care in whose lips you lock hereafter."

"Oh, you can find another viler creature for me to encounter, I'm sure," Darius said without effect, and spared a bemused heated glance to the stunned elder woman. "Though I'd venture, it won't be easy," he added and looked at the Baron. "Have at it, sire. Either I'll abide of my own free will or you'll force your own upon me, and either way, the result will be the same—I'll have tumbled with some wretched shrew." Anger still spiraling in his eyes, he commented, "You've left me with nothing but hatred and contempt, and it's no longer even inside of me to regret what I've lost."

Ahh, and what of your precious Jenna? the silky voice slid across his mind.

She was never mine, he answered knowingly. *A pawn in this game, the same as I have been from the onset.*

Now, and you will deny your love for her? Claim this hatred all that remains?

As you harbored your human emotions, so too will I, unless you snatch even the memories from this shell you've left me. I have loved her, and that you won't take from me without creating a different thing of me.

How sure of yourself you sound, son. An improvement, I'll mention, but . . . "Enough of this for now, my lad. We've a banquet awaiting us. Perhaps you'll be in a better humor whence you're sated."

The ability to respond verbally slipped from his control, but his mind remained active even as he nodded his assent.

CHAPTER 2

Alone for the first time since her early morning arrival, Jenna Windrow rested behind her desk in the Chateau Suites Hotel, unconsciously searching the room for something amiss. Rather than the overhead fluorescent panels in the ceiling, she'd turned on her desk lamp hours ago, and the soft light provided a warm glow that should create a comfortable ambience. Whether she would ever become comfortable within this room again remained to be seen. On the surface, everything had returned to order. A far cry from the disaster she'd encountered when arriving for work at the break of dawn. One of the hotel staff maids had cleared the clutter strewn about the room, and apparently, one of her cohorts had sorted and filed the scattered paperwork. The maintenance crew had repaired her window blind and replaced the screen. The file cabinets were neatly closed, the drawers locked. Personally, she'd repositioned her computer and arranged her knickknacks and whatnots, those to survive the intruder's rage. The room no longer looked as if a tornado had touched down and yet, the sense of violation lingered, trapped in the aether.

Something amiss, she considered while keening to the soft music from the lobby, listening to the more distant hum of traffic on the four-lane highway a half mile away. A Tuesday evening, one week before Christmas . . . and not that late. Barely half-past eight, she verified, glancing at her electric cuckoo clock. Miraculously, the clock had survived last night's blitz. She should find comfort in that detail. Most of her personal photos and wall art hadn't fared as well with the twisted frames consigned to a garbage Dumpster behind the hotel.

Her Christmas decorations had apparently met the same fate. A single bobblehead Santa perched atop her computer tower, a sad reminder of the small tree and red ribbons that had spruced up her private domain. Apparently, the intruder secreted a despise for Christmas décor, which could encompass a wide range of suspects in the von Hendricks corporation.

Atheists, the lot of them, and no one had bothered to mention that detail before Jenna had decked the halls from the front gates to the tower peaks.

Unconsciously, she touched her lip, rubbing a twitch, and flinched at the spark of fire. For a little while, she'd successfully ignored the lingering aches and pains, the result of a truly restless night. And horses fly. The condition of her bedroom, from tangled sheets to her brass bedside lamp lying across her pillow, spoke volumes about the intensity of last night's nightmares. She almost feared going to bed this evening, which might account for her present stasis. The break in—or break out, as the federal agents had decreed—was merely the icing on the cake. And at the thought, her muscles gripped, tension hiked.

A dream, a wicked dream, the likes of which she'd not experienced since childhood. She'd awoken in a mad scramble, heart racing, breath heaving, sweat dripping from her pores . . . and blood dripping from a corner of her lip. Assessing her physical ruin in the waking moments hadn't offered comfort, especially not while suffering lingering nightmare images of fighting for her life. Even now, fingering her puffy lip—compliments of a knocking her lamp nearly on her head—she suffered flashing images of a monster and shuddered despite the heater vents blowing hot air over her shoulder.

Lisa Blythe. If not much else came clear about this latest bout of night terrors, the monster's resemblance to her rival remained front and center. A monster, yes. Lisa, with her wild mass of neon hair to the cat's slant of her pale blue eyes enhanced with a string of painted black eyeliner, had featured in the night terror, but twisted. Rather than her pale, slender cheeks and pixie nose, her features had distorted to sharp, knife-like cheekbones and jaw. A feral shine had glowed below her horsehair-thick lashes and jutting brow. The sense of fear and disbelief lingered, compounded by the realistic ambience of the dreamscape. Hazy, now, she remembered spying Lisa through the peephole in her apartment door, and like all nightmares, in the next instant, Lisa had stood inside her apartment, already chiding and hissing taunting jibes. . .

Brow crinkling, Jenna stared blindly at the clock, her thoughts turned inward to remember Blythe accusing Jenna of sleeping with Darius to keep her job, The dream had begun like that. All normal and realistic since Blythe had admitted to trying—and apparently failing—to bed Darius for job security or advancement. With a memory of Lisa's bright, skimpy red dress at the Christmas—end-of-year PR—banquet, Jenna believed the words. In the six months Jenna had worked at the Chateau, she'd never seen Lisa appear more naturally dressed than at that banquet. With her tiny waist and oversized boobs in a living rendition of Barbie, she'd filled, and overfilled, the miniskirt and low V-neck sequins. On duty, Lisa dressed conservative, although she kept her options open, often loosening blouse buttons and letting her hair down if a wealthy, male guest arrived in need of a room and company.

The first time Jenna had caught Lisa slipping from a guest's room, she'd spoken with Mason. In his usual woebegone demeanor, he'd assured her, she couldn't possibly have read the situation correctly. All on the up and up. 'Maybe she was delivering fresh towels,' he'd said woefully.

That probably should have provided the first inkling of things amiss in the Chateau Suites.

"Damn it," she muttered, focusing on the cuckoo's hands to realize another ten minutes had passed. She needed to leave, but somehow, even the thought of returning to her apartment niggled at the edges of her mind, prickling her scalp.

Whether the threat of waking to another night terror or a thought of spending the evening alone distressed her more, she couldn't decide.

Darius was gone. Probably halfway around the world—or a quarter way, by now. Likely asleep in his bed. He kept a flat in London , , ,

But another segment of the night's terrors blasted to the foreground. Darius Brock. The man of her dreams . . . Lifelike, his image blasted into her mind, snatching her breath. Sprawled, lying in a scattered heap within the livid glow of lamplight, he wore the same black jeans and shirt minus the charcoal sweater he'd worn when she last saw him. Twisted, this nightmare to believe Darois lying on the familiar oriental design of the carpet in suite 606. Splattered on the floor, lean handsome face turned pale in the light . . .

Too closely, he'd resembled Lawrence Fradden and that image, though the thing of nightmares, remained too real. Fradden, a New York native from the von Hendricks Distribution Center, who'd attended the banquet . . . Deflated and twisted, Fradden had slumped in an armchair in suite 610, two rooms from suite 606, the rooms Darius occupied on the sixth floor. Shuddering, Jenna clasped her arms against the chill, the same chill to steel over her when she'd stood inside Fradden's suite three days past. She hadn't seen Fradden die, doubted her imagination could conjure that event . . . But in livid color, she'd recognized the luxurious colorful carpet, watched Darius's long, jean-covered legs twisted, kicking in death throes. One bare arm reached, stretched into the shadows above him as if besieging God, seeking salvation. As if poised within a spotlight while everything around him remained a dark blur, his handsome face sagged, his complexion turned gray in contrast to his dark mustache. His mahogany hair, appearing windblown, scattered across his pale, intelligent brow and his deep brown eyes stared blindly from beneath thick black lashes . . .

Jenna jolted with the panic, the memory terror, and reached for the phone. On dual planes, she grasped the receiver and realized the futility. Halted, she stared at the phone as if she might will it to ring . . . and suffered the memory flash of lifting her home phone, hearing his voice. In that second dream to counter the first, she'd spoken to him, verified him living and breathing, believed even now that she'd heard his voice, knew the relief . . . and the thrill of his invitation to travel with him.

She would have gone with him and in her dream, she'd agreed to join him. She would have abandoned her post as second in command at the Chateau Suites, would have left her family and friends regardless of their Christmas plans or their disappointment. To spend even a few more days with him, she would have forsaken all else . . . if he'd only asked.

Maudlin, she slumped in the rich leather chair, her gaze listing as she swiveled to gaze at the cuckoo clock, reading, registering the time. 8:45. By now, his plane had surely touched down in England. He could be sound asleep in his bed . . . He'd been so blasted bone-weary from the moment he'd arrived Friday evening, and the rat race over those three lousy days hadn't helped.

A day off. A single day off to do with what he pleased, and he'd chosen to spend every moment with her.

Far more welcome than that wicked memory, Jenna replayed the moments when they'd laughed over sausage sandwiches and cola in a small cafe on the Eastside, meandered through Carnegie Museum and debated the customs of the Renaissance period. Molded like a granite sculpture against the chilly wind, they'd stood on Mount Washington and watched the colors fade across the sky, the city lights igniting on the triangle of three rivers below.

Even now, she felt the warmth of his long coat wrapped around her, registered the beat of his heart at her back as she tried not to think about the coming moments, the day's end drawing near. Not a lifetime. At the very onset, he'd set that detail in stone. A single day to share memories to last a lifetime.

Unbidden, tears gathered in her eyes, and she muttered a curse, picking herself up from the slump. No promises between them other than the simple vow never to forget, and she hadn't needed to voice that promise aloud. She would likely forget her own name before ever forgetting Darius Brock.

Pushing off her chair, feeling far older than her 27 years, Jenna barely spared another glance over her office before collecting her coat and purse from the slight closet near the door. Sooner or later, she needed to face her fears—and the loneliness. Life must go on.

"Rebecca, my profound apologies," the Baron said as he flagged his free hand, keeping his son on his hip. "It's been a long journey and my young associate's been under a great deal of stress."

Taking Brian's arm as she turned, starting across the hall, she commented, "You've changed him, Amad."

"A slight adjustment, I'll admit."

"I'd imagine it was necessary," the Baroness spoke indifferently, as if discussing nothing more than a business transaction.

They were moving. Darius fell into the procession a pace behind his mortified cousin, who trailed after the Baron. Like sheep following a shepherd's staff, they crossed the hall and passed into one of the slightly wider, no-less-shadowy halls. Oil paintings, some probably lost hundreds of years ago, hung on these walls. The subdued light presented the images in perfect stasis of dark, brooding hues and swirled strokes. By the gilt frames alone, the oils reminded him of the moments in a museum, and something of his anger ebbed with a glimmer of a soft smile, a warm laugh, a spark of mischief in deep blue pools.

"I can't say that I'm surprised to see him here," the quaking voice continued. "I wondered if he had some bearing on your sudden trip to America. Do hope you arrived in time to salvage whatever damage he's apparently done."

"Do you doubt, Rebecca?" the deep voice played.

She laughed, a grating sound nearly lost entirely as she passed through an entrance alongside the Baron. "Suppose that was a foolish comment. I should ask more appropriately, how much have we gained with this turn?"

"A singular gain, I'm not ashamed to admit, my dear," Amad said loftily. "Some commodities cannot be weighed in silver and gold."

"So true," the shrew sighed, continuing toward the far end of the long banquet table.

Darius glimpsed the hand gesture and glance, but neither were necessary to direct him into the left-hand seat at the Baron's head of the table. Predating even the Baron, the heavy carved oak shined with a patina to effect glass. More than a dozen tall chairs with intricate carved backs and crowned end posts stood at attention around the platform. In massive chests and armoires against the walls, the silverware and porcelain rested in safe storage, and toward those chests, two stout young women hustled. The Baron liked his staff hardy, kept them all fatted like calves to be slaughtered . . . or cows to be milked.

Preoccupied, Darius rested in silent repose, but even across the distance, he sensed Brian's keen interest, his darting eyes. No kinship existed with this boy, and in Darius's mind this lad, too, was a boy though he'd lost the youthful smoothness of his teenage years. To each his own purpose, Darius considered. He'd understood that concept years ago. Young, virile, a budding Casanova at seventeen already well on his way to becoming the man of every woman's dreams. Brian was the alpha to Teddy's omega, the yin to the yang. Had the Baron chosen him to fulfill the role Darius had played in this madness, the boy would have accepted the offer with gusto and enthusiasm. Instead of a hundred women, Brian was condemned to please only one, and for that, in his human condition, Brian still believed Darius had robbed him of his rightful position.

Perhaps, now, the contempt would ebb, though Darius couldn't care less. In his enhanced or twisted nature, he sensed the boy speculating on the consequence of this transition.

Brian wondered if, alas, he would rise to his proper place and circle the globe to engender new life into their dying clan. He saw himself risen to greatness and, by his arrogance, condemned himself long ago with his visions of grandeur. Clinging to that macho image of himself, most assuredly prompted the Baron to destroy him at every turn.

Darius wondered what the boy thought in the dead of night after he fulfilled his obligations to the hag. How often did the lad wet himself in fear or lie awake and tremble as night brought its torment and monsters from the dark? Or did he truly survive by pining for the position Darius had held? Did those dreams sustain him when fear threatened to sink him into madness?

The twelve . . . or thirteen, if one included George Halbrook, who shuffled to the far end of the table, crawling from some crack in the wall to join the banquet feast and partake.

CHAPTER 3

They all maintained their place, their purpose. Darius wondered even now what new post he would fill and what torture the Baron would force him to endure. The Baron hadn't said, hadn't once alluded to what this new status would involve . . . but did it matter at all? He was dead and in a class of his own, no longer even one of the four sole survivors of that fateful night. Nor entirely one of the fallen who'd departed the castle and continued with their lives, oblivious of their sacrifices.

The kinship with his clan to sustain him for these several years . . . that too, was missing, now. Only contempt and hatred lingered, spawned anew as he found his mobility to watch the mottled old man cowering into a chair near the shrew. They were a pair. A match made in hell. The silver-haired spinster with her high, prominent gaunt cheeks and lifeless eyes, the balding academic with his rotund cheeks and liquid orbs. In an odd epiphany, Darius considered wringing life from either neck. They were human. George less so, but they both retained something of human occupancy. He could smell it in them, their corruption a flavor more vivid than the aromas from the kitchen.

Rebecca was evil, a daughter born of the Baron's lines. The taint thrived quick in her spindly limbs and veins, if not entirely in her black soul. She'd dwelt in this manse most of her natural life, a tyrannical shrew to keep the home fires burning for the monster who'd posed as her father, then uncle, then grandfather. She'd known the monster as long as her brother, Thaddeus, a lad who'd accepted all the riches and titles the Baron had bestowed on him, in exchange for only two things. Silence and obedience. The Baron was too clever to demand loyalty from his heirs. Darius knew well, neither living heir could be loyal. They were heartless creatures without the integrity to vow loyalty to any man or beast, only to themselves, their lust and greed.

Halbrook's corruption carried a unique flavor, but no less vile or offensive to Darius's keen senses. This wretched, portly chap with his soulful rheumy eyes remained a study in dereliction. Behind his injured posture, his pitiful sham, lived the guile of a self-serving beast. Darius had sensed it years ago when he'd stood in the hall. Separate and apart from the twelve, this aging academic had portrayed sorrow for luring them into that nightmare. A liar knows his own scent. Darius had survived behind his lies too long to be fooled by another of his own ilk. The bastard had stolen Dylan, would have sacrificed a five-year-old to save himself. Behind the dolt's posture of piety, he'd worn the attitude of a true disciple. Even Kevin had been duped to pity that nervous little man as he'd delivered the scrolls into their hands in the holding room. Brainwashed by years of higher education, Kevin had trusted his fellow academic. A damned fool. Darius had sensed the man's nature at a gut level . . . And would have killed him later that day, not fooled by the flood of tears. If that bastard had a heart, he would never have delivered Dylan on a silver platter.

Even now, the man proposed to be nervous and sorrowful, hanging his bald pate, darting his watery eyes behind thick glasses . . . His focus caught on Darius. His eyes widened slightly, affecting surprise when he might have expected no less than to find Darius here. This chap was the Baron's greatest source of entertainment, a learned man, a convert, a true disciple to whatever doctrine Amad proposed. The bastard had traded his soul merely to keep himself alive. In him, the taking was an afterthought, no doubt . . . a mistake, Darius remembered abruptly. Raphael had bitten the bastard at this very table, an act of defiance after the Baron had attempted to make Halbrook the lad's tutor.

What would that be like? Darius speculated as he held the rheumy gaze across the long distance, not distracted by the silver platters arriving at either end of the table. What would it be like to drink this bastard's blood and taste the obscene flavors of his life?

A shiver slid down Darius's spine, but he wasn't certain of its cause. Anticipation? Or fear that he might yet experience that wicked thought in all its darkness? To drink of human blood . . . if ever one existed to stir that thought, the more wary chap hunkering deeper in the chair was just such a lad. Darius could feel his senses quickening, aroused by either his thought or the more natural scents lifting from the silver servers. At the edges of his reeling mind, the presence observed him, no more distracting than the meal sliding in front of him. Like a large cat pinning a bird, Darius held the old man's widening eyes, his own as chilled and dark as his heart, his smile as beguiling as ever the Baron's had been. Just a quick bite, two tiny holes, a taste of this bastard's blood in retribution—

Enough.

The word slammed inside Darius's mind like a hammer striking hot oil. Flinching with the physical pain, he turned his gaze. The Baron studied him with a bemused smirk. *You lied to me about that too,* Darius realized as he recovered sense to know where his thoughts had led. *I won't be satisfied with nearly raw meat or warm juices dripping from a heated lamb. The hunger you mentioned won't be sated through ordinary means.*

Sadly, m'lad, you need live with those throes of depravation and starvation. You won't drink from Halbrook or any other in my keep. Let your hatred ascend whence it will. The Baron smiled more deeply, inside and out. *Passion in all its purity, an emotion so grand as to bring chaos to order, calamity to serenity. Ah, and I do enjoy you, Darius. Have from the onset, truth be told. You are a man of uncommon spirit.*

I'm not a man. I'm now the monster you created.

The Baron's eyes sparked fire and mischief, darting down the table to where Halbrook rested quaking in his huddled pose. "You've good reason to worry, George. M'young lad would like nothing better than to drink your blood and have his revenge for the injustices you wrought against his son. A pity, but you'll need steer clear of my charge lest he break the chains I put upon him."

At the far end of the table, Halbrook's lips parted, his rheumy eyes catching the light from the overhead crystals of three chandeliers, shining like glass. "No-oo, surely this can't be, Darius . . . You've an occupation—"

"We can't all be loyal disciples like yourself, George," Darius said drolly, sighing in disgust. "Some of us truly despise this lot you cast for us. In fact, you might say, some of us would have preferred death to the life you've had us lead. Your days are numbered, chap. If ever the chains snap, you're a dead man. Mark my words, if I live long enough, I'll shore the flab from your bones and lap what's left of you before it sinks through the cracks and returns unto hell."

In the stopped, stunned silence, George gaped. Teddy dropped his blond head in a deeper bow. Rebecca's thin lips twisted into a curious, wary smile. Brian stared and kept his mouth shut as his mind ran wild with the confirmation of this dialogue. Directly across from Darius, seated like a proper little gentleman wearing a dinner jacket of a lively color, Raphael merely gazed across the table with sad speculation in his ancient blue eyes.

The Baron broke the stillness with a low chuckle. "Son," he said in a tempered, still vibrating voice, drawing Darius's gaze. Devilment danced in the cobalt eyes. "We definitely need to review your table manners and people skills. These fits of fancy over dinner will truly not bode well in a boardroom or over cocktails."

"You don't believe I'm still the fool, master," Darius said in a mocked humble tone. "You'll find another to fill the position I've held. At least in the public realm. I could no more fulfill those obligations now than I could walk into the noonday sun. Or maybe I could," he said without missing a beat. "But neither the oracles nor decisions would be those of Darius Brock. Use this husk as you will, *Father*," he said with bitter emphasis. "But don't expect me to be disillusioned further by whatever course you steer for me. I'll play with George and revel in my effect, but I'm not a fool. I know the impotency of my threat. The bastard's as safe in your keep now as he ever was."

"We'll see then, won't we?"

"Predilection based on hindsight," Darius spoke in a lower voice. "If I couldn't break the chains in love, I won't break them in hate. If my threat bears fruit, it will be at your command and toward your desire, not by my design. Bluntly, if you want him dead, I'd see to it with raging enthusiasm and therein lies the bastard's safety. Never would you allow me such a wild pleasure as I imagine those moments would be. Senseless slaughter . . . that's not your way. If you ever need your day spiced, you'll grant me that uncommon pleasure." A smile curved into his mustached lips; his heated glance fleeted toward the more terrified man and back, amused, "At least that's something to look forward to. For such hope, I should be overjoyed, eh?"

Far more darkly amused, the Baron flicked his hand, gesturing to the dripping steak which rested on the plate in front of Darius. "Partake, lad. You've spiced the meal aplenty for the moment."

In a courtly nod, Darius turned his attention to the thick slab, slicing and dicing with the flair of a gourmet chef. In proper manners, the linen napkin draped his lap, and he handled the utensils with practiced aplomb. If Teddy even noticed Darius's skill, the boy failed to acknowledge or appreciate the talent. Across the table, seated next in line to Raphael, the boy ate in dreary silence. His young cousin would rather see him dead than see him at all now. A pity, that. Even if the lad had the balls to attempt murder, Darius would no longer accept that end.

Far more warily, however, Darius glimpsed the child directly across from him, not fooled by the innocence or sadness on the cherub face, resting in a bow. The little devil might yet make the attempt, but unless the Baron sanctioned that end, the boy would fail. In nearly two hundred years, unless the little devil lied, he'd never found heart or soul to fully take a human life. Darius doubted himself to become the exception. With his new perspective, he understood how easily the child could deceive himself into breaking that promise, and in a moment of greater clarity, Darius knew for the boy's own sake he should break that promise.

With the conversations stifled entirely around the long table and the human fare delivered, the Baron brought his meal to the table. Without reservations, he sat the plump maid on his lap and set her to cleaning his plate as he nipped her shoulder. Raphael refused the similar fare, waving the second maid away and continued staring toward the floor past his father as the stout woman nibbled from his plate.

"Raphael," the Baron sighed while unseating the maid, waving her away. "I'm no more fond of your brooding and stubbornness now than ever before. If you have a complaint, have out with it, lad, or do not annoy me by rejecting your dinner again."

"I could survive twenty years without a meal, and you're knowing sooch, pappa," the boy growled with a stubborn edge, his eyes lifting with a shine of anger. "If I dinnae want to dine on that fat cow, then there it is, then, I willnae."

"A trifle mad at me, are you?" the Baron feigned sorrow.

"Aye, and that covers it, then," the boy agreed boldly.

Without fully grasping his actions, Darius rose from the table, waking to the internal tug and the intentions, merging the decision with his will and striding more freely around the table. Anger spilled across his mind as he tugged his shirt and sweater sleeve off his wrist to his forearm. With a heated shine in his eyes, he looked down at the wide startled eyes even as he stopped alongside the child's chair and offered his arm into the boy's striking range.

Wariness crept over the blue orbs; a thin sheen of tears rose under the thick lashes. He shook his head slowly, barely moving the tussled curls at his knitted brow and collar. "No, Darius. I willnae dine froom you either."

"Have at it, l'il, chap," Darius coaxed snidely. "You can't hurt me, and I believe that's what your father wants you to understand."

The blue eyes turned, far more glittering with the moisture. "Dinnae make me, father. I'm seeing him clearly. I dinnae need further proof of his damnation."

"Ah, m'lad," the Baron said sadly. "This wouldn't be the first time he's fed you. Go on, then, have a taste of all those wondrous scents you've so enjoyed. A bit tainted, now, I'll grant, but you may be pleasantly surprised."

"I willnae do it!" he snapped, and in one swift motion, spun off the opposite side of his chair, snaking past the maid and darting nearly to the other end of the table. Without pause, he swept under George's arm and pivoted, snapping his teeth into the fat palm. Belatedly, George gasped a cry and tried pulling away, but the boy was like a dog with a bone, merely wrenching his neck with a snarling sound and sinking his fangs deeper. Across the distance, his eyes glowed red and feral, darting over the appendage to lance both Darius and the Baron as he continued to feed. George had frozen, his eyes glazed and staring in silent repose at the tussled black curls.

Retribution, Darius realized, and nearly suffered a smile at the child's unruly temper, more intent on the Baron's mild conflict of annoyance and amusement at the edges of his mind. In mocked disapproval, the father watched the son.

In slow motion, the cobalt gaze lifted, and the lips snarled in a smile. "Appears you've been rejected, Darius. He prefers his governor over his brother . . . and a pity that, as I've decided, you will fill both roles in his life." The Baron paused, glancing toward the other end of the table before continuing with a more contemptuous smile. "You're an educated man, and you're more than capable of adhering to his schedule. Hence, lad, I'm placing my little lad in your charge. You may need to consult your cousins to grasp the routine. Specifically," he paused, if only for effect. "Your cousin and colleague, George, as the chap's had the most experience."

"I've ventured a tad closer to hell with this turn," Darius mused, glimpsing the boy sliding from under the limp arm. George had sunk deeper into the chair, his eyes fluttered, dazed; he collected his hand to cradle against his bulging stomach. Raphael sauntered forward, hands tucked in his pockets, his eyes glittering with the challenge.

The Baron glanced between them, entirely enjoying himself as it would appear. On his child, he settled a dead glare and spoke smoothly, "Hence forward, as you've so chosen, son, your governor will provide for you. Obey him, as you would me, and do not annoy me with any further stubbornness or childish temper. You've wanted him here. He is now, here. Let us see if he's as kind to you now as you were to his creation for all these years, shall we?"

"You're a cruel one, Pappa," the child said drearily and shook his head in sad repose, a near desperate abandon haunting the deep blue pools. Lifting his gaze to Darius, he slid his hand upward and captured Darius's palm. "C'mon then, goov'nor. I'll show ye to your quarters."

Before Darius took a step, the Baron reached and clasped the boy's shoulder, halting them both. In a low, dark tone, the Baron stated smoothly, "If you refuse to take from the father as you have the son, lad, I shan't be kind to either of you. Bear that in mind before you choose to defy me."

"Aye, father, I'll bear it in mind, ye can rest assured," the boy stated grimly.

CHAPTER 4

B y no surprise, the two federal agents, Reichley and Miller, waited outside the office door in the executive wing of the Chateau. In unison, they came to attention as Jenna pulled the door closed and engaged the lock. Not that their presence would do any good. They'd been with her this morning, when she'd discovered the break-in.

If, as the authorities believed, Lisa Blythe was responsible for Fradden's death, along with the assault on Jenna's office, the psychotic young woman wouldn't likely return to the scene of the crime. And if she did, a single lock wouldn't thwart her. Lisa Blythe, after all, carried a master set of keys to access any room in the Chateau, including room 610 which allegedly added weight to the Bureau's belief.

If nothing of the past dozen daylight hours remained clear, Jenna wouldn't likely forget Rita tracking her down in the hallway to share the breaking news on the noon broadcast. According to the report—which even Mason had failed to mention—Lisa Blythe, an assistant manager at the hotel for ten years, had become the prime suspect in the murder of Lawrence Fradden, a New York businessman. And Jenna could believe at least part of that scenario. With the woman's history of climbing the corporate ladder one bed at a time, she could have tapped on the mid-aged executive's door to gain access, wouldn't even have needed to engage her master key. Married or not, Fradden, wouldn't have rejected Lisa's offer. Jenna had encountered him only once, during the banquet, when the fellow had intruded on the dance floor. She hadn't known Darius for more than two hours, but she'd read the annoyance to light his handsome dark eyes as he'd stepped aside to address whatever problem Fradden had deemed of utmost importance. Under Darius's harsh reprisal, the fellow had appeared to shrink and back off, but those moments, apparently witnessed by a dozen others, had made Darius the prime suspect, however briefly. Lisa was a more viable suspect in Jenna's opinion, although watching Darius back the New Yorker against the wall, Jenna had suffered a chill . . . and a little thrill, if she were honest.

The Henchman.

Darius hadn't gained that nickname by kowtowing to any man, let alone a fellow who'd looked like a mafia thug while demanding Darius's immediate attention. Whatever Darius had said to him had sent him stalking—hurriedly—from the room. Fully composed, Darius had returned to her seeking a dance . . . and she'd declined. He'd looked so blasted tired. More exhausted than angry or disturbed by whatever Fradden had told him.

Glancing between the agents, both of whom hid their boredom behind stoic expressions, Jenna commented, "I could use a lift home."

"Whenever you're ready, ma'am."

She was past ready, but kept the thought to herself as she followed the older agent, Reichley, with Miller on her heels. Emerging from the administration wing, Jenna spotted Evan Trevane lounging in the lobby. With the influx of reporters and officials, not to mention irate guests, the PR man from the Pittsburgh branch office of the von Hendrick's corporation, had kept busy. Still, he appeared no worse for the wear. Blond waves slicked off his brow, tie loosened but not removed, and top button freed, he posed as the epitome of nonchalance. Ready-made, the smile slid into his light-colored mustache as he rose from the chair near the crackling hearth and appraised her in a glance. His hundred-watt smile dimmed.

She'd only met Evan on Friday—about five minutes before meeting Darius—and the latter thought stifled her attempted smile. If not for that blasted party, she wouldn't have caught the henchman's eye or interest when he'd acknowledged the abundance of Christmas décor. She never would have fallen for his overwhelming sadness . . . Damn it. The damage was done and aside from Fradden's demise, Jenna wouldn't change a moment of that evening. All things considered, the party had been a roaring success, although Mason, if no others, could have warned her of agnostics in the upper echelon.

Evan had enlightened her right after complimenting her on the stunning festive décor.

Preoccupied, Jenna continued toward the glass doors, offhandedly flagging a wave and weary smile toward Rene, the young registration attendant. The past several days had taken a toll on all of them, but if Rene even responded, Jenna missed the moment. Startled, she stopped when Evan intercepted Miller, halting their slight procession. Tossing his coat on the back of the nearest velvet chair, one of a dozen in the parlor setting of the lobby, he reached for Jenna's coat. "Allow me, honey . . ."

How Evan convinced her to accept his company, Jenna couldn't decide. 'Chinese takeout,' he'd suggested and included the agents in his offer to pick up dinner. Sitting in the backseat of the agent's dark sedan, Jenna considered the whirlwind to encompass these von Hendricks employees. Masters of manipulation, the lot of them. But maybe having company for a little while wouldn't be such a bad thing, not when the loneliness and lingering fears threatened the edges of her mind.

Lisa Blythe . . . Somewhere in the chilly darkness, Lisa hid, waiting, plotting . . . and that nightmare . . .? Jenna couldn't shake the feeling of foreboding, or the sense of danger. Even in her office and traveling through the hotel throughout the day, she'd suffered wicked moments of ill omen, and a sense of something, someone hovering just over the horizon.

As a child, she'd suffered night terrors, and too often, bad things followed from earthquakes in California to wildfires in Florida, and many an odd thing in between. She hadn't foreseen Fradden's demise, but then, she hadn't suffered a serious terror in years . . . not since her best friend lost her parents in a car crash at the age of sixteen. She'd woken sobbing, she remembered, great wrenching sobs of grief as wicked images had sailed through her mind. And that seemed only the beginning. Crashes . . . house fires . . . mass shooting and bombings . . . for nearly two years after Lonnie's parents died, Jenna continued to wake sweating, screaming, and seeing monsters as if a living, breathing entity stood behind those violent deaths. Even now, she couldn't be certain how she'd shut those visions down, locked them away. For her sanity, she'd found the means to shut off those visions . . .

And if last night was any indication, she might need to find the means again. She certainly couldn't afford to share her fears or admit a sense of premonition. She truly hadn't seen Fradden's demise . . . but somehow, that fellow's death had cracked open the vault to her wicked gifts.

Too lost in thought, Jenna glimpsed the Terrace Apartment entrance, wishing suddenly she'd stood against Evan's persuasion. She wanted nothing more at this moment than to run a hot bath and soak in scented salts to lift the day's dirt and pain away. But nearly at the same time, she suffered an internal chill. Something bad. As if a clock ticked, counting down at the fringe of her mind, her muscles gripped, her hair follicles lifted.

Too much, too damn much thinking, worrying, fearing for her life, Darius's life. If she wasn't shivering with the willies, she'd be more alarmed . . . and she was alarmed enough.

Neither agent had intruded on her silent commiseration throughout the short drive, but then, they probably weren't thrilled to pull babysitting duty. If she were in their shoes, she might hope for an encounter with a mania if only to spice up their evening.

Damn it. She should have rejected Evan's offer. She could have accepted the agents' escort then sent them on their merry way. After all, the Terrace boasted a half decent security system . . . which hadn't stopped Darius from arriving on her door undeterred, and undetected by the agents currently stepping from the front seat.

Resigning to both her escorts and the ensuing company, Jenna slid from the back seat at her apartment entrance, and strode between the agents to the brightly lighted cove. Only by luck, she'd found this apartment close to the Chateau, but she might have preferred a duplex and fewer neighbors.

Maybe less highway noise. As she punched the code at the door panel, she became starkly aware of the distant engine sounds, keen to the stillness of the parking lot. With the abundance of vapor lights, the lot glowed as bright as daylight, with enough unmarred snow under the scattered tree bows to create a white glow. For a moment, she appreciated the winter wonderland ambience, halfheartedly thinking of her family and Christmas, and hoping this sense of ill omen passed soon. The party, that damned party, was supposed to be her last big event. She'd planned to spend the week with her family for the first time in several years. No fighting O'Hara traffic to catch a plane, no airport craziness . . . she'd simply pack the presents in her Lincoln and drive the ten miles to her parents' homestead and arrive in time for breakfast. She planned to help her mother dress the turkey and peel potatoes.

A chill stole over her as she stepped into the receiving room and veered toward the bank of mail slots.

Automated, she unlocked her box and extracted a short stack of colorful envelopes. Distracted, she identified the cards, halfheartedly thinking maybe this evening, she'd try writing out the Christmas cards awaiting her on her kitchen counter. Fleeting, an image of her cards sailing off the counter stifled her step. Had she sent those cards flying? Damn it. If she postponed writing and addressing those cards much longer, she might as well write 'Happy 1998' instead of 1997.

If either agent questioned her slightly cynical smile, neither commented as she jabbed the codes alongside the second set of glass doors to access the apartments.

Halfway to the elevator across the connecting hall, she glanced habitually at the next door, and the discrepancy registered. Just one more change. As regular as an eight-day-clock, her neighbor and not-so-secret admirer, Matt Cord, timed his arrivals and departures to coincide with her own and she hadn't seen him since Sunday afternoon. Not since Darius had picked her up in his limousine. Matt was probably heartbroken, or worse, too intimidated or insecure to make an appearance.

Uncomfortable suddenly, irritated by the absence of a natural routine, Jenna veered toward his door, then reconsidered. Motioning to the agents, she reversed her course. "There's something I need to check," she commented and strode through both sets of entrance doors, drawing her coat closed against the chill. A single step into the blustery breeze offered a clear view of her Lincoln alongside Matt's Grand Am. Between the parking lot lights and the glow from the upper balcony doors, she identified the frosted glass on both vehicles. Neither car had moved recently and in a fleeting instant, she recalled spotting Matt's car in the slot next to her Lincoln in the early morning hours. He should have left for work shortly after her departure this morning.

Far more uncomfortable suddenly, a prickle of alarm lifting under her collar, she reached a decision before reversing her course, striding through the entrance. One more for dinner. It was the least she could do after crushing Matt's hopes. And hopefully, Matt's presence would alter Evan's aspirations toward an intimate relationship. Friends. As much as that thought disturbed her, she would never offer more. Regardless of how quickly she'd fallen for Darius, or how swiftly their relationship had ended, she loved Darius Brock, and in a weird epiphany, she knew that would never change.

At Matt's door, she knocked and glanced at Miller, who stepped closer, perhaps intending to shove her aside. "It's all right. Matt's a friend."

"Miss, this might not be a good time to visit anyone," Miller stated, and Reichley agreed, "We shouldn't be standing in the hall."

"Just give me a moment," she interrupted. "I'd like to invite him to dinner."

"Miss, really, that's not a good idea."

"I'm not about to explain this to you," she said while listening, hoping to hear the bolt latch disengage. No sound registered through the door, and that wasn't like Matt Cord. The man was nearly as obsessed with the television as he was with her schedule. She knocked again, more firmly. "This . . . there's something wrong here," she whispered and looked to Reichley, whose naturally bland featured firmed a notch. "His car's outside. If he's home, his TV's turned on—it's too quiet." *And he never misses my car pulling in regardless of the hour*, she added silently.

Reichley nudged her aside, asking, "What's his name?"

"Matthew Cord."

Glancing at his partner in silent communication, Reichley rapped his knuckles on the solid wood door, calling, "Mr. Cord? Open up! FBI!"

Silence. Not a single sound breached the door and Jenna clasped her arms, hugging herself as she glanced worriedly between the staid-faced agents.

"It might be nothing, miss," Miller stated gravely. "Maybe he went out with friends or he's having car trouble. Why don't we check back—"

"Look, I know this sounds paranoid," she said honestly. "But I'd feel a lot better if we could make sure he's all right. This isn't like him. I always run into him at least once a day. Generally, we're passing in the hall or leaving for work at the same time. Granted, I went in late today, but his car was still in the lot then, too. Mr. Tormen has the keys. If we could just ask him to open the door?"

"Miss, I know you've been through a lot over the past few days," Reichley said understandingly. "But we can't break down a door or search an apartment without justifiable cause."

She considered a half second before deciding, "All right. Let's go up to my place. Maybe he left a message on my machine. If not, I'll see if I can find the number for his firm. Maybe he's working late."

Antsy, her skin prickling, Jenna rode the elevator, watching the floor lights above the door. That awful sense had returned in spades; prickling and tingling, lifting short hairs. Barely loosening her long coat, she ignited lights as she passed through the living room and dining room, collecting her address book lying alongside the stacks of Christmas cards. Leafing through the book while rounding the island, No messages blinking on her answering machine. She found Matt's name in her book, glad she'd had the foresight to jot the name of his advertising firm along with the number he'd insisted on offering her in the event she ever needed to reach him. For what, she'd wondered at the time, and thanked God for his offer now.

Listening to the recorded message of Matt's firm, she shivered internally while hanging up, rounding on Reichley who'd followed her into the kitchen. "Either you help me find him, or I am phoning Mr. Tormen to check that apartment."

"If you can convince the super to let us in, one of us will go have a look," Reichley decided.

Linc Tormen agreed in less than a minute, needed only to consider the FBI activity in the Terrace to offer his cooperation. Jenna refused to sit and wait inside her apartment. Riding to the first floor between the two disgruntled agents, she stood her ground. If, by some chance, Matt was inside sleeping, she 'd rather be there to explain her concern. She might not share his attraction, but damn it, she liked him . . . and she was worried.

The sense of alarm niggled at her nape as she stood aside with John Torman, the Terrace super, while Miller engaged the master key. At nearly the same moment, Miller opened Matt's door, and Evan Trevane entered the glass cubicle entrance. Spotting Jenna, Evan bypassed the buzzers and knocked on the glass. Reichley halted her from striding forward and started toward the doors. In a split second, Jenna drew a rancid breath, and Miller snapped a curse to spin Reichley in his tracks. As the agents exchanged glances, Jenna backed a step and shook her head. That smell . . . she knew that smell! The same odor to slam her three evenings ago when she'd entered room 610. Matt! "N-no," she uttered, spying Miller's grim, tense eyes. He pulled the door closed and started toward her. "No! Don't tell me—"

Already, Reichley lifted a portable phone from his pocket. Miller clasped her arm, moving her backward and motioning Tormen as well. At the glass doors, Evan grasped something happening and snapped his palm more fiercely against the doorframe. Reichley started toward the doors even as he pushed the buttons on the mobile phone.

"Miss, just stay back here for a moment," Miller stated and included Tormen in a glance, then turned to Matt's door. Sliding his gun from under his jacket, he stood aside and nudged the door in classic style. Even over the distance, the rancid odor wafted through the open door as Miller sidled into the shadowy room.

She needed to know! No other thought started her from the super's grasp, and as if wading through sludge, she entered the doorway. In the center of the living room, Matt sprawled wearing one of his athletic sweat suit ensembles, arms and legs askew, his running shoes tilted at awkward angles as if kicking air. With his head of premature-thinning hair rolled sideways to face the open door, the hall light reflected a white glow in his open eyes. Covering her mouth, she backed and spun, stumbling several steps as tremors raced through her and tears erupted. Matt—shy, introverted Matt Cord lay on his floor, dead . . . because of her. Somehow, she was the reason! Her . . . the Chateau . . . Darius . . . Lisa . . . Somehow, they were all to blame and Matt Cord, a mediocre little man with a harmless obsession, was dead because of them.

Juggling bags, Evan hurried to her, clasping her arms, speaking, but none of his words registered.

She wanted this stopped! Wanted never to see another dead body! Wanted never to hear the word 'murder' . . . or 'forensics'. . . or FBI.

Already numb, Jenna accepted the arm about her shoulder and entered the elevator under Evan's firm persuasion, wracked with shudders as she rode to the fourth floor. Matt . . . poor defenseless Matt who'd never gained the courage to mention a date, who needed an excuse to say hello or to pass her in the hall. She hadn't seen him . . . not since rejecting his offer to help her carry her shopping bags on Saturday night. And that seemed so long ago. He phoned her later . . . invited her to watch a movie.

When had this happened to him? When? Why . . .?

No answers came, not swiftly. She accepted the drink that Evan slipped into her hand and continued to tremble internally. How much more of this madness could she stand? How could she handle any of this . . . without Darius here to hold her?

And, suddenly, that seemed the most important question in her mind. He wouldn't be here to hold her. She couldn't phone him and hear his voice. She'd needed to phone the airport just to verify his departure. Not once had he offered the phone number for that ever-present annoying instrument he carried in his jacket. When she needed him . . .

Never once had he suggested or promised to be there for her.

As much as she loved him, he could never love her half as much.

A one-night stand. A damned one-night stand which would last forever in her heart. If ever she felt more cheated, more robbed by fate and damned by her nature, never more than now. She needed him here! Needed his arms, his voice, and that half sober smile, the quick intelligence in his mahogany eyes to heat her against this unearthly chill.

Instead, she sat on her couch, staring at the wineglass in her hand with Evan's arm wrapped around her shoulders and his worried voice chanting reassurance in her ear. He would never replace Darius. No one would. And for that single fact, she truly was damned.

"Honey, I know what you're thinking, but this isn't your fault," Evan chanted softly, rubbing her shoulder, holding her against his chest. "Talk to me, sweetheart. Don't just stare into space. You're worrying me, here. Please, at least acknowledge me. Do you need a doctor? Would that help, dear? Should I ring for a doctor—"

"I'm . . . fine, Evan," she managed tonelessly. Murky, her eyes lifted, and she found his intense blue gaze. "I truly am alright. It was just a . . . such a shock."

"Honey, I know you're not alright," he said consolingly. "Something like this—"

"I'll survive," she said and pushed smoothly from his arm, rising and striding into the kitchen. Finding a wine bottle on the counter, she refilled her glass, then set it aside and began making a pot of coffee. Business. Details. If she truly meant to survive, she needed to concentrate on things she could control. Making coffee, running a hotel . . . maybe it was time to start seriously considering her future, time to toughen up and play the game as ruthlessly as all others. Perhaps she'd lied to herself all these years, pretending to feel compassion and joy, only pretending to care for others. Maybe she'd needed to fall in love with a man like Darius Brock, a man who could smile despite his hardened heart. The Henchman. He wore that nickname well. He'd probably arrived at that party five days ago to fit her neck in the noose over those lousy Christmas decorations . . .

Death had intruded. First Fradden, an executive from the New York distribution offices. . . Now Matt Cord, a harmless, shy young man with an unhealthy infatuation . . .

She needed to take lessons from Darius. Run her life efficiently and methodically, steal a forbidden pleasure, and walk away.

Ruthless. To survive, one needed to be ruthless, and he was. That she loved him remained a fact, and he'd loved her in return, however briefly. Nothing else mattered. Missing him already, deeply, she'd managed a full day's work and handled every shred of chaos thrown in her direction. Ruthless. She wasn't the exception.

As she set the coffeemaker to brew, she turned and collected her wineglass. Her gaze drifted and landed on boxes of Christmas cards stacked on the counter. Absently, she wondered what the great Baron von Hendricks had thought of his hotel, a decidedly atheist hotel, all decked in glitter and glitz. Maybe she should heed a few lessons from that corporate giant and broach an agnostic stand toward the holidays, any holiday, every holiday. Nothing of joy or cheer lingered inside of her. Darius was gone, and she might never see him again. Matt Cord was dead; she would never see his shy smile again. Lawrence Fradden was dead, but she might never stop seeing him in her mind. Lisa Blythe . . . Jenna wished she had about ten minutes with that crazy bitch. Ten minutes to rip her hair out and hammer her ruby red lips, and for just a second, Jenna imagined doing exactly that . . . with a candlestick . . .

Imagination and nightmare. Where one ended and the next began, she wasn't sure and only one clear thought remained . . . unless she wanted to land in a nut ward, she had no choice. She needed to concentrate on business, on her career, on her business life. Nothing else could matter.

". . . There are no visible signs of forced entry," Wharton was saying, sitting across from her at the dining room table. "We think Blythe probably rang his doorbell to gain entry to the building. She probably lured him into his apartment with every intention of removing an eyewitness before coming up here . . . Reichley and Miller outside your door probably saved your life, miss."

"Then you won't mind if I ask them, or whoever you leave here, to remain in the hall again tonight, will you? And if you're finished, I'd like to be alone . . . Evan, thank you for being here," she said while pushing off the chair, offering him a faint reassuring smile which affected nothing of the thoughts behind her eyes. "I'll speak to you tomorrow."

"Honey, you shouldn't be alone tonight."

"I'll be fine," she stated. Tonight, tomorrow night, for the rest of her life. If not Darius, then no one. And with that simple, silent benediction, she escorted the troop of men to her door. If she wanted company, she would phone her parents, sister or brother . . . she wanted no company. If not Darius, then no one.

Braced against the chilled night air, Darius rested on one of the listing stones, watching his new charge, his albatross, kneeling in front of the next stone. He'd stood on this knoll once before, had stooped with the lad and read the inscription under moonlight then. No brilliant silver sheen assisted his sight now. Adapted to the darkness, he could make out enough of the boy's features to see the pensive expression, like a natural child wrestling with a complexity too great for his young mind. They were both trapped, but Darius had nothing remaining inside of him to feel sorrow or sympathy for this night child. His contempt lingered, as chilled as the air slipping through his drawn lapels and sinking through his flesh. If the boy had meant to torture him, he could have chosen no more effective means. Not even winter. Already his bones rattled from the mountain chill.

"You'll need to accept the cold, Darius," the child nearly muttered, tipping his head and looking up with a twilight shine. "It willnae be easy, I know—"

"Do me a favor, will you, lad?" Darius interrupted smoothly. "Do not propose to offer me any sound advice or comforting words, not now, not in the future."

"You hate me now."

"As much as I once loved you, lad, if not more," Darius answered honestly and read the hurt, immune to the effect. "And I won't disillusion you or lie to you. That's all your father's left inside of me now. If it's any consolation, I hate myself, my circumstance, and all else living and dead with equal measure. As for acclimating, I'd rather not. Better to feel half dead from the cold than nothing at all. It's a human condition I can embrace with your father's apparent blessing."

"Aye, you hate me now," the boy said morosely, and lowered his head into a bow. "And I dinnae blame you, m'friend. I've a powerful hate inside me, too. Whether I am lucky to have else left to me, I cannae ever decide. I can love you, even when you hate me so."

"No blessing on you, lad. Love can hurt you more than hate ever could."

His eyes lifted. "Is that what happened tae you, Darius? Is it your love turned to stone now? A defense against the hurt?"

"Don't propose to understand a concept beyond your grasp, lad," Darius said smoothly.

"Aye, boot I'm not, sir," Raphael said quietly. "I understand love."

"Suppose you do," Darius conceded. "You certainly loved your dinner."

"I was a human boy once, Darius, as you were once only a man."

"We are a self-serving lot, lad, and if you've not learned that by now, grasp it now. I really don't give a damn what you were, where you came from, what you think . . . I really just don't even give a damn about what you are. I'm under orders to govern you. When you're hungry, I'll feed you, but we should reach an understanding about that. If you ever bite me without asking or attempt to take more than you should, if it's in my power, I'll slap you senseless. An idle threat, but once spoken, there's no retraction. If he has you sneak up on me, now, then you better be sure he holds dominion, or I won't be the only one suffering the shock."

"Ahh, m'friend," the boy said sadly, lowering and shaking his head in the moonlight. The breeze caught the ends of his hair, fluttering the curls to twine like Medusa's own hair. "Do you even remember the promise you made me vow to you, I wonder?" he uttered deftly.

"I do, indeed, lad. But promises are meant to be broken. Break that one or it may be the last you ever speak," Darius said grimly, aware of the Baron at the edges of his mind.

"Tis nae my imagination then," the soft voice nearly whispered, and the eyes lifted again, a wet shine on the surface. "You know—fully—what's been done tae you."

"I've been gifted with semi-eternal youth," Darius said with a bitter edge to his humor. "You were a prophet, lad. Are a prophet. I've died young."

"You're not dead."

"Oh, not technically, but I think to be on the safe side, I'll refrain from napping in public places. I'd not like to wake up in the middle of my own autopsy. Afraid that would be more than even my solid constitution could withstand."

A smile flickered on the full lips.

"Hmm, reduced to court jester," Darius said with a smirk twitching his mustache. "Or is it elevated to such a status, I wonder? Certainly, a slight improvement over being an animal in a round pen. Or is it? An animal has no ability to comprehend the conditions of his circumstances. Ignorance was bliss upon a time. Ignorance would be bliss now. Unfortunately, I'm freezing to death in a fucking graveyard. I'm dead and I can't die. A paradox."

"You remind me of Algen Brock even now," the boy said and turned his gaze. His palm lifted to the stone in front of him. He knelt, worshiping the slab. The engraving had nearly weathered into extinction, but the child had recited the words from memory eight years ago. Algen Brock. Dead more than a hundred years, his bones consigned to this mountainside, damned to linger eternally in direct view of the legacy he'd perpetuated. Darius hated him, too. Would tell him so if the bones rose from the ash.

"He was a good man, Darius," the boy said, apparently taking the liberty his mentalism provided. His hand remained flat against the stone, lost in the shadows, but his gaze lifted. "Like you."

"Sadly, lad, you are wrong on both counts. Algen was a wicked chap, and I've never been a decent man. Even in life, I was a self-serving, calculating beast. The only surprise is that any of us survived our own evil and lived into this century. A pity we weren't all slain when we wronged your pappa. You might not be here, I certainly wouldn't be, and what a better world that would be."

"I willnae stand for ye insulting Algen, Darius," the boy said in low tempered voice.

"You've told me the story, lad, how he looked after you in those early years. Alive and dead, as I recall. Your first grand association to a Brock, to have yourself dished up to a monster on a silver platter, as innocent and trusting a lad as ever lived. You wanted love and kindness; he offered you eternal damnation and pure hell on earth. I couldn't insult my ancestor, lad," Darius said in mocked sorrow. "His existence was insult enough to last you forever."

"He had no more choice than you did, Darius," Raphael growled. "And he taught me more aboot love than any oother living soul alive then."

"Oh, I've learned that lesson myself recently, li'l lad," Darius mused darkly. "If you truly love someone, damn them for all time and deliver them to the hounds of hell. Don't fool around just making their lives miserable. Hell, take their human soul. It's easier that way. You can be sure to see them again."

"Did you love her so?"

"Who can say, lad? Not I," Darius admitted. "Where did your father's plan begin and end? Where did his influence and orders begin and end? He says I wasn't tainted before yesterday, but should I believe either the father or son of lies? Does it matter? I have living memories I wouldn't have enjoyed without that twist of fate. For those, I can be either outrageously pleased or pleasantly outraged. Either way, the memories are mine and I've found in myself a great propensity to be selfish and greedy. I'll accept what I can get."

"Take care in what you say and think, Darius," the boy said gravely, his gaze intense even in the darkness. "You could be dangerous, and father knows it."

"Lad, I'm a condemned man," Darius said quietly, soberly. "Do you think it matters from here what I say or think? Do you truly think I have any more control now than yesterday or the day before? If he strung me to a lamppost and left me to the sun, I'd fight to my dying breath before the fires consumed me, but I truly wouldn't give a damn. He's freed me from moral concern, from human fear and terror. I may scream in agony or defeat, but nothing truly matters to me. There's nothing he can take from me now that he's not already taken, other than the other half of my life, and as my foppish cousin would say, *c'est la vie*."

In slow, smooth motion, the boy flowed off his shins to his feet and eased a step closer. His finger lifted, worrying between his teeth as he appeared to judge his safety. He sidled another step closer, then lifted his hands, demanding to be carried.

Caring neither one way nor another, Darius leaned and caught the body beneath the lifted arms, bringing Raphael to rest against him and gathering a better hold. The arms swept around his neck, holding on tightly as the boy buried his chilly cheeks inside Darius's collar. For an instant, he believed the child drawn to his warmth; in the next, he knew the boy's intentions. In one quick motion, he ripped the body from against him and tossed him several feet. Feral, the wide eyes shined, and the drawn lips parted, emitting a hiss and snarl of anger and frustration. Unconsciously, Darius lifted his chilled hand and rubbed at his neck where the tiny incisors had scraped him. "Don't expect to be held again, lad."

The boy firmed his stance, seething and whining through his drawn teeth, his eyes flaring with the feral shine. "I have tae killl you, Darius!"

"Suppose you need to try," Darius said indifferently. "But as your governor, I'm obligated to tell you, it wouldn't be a good idea to try again. I'm a tad faster than you at the moment and where my talent fails, your father's power begins. He's inside of me now, lad. In my head, in my flesh and blood. The man you knew as Darius Brock doesn't exist any longer and there's not a damn thing you or I can do to change that."

For a moment, the boy poised as if to attack, but with a panted breath, he pivoted and bolted, flying toward the ascending hillside and fading into the darkness.

Darius barely followed a step when his direction veered, and he started down the hillside instead. The master's call. If nothing else, he'd adapted to that sense of vertigo that accompanied his mindless impulses. Why fight it? His feet would fall wherever the Baron placed them and to battle the propulsion would be rather like trying to walk against a merry-go-round again. Resignation. Blind obedience. He fought nothing against the internal mechanism, strode down the hillside, watching his step and moving vines in his path merely by reflex and instinct. In the garden maze, he walked without a sense of direction, circled twice through the same stretch of hedge, passed the same stone sculpture and granite bench. Killing time, possibly, or merely playing another mental game. Darius escaped the maze and continued toward the rear entrance of the forbidding monument, passing through the servant's entrance and continuing in the halls with a preordained destination.

CHAPTER 5

To avoid the media circus awaiting outside the main doors of her apartment building, the agents shuffled Jenna through the side door, one of them bringing the car to the curb, the other ducking her into the backseat. Neither were pleased when one camera crew hustled down the shoveled sidewalk, shouting and firing questions through the chilled air. Condensation spewed off their lips, lending the foursome the appearance of charging bulls . . . like the kind seen in cartoons with steam blowing from flared nostrils.

Already desolate, Jenna settled into the bench seat, tempted to phone Mason and call-in sick, which wouldn't be a lie. She was heart-sick. But with Lisa missing, presumably on the run, and several of the staff members too spooked to report for work, she didn't dare abandon Mason. The poor fellow had enough on his plate for ten people.

The news reports had broken into regularly scheduled television programs shortly after ten last evening, and Jenna had begun receiving irate phone calls from her parents, sister and brother by 10:15. At the mere mention of The Terrace Apartments they'd all made the proper connection, and Jenna had needed all her persuasion to keep the lot of them from busting through the troop of reporters and crime scene tape.

Matt Cord was dead. Like an unholy mantra, Jenna played those words inside her head . . . Because of her, sweet, shy Matt lay on a slab—or more likely, a metal table within a stark, utilitarian room as depicted in one too many crime dramas and forensic TV programs. If only last evening were a rerun of Quincy, M. E. or an episode of The X Files.

Readily, Jenna cast Lisa into the role of a deranged monster killer and the continuing news coverage had enhanced that image. If Blythe had harbored any desire to become famous, her hopes had come to fruition. Her name landed front and center, synonymous with murder.

Out of the corner of her eye, Jenna glimpsed the familiar, rosy-cheeked reporter dressed to the nines. Oblivious of the cold and ice, she attempted to catch up to the car wearing spiked heeled fashion boots. Quite a sight, that one. Luckily, the cameraman hurried at her heels, catching up in time to catch her arm and halting her from face-planting in the slush alongside the sidewalk.

In Jenna's dark mood, she might have enjoyed that event, then cursed her thought. That pleasant celebrity hadn't done a thing to deserve her ill-will. Eventually, as Evan had mentioned before departing last evening, Jenna would sit down with the evening anchor, or another of her ilk, and offer a statement regarding the hotel's position on Blythe and the safety of their guests. Evan had assured her, he'd write the news release and assist in the delivery . . . 'No worries,' he'd promised. She could count on him.

Silently, she'd countered then, and now, no one could she count on. If or when she offered a statement, she would do so on her own time, in her own words.

The crowd at the hotel entrance was worse than the Terrace. Jenna identified two news vans parked at the curb before spotting the collection of reporters stationed outside the doors under the portico. These harbingers of bad news were relentless beasts.

"Take the back entrance, gentlemen. We can go in through the pool area," Jenna advised and kept her head low as they bypassed the loop and continued through the side parking lot. If any reporters had considered this route, they'd opted to avoid the chilly wind sweeping through the surrounding forest and cutting across the delivery entrances.

Inevitably, whether Jenna entered the rear door or the main entrance, she experienced the same attraction and sense of belonging, but as she passed through the delivery doors, another sense of foreboding darkened the fringe of her mind. *The time had come.*

Slipping off her coat, traveling through the empty rear hallway, she reached a single conclusion. Today. Today, she would submit her two weeks' notice. Two weeks was long enough to hire and train her replacement and resolve whatever disaster resulted from Lisa Blythe's guilt. After that, maybe she'd take a vacation, travel south and sit on a beach for a few weeks. She could always return to Chicago and ask for her old job back. Losing a little seniority wouldn't hurt. She'd never burned that bridge, never limited her options. One certainty, she wouldn't remain in this area, no matter the proximity to her family.

Halfway through the arch into the lobby on route to the administration wing, Jenna glimpsed the gentleman lounging in one of the nearest leather chairs. The intensity of his dark blue gaze locking on her stifled her step. A reporter . . . A guest. Just a nice-looking male guest, probably waiting for his wife to join him for breakfast. Jenna continued into the lobby without missing a stride.

"Miss Windrow?"

Stopping, she found him rising, already turning in her direction. Both agents stepped past her, sidling in front of her as if to block a frontal assault, halting him three paces away. He was tall, square-shouldered, without shoulder pads in a crisp tailored blue suit, a shade lighter than his dark, piercing blue eyes. With his firm square jaw twitching and neat-styled black hair tilting, his annoyance remained apparent. Mid-thirties, Jeanna judged and again guessed his occupation as a reporter—maybe one from a national syndication. Doubtful any locals would wear a tailored suit of exquisite French cut and fabric.

Her second guess was likely more accurate, judging by his taut expression. Another disgruntled guest intent upon lodging a complaint over the inconvenience of the past five days' events. "Can I help you?"

"I'd like to speak with you," he said in a quiet, cultured voice, lifting his gaze to dart between the agents with lofty indifference. His gaze returned to her smoothly, and he managed a smile that might have enhanced his charisma if not for his eyes. No smile there. "Under the circumstances, I can hardly fault the security measures in evidence," he spoke aloofly, as if he held a right to judge.

Before she reacted too quickly to his arrogance, Jenna glimpsed at the two broad-shouldered men stepping from different directions, one from alongside the glass entrance, the other from the elevator cove entrance. Both of her escorts coiled for action before an agent near the registration desk hustled forward, stating, "Coleman, Lystrom. Stand down."

As both agents halted and the visitor advanced another step, Jenna decided she'd rather not endure another introduction regardless of this fellow's status. In a fleeting glance, she identified the two suited fellows as bodyguards. And the bulges under their jackets weren't handkerchiefs. Whatever his authority, he apparently possessed a few enemies, real or imagined. Did he fear an encounter with Lisa, or landing on her list of targets?

"Miss, I apologize if I've upset you. I'd have waited in your office, but I'd prefer a less formal setting under the circumstances." He barely paused for a breath, not awaiting a response. "Perhaps you've heard of me, miss. My name's Hubert von Hendricks. I'd prefer you call me Hugh," he said and offered his hand.

In the bright florescent light, ornate gold rings and gems glittered on several fingers, a fact of which he appeared aware if the tip of his hand was any indication while clasping her palm.

Slightly surprised by his announcement and the firm clamp on her fingers, Jenna accepted the handshake. She'd heard of him. Recently, in fact. Darius had spoken the name Friday evening in his speech, mentioning Hubert von Hendricks hailed from New York and controlled the winery bearing the von Hendrick's name,

With her fingers still trapped, she offered politely, "Mr. von Hendricks. Pleased to meet you."

Annoyance flashed in his livid eyes, but he maintained his smile. "I understand you've endured a great deal of stress over these past several days, miss, but I hope you'll join me for a few moments."

Deciding against offending him, she glanced toward the circle of lobby chairs, agreeing, "Here?"

"I'd prefer the dining room," he said and released her hand, intending to clasp her elbow instead.

Deliberately, Jenna eased distance between them while turning, not intentionally annoying him, merely reacting to her natural instincts. She wanted absolutely nothing to do with men, not strangers, not friends, not any man affiliated with the hotel, much less a von Hendricks. Apparently, he caught on, keeping his distance and finding another place for his hands as they walked into the side hall toward the dining room. Despite the early hour, several guests had come down for breakfast, but a table toward the rear corner, near the doors, sat separate from the hub of activity. Not since Friday night with Darius had she entered the dining room, and she would have preferred not to change that detail. The crackle of the fire, the quiet ambience, the snow outside the doors . . .

The Christmas tree in front of the French doors had captivated Darius from the moment he'd settled into the chair alongside her. That's how the evening had begun and with the memory, a dim smile curved her lips. For several silent moments, he'd studied the tree, his handsome dark eyes shaded as if drawn to some distant half-painful place. He'd appeared haunted—

Interrupted by one of the morning waitresses, Jenna offered a glance and answered the pleasant, nervous amenity, reassuring the young woman with a faint smile. The arrival of another von Hendricks had circulated despite this less ostentatious visitor. The corporate giant who'd breezed into the hotel Sunday evening, Amadeus von Hendricks, had arrived in the flesh, unannounced, and turned the hotel staff on its ear. Listlessly, Jenna recalled her initial thought when hearing of Lisa Blythe's tardiness. Like Rene and Lucy, she'd believed Lisa had resented missing their visitor and might have retaliated by not showing up for work. If only life had been so simple . . . and in hindsight, Jenna shuddered despite the warm ambiance. Matt Cord . . .

Sometime over the past two days, Blythe had entered Building Four of the Terrace Apartments, and Jenna wondered again—had Blye killed Matt in Jeanna's stead after finding the FBI agents stationed outside the door?

Turning her attention to adding cream to her coffee, Jenna glanced at the man who studied her as if judging her every move. Leaning, she put the cream pitcher in his reach, then met his direct gaze.

"Pardon me if I seem forward, Miss Windrow," he said smoothly, reaching for the cream and adding a dab, barely distracted. "I feel as if we've met before now, and I'm ashamed to admit, I don't recall ever receiving a formal introduction."

"I don't believe we've ever met, Mr. von Hendricks," she said with a slight smile. "I think I'd recall if we had." He liked that. She could tell by the light fleeting in his eyes. "What is it you'd like to discuss, sir?"

"Please, I truly wish you'd call me 'Hugh,'" he said in quiet authority.

Refraining from an entire string of jokes concerning 'you' and 'Hugh', Jenna maintained her calm with a smile. "I have the distinct impression you're stalling," she said directly.

He smiled with a wry twist that softened his eyes to a degree. "You've caught me then," he said lightly. "I'd like to share your company over breakfast, and I have the distinct impression that you'd rather be on your way swiftly."

"I have mounds of work to do, and I assume you're aware of our current situation."

He sobered immediately. "Yes, I am. Which, as you suspect, is one issue I need to discuss with you."

"By all means, then, sir, let's discuss it," she said with a careful edge to gain her another piercing direct gaze.

"Perhaps there's something I should explain prior to launching into that discourse," he said instead. "I'm not directly affiliated with the hotel chain. Nor many other of the von Hendricks holdings. Frankly, miss, my personal holdings are based in New York. You may have heard of our wine. We've recently ranked—"

"Mr. Brock mentioned the contests and awards, sir. Congratulations and personally, I'd like to admit, I agree with the experts."

"Thank you," he said dryly. "That said, I need to mention, I've come here as a personal favor to Darius and by extension, my brother, Amad."

Only one of those names captured her attention and quickened her heartbeat.

"I've gotten to know Darius well over the past several years. He usually stays with us at the winery when he passes through. I respect his opinion and value his intuitive senses immensely, miss." He tried another smile. "I was tempted to believe he exaggerated when he mentioned you were lovely. If you'll forgive me, I was rather taken by surprise by his accuracy and honesty. You are lovely, Miss Windrow."

"How is Darius?" she caught herself asking, ignoring the compliment entirely.

"Oh, fine, I'm sure," Hugh said dryly, slightly piqued by his tone and gaze. "I know he feels terribly about abandoning you and with this latest development . . .? You have my sympathy if the neighbor was a close friend, Miss Windrow."

Back to reality. "Thank you."

"Was he, then?"

"A close friend, do you mean?" she wondered, studying the strangely tense eyes. Perhaps he'd snorted a line of cocaine recently. He wore wild, shiny eyes without the manic darting and flickering generally related to a perpetual user. No telltale signs of inflamed nostrils. Still, the shine . . .?

"Yes, a close friend?" he said dryly.

"We were friends," she said simply, annoyed by the obvious implication in his question and penetrating gaze. "Is that important?"

"Well, no. Actually, it's not, miss," he quipped. "And now I do need to apologize. Knowing Darius as I do, I wouldn't be surprised that he'd . . .? Overstep his bounds with a woman who's currently involved with another. That's where he's placed me in a delicate position, miss. I know you couldn't have spent much time with him, and he's . . . rather uhm . . .? Promiscuous, I suppose, for lack of a more gentile word. The man can't seem to help himself . . . And now I truly must apologize," he said with a sigh and his gaze distracted to lift his coffee.

Was he attempting to tell her the relationship was finished? If so, he was a little late. "Sir, if you don't mind . . .? Why exactly are you here?"

Direct and honest wasn't this fellow's normal mode of communication. She'd thrown his rhythm again, and he swallowed a gulp before setting the cup aside, meeting her gaze with a tainted smile. "I can see that I'm making a mess of this, Miss Windrow, but I've been placed in a delicate position," he said grimly.

"So you said," she commented, becoming annoyed behind her direct gaze. "I'd prefer your honesty and directness, Mr. von Hendricks. What is your position?"

"I've been asked . . . Or, I should say—ordered to insist you accept my invitation to visit my home in New York for an extended visit," he said candidly. "Apparently, Darius believes—and circumstances suggest his accuracy—that he's put you in danger. Until last evening, both Darius and my brother felt that you'd be safe here after Darius departed. Regrettably, had he been more discreet in his association with you, as he is by normal routine, they might have been right. As you probably know, he doesn't become involved with single women. In any event," he spoke with a sighing disgust, a change in pitch as if he needed to hurry. "I must insist you accompany me. I have a plane standing by and I've avoided the media thus far—"

His gaze distracted, and Jenna followed his focus as Agent Wharton paused at the restaurant entrance. Spotting them, the agent started toward them. Von Hendricks continued with a sigh, "Frankly, dear, I'd hoped to speak with you longer before this gentleman arrived. I hoped to convince you personally before he told you . . . the arrangements are made. Discreetly, of course. Only the top personnel in the Bureau are privy to where you'll be staying. Two agents have already received authorization to accompany you and act as your personal security."

With Wharton's arrival, the shocking words and details quickened. The arrangements were made. And apparently, final. She had two choices—accept the personal invitation and sanctuary offered by von Hendricks/ Or the FBI would take her into protective custody and shuffle her into a safe house for the duration. Either way, they forbade her to tell anyone. Not even her family could know her destination. If, as the Bureau suspected, Blythe belonged to a cult, Jenna could jeopardize her family by involving them.

"I may have already jeopardized them," she realized.

"Once you're away, we'll circulate the knowledge that you're in protective custody, and we'll keep surveillance on your family."

"For how long?"

"As long as necessary, Miss Windrow," Wharton promised simply.

Under discreet FBI escort, Jenna returned to her apartment long enough to pack a bag. This wasn't the vacation she'd anticipated. Traveling north into a colder climate hadn't made the cut of possibilities. Almost changing her mind and opting for the government facility, Jenna remained preoccupied as she meandered through her apartment, stalling until she ran out of excuses and concentrated on packing. Like déjà vu in reverse, she felt as if she'd packed only a day past, and realized the damn night terror still haunting her. Leaving her apartment might not be an altogether unpleasant idea, but to accompany Hubert von Hendricks.

Her scalp prickled, her senses keened as she folded dress slacks and a single pair of jeans into her leather bag. Without needing to concentrate, she packed business casual, with warmth in mind, but on a whim, she drew a black cocktail dress from her closet. Cursing her foolishness, she added a set of high heels, silently calling herself every kind of fool.

She wouldn't see Darius, not in the next few days, probably not in the next several decades.

No strings, he'd established at the onset, and never needed to elaborate. His commitment and dedication remained with his employer.

Still, it never hurt to hope—or to be prepared.

A few days. She'd packed enough to last for three or four days, which was the extent of how long she would remain with Hubert von Hendricks in upstate New York. If the FBI needed longer than that to track down Lisa, they would need to provide a safe house on a beach somewhere—one below the equator.

Halfheartedly, she considered taking a box of Christmas cards and her address book, then dismissed the thought. With less than a week remaining, even if she managed to write the blasted cards, doubtful they'd reach their destination before the 25th.

Sighing, she scanned her apartment once more before glancing between her escorts, already waiting near the door. "Looks like I'm ready, when you are."

"If there's anything you need, I'm sure we can arrange to have it sent."

"Agents Reichley and Miller are coming with me, right?" she asked, while collecting her smaller bag.

"They'll meet us at the airport," Lystrom, the stockier of the pair, confirmed indifferently. If he envied his cohorts for their babysitting assignment, nothing showed—not on either one.

The reporters had abandoned the Terrace, probably joining the swarm at the hotel entrance. Following protocol, however, the agents shuffled her into their plain black sedan and wasted no time tossing her bags in the trunk.

No words passed between them. Lost in thought, feeling as if she'd left something—a lot of some things—undone, Jenna ran through the list of details she should have handled before leaving, only beginning with assisting Mason. Over and above business, she regretted not phoning her mother, and vowed at the first opportunity to make that call, regardless of what the FBI ordered. If Lisa Blythe had found a means to tap into the phone lines, then more power to her. Jenna wasn't about to disregard her entire family to accommodate one crazy bitch.

With the mid-morning sunlight glinting off bumpers and windshields, Jenna paid little heed to the direction, barely glimpsed passing cars other than to note the increased holiday traffic on the four-lanes. At least twice, the sedan sped off the interstate, traveled through residential neighborhoods and returned to the highway, apparently allaying the agents' concern that someone followed.

Perhaps their vigilance should add creed to their fear of danger, but their evasive tactics only offered the opposite effect. By the time they reached the municipal airport in Beaver County, Jenna considered pulling the plug on this ordeal. Even if Blythe had joined a cult or accumulated a wicked following, the FBI should possess the resources to catch her.

A whirlwind. Another whirlwind, compliments of another von Hendricks. Before Jenna caught up to the transition, she, the agents, and her luggage had joined von Hendricks and his husky escorts aboard the private charter plane. Luckily, the plane seated six, excluding the pilot, who looked more like a bush pilot from Australia than a commercially licensed pilot.

He even sounded like he hailed from Downunder while addressing them over an intercom with a jolly, 'Buckle up, mates!'

The craft didn't hold a candle to the sleek private jet that had carried Darius into her life. Clearly, she recalled the black Pegasus mural flowing across the haul. She'd taken Agent Whartons' suggestion and visited the airport to look at Darius's chariot, but the sight of that craft, inscribed with the name Night Rider, had impressed rather than stymied her interest in Darius. She'd already been half in love with him by the time she'd seen his ride, and his obvious wealth hadn't deterred or impressed her. The craft had merely represented a concrete visage of the man, sleek and powerful, and darkly alluring.

She would have ridden anywhere with him on that jet, if he'd only asked . . . and she couldn't shake the feeling that he had asked. A dream, perhaps. But so very real in her mind.

Unconsciously sighing, Jenna woke to the sense of the intense blue eyes studying her, and colliding with the shiny blue eyes, she replayed the last several moments. Hugh had once again addressed her, apparently, and she'd missed her cue. "I'm sorry," she admitted, a little annoyed by her preoccupation. She hadn't intentionally been rude, but by his expression, he believed otherwise.

"I wondered if you'd ever visited a winery before now?" he said dryly.

"Once. A few years ago, with some friends," she offered, and refrained from mentioning, she'd prefer not to visit one now. In twenty-twenty hindsight, she wondered if she'd offended him when arguing with Wharton over this destination. Visiting a winery in the dead of winter, with a strange fellow who set her teeth on edge, wasn't her idea of a vacation—or a good time. And a von Hendriks, no less.

Perhaps she was being unfair, or too critical. Hubert von Hendricks might not follow his relatives' trend toward arrogance and entitlement. As she'd heard from several of her associates, the older brother Amad who'd swooped into the Chateau, larger than life, had carried himself with a charm and charisma to dazzle everyone on staff, male and female alike. Mason had certainly swooned while mentioning his incredible height and handsome features, and Rene, part-time employee, full-time college student had elaborated to describe the billionaire as 6'7" of drop-dead gorgeous—and that young lady wasn't easily impressed by the male species, not after a seriously bad break-up recently.

Jenna had done it again—dismissed her host without a thought.

Jenna's focus cleared to a mantel of dark gray clouds, like a boiling gray awning overhead, and a sudden concern sliced into her preoccupation. Finding Hubert studying her critically, Jenna nearly lost her thought under the heated blue lasers. "Are we flying into a snowstorm? Do you know?"

"I'd imagine so, but it's certainly nothing to fret about," he said dismissively—as if her concerns were foolish with him aboard. A snowstorm wouldn't dare interrupt Hubert von Hendrick's travel plans.

Something about this fellow truly set her teeth on edge, and Jenna decided on the instant—she wouldn't remain long in wine country.

The Aussie announced, "If you loosened your seatbelts, mates, buckle up. We'll land shortly."

Luckily, the shifting altitude spared Jenna from a retort, and she turned her gaze through the glass as the plane dipped. Rather than a city, or a genuine airport, the craft banked like a hawk swooping to snag a hare, passing over frosted tree tops and stark white blankets. Paying closer heed, she identified row after row of mounded snowcaps with black, barren vines jutting like spiked hair in sharp contrast. The grape fields. And if this was all von Hendricks' arbors, the size of the winery was impressive without a town in sight.

In mere seconds, it seemed, the compact craft shot down a short strip of tarmac better equipped to accommodate crop dusters, or so it appeared. A single gray concrete block building apparently doubled as the terminal and control tower. Wind-socks ballooned from waist-high posts alongside the wet pavement, freshly salted, probably by a municipal plow and dump truck. Snow clung to the outer edges between the runway and a tall iron-link fence. Beyond the fence, a black stretch limousine appeared as out of place as a tiger in a petting zoo, crouched alongside several ratty-looking pickups and economy cars. Snow-laden black branches circled a small parking lot and wouldn't likely provide much cover from either the wind or a stalker, as if the latter were even possible.

Pulling her coat together, vaguely aware of keeping it on throughout the short flight, Jenna reiterated her silent decision to return home soon . . . even before Hubert rose in front of her. Deliberately, it seemed, he blocked the aisle between her and her escorts. Beyond him, the bush pilot had already emerged from the cockpit and began unlatching the door.

"Welcome to wine country, Miss Windrow," Hugh said haughtily, tilting his head as if he towered over her, when in fact, he barely stood 6'1".

Compared to her 5'6", he might consider himself a giant, and in an odd epiphany, Jenna realized his stature mattered to him, as if his height posed an advantage. An inferiority complex possibly. After all, his brother allegedly stood half a foot taller.

As if put upon, he offered his arm in courtly fashion to escort her from the plane and Jenna obliged, preferring not to antagonize him any more than she might have already. He was a von Hendricks, and by his manner, just as haughty as all the others she'd met.

A day or two. She could endure his arrogance for a day or two, but she intended to speak with her bodyguards before the day ended.

CHAPTER 6

Whether Raphael had returned to the castle or romped in the surrounding black forests, Darius neither knew nor cared. His feet carried him from the hedge maze and over the black stone path, leading him on a deliberate course through the rear entry and arches. He hadn't lived here long—not of sound mind—nor visited often enough over the years to navigate the labyrinth of passages. A summons, apparently, and not one he could avoid by getting lost in the matrix of dark hallways.

Automated, Darius strode into and through the grand entry, identifying the gaunt manservant, Alon, who opened the door ahead of him. Without pause, he stepped into the receiving room and several senses awoke at once. From the natural scent of human essence to the sight of Kevin rising slowly off a large settee, Darius' attention fixed.

They hadn't come face to face in several years, but Kevin seemed not to have aged. He stood a solid 6'3"— as equally tall and solidly built as Darius, with the same dark eyes and hair. They might have passed for twins if not for the dozen years to separate them. By the time of the gathering, as Darius had come to think of that initial assembly, Kevin had already established a thriving law practice in New York City, one dedicated to corporate law, which likely offered an irresistible addition to Kevin's placement in the ensemble. Ready-made, Kevin had stepped into the executive position in the von Hendricks Corporation, rising to hold the second highest position at the Baron's side despite an abundance of von Hendricks vying for that slot. If not for the Baron's tight rein on his property, Kevin might have become a casualty long before now.

These living von Hendricks were not to be taken lightly. Scattered around the globe, not one could be trusted, Darius could attest, having met several of them over the years.

The dark shine in his eyes enhanced as Darius read Kevin's halted pose and ebbing relief. At the Baron's internal persuasion, his gaze shifted, and Darius' thoughts halted, stilled. His focus landed on the boy sitting stiffly, tensely at the end of the settee that Kevin had occupied. In a heartbeat instant, Darius knew his cousin had meant to shield the child from view, perhaps soften the initial shock for both of them.

Nearly a teenager, now. A stranger.

No denying the likeness. The child's hair rested in a neat style, the color several shades lighter than his own. The eyes, too, were lighter, presently imbibed with a wariness to justify the set of the sturdy jaw, the cut of the sculpted chin. Darting, the boy glanced at Kevin, then to the Baron, apparently deciding on the latter for an explanation, "Father?"

Anger spiraled through Darius's coiled limbs to hear the fine resonant young voice speaking that address toward a vampire, as if it were the most common of all circumstances.

Smiling faintly, a troubled frown on his brow, Amad looked at the boy with a calm human gaze. "Do you remember who this is, Dylan?"

The brown eyes lifted, more wary and darker with his anger. "I don't remember you, sir. But I know who you're supposed to have been."

The accusation and temper in the voice set off another heated wave and Darius turned his gaze to the Baron, his thoughts and mind on hold. Eight years, formidable years, had passed since he'd lost this child, his child, and the boy held him to account.

"Suppose I should have warned you, Darius," Amad sighed in mocked dismay. "You mentioned you'd like to see the boy, and since he'll be going off to school soon, I thought now might be a good time."

Silence. To open his mouth or mind to this torment could only damn him further. Warily, Darius turned only his gaze to the hostility growing in the young man's eyes. Not a child. Not the child he'd held for the last time eight years ago before putting him safely on a school bus. A young man now, a pet in the possession of a vampire lord.

"Darius," Kevin started forward, his dark eyes far more intense, a mask of worry growing across his handsome features. "It's good to see you, cousin," he said smoothly and offered his hand, his gaze searching as he halted within arm's reach. "If it's a shock to me, I can't imagine what you're feeling."

Did he mean about the child's surprise visit? Or did he know the extent of this latest transgression? "I should hate you, shouldn't I?" Darius asked and watched the tension increase, conveying his growing rage in slow degrees despite his smile. If ever he strained against the Baron's leash, never more than now.

"Come meet him," Kevin said carefully, trying a tad of sorrow and reassurance in his tense smile and eyes. "As soon as he's over the initial shock, I think you'll—"

Darius held firm. He neither lifted his hands from his pockets to accept the handshake, nor budged under the hand clasping his elbow. Only his eyes moved, returning to the teenager. The young stranger planted an arrogant smirk on his lips and braved the shock with a stiff upper lip, loftiness in his raised chin. A lie. This shell of a natural child wasn't his son, not now, if ever. "Hate me, do you, lad?"

"I don't know you to have that privilege," the boy answered arrogantly, just a slight edge of sarcasm in the voice.

A smile slid more deeply into Darius's lips; his temper ascended. "Ah, well, let me assure you then, you have every right and privilege, and I give you full authority to do so."

"How kind of you," the boy said snidely.

Darius turned his gaze to the Baron and his grin deepened. "You've had your thrill, now, and given me one in return for which I'm grateful." The hatred lingered; an echo of his humanity coursed through his mind. No matter what words he offered, the boy would hear or remember whatever the Baron granted him. Enthralled. Faint and mixed with the flavors of youth, Darius drew the familiar scent wafting off the boy. He recognized the condition and suffered no relief to recall he'd lost his right and privilege to love this child. In a weird epiphany, he knew he couldn't protect him eight years ago, could do nothing for him now. "A court jester," he said benignly, ignoring Kevin's growing concern and budding enlightenment. Turning his attention to the Baron, he wondered, "What dance should I perform for you now, sir? Should I fall to ruin at the sight of him or regal you with curses? Or worse, regal him with a few? Do tell. I'll be happy to oblige."

The Baron turned his gaze almost sadly toward the boy, who appeared only more angry and confused. "I hope you'll forgive me, lad," Amad said quietly, sympathetically. "Had I known how he'd react, I would never have sanctioned this reunion. I thought perhaps that seeing you would help."

"I . , . I don't understand, father," the boy said carefully.

The Baron sighed and reached, clasping the boy's shoulder, appearing only saddened. "I hadn't realized how badly the stress was getting to him, Dylan. Even the best of men can buckle under too much pressure. He's . . . suffered a breakdown of sorts, lad. I'm sorry I brought you here to see this, but I truly hoped that seeing you would help him. I knew you'd be strong enough to handle seeing him."

"You're . . ." the boy's more stricken eyes darted off Darius then back to the Baron. "You're saying he's suffered a nervous breakdown? He's ill?"

"Afraid so, lad. I wasn't sure how serious, until now, I'm afraid. I didn't want to believe what the doctors were telling me, but I suppose," his gaze shifted to Darius with a heartfelt sorrow haunting his brow and eyes, a beguiling smile in his lips. "I should have understood, Darius. Go on, now, lad. Go on up to your room. I think you've had enough of the cold for one evening."

Darius dipped his head in a courtly gesture and turned, amused at Kevin's more ghastly expression. Winking, Darius leaned and whispered against his cousin's ear, "Snap the leash, Kevin. Kill us all. You'll do the world a favor."

Kevin glanced over his shoulder at the Baron, asking, "Do you mind if I walk with him, Amad?"

"No, not at all, Kevin. I'm sure he'll enjoy your company."

Darius emitted a humph and continued his turn, his hands still in his pocket as he moved to the door. Kevin caught up and reached ahead, opening the panel, eyeing him as he passed through the opening into the hall. When the door closed and they were earshot from the parlor, Kevin hissed, "What's wrong with you, Darius?"

"You doubt the master?" Darius asked in a natural voice.

"This once, I'm not at all sure that I do," Kevin said warily.

"Kevin," Darius said and turned to face him soberly. "Believe nothing. And everything. That way, you'll never be wrong."

A flicker of doubt creased the drawn brows. "Darius, what's happened?"

"Nothing. Everything," Darius answered with a smile and winked. Glancing back to the parlor, he commented, "Cute li'l chap, huh?"

"I . . . thought you'd be more . . . glad to see him."

"Then," Darius said lightly and met his cousin's eyes, his own heated to a black shine. "You're a greater idiot than I ever would have believed. See him? Glad? Oh, thrilled? Yes, I am. Can you tell? I could have him run into my arms and warm me with his embrace . . .? You are a fool," Darius said. "We're all just cattle in his keep, cousin, and I no longer live with illusions. What the Baron does with that calf isn't my business or my concern. He's not a child. Not my child. Not any man's child any longer. To bloody hell with him and to bloody hell with you," he finished and started to turn away. At the hand brushing to clasp his arm to halt him, Darius spun and sent his flat hands against Kevin's suit jacket, striking the broad chest with a speed and force to send the man staggering and gasping for breath. Halted, Darius stood his ground as Kevin slammed the wall. Dropping his hands to hook at his pockets, Darius watched as his cousin recovered his footing.

Braced against the wall, still heaving for a clear breath and rubbing his chest with one palm, Kevin eyed him more critically. "I . . . wondered."

"Well, and now you know then," Darius said simply. "I wouldn't dwell upon it or react too severely were I you, cousin. A mere fact of life and we all have our crosses to bear."

Beneath the anger, Kevin's sorrow ran true, his frustration as grave as any past. "Darius, how . . .? Why? Do you know?"

"Do you know what it's like to have your every word and breath dictated, cousin?" Darius asked with his attitude running toward indifference. "No," he ventured. "You don't, yet, or you'd not ask such an asinine question. As if any of us could ever trust knowledge. Ah, fact. I live and breathe. That's enough for me, and if you're half as smart as I once believed, you'll revel in the illusions beyond that single fact."

"You're . . . telling me, you don't know."

"I've taken a new station. Have you heard? Quite a twist," he said with a wry smile. "A bit of reverse role modeling. I've taken my lad's place as the palace pet. Rather looking forward to it, too, so I am. My ward's only tried killing me once, thus far. A wonderful life we lead, Kevin. Waste not a moment. Do take care of yourself, ole chap. I'm sure I'll be seeing a great deal of you, though. Perhaps, we'll really get to know one another. I've never met your wife or sons. Seems odd after all this time." With a lopsided smile and shrug, Darius flagged his hand and turned again to walk away. "A fond hello to the missus—"

"Darius, wait," Kevin said and hurried a step, halting himself from reaching. As their eyes locked, Kevin hesitated, then nearly uttered, "I'm sorry I couldn't help you."

"Lose no sleep on my account, lad. Sorrow is for the faint of heart and we Brocks are a sturdy lot."

"He's damned us all to mortal hell by taking you, Darius," Kevin whispered. "You were hope, cousin. You were the promise of our future."

"Perhaps, therein lies the key to my damnation, eh?" Darius ventured idly. "Hope and promise, bedamned. I'd have killed us all before long, and what fun is that? Don't weep for me, Kevin. Cling to your shallow hope and feed the beast as I feed him now. There's little else in this world to live for."

"I will weep for you, cousin. For all of us."

"By all means then, and who knows, perhaps, when next I see you, he'll have me weeping with you," he mused and completed his turn, not stopped again. Kevin let him go and in the back of his mind, Darius felt the Baron's dark amusement, a shadow at the edge of his mind that he couldn't shake. Why bother even to try?

Wine country consisted of rolling hills, miles of fences interwoven like a latch hook rug, and strips of barren forests to separate the crops. Through tinted glass with a threat of snow in low-hanging clouds, the country seemed forsaken, if not merely as dormant and tragic as the endless rows of gnarled dead vines laden in mounds of snow. In a running commentary, the dialogue had begun nearly the moment Jenna stepped into the limo and by the time she viewed the first grape arbors, she'd successfully tuned out Hubert von Hendricks' monologue. She understood very little beyond the mention of Concord, a word she readily associated with the labels on her jelly jars than fine wine.

When exactly the commentary switched from a lesson in wine making, Jenna had no idea. As the car slowed, and turned onto a lane between black stone markers, she grasped Hugh's words and tuned in to the conversation.

". . . The original house still stands, but we've opened it up as a museum and it's included in the regular tours of the original winery. You'll be surprised at how much of our history we've been lucky enough to preserve," he said dryly, as if aware of her renewed interest. "My great-great-grandfather settled here in the early part of the last century and the homestead predates his arrival by nearly fifty years. A Frenchman built the house in the latter half of the eighteenth century and allegedly. shucked it all to return to his homeland. Needless to say I'm proud to admit, we're probably one of few families who've held title to American soil nearly as long as the Constitution's been around. I certainly hope you'll give me the opportunity to personally escort you on a full tour while you're here."

Despite her tension and descended mood, Jenna agreed with genuine interest. "I'd enjoy that very much, Mr. von Hendricks. But I'm sure you're a busy man." She wouldn't mind taking the tour alone, fleeting a thought of Darius' speech and his suggestion for everyone to take the opportunity. At the time, she hadn't ever considered the possibility, had become more fascinated by the man of the hour. He'd detested stepping up to that podium and into the spotlight. A faint smile haunted her lips as she remembered the dread passing through his handsome dark eyes. Would it ever stop? This madness blindsiding her by a mere thought of him.

"I'll rearrange my schedule," Hugh spoke in a condescending tone, as if it might be a burden, but he'd make the sacrifice.

If only to avoid his gaze, Jenna glanced through the tinted glass, uncomfortably aware of the thick tangled briars and trees crowding the snowplowed lane. Even through the windshield, the lane appeared shaded, barely sprinkled with gray light particles breaching the gnarled branches overhead and littering the wet black pavement ahead. Isolated. Secluded. The lane wove into the forest, appearing endless until passing through a series of S bends.

Disorienting, the two-story colonial rose against a backdrop of forest, but this wasn't the original homestead. Sprawled beyond an acre of unmarred snow, the house reflected a conventional, modern style, from gabled roofs to aluminum siding and black shutters. Black and white. By size, the house remained impressive, glowing neon white, from its porch rails to the pillared posts that rose as if propping up the mantel of gray clouds hanging just above the trees.

More snow. Definitely more snow on the horizon, but at least the weather had held off until the plane landed. Were there blizzards here, though? Could she be trapped here? In this white, isolated world, surrounded by woods and hills? Miles from the nearest city—or even town?

The limo swung wide in the circular drive, rolling to a stop perpendicular to the short, wide sidewalk leading to three equally wide steps ascending to the covered porch. The first dots of snow began to fall as the chauffeur, a lean, stoic fellow wearing a traditional black coat and cap, strode around the car to reach Hugh's door. Protocol apparently dictated that Hugh receive attention before all others, and somehow Jenna wasn't surprised when Hugh awaited his door to open rather than reach for the handle. As Hugh stepped first from the car, he spoke offhandedly, ordering the chauffeur, "Take their bags to the service entrance and ring for Randal to collect them."

"Yes, sir, Mr. von Hendricks," the man said while sidestepping to open the rear-facing door for the agents.

Offhanded, over the past two hours, Reichley and Miller had spoken with von Hendricks, enough to verify they would share accommodation in this main house, in a guest wing equipped with the essential two beds, a private bath, and a sitting room. They'd take shifts, they'd informed Hugh, who'd merely sighed indulgently, as he'd countered, 'I'm sure you'll find that's not necessary, gentlemen . . .'

In courtly style, Hugh stood close and offered his hand to assist Jenna from the car, although, as he'd done in the plane, he stood close, granting her no choice other than to accept his escort.

If he intended to make a habit of this brand of chivalry, Jenna vowed to set him straight soon. She was certainly capable of walking from one location to another . . . and that wasn't fair. If his brother and Darius had arranged this visit, the poor guy was likely trying to be civil. Under the circumstances, she should at least attempt to be grateful. Over and above the potential danger she could bring to his door, opening his home to a stranger was going a little above and beyond.

As they started across the sidewalk, Hugh flagged a hand toward the left. "We have a private lane that connects with the winery beyond the house. The homestead is about a quarter mile further. I'd prefer you don't try visiting on your own—or with your escorts—until I arrange for transportation and have the opportunity to show you around."

The unofficial tour of his mansion began when they stepped through the elaborate double doors and Hugh pointed out the security system to the left of the stained-glass skylights. He didn't share the code, merely addressed the agents, offering, "Ring the bell inside or out and George will disengage the alarms for you."

Slightly too obviously, Hugh didn't extend Jenna the same suggestion or courtesy, and she wondered about that. Surely, he wasn't as chauvinistic or condescending as he portrayed, to believe her incapable of walking from his house without an escort? She wasn't a prisoner here . . .

The main house was neither as small nor modest as it first appeared, and Hubert von Hendricks wasn't a man who embraced the concept of modesty despite how well he attempted to convey the opposite. Wide spaces, hand-carved and skillfully reproduced renditions of the colonial era, varnished tongue-and-groove oak panels in the walls, lace and linens, curtains and drapes imported from the finest designers in Europe . . . The house reeked of wealth, complimented by a full staff of servants, the elder pair of whom presented themselves for her inspection, or so it seemed. Several others hurried to take coats, and in Hugh's case, his brimmed hat. The tour began without preamble, a task which Hugh might have assigned to any of a dozen servants at his disposal, including one stout woman with dull brown eyes who trailed after them like a ghost. Apparently, if Hugh needed something, he need only snap his fingers to call her to service.

He was polite, formal, if not cordial. Whether he feared offending Jenna or feared to be offended, he refrained from touching her arm, but his smooth pale hands fluttered in a constant wave, indicating a direction or highlighting his most prized possessions.

By the time Jenna stood alone in the guestroom on the second floor, gazing through delicate drapes and curtains to appreciate a lovely view of the surrounding forest and hills, she reached only one conclusion—she should have accepted the FBI's option. Regardless of his subtle flirtations, Hugh's interest remained obvious. He was, he'd mentioned rather smoothly, single and available. With a self-deprecating laugh, he'd admitted his self-sacrifice and dedication to improving the winery. As if put upon, he'd boasted his singular goal to expand the market, determined to distribute his wine to the finest houses on an international market. When he spoke of his business, his eyes sparked with ambition and enthusiasm; when he mentioned his life, his gaze hooded with inhibition. Doubtful he was shy or introverted . . . and inevitably, she thought of Matt Cord.

Matt was shy; Hugh von Hendrick's was something else.

Slumping into one of the three cushioned parlor chairs in the sitting room, Jenna stared blindly through the French doors across the room. Spindly gray branches jutted just beyond the cast iron rail of a faux balcony, an odd reflection of her apartment's sliding glass doors and balcony. The image of Matt splayed on his carpet struck again, and Jenna drew a soft breath as if physically gut punched. Matt was dead. Because of her. Because of her affiliation with the Chateau Suites, and ultimately, Darius and the von Hendricks clan.

And here she sat, a guest in a von Hendrick's house.

Shivering internally, she thought of Hugh and his lofty tone while showing her through his abode. Several times, she'd caught him eyeing her, speculating, as if judging her. Single. Available. He'd said those words with a wry twist as if his interest should flatter her—or dazzle her. Mid-thirties, single, attractive, ambitious . . and Hugh appeared a little too smug, as if he were privy to a secret.

Somehow, Jenna couldn't imagine Darius confiding in this fellow or boasting about their affair, but Hugh's demeanor lent her cause to wonder. Just how long had Hugh spent at the Chateau before her arrival this morning. If he'd arrived late last evening, following in his brother's footsteps, he might have heard any number of rumors . . . or genuine gossip entrenched in fact. And did he assume, then, she was easy? Had someone—other than Lisa Blythe—fed Hugh enough truth and lies to suggest Jenna would fall for him as easily as she'd fallen for Darius?

If Lisa were about . . .

Another shiver swept through Jenna as she considered the possibility of Lisa and Hugh connecting. What if Lisa had come to Hugh seeking refuge?

No. No, impossible. Darius wouldn't have sent her here if he suspected Blythe and Hugh of a liaison, but in the same regard, Hugh's behavior suggested more than common knowledge of Jenna's personal life.

Did the rich son of a bitch think she'd agreed to his hospitality and automatically accepted the position of mistress?

What the hell have you gotten me into, Darius? She asked silently, feeling only more miserable. Married women . . . discreet affairs . . . affairs where he could feel entirely safe from long range commitment? Was he attempting to tell her something? Had he involved his apparent von Hendricks friend with an ulterior motive? Was the man daft? Did he even for a moment believe she could turn her affection for him toward another?

Feeling alone, isolated, Jenna focused on her reflection on the French doors. What was she doing in a stranger's home in the middle of nowhere . . .? In a state that boasted the largest city in the United States? She would have felt safer, decidedly, in a penthouse suite in New York surrounded by millions of strangers.

Whether Darius had meant to protect her or hurt her by suggesting this sanctuary, he'd succeeded at the latter. What she felt for him, what she believed he'd felt for her despite how briefly they'd known each other, wasn't a feeling to be pawned off on another . . . And that was exactly how this felt, regardless of the circumstances.

A few days . . . she would remain a few days in Hugh's company and allow the Bureau time to find Lisa Blythe as she agreed only yesterday. Saturday. She would remain until Saturday, then either return to her home and spend the holidays with her family or catch the first flight to Miami. She'd spend her afternoons under the sun and her evenings watching Christmas lights twinkling on palm trees.

That's what was missing here. A Christmas tree.

Not a single sprig of holly or pine, not a red ribbon or wreath, not a single sign inside or out of this immense lovely house existed to suggest that Christmas was only a week away. Atheists . . . or Jehovah's Witnesses . . . or some other offbeat religion where the son of God had either not arrived or existed. The von Hendricks weren't Jewish. Even a menorah would have provided a welcome addition to the elaborate oak mantel above the fireplace.

Far more depressed, Jenna fanned her gaze through the parted curtain. Snow or rain, one or the other, lingered in the clouds with the gray light filtering into the room. Where was he? What was he thinking? Was he thinking of her at all? Or had she provided a simple diversion against the chaos abounding over those few hectic days?

With a thought, Jenna remembered the haunted shine, the sadness in his eyes, the sorrow in his voice when he admitted never feeling for another as he felt about her. He hadn't lied to her. She'd grasped the integrity of his words and the strength of his conviction in his arms. Not a lifetime. By whatever instincts tricked her into reality, she'd known they'd never share a lifetime . . . and that had been enough. She'd agreed to those terms. He'd told her not to wait for him, not to pin her hopes on him. Commitment and responsibility remained his priority, and he'd steeled his voice with that claim.

Fingering the earring at her lobe, feeling the weight of the necklace tucked under her blouse, she heard his words against her ear as his fingers tingled at the nape of her neck to fasten the gold chain. '. . . Just think about me,' he'd asked, but needn't have bothered. She'd think about him, had thought about little else in every dormant moment. The hunt for a killer, the death of Matt Cord . . . wine country and a house full of strangers . . . Nothing else stayed long in her mind. Darius Brock with a wry smile in his mustached lips, a spark of mischief in his eyes, a laugh in his deep voice . . .

CHAPTER 7

E verything missing in Hubert von Hendricks' main house existed in the reconditioned homestead and from the moment Jenna glimpsed it through the branches ahead, the black stone mansion beckoned her. From its high-pitched roofs to the balconies to wrap about its rear walls and join the limbs of nearby trees, permanence and history abounded, drawing Jenna with an odd magnetism.

Even Hugh's haughty presence couldn't detract from the instant attraction. Mesmerized, Jenna accepted his arm, striding up the stone steps onto the expansive porch. Like the first time she'd entered the Chateau Suites, the sense of familiarity wrapped around her, more effective than her coat to offset the winter chill penetrating her wool slacks. Here, for the first time since reaching wine country only a day past, Jenna drew a sense of safety and security.

"The doors don't open to the public until noon," Hugh said offhandedly as he unlocked the ancient oak doors. Boasting, again, by his tone, he expected her to be grateful and impressed with his power to grant her the privilege of this private tour. "We'll begin here, but the real tour begins in the cook house . . ."

Merely stepping through the front doors, Jenna swayed, overwhelmed by the déjà vu sweeping over her. She'd stood in this parlor before, surely. From some distant place, a grand piano played, mixing with the notes of violins and harpsichords. Soft voices, young and old, laughter . . . like a half-remembered dream, she heard the sounds at the edges of her mind and shivered against the whisper of winter chill seeping under the doorsill. Another place. Another time.

Even as Hugh began his droll litany, Jenna's gaze drifted, capturing hazy images as she drew scents of beeswax and burning candles. Not since her teenage years—not since the plague of nightmares—had she suffered a stronger, visceral sense of another era. On dual planes, she heard Hugh mention his ancestor, a titled baron occupying this mansion, and imagined she saw him there. A tall, lithe figure, a titled baron sweeping into the foyer, tossing his elegant accouterments to a waiting butler like the fellow—Carl—who stood inside Hugh's house awaiting Hugh's arrival. With a mere tip of her head, she identified the top hat and long black coat hanging within a glass display case inside the doors . . . but the walls protecting those ancient linens vanished. As if newly minted, the fine soft wool and silk glistened; the brass handle of an umbrella protruded from a tall, oriental urn, likely shipped with the baron's personal trappings more than a century past.

Fascinated, floating between worlds, Jenna barely understood Hugh hustling her through the foyer as if adhering to a schedule . . . or chased into the next room.

"Baron Amadeus von Hendricks," Hugh said while drawing her attention to an oil painting above a magnificent fireplace.

"Amadeus. It's a family name," Hugh continued tediously, threatening to break the spell swirling through Jenna's mind. "You'll find it scattered liberally throughout the von Hendricks family. My brother is actually at least the third von Hendricks to wear both the title and the name, but we've had several others in the mix. There was a Raphael for a time, and if you'll note the painting . . .?"

Jenna's attention riveted, drawn to the painting, focusing. At the bottom right hand of the stately gentleman, the artist had captured another image in fine detail. Standing firmly against the Baron's hip, one of the man's hands resting on his outside shoulder, a young boy hovered, his black velvet jacket and knickers blended in the dark strokes of the elder's topcoat and trousers. The likeness remained unmistakable between the pair. Stark blue eyes peered from beneath thick black lashes. Where the elder wore a thick mustache in a curve; the child's soft, full lips tipped in an impish smile. The artist had captured those eyes, gifted the oil orbs with the power to follow anyone who ventured into the room. And Jenna wasn't the exception. From the instant she locked her gaze on those orbs, it seemed she felt them looking into her, studying her. Raphael.

"The boy's name was Raphael and his is a rather fascinating story," Hugh continued, enjoying his captive audience of one. Like Jenna, he'd apparently forgotten their escorts who lingered near the entryway, never far from earshot. Continuing, even as he gripped her elbow in a more possessive hold, he admitted, "It's rumored—and documented actually—that the baron—my great-great uncle veered an entire ship toward the shores of Scotland, paying the captain handsomely to delay a few days before setting sail for America. Allegedly," Hugh continued dryly. "The Baron's younger brother had disappeared in a port city and before setting off on his journey, Amadeus hoped to discover his brother's whereabouts. Instead, he found his brother's illegitimate child working in a livery owned by the child's maternal family." Sighing, sounding oddly disgusted, he continued. "Allegedly, he'd paid the boy's guardians a handsome fee and adopted the parentless boy himself. With no children of his own, having lost his young bride during childbirth, Amadeus raised his brother's son in America and bestowed the title on him without reservations."

Uncontrollably drawn by the scathing tone, Jenna drew her gaze from the handsome pair to eye Hugh directly. An ancestor, perhaps. The familial components remained apparent from the angled jaw and slender, patrician nose to the dark blue eyes . . . but on Hugh, the lashes slashed, the jaw cut at a sharper edge, the chin jutted, thrust for dramatic effect and left him with lofty persona.

"Technically, the title found its rightful heir," Hugh continued haughtily, oblivious of Jenna's scrutiny—or misreading it as approval and awe. "Had the brother survived to marry the child's mother, in the event of Amadeus's failure to reproduce, Raphael would have succeeded his uncle anyway." Disgust lingered in his tone and sighing, he continued, "I've often looked at this picture and wagered the child was genuinely delighted with his uncle. But then, having been lifted from poverty and strife, I wouldn't think it otherwise. As the story's told, the boy truly adored his adopted father. But as in all life, a little cloud followed them. Rather sadly, the child, like Amadeus, suffered a malady that's plagued my family for centuries, striking seemingly at random throughout our generations. I don't imagine Amadeus realized the illness in the child until it was too late."

Jenna had turned her gaze to the painting, but turned her attention to Hugh in time to see the pensive set on his jaw as he'd glared up at the painting. By his expression, his tone, he seemed to accuse this ancient ancestor of some social faux pas . . . and the ancestor, with his intense blue gaze appeared to mirror the cynical smirk in Hugh's mustached lips. If ever she questioned the family resemblance, she'd need only consider this moment. To break the silent dual, a shiver slipping down her spine, Jenna asked, "Was the little boy lost?"

Distracted, Hugh returned his gaze, caught between a conflict of near hostile proportions that enhanced his attempted smirk. "No, unfortunately, he wasn't. In fact, so smitten was my ancestor, he protected the boy long into his adulthood and exulted in the lad's ability to produce a child. At times, I'm tempted to believe my family's cursed," he'd said with a hint of humor that didn't reach his intense eyes. "To continue the story, however, Raphael managed to produce a single heir to carry the title, and I suppose, if he hadn't, we wouldn't be standing here."

Continuing on a sigh, as if the tale bored him to tears, he idled, "It was his son who later married my great-great grandmother. By then, however, both father and adopted son had returned to Europe. Technically," he said with a kinked smirk. "Amadeus von Hendricks only lived in this house for about eight years. He and Raphael spent the next several years traveling between the States. As the story goes, Raphael fell madly in love with a Lady Helena in Romania, but there's not much to be said about her. She died in childbirth, and it's said Raphael was so devastated by his loss, he spent years locked up in the castle von Hendricks mourning her loss and raising his only son. That too, I'm afraid is a malady inherent in my family. My grandfather, though you won't find this in the public realm, suffered horribly after my grandmother's demise."

"She died in childbirth?"

"Nothing quite that noble," he said with a twist. "If you've heard anything about my family at all, you may have heard the story. That, unfortunately, wasn't kept a secret, and it happened in recent enough history." Whether delighted to share this story, or put off by the same, he continued freely. "My grandfather never talked about it, but then, he was never the most approachable man. My father told me the story, though. After all, it was allegedly the reason my grandfather packed up his entire family and returned to the United States. Apparently, my grandmother was a rather fragile woman from the onset. My father, being the oldest son, remembered her as a delicate woman. To make a long story short, dear, she didn't have the mental or physical constitution to live in the Carpathian Mountains. Which condition attributed more greatly to her demise, I've never learned. She died about twenty years ago. I remember my grandfather weeping when receiving the telegram. She spent more years in a mental institution than I've spent upon this earth. I don't think my grandfather ever quite recovered from committing her. Although," he said with a cagey smile. "The old goat certainly made the effort if half the stories of his affairs are to be believed."

Jenna understood the implication and smiled sadly. "Perhaps he was looking for the love he'd lost."

"Well, he certainly looked in a variety of places," Hugh mused. "If you've ever seen a picture of my grandfather, you'll certainly not see him alone or pining. I think that's one of the reasons I haven't married yet," he said with an ebbing smile and reached his hand to her elbow, gesturing for her to continue the tour. "My father was a great deal like my grandfather, despite my mother being very much alive. I'm not sure if I blame him, though. My mother was never the most . . . lively soul. Even now, she pines away her hours doing little beyond watching television and gaining weight."

"Where does she live?" Jenna asked in casual interest.

"At the moment, she's staying in our beach house in south Miami."

Delicately, Jenna pointed out, "She may not have recovered from the loss of your father, Hugh. Do you ever speak with her?"

He seemed to find her words amusing. "Believe me, dear, there was no love lost between them. She may feel a little guilty that she survived him, but doubtful she misses him tremendously. I often wondered how they managed to bear five children, and that, lovely lady, is all I intend to divulge of my personal crosses." He nearly rolled his eyes. "I can't even believe I've told you that much," he said with a worried frown. "I truly don't ramble on like this as a rule, dear. You are . . . extremely easy to talk to."

Undoubtedly, he'd omitted an abundance of details, but Jenna wasn't certain she minded. The last thing she wanted, or needed, was Hugh sharing family secrets and intimating private details of his life. The less she knew about the von Hendricks family, the safer she might be.

With the spell broken, she scanned the immense dining room, more naturally impressed and awed by the attention to detail and preservation of the family artifacts. Darius had been right. Anyone even remotely interested in wine making—or history in general—would truly enjoy this tour, and she could admit, a genuine fascination with the history. Particularly the mention of a Raphael in the ancient past. Like Amadeus, she supposed the name Raphael had carried through the family lines, although Hugh refrained from mentioning that detail as they continued through the house.

Returning to the foyer, feeling oddly slighted, Jenna lingered near the reception desk where the public tours obviously began. A tall swiveling rack of brochures stood near the tall oak counter boasting nearby attractions from other wineries to at least two amusement parks within a hundred miles, an Indian-owned casino, and several hotels. Despite its feeling of isolation, the winery boasted two direct routes to nearby interstates and offered some relief.

If the need arose, she could commandeer one of Hugh's vehicles and . . .

And that was a weird thought.

Without a clear thought, Jenna spotted the Winery brochure and pilfered one from the slot, slipping it into her coat pocket as Hugh rambled on about a pair of Tiffany lamps, admitting they were replicas, assuring her.

"We certainly wouldn't risk displaying the originals with the amount of tourists already coming through here." But the originals existed, he assured her with another of his self-deprecating laughs to prick Jenna's nerves. "Bundle up, now, dear," he suggested—or commanded—while flagging a hand, again clasping her elbow to direct her toward a rear door. To the agents, he commented, "One of you gentlemen could go direct our driver to bring our car around to the main building. We'll cut through the back breezeway. It's not far," he assured her.

He'd dressed for a hike, Jenna noticed. From his plush boots, long coat, wool scarf and hat to his fur lined leather gloves, he was likely warm as toast and accustomed to the cold. But then, in the latter regard, she was likewise equipped after spending the past half dozen winters in Chicago. Style and versatility, her calf-high boots sported enough fur to keep her warm and dry, although her wool slacks might take a beating if he ventured too far off a shoveled path.

Barely stepping from the rear cove, likely a servant's entrance in a bygone era, Jenna grasped her foolishness. Hugh would no sooner step onto a slushy walkway than he'd travel too far afoot. In anticipation of this tour, Hugh had likely ordered the covered breezeway shoveled and doused with enough rock salt to form puddles between the flagstone. Still, Hugh stepped lively, avoiding the cracks, and Jenna refrained from smacking her soles or heels into the puddles, though the thought crossed her mind. Why she suffered an almost insatiable desire to annoy him, she couldn't decide. His arrogance could account for part of it, with his haughtiness taking a close second.

Over breakfast, he'd demonstrated enough of his arrogance and misplaced entitlement to last Jenna a lifetime. If she'd needed to endure even one more sausage link sliced into perfect one-half inch circles, she might have tossed a blueberry across the table. In all her years of dealing with the upper echelon in one of the finest hotels in Chicago, she'd never encountered another of Hugh's ilk. Undoubtedly, a case study in idiosyncrasy, or just plain crazy, he'd rejected his sunny side up eggs twice, claiming the edges were too crisp, then not crispy enough. The sausage arrived undercooked—overcooked. The toast not browned enough, then too brown. If he'd intended to impress his guest with his demand for perfection, he'd succeeded. Jenna had never imagined another human could be such a horse's ass. Impressive, indeed.

Through the thick wool of her coat sleeve, Jenna felt the bruising grip on her elbow and wondered if—as it seemed—Hugh intended to make another impression. This one, however, wasn't as annoying as it was unsettling, with the bite of his fingers pressing into her forearm. Overzealous, perhaps. Or overly anxious to appear chivalrous. Either possibility might be innocent, but in an odd instant, Jenna caught his side-eye and questioned the kink in his mustached lips, the speculation in his glance. A test, perhaps, or a show of force? A sample of his strength?

With a prickle lifting under her hairline, Jenna barely flinched, a prelude to yanking her arm free when his grip relaxed, and he spoke in a casual, droll tone in a continuance of his tour guide voice.

"Back in its heyday, this entire back area comprised a garden area where—I'd imagine—my ancestor entertained a great deal . . ."

Perhaps he hadn't meant to grasp her arm so fiercely. He might have genuinely intended to steady her on the slippery stone.

"We've only begun the renovations," he commented, then emitted another irritating laugh. "Not that you can see any progress with this latest storm."

Nearly eight inches of snow had fallen during the night, creating a winter wonderland throughout the forests between Hugh's house and the museum/homestead mansion, but here, in this alleged ancient garden, shadows clung between the trunks of trees and snow-laden branches. Not even the morning sunlight penetrated the newly constructed overhead tress or sagging snow-laden vines and limbs stretching beyond the lattice walls to create the tunnel. Despite the absence of wind, the chill enhanced tenfold, sending a shiver down Jenna's spine.

A breezeway, Hugh had called this path, and perhaps once, long ago, it had served as a direct trail to reach the main buildings and might have worn a covered bridge path through a garden. Presently, where the tangle of snow-covered briars ended and the cultured grapevine began remained a mystery, as ominous as the phantom images Jenna glimpsed through the basket weave walls. A tunnel. An illusion, perhaps. Like a prop in a carnival funhouse, the tunnel appeared endless—or ended, she corrected silently as she swayed mentally, physically, barely halting her reaction to accept Hugh's arm.

Like those first moments in the foyer, the images swam lifelike in her mind's eye, overlapping on dual planes. She heard Hugh's monologue about upcoming renovations, but he sounded far away. Closer, clearer, wagons trundled, and horses' hooves clomped on cobbles. Where snow covered the vines in her sight, thick emerald leaf twined through waist-high wood fence and rustic posts. Rather than walls, fences had lined this path, covered in grape vine where the original vineyard had begun . . . but darkness shrouded this grove. In darkness, the visions overlapped in the morning light.

Not a garden, Jenna might have enlightened Hugh. Beneath these snow and ice encased vines, the remnants of granite stones crumbled, hidden, marking dozens of graves. Transient workers, estate servants, winery employees . . . and others. The villagers. In passing, Hugh had pointed out the copse of trees and a bisecting lane leading to a dozen stone huts where the equivalent of a small village accommodated the estate dwellers. Even now, the houses remained occupied and supplied over a dozen permanent employees, including those hired to reconstruct the grounds and return its structures to the original grandeur.

Privy to the past, Jenna matched her pace to Hugh, trapped between worlds with a gray pall hanging over the images and creating prickles down her spine. Rather than a winter chill and threat of snow, she tasted the balmy heated thermals gathered beneath a canopy of young oaks. Summer heat . . . and midnight.

The dwellers here had lived by night, and the thought sent another internal shiver down her spine.

A disease, an inherent malaise to infect the von Hendricks . . . but such a condition might not have boded well with the townsfolk of another era. As if Jenna walked among the living of a century past, she suffered an undercurrent of apprehension within the dwellers—both the Baron and his adopted son and the commoners.

Whether her thoughts affected her or something else tap danced at her nape, Jenna drew from the past to catch up to Hugh pointing out the piece de resistance, the immense two-story barn where it had all begun. The Cookhouse. Restored or preserved, the structure could pass for a carriage house or barn with its wide oak beams, roughhewn in reflection of a log house. Modernized, the cleared wet pavement spanned the front of the building, wide enough to accommodate two sets of swinging wood doors, and two impressive man doors, one at either end of the building. Keeping with the era and style, signage dangled on cast iron poles and etched in the bulkhead planks above the entries.

'Office, Employee Entrance . . . Shipping, Receiving Entrance'

Presently all the doors remained closed and only two cars, late model SUVs encased in snow, occupied the employee lot . . . before the limo emerged from the private lane.

Cobbled . . . cobbled stone had once spread across this courtyard-style entrance . . . but only hints of the original lane lingered at the edges of the cleared lot to form a neat stone border at the base of the plowed snow.

Despite the smooth surface, Hugh maintained his hold on Jenna's arm as they crossed the tarmac and he continued his running dialogue about his 'vision' when transforming the winery and concentrating his efforts to build a wine making dynasty.

"Technically," he spoke with a scoffing tone. "The winery remains part of the von Hendricks Corporation holdings, and my brother holds the controlling interest . . . Luckily, our visions align in its regard, and of course, I own my chateau . . ."

As in 'castle,' Jenna understood, uncertain now what affected her more, the chill in the air or the shiver in her bones as she panned the shadowy forest encircling them. From here, at the winery doors, not even the immense old homestead remained visible, lending the impression of being encased in an ice fortress. If not for the sense of perpetual shade and the pall of sadness to linger here, she'd find the view enchanting.

Surprisingly, Hugh opened and held the door rather than await his driver as he had at the house. But whether he meant chivalry or intended to keep her close, Jenna didn't ponder long. Instantly awed, she panned the sights of immense stainless steel vats, three to either side within her immediate view with a sense of others spaced beneath the high overhead beams and iron walkways. She'd never paid much heed to the wine production on any of her previous winery tours. Along with her friends, she'd never traveled much further than the tasting rooms.

Only a hint of grape flavored the air, and as if the shadows had followed her inside, the overhead lamps barely lit the stone floor. She sensed rather than saw others about and barely glimpsed a man ambling past one opening between the vats. Like the homestead, some of the original stone walls remained at the edges of the building, but unlike the home, immense oak beams held the rustic rafters aloft and sections of bare stone created a matrix of rooms or compartments.

"I must show you the fermenting room," Hugh insisted and lead her deeper into the maze. Rambling in his monotonous tone, he reiterated the finer points of wine making that he'd mentioned on the drive from the airport. Obviously, he viewed himself as an authority on the subject and meant to impress her.

To his credit, she admitted silently, he appeared to know his stuff, but his condescending deliverance countered her interest. Once more, she glimpsed a body in shadows and shivered unwittingly with the sense of eyes upon her . . . like that blasted painting in the dining room. Except these eyes, she feared, were very much alive . . . and intense.

"Here we are then," Hugh spoke as they stopped in front of a wide, shined oak door—either original or a splendid replica of a by-gone era with the heavy planks tongue-and-groove patterned and the patina shimmering like glass even in the dull light.

Despite their entourage, Hugh addressed a party of one and maintained his hold and manners while engaging the scrolled iron handle to push the door inward.

"This is where the real magic happens. Our tasting room," he announced while they entered another poorly lit room. Here, the dull watt bulbs dangled from copper fixtures more suited to an ancient train station. In neat rows, as straight and uniform as the oak barrels stacked five high to either side, the lights offered an ancient atmosphere while allowing for the safety of the paying public.

Through the direct center, two rows of barrels stood on end, supporting wide oak planks with a runway through the center, and Jenna recognized the shelving and glistening glasses, the rustic trays and refrigerated cabinets beneath the planks. The tasting room could accommodate at least two dozen customers, with at least two hosts or hostesses attending at either end of the planks. Swing-shelf doors blocked the customer access to the center aisle, and Hugh sent one aside in a flourish, releasing her arm for the first time and motioning her to the receiving side.

"What do you say we begin with a nice sweet red?" Hugh suggested.

Somewhere, she'd heard that only an untrained pallet preferred sweet wine over sharper, more heady whites or rose' but she chose to ignore the slight jibe. "It's a little early for me, Hugh. Perhaps, the next time?"

"Oh, don't be silly. It's nearly noon, and it's not as if you need to report to work anywhere," he said while collecting wares from beneath the plank top. "Besides," he said with a sheepish smile. "We need something to lift the chill after our jaunt. A few sips certainly won't make you tipsy . . . Though, I should admit, after a taste, you'll likely want the entire bottle."

Why every word off his lips sounded like an insult, she had yet to decide, but she suffered the distinct impression that he implied she was either a lush or easy. Just what the hell had Darius told this dolt when suggesting he open his home and propose to rescue her?

As much as this historical atmosphere appealed to her, Jenna suddenly wished she'd remained in Pittsburgh—or accepted the FBI's safe house. With her thought, she found her escorts—both of whom stood just inside the closed door, watching her with varied degrees of intrigue and amusement, as if they questioned her morals as well. And this wasn't the first time.

Clearly, she recalled her first encounter with the FBI agents in the Chateau Suites, and Agent Wharton's instant judgement. They'd believed her swapping sexual favors with Darius to rise in the chain of command, and at the time, jumping in Darius's bed had been only a fleeting thought for her own personal satisfaction. As second in command of the Chateau, she'd considered her goals met . . . and she really should call the Chateau and speak with Mason about the mess she'd left behind.

Hugh had brought several bottles from shelves under the planks, along with a rustic wooden tray and half-dozen shot glasses in place of the disposable thimble-sized plastic cups for tasting.

"Hugh, seriously," Jenna said lightly. "I appreciate the offer, and judging by the wine last night at dinner, I'd enjoy it, but it really is too early for me. I prefer wine with dinner or as a cocktail afterward. I'd truly appreciate a raincheck."

His blue gaze held momentarily, either nonplused or annoyed. Clearly, not accustomed to rejection.

Before the crawlies set in under his scrutiny, Jenna watched him turn his undivided attention to the bottle he'd lifted in prelude to opening.

Too carefully, as if he need exercise restraint, he set the bottle aside and his lip twitched in clear derision as he sighed indulgently. "Another time, then," he said with a subtle edge and turned to the swinging gate, leaving the tableau on the counter for his employees to clean up.

Somewhere outside the tasting room, equipment purred at a low volume, and more distant sounds breached the door to suggest human occupancy. Sounded like heavy machinery, a skid steer or back loader, which would make sense considering the size of the oak barrels. Human hands wouldn't lift those barrels onto the top racks, nor carry the cases of wine on the pallets in the next room.

With the harvest season well past, Jenna would have thought the winery would become as dormant as the plants, but offhandedly, Hugh mentioned the production of an ice wine, as well as the bottling process and shifting wine in the barrels. The tour, however, had ended. Jenna caught only an impression of other areas of the winery buildings sprawled high and low, noticing another three doors within the stone walls as Hugh escorted her silently on a circuitous route to the entrance. Twice, Jenna spotted a laborer watching them pass and wondered what explanation Hugh might offer for his visitors. Maybe potential customers checking out the facility toward future sales . . . but on second thought, she knew he was above offering any of these men or women an explanation. Either invisible or beneath him, Hugh failed even to acknowledge those they passed and in like regard, none offered a greeting.

Not a nice place to work, this winery. Dismal, half hidden in the faulty light, the faces—male and female alike—appeared lax, like the waitstaff within Hugh's castle. Seen and not heard. Almost robotic in their servitude. And unsettling.

If she never visited this winery again, it might be too soon. Something truly disturbing lingered here within the shiny vats and spiderweb tubing. Although, to be fair, the company likely accounted for her attitude. At the entrance, where the chauffeur stood waiting like a guard at attention, Hugh addressed her, barely restraining his irritation. "My driver will take you back to the house. Lunch will be served in the dining room at noon and if you need anything, speak to Harlan or Laura. Dinner, as I said last evening, will be served at six, but I'll anticipate seeing you at five thirty in the parlor . . ."

CHAPTER 8

One visit to the homestead was not enough. As if the house called to her through the windows of her guest room suite, Jenna had stood once too often at the balcony window, gazing through barren branches, hoping for a glimpse of the ancient black stone. Like the Chateau Suites, the house touched her at a primal level, stoking even more curiosity and fascination until the allure had become too strong.

According to the brochure she'd pilfered on her first tour, the Old Homestead offered tours five days a week, beginning at noon. Making her excuse after lunch, telling her dogged escorts that she intended to spend the day in her suite, curled up with a good book, she'd slipped through the rear stairwell and out the back door. Why she'd lied, she wasn't certain, although she suffered a sense of those agents reporting to Hugh about her activities, more often than even their superiors.

Luckily, the back door, likely considered a servant entrance, opened into a hedge-shrouded cove, as if Hugh found the necessity of a waitstaff entrance offensive. Well away from the house, Jenna passed several economy cars and one cub-cab 4-wheeler before she strode onto the slushy gravel lane connecting the Hugh's mansion to the original homestead and the winery. She'd worn ankle boots with the snow in mind, although ski boots would have been better. She hadn't packed for a blasted ski trip . . . and the short drive in Hugh's limo from the house to the homestead hadn't prepared her for the slush. As she'd noted at the onset, Hugh meticulously maintained his private—paved—driveway at the front of the house, while all other gravel lanes and paths were lucky to rate a plow and a dash of salt.

She probably could have asked for a lift, but that would have involved speaking to Hugh. Besides, the crisp chilly air felt good. Cleansing. Hugh's house carried an overwhelming scent of potpourri, a smell she might forever associate with slimy glances and snide remarks.

Asking Hugh for another tour wasn't even an option. The more time she spent with that fellow, the less she cared for him. Between his droll monologues and self-deprecating laughs, his arrogance remained evident, and she'd caught one too many of his sly glances to remain comfortable in his presence.

The land, however, was lovely, from the wild undergrowth of the forest to the sun glinting on the white-capped branches. As she'd noted from behind tinted glass, cottages stood back within the trees, with lanes and paths jutting in either direction, likely connecting the homes like a pencil-dot puzzle. As Hugh had mentioned in another of his monologues, more than a dozen families still occupied the small houses—some as old as the homestead—and remained employed by the winery, no differently than the families of yesteryear. Sounding almost disgusted, he'd admitted his ancestors—meaning the Baron Amad von Hendricks—had employed and housed dozens of families, even providing schooling and medical care, however limited.

In Hugh's opinion, the amenities were a waste of money and effort; after all, the Baron had provided well enough just by employing them and paying a stipend. They could have squatted elsewhere and invested in a horse and wagon to report to work.

In effect, the equivalent of a village sprawled through the woods between Hugh's house and the original the winery

By the time she reached the stone courtyard, the chill nipped at her cheeks and nose, but Jenna paused a moment within the quiet cove to appreciate the tranquility. Unwittingly, she'd veered off the lane, onto a narrow path leading to the rear of the sprawling ancient mansion. And again, a sense of déjà vu struck as surely as the sounds drifted into the cove. Halted, frozen, she heard the children's laughter transcending time, imagined the youngsters darting between their elder and the wagons forever hustling in the cobbled lanes.

The sound carried over time, as surely as the taste of grape and sugar flavored the whistling wind between tremendous branches surrounding her. Despite Hugh's dry rendition of the bygone era, Jenna experienced the bustle of activity, from wagons and coaches arriving to the haggard workers trailing on the lanes from a hard day's labor in the groves. As if she stood, overseeing that chaos, she heard the hail of workers, the clamor of hooves and the rattle of tresses. So vivid was the imagery in her mind that she jolted at the modern engine sound and again started at the sound of chiding voices filtering through the deadfall from the front of the house.

The tour. She'd come to hear the details that Hugh had undoubtedly neglected in his telling. As she'd noted days ago, pall hung over this winery, a darkness she recognized and sensed on every plane, and in odd epiphany, she felt a connection as strong here as at the Chateau Suites. She'd never been here, but déjà vu lingered at the edges of her mind.

In another scan through the gnarled branches overhead, she recorded the half-dozen windows on the upper floors and again judged the likeness to the Chateau with the heavy drapes drawn, not a hint of internal light leaking at the edges. Unlikely, any daylight touched the rooms, but if lamps lit the interior, no evidence existed. And that was like the Chateau. Forever, by hotel policy, the drapes remained drawn between occupancy, as if to conserve heating and cooling bills.

With a fleeting thought of Darius donning glasses against the breaking sunlight, Jenna remembered his light sensitivity . . . the drapes drawn in his suite at every hour of daylight. Was he the reason for that mandate? And how did that relate to the story Hugh had told? The von Hendricks inherent malaise?

Was he a von Hendricks that he would suffer the same affliction?

Muttering a curse, Jenna shuddered with the sudden chill, and turned about to retrace her steps to the lane. She needed to stop thinking about Darius . . . but inevitably, the mere thought of him niggled at her mind. He was in danger—

Another car turned into the gravel lot, luckily plowed to accommodate visitors, and Jenna reached the tall cast-iron gates in time to fall in line behind a mother and two rowdy young boys. With Hugh, she'd barely had time to glimpse the ancient gates or notice the flagstone underfoot. She took time now, ignoring the boys' chatter while ascending the wide stone steps. The covered spindle-railed porch spanned the front of the house; leaded glass skylights framed the ornate double doors. Mahogany, the wood shined with a dark patina nearly the color of Darius's vivid brown eyes. And Jenna barely stifled the curse with her thought. She needed to stop that, stop blindsiding herself with his every thought, but even as she chastened herself, she woke to the museum ambiance, and remembered meandering through Carnegie Museum alongside him. She could only imagine how he would love entering this ancient stone house. Like a castle, she imagined while recovering her balance, stepping into line behind the mother and sons.

A glass case, likely preserved from a department store from another era, served as the registration desk, and a sprite-like older woman stood behind the glass, chatting up the trio of young people. Befitting the era, the woman wore a chambermaid ensemble, from an ankle-length blue dress to crisp white apron with frilly lace trim. A bonnet capped her short white hair, and her pale blue eyes twinkled in the simulated light from an overhead chandelier—electric candle equipped—and several ancient lamps. Despite the touristy flair of wooden racks offering a variety of pamphlets and brochures, and the multitude of souvenirs on display in the glass case, the woman's theatrics soon distracted from the modern age.

Behind the mother and sons, Jenna paid her eight dollars, returning the older woman's pleasantries and stepping aside. She probably could have skipped paying the fare by mentioning her visitor's status but preferred to remain incognito.

Alongside her fellow tourists, she meandered about the receiving room—a foyer—appreciating the artifacts. Like the top hat, coat and umbrella, anything of significant age or value remained under glass, and Jenna paused a moment, reading a ship's lading within a glass case, taking the time now to appreciate the details without Hugh hustling her along.

She wasn't alone here. Around her, the boys chattered incessantly, and three young college-aged men chided their single female companion. The young woman had probably initiated this visit with a serious interest in history, and an older couple, linked arm in arm, awed over the antiques.

Unpretentious, the little woman stepped from behind the glass case and began simply, "Hello, everyone. If I could have your attention, please?"

Jenna, like all others, turned and offered her attention as the grandmotherly woman continued.

"Before we begin, let me just introduce myself. My name's Emma Chauncy," she began, and admitted that she was the youngest daughter of a woman who'd worked in the main winery at the turn of the century—and into the roaring twenties. Currently, Emma was a retired historian—a college professor, she added with a quick, knowing glance and smile to the students. Jenna liked her at that instant, appreciating the wry humor and simple style promising to shine throughout the tour. "Keep your coats with you, but please be careful not to put them down anywhere or touch any of the furniture . . .

"I know some of you are eager to get underway," again a glance to the young men, one of whom had the wit to appear abashed. "But I'd like you all to look around this room for just a moment . . ." In a quiet tempo, Emma began with the facts. A Frenchman, who'd allegedly amassed a fortune in the pirate trade, had built the house in 1781, only five years after the signing of the Declaration of Independence. She didn't elaborate, but she caught both small boys' interest with the mention of that romantic enterprise; both stood and gaped up at her, riveted in their front row station. By 1795, the Frenchman suffered failing health and returned to France, where title to the American land fell into Baron Amadeus von Hendricks' hands. With that bit of history concluded, or so it seemed, Emma called their attention to the construction, dating the crown moldings, the paintings, the ceramic umbrella-stand from the orient . . .

Most of what they were about to see, she promised, were the original possessions of Baron Amadeus von Hendricks, preserved through the sheer will and determination of the von Hendricks family. The von Hendricks, she boasted, maintained private ownership of the land and artifacts. The house and winery, in the interest of history, remained listed in the National Historical Society registry, and opened to the public for appreciation in 1981. "But that's getting ahead of ourselves," she said as if catching herself from rambling. "Why don't we take a walk this way and I'll introduce you to the Baron Amadeus von Hendricks . . ."

Having already seen the painting to which Emma led them, Jenna stood toward the rear of the gathering, not entirely immune to the effects of those blue eyes piercing the soft indirect light to shine from a hooded lamp above the elaborate gilt frame. She shivered unwittingly with a sense of those eyes, and the child's eyes, watching her, not relieved to hear the teenagers sharing her discomfort.

"I hate those kinds of pictures," the young woman whispered to her boyfriend. "Feels like they're looking straight into me."

Emma had overheard and smiled to the young woman. "You're not alone, dear. As stories and documentation collected suggests, this artist's rendition of the Baron is strikingly accurate. He was an extremely striking young man, and exceedingly tall for that era. Our records indicate, he stood well over six foot seven at a time when the average height for men was about 5'5". Between his height and his piercing eyes, I'd imagine he was a sight to behold even without this painting to assist our judgement. This oil, by the way, was painted in the year 1812, only a few months after his arrival.

"If you'll turn your attention to the child at his side, there's a little story I'd like to tell you," she dropped her gaze to the youngsters who froze under their mother's hands. Her smile put them at ease. "This little boy was probably not much bigger than either of you two when he made the journey to America. I believe, and documentation suggests, the artist took liberties in his rendering, perhaps, on his own, more likely at the Baron's request," she said with tongue in cheek. "In this rendering, the boy appears to be natural height for a ten-year-old when standing against an average man. Several letters tell us that wasn't quite the case. The child barely reached the Baron's waistline when he arrived. His name by the way, is Raphael. At the time of this sitting, he wore the name Raphael Donelly. . . and I suppose I'll need to explain that now," she said, as if she'd backed herself into a corner.

In a rapid pace, she covered the Baron's decision to visit the country where he'd become a land baron beginning with his travel preparations. Sending servants ahead along with a great deal of furniture—a few pieces she pointed out while moving them around the room—the Baron planned his trip over the course of nearly two years.

"At that time," she told them, "He was still living in a castle in the Carpathian Mountains in Romania. If you look, I'm sure you'll notice a little of his gypsy heritage, although his ancestry would indicate a German heritage as well. With most of his necessities sent ahead, he began the trek, traveling by coach across Europe and eventually reaching London, England. According to the ship's manifest, the Baron and his manservant, a man by the name of Algen Brock, boarded a packet ship in Liverpool . . ."

Jenna lost track of the words; her attention riveted on that single word—Brock. A Brock, a manservant, had set sail in the company of

Baron Amadeus von Hendricks almost two hundred years ago? This story suddenly took on new meaning and significance in her mind.

"No one knows exactly what happened aboard that ship. The details, as you may well guess, have been lost if an explanation was ever documented. In those days, it wouldn't have been difficult to imagine a plague spreading, possibly brought on board by a rat in the food supplies. What we know is that little more than a week later, the ship sailed into a Scottish seaport in need of crewmen. The captain, a rather wily fellow if you ask me, apparently lied well enough to the harbor master to gain access. In those days, if a ship was suspected of carrying a plague, it most assuredly wouldn't have gained entry to a harbor. Captain Malcom Friemont not only dropped anchor, he convinced the harbor master that he'd left England with a skeleton crew over some fracas or another on the docks. The records show eleven men and the captain's cabin boy died on that comparably short voyage. As I said though, Capt. Friemont was not a nice man," she said and eyed the small boys, holding them with her tone. "He managed to replace the men easily enough. Seaport cities were loaded with sailors awaiting a ship. The cabin boy, though, was a different matter. As the story has it, he rejected several before spotting a boy who caught his fancy. None other than the little boy in the painting you see here, Raphael Donally who at the time, worked in the town's livery stable, little more than a servant in the house of his own mother's brother.

"There's a great deal of speculation about the facts," Emma said smoothly. "What we know is that the Baron's brother disappeared on the shores of Scotland and that he'd been a sailor. We believe, from later correspondence, the Baron had a hand in the ship docking in that harbor, that he bypassed several larger ports. As the Captain's later endeavors indicate, he could have been persuaded to limp his ship along for a few silver coins. Whether the Baron went ashore remains a mystery. We believe he asked the Captain to inquire about his brother. Wily as the captain was, he not only found out the brother had been murdered, he found the brother's illegitimate son. Raphael had neither father nor mother to look out for him," she said to the children, captivating them. "And he lived with a very mean uncle," she added. "That captain? Well . . . he simply offered the uncle a few coins and indentured the little fellow. What that amounted to," she clarified. "He bought Raphael from his uncle, undoubtedly, with every intention of selling him to the Baron, but Capt. Friemont, as I said, was a wily fellow. He was sneaky, and he needed a cabin boy. By and by, the Captain kept little Raphael away from the guests. Locked him up in the cabin. It wasn't until the ship reached the shores of Maine, that the Baron finally saw and recognized his heritage in the child's face. We don't know exactly what he paid to buy the little boy's papers, but we know the child landed in the lap of luxury," she said with a smile. "As we continue through the house," she addressed the children as avidly as the adults. "I'll call your attention to quite a few details concerning Raphael.

"And not just to hear myself talk," she said to the students. "Frankly, a great deal of the history of this house and the winery itself reflects the relationship between the Baron and his adopted son, who, by the way, became a legitimate heir to the von Hendricks fortunes. It's said on the eve of the little boy's eleventh birthday, he officially and legally became Raphael von Hendricks, which was just one of the surprises the Baron had in store for him.

"If you'll come this way," she said and motioned her enthralled audience toward the study.

When Jenna had asked Hugh about the books lying open on the library table, the stool and lantern, He'd merely offered an offhanded reference to Raphael. Emma, however, elaborated, twining a history lesson concerning the books to line the walls from floor to ceiling with the story of Raphael, who'd spent countless hours with Algen Brock within the library. Algen Brock was slightly more than a manservant, she admitted. He was the Baron's righthand man in business, a counselor and trusted friend, and with the arrival of Raphael, he became the boy's governor and tutor.

Raphael, Jenna considered time and again, recalling those moments in the suite when Darius had spoken to a child on the phone . . . Raphael. Was history so wily as to repeat itself of its own accord? Was this part of the story Darius might have told her? That his ancestors had worked for the von Hendricks, that the two families were somehow connected throughout history? The probability seemed unbelievable, and yet, the facts were here.

An Algen Brock had lived in this house. Jenna viewed his room on the second floor, entering no further than the others, three steps into the stately accommodations, barred further entry by a red velvet cord. Algen Brock had been a scholar. Books lined a cabinet in his private room. An oil lamp still stood on the desk where he'd spent countless hours composing letters or arranging business ventures for the Baron Amadeus von Hendricks . . . no differently than Darius apparently dedicated his life to the present Baron . . . who wore the same exact name and title, with a great deal more wealth and holdings to his credit. How was this possible? And who was Raphael? Who was that child who'd phoned the suite in a panic? Who was this boy 'Raphael' to whom Darius had spoken with such simple, honest affection?

Hugh hadn't elaborated on the child in the photo. Emma showed them into the boy's room, a room of incredible wealth and class for the era. His room sported a private desk, and an immense poster bed draped with velvet curtains. Glass doors opened onto a balcony to overlook the gardens. A private clawfoot tub stood behind a standing screen. A full-sized dressing room still contained the collection of suits behind glass cases, and shoes galore.

"The Baron had a lot of years to make up for, you see," Emma said, while rumpling one of the children's heads and pointing out the shelves of toys. Carved and painted wooden toys, tin toys. All manner of toys stood on neat displays on a half wall of shelves, and Emma pointed out the footstool that Raphael had apparently needed to reach the upper shelves. "The little fellow never lacked again for material comforts," she said smoothly. "As the story's told, and several documents support, the Baron spent a small fortune just in the child's clothes. We do know a tailor arrived nearly every three months and the material for his wardrobe was all imported. They were, as it was said in those days, the two best-dressed gentlemen in New York, barring none, which later reports show, never changed. The two of them attended countless parties all down the east coast . . ."

The words led into the Baron's private suite, which was in fact, a collection of rooms, from a sitting room where he'd spent hours behind a magnificent oak desk, to the sleeping quarters, to an immense dressing room which bespoke of all the latest fashions of that era.

"He loved hats and long coats," Emma said while pointing out an impressive collection again under lock and key. "Even in those days, it was quite fashionable for a man to take a great deal of pride in his wardrobe, as much as he prized his horses and carriages when he went out on the town . . . Why don't we come this way? We'll take the servant's stairway . . ."

The story and history lesson continued, covering a range of subjects, from food storage and preparation to the European style which the Baron had brought into their everyday life, preferring formal dinners each evening, served on silver platters and the finest imported china to be found. And to support that detail, the immense dining room table, a length to give any normal family pause, remained perpetually set in full regalia from one end to the other . . .

"Most often, it was just the Baron, Mr. Brock, and Raphael at the table, except, I'll mention, when guests arrived, which wasn't that unusual. There are records to suggest the Baron entertained guests regularly as I mentioned upstairs when pointing out the guestrooms . . ."

The tour was nearly finished on the inside. Emma paused long enough to tell the story of Raphael's eleventh birthday, seeming only to entertain the children in her company, which Jenna suspected was only half true. Emma Chauncey had a rhythm and flair, one room and story leading to the next. The three-day bash which had marked Raphael's introduction to highborn society wasn't the exception. "Some guests had traveled as much as a week to attend that party, but then, more than a few of those society families had come with an ulterior motive. The Baron was, after all, an extremely eligible bachelor. Every parent with an unwed daughter within three hundred miles made the trek to present her for the Baron's hand." She smiled at the older boys, none of whom had lost interest or rolled another eye. Winking, she stated, "He played the field, although there was a young woman who caught his attention and favor. . . a mere peasant compared to some of those who came to flatter him. For years after he left the area and even after he returned to Europe, they corresponded regularly. He never remarried, nor did Rosemary ever accept a marriage proposal, although . . ." she pointed out the only single female portrait on display.

In a gold frame, on a canvas no larger than a piece of writing paper, the painting hung above the mantel in the dining room, an accent to gold candlesticks and ceramic vases presently overflowing with cloth wildflowers. Wearing a simple ensemble of a milkmaid dress for the era, the woman had posed with her lovely face tipped back, her hair spilling down her back in a fiery red tint, her eyes piercing. The artist had captured a tiny seductive smile in exquisite detail, and she appeared to laugh behind her glittery eyes.

"As you can see, she was a very beautiful young woman. If you'll put on your coats now, I bet you little men would like to see the stables where Raphael received his first pony . . . another birthday gift . . ."

As they herded through the backdoor, Jenna manipulated her position closer to Emma and availed herself to ask, "Whatever became of Mr. Brock?"

"He stayed with them for years, dear," Emma said. "In fact, it's believed that one of the reasons the Baron returned to Europe concerned Mr. Brock's failing health. If the history's accurate, Algen passed away shortly after they returned to the castle."

"Did he have family?"

"An extensive family," she said with a smile. "And ironically, the friendship between the two families has endured for nearly two centuries, if not longer. As I understand it, there are still several Brocks who work in the von Hendricks companies even today. In fact, I've personally met one of Algen's successors, who holds a prominent position in the Corporate offices . . ."

"That seems odd," Jenna admitted, walking through the door a half step ahead of Emma.

"Fascinating, actually," Emma said lightly. "I can't imagine a family with so much history, much less two so intertwined. I'd often thought I should write a book on that subject alone. I don't think there was ever a time when the von Hendricks name could be found without a Brock name at the same time . . ."

These were the details Darius couldn't explain, Jenna realized. Responsibility, loyalty, commitment. For whatever reason, he felt obligated to the von Hendricks family . . . or bound to them. Enough to give up his own son to be raised by his employer? Enough to dedicate his entire life to the corporation with no time for his own life?

She was missing something, and nothing in the remainder of that tour offered further insight. Only half listening, she barely finished the tour, when two irate Federal agents arrived in search of her. Neither were pleased, but not nearly as distressed as Hugh when he learned of her walk and confronted her over dinner.

"Jenna, for your own safety, don't do something like this again," he nearly growled. "We don't know if you're entirely safe here. We've taken precautions, granted, but there are no guarantees. Anything could have happened to you, and I'd never forgive myself if I didn't prevent that. Please, dear—"

"Nothing happened to me, Hugh," she interrupted flatly. "I'm perfectly fine, as you can see, but I am curious. Are you truly an atheist . . ?"

The question so startled him, he merely stared at her across the dining room table where they'd shared their meals since the first evening. "Well . . . no. I don't suppose entirely."

"I would think just for commercial appeal, you'd have the homestead decked out for the holidays in the traditional sense. You could have built an entire advertising campaign out of it and had people flocking to the doors for a tour of a 18th century Christmas display. Not to mention, you might spruce up this lovely house with a single Christmas tree."

"I . . . well, uh. . . We just never celebrated Christmas, Jenna. Even without the religious portent, it's just not—"

"Do you mean to tell me you've never had a Christmas tree or received a Christmas present?"

"No tree," he admitted, appearing slightly uncomfortable. "I suppose I've received the occasional gift, and I find it an opportune time to distribute bonuses for commendable service in my winery."

"That's a plus. I wondered if I'd need to call you the modern day Scrooge," she commented with a wry smile which put him slightly off guard. He appeared wounded. "Really, Hugh, a little holiday cheer wouldn't hurt," she said with a fading smile, her mood descending. Trying to remain up when she felt so blasted depressed had taken most of her energy. "But it's certainly not my business," she said, letting him off the hook entirely. "And on that note, hon, I think I should mention, I plan to leave tomorrow."

"That's out of the ques—"

"I intend to contact Agent Wharton in the morning," she continued smoothly. "Depending on what he has to say, will depend on where I intend to go. If the situation hasn't improved in Pittsburgh, I'll probably fly south."

"Jenna, that's truly out of the question," he said quietly. "And I'm not saying that simply because I love having you here, which I do, as a matter of fact," he said with a cagy smile. "But I've already spoken with Agent

Wharton, only a few hours ago, in fact. The situation hasn't improved. They've confirmed that Miss Blythe was in your neighbor's apartment, and they've connected her to an occult in California who might be responsible for two murders in Los Angeles . . . Why don't we discuss this after dinner, dear . . .?"

CHAPTER 9

Already, Darius had lost track of the days and nights he'd spent in the keep. One ran into the other, his dusk and dawns lost as efficiently now as ever before. He supposed he slept, but never soundly. Even in dreams, he felt the presence hovering over his shoulder, looking in on him, invading and intruding at whim and whimsy. From an otherwise sound sleep, he could wake in a cold sweat with the echo of the deep, sensuous voice still trailing through his mind. The daylight was nearly lost. His internal clock remained governed by another and there were moments when his eyes burned or his senses floated with the effects of too many waking hours, and other moments when the lights simply vanished and he lingered in a nebulous, aware of every natural sound from voices in other rooms to the caw of a crow outside the windows. Immobile, he could neither rise physically nor fall consciously. Cursing, raging, halfheartedly pleading, he lay trapped in an empty shell, hearing his natural breath, aware of his body splayed on its back on an uncomfortably hard mattress. He could feel the light in those moments, could sense the sunlight probing at the dark curtains to hang over his private window. In a room no larger than the haul of his former jet, he retained all the comforts of home. A closet for his wardrobe, a chest for his underclothes and colognes, a small private bath with a clawfoot tub and a coiled hose to offer a shower. Unfortunately, the hose connected only to the cold-water outlet and his baths were never much warmer with the faulty water system. Physically, mentally, the Baron granted no reprieve in his circumstance.

Awake, by no choice of his own, he moved through his morning routines with a heaviness that followed him throughout every mobile hour. Inevitably, Darius arrived in Raphael's room within moments of the boy's waking. A hellish price to pay for his human error, Darius considered more often than not, to be chained to this night child who'd tried more than once to fulfill his promise. A hellish price, to find himself playing hide 'n seek with a child who could simply spin away and appear a half second later with his teeth sinking smoothly into flesh. Or worse, to suffer the crack of a wooden bat across his head and wake to the little monster a half step from plunging a knife in his heart. If he wasn't so blasted weary, Darius might find the situation amusing. Not amusing, and less so when he thought of the first lesson the Baron had taught him in the Chateau's suite. A lesson of fighting power for the simple sake of avoiding the lethal intentions of an eleven-year-old with a warped sense of integrity. The lad had promised to take his life if or when Darius suffered the change, and Raphael fully intended to keep that promise.

Far more warily, Darius entered the boy's dark room, flicking the lamp switch and searching the shadows around the shrouded bed. Not again would he stride confidently through that door, only to have the little devil launch off a chair from behind the door. Reasoning with the lad was useless. After one such attempt, nearly certain his troubles were over by the solemn oath the child swore to 'cease fire,' Darius had barely relaxed when he caught the scent of poison lacing his wine.

Raging, the imp paced back and forth, his hands locked at his back and head shaking like a dwarfed professor cursing a failed experiment. "How the bloody hell am I suppoosed to keep me woord, when you willnae go and die, damn you?"

"Forget the bloody promise, lad," Darius had snapped, despite his dark amusement. "I'm sorry I ever tricked you into it!"

"Ah, was noo damned trick, and ye'd know it if ye weren't soo bloomin trapped!"

For his safety, Darius backed to the closed door and waited now, watching the curtains for the first sign of life. Depending on the child's mood, Raphael could blast through a crack in a flurry of motion or slip his bare toes to the floor and slink from behind a draped panel. The boy followed a routine of sorts, as described by George Halbrook, who quaked in his boots when offering advice. With the tight rein inside his skull, Darius had forced his concentration, but wistfully, he recalled how close he'd once come to strangling the fat neck. If justice existed in this black world, Darius would have his way with that quivering blob soon, but just as often, Darius knew the opposite held true. Halbrook would probably depart of natural causes long after his due. A true disciple and a thorn in a certain chained chap's side. Either reason could ensure Halbrook's safety for the next twenty years.

Fully dressed, wearing blue jeans and a pullover blue sweater which matched the livid color of his eyes, Raphael strode from the bathroom at a normal pace.

Startled, as much by the direction of his arrival as the disorienting appearance, Darius leveled his wary gaze on the boy as he stopped several paces away. At times, Raphael could appear as normal as any other child of eleven years. Sightly small for his age. Slightly more pallid and delicate than most. But a handsome, healthy child all the same.

He wore a slight smile on his full lips, but his brow notched in sober speculation. Something serious weighed his mind. "G'd moorning to you, sir."

"Likewise, I'm sure, lad," Darius said smoothly, not moving off the door.

"I've decided I willnae try to kill you today, Darius," he said bluntly. "And if you want, I'll swear to that and give ye my word."

"Seems I've heard a similar word spoken a time or two recently," Darius commented.

"Well, you're stubborn aboot dying and I'm in nae mood to fight with you aboot it today."

"Grieves me to hear you forfeit so easily, lad. Perhaps I should lend you a few pointers to improve your technique."

"Aye, and make a jooke of it then, lad," the boy stated with mild irritation. "Boot keep yer advice to yerself. I'll coome up with a good plan a me own when it's time. Today, I've other things on my mind."

"I hope those include a few hours of history and geography."

"Nope," he said and continued forward, a smug set to his lips. "I've a visit to pay and yer cooming along," he stated and motioned to the door. "Let's go then."

"Do believe you're forgetting something, li'l chap," Darius said and offered his hand. The shadows whipped across the blue eyes; the smile turned to a frown. Darius need not bother to admit he felt no better about this ordeal than the child. On the periphery, the Baron watched, apparently enjoying the boy's stubborn will as well as the flash of frustration as he came forward, clasping Darius's hand with a near gentle grip.

"You shoould have been a smaller man, Darius," the boy grumbled in annoyance. His wet eyes lifted, evoking his distress. "If you were, I could never do this tae you so ooften."

"Get it over with, lad," Darius stated indifferently and watched as the boy battled his will before resigning to his hunger. A hellish price, Darius mused even as he flinched with the razor pain in the side of his hand. Never a thick vein or major artery; those were the Baron's rules defined in those first days or hours. Only from a muscle could the child draw his sustenance, and the rules worked twofold. The process took longer than it ever should, throughout which time Darius stood gripped in pain, inevitably thinking of a calf sucking a cow's udder, and the child growled with his frustration as he shared the thought. Second, not least, the boy couldn't possibly drain his source in an eye-blink, and if the lad made the attempt, as he had once at the onset, the Baron could intervene with time to spare.

With the pain still spiraling through his wrist and into his shoulder, Darius watched the curly locks withdraw, sensing the little boy's shame in the downcast eyes and posture. Bringing one hand into the other, Darius rubbed his thumb over the dual punctures rather like the holes made by a lead pencil, both holes bubbling red. By no surprise, the weariness tugged at his mind. Even in slight degrees, Darius knew the lingering effects of the regular losses, knew his physical strength lingered in a perpetual low, a near constant heaviness. In another life—in any life—a doctor would diagnose him anemic.

"I'm sorry, Darius," the boy said morosely and sidestepped, clasping the door, not lifting his gaze.

"Don't be," Darius stated in a low tone and clasped the upper panel of the door, tugging it open wider for both of them. "You're a kid, and I'm the goat. And all's right with the world."

"You're mad at me now," Raphael pouted as he moved out and took the lead in the upper hall, starting toward the rear stairs.

"I wonder if a goat suffers a pounding headache after it's milked," Darius said offhandedly and caught up to clasp the boy's shoulder. "The library's more accessible through the main hall."

"If you've a mind to read, go on then," Raphael stated and tugged away, darting a step ahead, pivoting and backing down the hall. Angry, he glared up at Darius. "I told you, I've a visit to pay. You can either coome along or go aboot your own business."

"You are my business," Darius stated and continued his natural stride, not bothering to plot a quick advance. The son could look into him nearly as easily as the father, and Darius had learned the futility of his actions early in this enterprise. If the father wanted the son halted, the action would come. Caught between them, Darius had resigned. Right and wrong never existed in this realm of perpetual night and misery. He could pay as swiftly for acting against the child as he could pay for failing to act.

As the child pivoted and bolted toward the narrow stairwell, a curse slid off Darius's lips and he lurched into a trot to follow. Apparently, catching him wasn't essential, but keeping within range was an undefined rule.

Passing through the arch, Darius followed the scent as easily as the brush of soft soles and the rush of air in the child's wake. Another lesson learned . . .

In a spiral descent, the stairs wove through three floors and opened into a hallway connected to the servant's quarters. By the time Darius passed through the arch, he barely glimpsed the shadow passing through another connecting hall, tempted to demand the devil's halt. Why bother? Most nights passed in one game of chase or another. He should be grateful the boy hadn't shot toward the rear entrance and the outdoors. Whether Darius wore a coat, thick sweaters or three layers of shirts, the cold penetrated and settled into his bones. Resignation. He had opted a turtleneck and black sports jacket, black jeans and tennis shoes. A pair of leather gloves tucked into his jacket pocket remained his only constant concession to the cold, and thus far, the Baron hadn't forbidden that comfort.

Passing through the same arch, Darius continued his pace, tracking the youngster by instinct and not entirely pleased when he traveled into a narrower corridor that he'd never seen before. Doubtful, he'd traversed more than a third of the entire collection of dark rooms and passages. His senses keen, however, he caught the scent of dust and mildew, dampness and a fetid odor wafting from a mere crack in an ancient plank door. Even with his night vision adapting, the shadows thickened. A single sconce at the entrance barely reached the surrounding walls. Raphael had passed this way, and nothing in his mind forbade Darius to follow.

Uttering a breath, Darius pushed the door ahead of him, hearing the same faint scratch of hinges that had reached him as he had entered. The boy wasn't far ahead, but the darkness had thickened yet again. By no sense of his own, he landed a sole smoothly on the descending step. The walls had closed in, or so it seemed. His palm rode the rough edges of chiseled stone. The scent of lamp oil registered more readily than the flicker of pale-yellow light lingering always just ahead of the next bend. Either Raphael carried a lamp, or an illusion played at the corner of his optic lenses. His breath weighted with dust stirred beneath his and the child's soles. His nostrils cringed at the fetid odor belying the grit in the cloying air. Rancid, that bitter scent. Something rotting, Darius knew and needed very little else to judge the essence of decaying flesh and human waste.

Apparently, the Baron sanctioned his curiosity and interest. Silence prevailed despite the whisper of his footsteps. The light stayed ahead, circling downward, winking and flickering, stretching across the pitted stone to create illusive shadows and images in the crevices. Human eyes winked and blinked on the ridges, glaring black in perfect round orbs as if windows to eternal darkness. A walk into hell, he ventured and wondered belatedly who the lad intended to visit.

When it seemed like the stairs would lead directly into the fires of hell, Darius stepped onto a solid floor, a corridor of soot and sand indigenous to the lower realm of mountains. How far he had traveled, he couldn't fathom. Depth and perception faltered miserably within the darkness. He heard water trickling, felt the dampness under his palms where springs emerged, following their own path and cutting veins into the ragged surface. On a steady decline, he traveled into a natural cave, his senses keening for any sound, the scents enhancing with every step. Passing around a single sharp curve, he emerged into a wider corridor, momentarily disoriented by the flickering candlelight barely penetrating the darkness.

Halted, the boy stood holding a lantern at his side, his face masked in shadows and a soft glow. Naturally, Raphael gripped his index fingernail between his even white teeth and quivered a nervous smile, nearly stammering, "You're really mad at me now, aye?"

Rather than answer, Darius scanned the corridor, breathing in the collection of vile scents and taking in the shadowed fissures in the walls. Those inlets remained far too uniform to be natural. Moving closer, he stopped alongside the boy, who stood in front of the first door. Like the door above, these doors were made of solid oak, wood pinned and grooved, equipped with stout iron bolts and ancient heavy locks dangling free from a chain pin and latch. Breathing in the scent, Darius realized before he ever looked down into the blue eyes, "Your grandfather's quarters?"

"I cannae call him that anymore," Raphael said in a hushed voice, lancing the door a quick glance. "He's noot the man I once knew. Naw even a whole man a'tall anymore."

"But you still visit him?"

"Aye, boot not so often as I did," the boy said gravely and looked again toward the door, appearing slightly uncomfortable. His eyes lifted, haunted in shadows. "This is a thing you should see, Darius. Noot a thing I'd bring a man to see, boot a thing you should see."

An inkling of the boy's intentions surfaced swiftly, and Darius nodded slightly, all too aware of the silence inside his mind, not fooled by that dormancy. "By all means, lad. Appears I'm here, and it's no man you've led on this merry chase."

With slightly more discomfort, the boy nodded and turned, lifting on his toes to reach the chain and pin, to throw the bolt. In his other hand, he still held the lantern, raising it slightly as he pushed the heavy panel inward. As the light lanced the darkness within, a low hissing sound erupted, and a clatter of chains rattled as if shaken.

Over the boy's head, Darius saw it clearly, not certain what it was. The smell nearly gagged him, which struck him funny considering his own transgressions. Stepping closer, prepared to latch onto the child and tug him away—by what reason, he could not imagine—Darius took in the collection of spindly limbs, a human skeleton, folded into itself. Boney knees clung to a rack of shoulders, filth holding the skin to the protrusions. Forearms and elbows dangled toward the floor at the hips; long knobbed finger-bones splayed on crusted filth. Ever the curious, Darius took in the slowly rising and falling head. In long twisted tendrils colorless hair caked to the high-boned brow and gaunt cheeks. Long snake-like coils clung to the tangle of filthy fir coating the prominent jaw. The eyes were most impressive. Round as silver coins, the blue orbs caught the shallow light to shine like colored glass. The chap was blind, or nearly so. His head cocked, poised and dipping like a beast catching a scent, keening as if he meant to attack whatever came within his reach. With the manacles sagging at his wrists, possibly holding his hands to the floor by the weight of chains pooled at his side and dangling from tremendous rings in the wall, his reach remained a mystery. Haunting, the fellow carried a vague essence of familiarity, a mere shadow of the sophisticate Darius had met only once before. Almost in harmony with his thought, Darius clasped the small shoulder in front of him, tugging Raphael back from a started forward step.

Liquid blue, the lively eyes lifted to Darius. "He cannae coome this far."

"Yooouuu!" the ancient voice shrieked, and Darius felt the quick grip under his hand.

"Aye," the child said in a disorienting low tone. "Tis me, Thaddeus. Coome to see if ye're still with us."

"Deeevvvilll's ssspaaawn!"

"Aye, ye've life and mind to ye then," the boy spoke as if the thought disgusted him. "We'll nawt disturb you further then, sire. Sorry to be bothering ye then."

The sounds screeched, not entirely human nor words to be understood, but Darius grasped the portent, sidling and accepting the child's decision to step out. Thaddeus von Hendricks. Darius caught a last glance of the beast rattling its chains, pitching onto its knees as if to attack. Pulling the door shut, taking the initiative, Darius affixed the bolt latch, though it seemed a wasted effort. Thaddeus von Hendricks. The last time Darius had seen the old man, the Baron had led the old chap down the path from the graveyard. One sturdy arm had slung over the drawn shoulders, the silver moonlight had shimmered on both heads despite the gray gloss on Thaddeus's crown. Eight years . . . it seemed like only yesterday. Darius remembered the Baron's arrival on that knoll . . .

He and Kevin had been following the child, an odd little boy darting in and out of the moonlight as they raced in his wake. A nightmare, Darius remembered. He'd believed himself suffering a nightmare, or a prolonged hallucination brought on by hysteria . . . The child had been commanded by the man, the monster, his father, Darius had decided. The boy had meant to take them to see where their ancestors were buried. A full moon, a graveyard, a devil-damned child who ran faster than their eyes could see. They had come upon the elder lord, the graying-haired sophisticate who'd stood inside that receiving room, appearing only intrigued and amused.

Oh, but the fellow wasn't smiling or gloating, though he'd appeared rather amused, like a cat toying with a mouse. He'd struck the child a fierce blow, sending him flying and slamming, cowering.

Kevin had grabbed him, held Thaddeus from another strike, but the old man continued taunting the child, chiding him to come forward, hissing wicked curses. In front of Darius, the child cowered yet again from another wicked blow across his face . . . and Thaddeus laughed, hissing bitterly and boasting his plot. ". . . if the bastard had followed my orders, you'd have been dead before we'd have arrived."

"Thaddeus," *the single hissed word slid out of the darkness and Kevin stumbled back as the image appeared. Already draping an arm around the stiff shoulders, the Baron manifested in all his wild bearded glory looking as he had inside the dining room, a great roaring lord from some ancient medieval lore. In the moonlight, the images twined, and the low silky voice hissed against the old man's ear.* "After all I've done for you, all I've given you, this is how you would repay me, son? By attempting to destroy the only thing that means more to me than my own damnation? The only thing—the only living entity which allows me to feel human—to remember humanity—to give me the balance to be kind when I would prefer only to be cruel?"

"I would have killed him myself to be free of you," *Thaddeus snarled.*

"And you consider yourself human?" *the Baron seethed.* "My undead son is more human than you, Thaddeus, with a greater propensity to love and be loved than you have ever had. Your greed, your lust for power, your desire to be more than you could ever be . . .? You are the abomination, but what a pleasure it has been to watch your wiles . . . and a greater pleasure it will be to watch you stand in witness to the prices you will pay."

"There's nothing you can do to me. Your hold over me ended long ago," *Thaddeus chided.*

"Tonight you have witnessed the justice meted upon your accomplice . . . for Levine's betrayal. In silence, you watched as I nearly destroyed his clan these two years . . . Ah, and the guilt remained your burden, puny man. You are nearly mad with that guilt now. But such a quick release is not to be, son. Nothing I can do? Prepared to meet your death, believe your death to be your freedom from me? Aye, and we will see, but know this, lad, by your own vile nature, you have condemned your offspring to the fires of hell."

In memory reflex, Darius cringed as the great black head had dived and the eyes glowed brilliant red, teeth sliding and slashing, lashing into the wrenched throat. As the image faded, ebbing, Darius remembered the man thrashing . . . Too like his own experience of late. The image sent a shiver through him.

Eight years . . . for eight years, the old chap had lived in this darkness, his comeuppance for plotting to kill the child, and by extension, the Baron. What had become of Levine Brock, the weak idiot who had fallen in with this crazy old fool? And in so doing, condemned their entire clan.

A half step ahead, a shudder coursed through the dwarfed body and the lantern shivered the light against the walls. Already, the boy started them toward the cavern, his step hastened noticeably.

"What became of him?" Darius asked, knowing he need not mention Levine. The child had reacted to the mere thought.

"He's still aboot," Raphael answered grimly. "Er . . . maybe not now. I dinnae know. Dinnae care."

A lie, undoubtedly. If nothing else, Darius knew the boy had been terrorized and terrified, nearly killed by the betrayal of Levine Brock. The Baron had known . . . had undoubtedly known from the onset, what plot Thaddeus conceived. Too well, Darius remembered the Baron hissing the tale of Levine's wickedness, how he'd battered the child relentlessly and driven him to the cliffs, driven him off the cliff. Broken and battered, unable to die even then, the child had lived for two years at Levine's mercy, chained to a floor in a twisted heap . . . And still the Baron had waited, taking no action until the last moment when Levine might have driven a stake through the helpless body.

On that night, Darius knew, a night more than ten years past, the curse had spilled out like a virus from the enraged mind of the Baron von Hendricks. Otherwise healthy men, women and children fell prey to the infection, their only connection being a relative genetic code, a bloodline springing from two single men born nearly four centuries before their own birth. Without explanation or detection, the madness struck at the darkest corners of the mind, igniting senseless violence, hopelessness, hatred and depression as spontaneous and deadly as any biological virus created by nature or modern science. Entire families killed in an instant as a father veered his car headlong into another; an office manager carrying a weapon into work and opening fire . . . One after the other, those deaths had compounded, and the scribe, the man who'd inherited the watcher's post, should have been alarmed by those rising statistics. Instead, he'd remained dormant and ignorant for nearly two years.

George Halbrook or Levine Brock . . . one was as guilty as the other in Darius's mind. One through action, one through inaction. Degeneration and dereliction.

In a weird epiphany, Darius realized the conflict still inside of him. In front of him, the child walked at a clipped pace, possibly suffering doubts and concerns regarding the monster who still wore the name Brock. As much as Darius wanted to hate this little devil, the outrage festered over what Levine had done to such a desperate child. The contradiction, be-damned. Raphael was a child, a child of the night, but a child still. Against a grown human man, the child was nearly defenseless, made worse by his shackles of decency. Because Levine was a Brock, because of an oath vowed before the child breathed life, Raphael had restrained his base instincts, chained his penchant toward evil and spared Levine's life.

Who was the monster in that travesty of evil intentions?

Annoyed, Darius realized the lingering effects, if only echoes of his own humanity. A twisted humanity. He would like a few moments with Levine Brock, a few moments to mash that betrayer into a bloody pulp. Thaddeus von Hendricks would fare no better. If the man lived to be two hundred, he would have been released too soon from his punishment.

"Why did you bring me here, Raphael?" Darius asked in a low tempo, his mood seeping into his tone and sending a shiver through the child in front of him.

"Doesn't matter," the boy answered glumly. "Mee plan backfired."

"English, lad. My plan backfired," Darius corrected if only to soften his tone, distract his building rage. "And what plan was that, I wonder?"

They'd reached the steps. The child stayed three steps above, dangling the lantern at an angle to spread light between them. Without a need to wrench his neck, he looked over his shoulder, a shine caught in his eyes. "I wanted you to see, Darius, to understand what you've waiting in store for yourself." A subtle whine inflected his voice. "'Tis the way of all men upoon a time. Aye, and there's your fate, staring you in the face, but you dinnae see it."

"Irritated with me, now, are you?" Darius mused.

"Aye," Raphael growled. "You're already daft, lad. There's no hope for it or you."

"Do you feel badly about Thaddeus, lad?"

"Sometimes yes. Sometimes no," he said in rolling pitches, again watching the steps ahead as he climbed. "I coome down here to remember. Aye, and I've memories of suffering—human suffering aplenty. And my oown. Was a time, I lived down here. Many a year passed as I rested in undead sleep. I'm knowing the terror of the rats and spiders and sooch. Aye, and you've slept that way, too, now, Darius. Undead."

Curious, Darius considered the words, commenting, "Have I now?"

"Aye, tis the state pappa creates in you, lad," he said offhandedly. "Tis life in you. Tis your own heartbeat you hear and a half-wake mind turning in chains. You'll end up like that ancient back there," he said with a careless wave of his hand toward their wake. "In half mortal chains, living in human terror."

"Raphael, were I ever to betray another man as he did, or plot such evil on one like yourself, I'd deserve that fate, don't you think?"

"You're a good man, Darius," the boy said gravely. "Aye, as fine as any I've ever met. As good as Algen in my mind, boot you've no choices left to you. Aye, and you never did. There's a fact. Pappa played with you froom the start. And so have I." His gaze came over his shoulder, glittering with menace which might have given Darius a start in another life. "I've had my foon at your expense."

"You're a child," Darius said smoothly, heating his own gaze and giving the child pause, if not a quick fright. "Even in my purely human condition, I knew that at the onset and took into consideration, your circumstance. Your games were nothing more than childish pranks. Enhanced a hundredfold, I'll grant you. And dangerous, I've no doubts. But pranks, just the same. I'd no more fault you for those than I'd fault a human child for behaving as such."

"I'm a damn sight older than yourself, lad," the boy stated in offense. "And I could do you harm, too, you'd better believe."

"I've a lump on my skull to remind me," Darius mused. "Perhaps, the next time, your pappa will give me rein to swat your rump for your trouble."

"Well! And he better not, I can tell you!"

"Worried you, have I?" Darius idled and reached over the child's head to push open the door in front of them.

"I willnae stand for it, Darius," Raphael warned and dropped his attention, fumbling with the lantern, turning the wick asunder and throwing them into near total darkness.

As the boy set the lantern down on the step and ducked through the door, Darius clasped his shoulder, bringing the faintly glowing eyes about. "I'm not Levine Brock, Raphael, nor Thaddeus von Hendricks. I've no desire to strike a mortal blow against you . . . nor your father, as well he knows. I am as bound by my word as by blood, lad. Should ever your father change that inside of me and land me in that dungeon because of an evil deed, I'd no longer be Darius Brock in those chains. Do you understand what I'm saying?"

"Aye, Darius. If it happens, I'm not to suffer for you."

"Or visit me, lad," Darius confirmed. He wouldn't welcome that end but if it happened . . . "The beast you'd find wouldn't be the man you knew."

"Can . . . can I hug you, Darius?" the soft voice quivered with need.

A smile quirked his lips. Darius sighed, "About the waist if you must."

In a swift launch, the child came against him, wrapping his arms about Darius's waist and holding on tight. "I still love you," he uttered in a half-sobbed breath.

Hating the lad truly was impossible. Whether the thought was his own or sent through the shadows in his mind, Darius couldn't deny the connection. Clasping a hand over the curly head nearly buried under his jacket, Darius sighed, "I can't love you in return, lad, but I'd want revenge on any man or beast who did you harm, if that's any consolation."

Sniffing, the boy eased back and ducked his head, wiping his cheeks on his sweater sleeve like any natural child of the light. Lifting his twilight eyes, he uttered, "I . . . I understand, Darius. W-was only the Brocks I could dare to love, only the Brocks were safe from pappa's wrath. Aye, and he can be a cruel one," he said gravely. "Boot . . . boot he is my pappa, and I love him."

"As you should," Darius said and scuffed the curls, nudging the boy through the doorway into the hall and offering his hand. By whatever strangeness existed inside this elf, the lad could never reject an offer of friendship or a kindness. He was more like a golden rock with a vein of evil running through him, than a mountain of rock with a strip of gold. By no surprise, not even the Baron could deny him completely. The injustice of what Thaddeus von Hendricks had attempted burned deeper as Darius felt the quick grip on his fingers. If the child had not survived, if the Baron had arrived too late, Darius wondered what cost the Brocks would have paid.

Hell on earth, not for a dozen, not for hundreds. The death toll would have risen a great deal higher.

Retribution.

A vicious circle, or cycle, Darius considered as he led the boy through the dim light toward the entrance. Other doors and passages branched off this artery, which undoubtedly formed a maze through the entire castle. The structure was designed to fend off attack and protect the king, if a king had truly lived here once. A vicious cycle. A king lived here now, regardless of what realm he ruled, and this chap would protect what belonged to him, whether land, riches, or human bounty.

The Brocks had paid. Justice had been dealt a quick and wicked blow, meted out to affect an entire clan through the blood and misery of a dozen. More effective than a virus, more diverse and efficient than a few dozen satellite dishes orbiting the earth. From the receiving room in this black castle, in a single night of horrors, the curse and the cure had twined, spanning the globe, touching every man, woman and in at least two cases that Darius could testify, even the unborn children who contained the Brock lineage. In groups of four, divided in thirds, the Baron had cast his spell, taken his revenge and cleansed the bloodlines. 'Father of your clan,' the Baron had decreed on that night of horrors, placing the responsibility of creation on Darius's shoulders, dubbing Kevin, 'Patriarch.' Only four potent males were left standing at the end of that eve. Only two had retained the right and privilege of creation.

The Brock clan would survive regardless of present circumstance. For a time, the births would lull, their numbers dwindle, but they would revive in time.

What of the von Hendricks? Other than Thaddeus, no others had seemed to suffer an ill or a harm. Were the others all exempt? Spared if only out of the Baron's blue blood in their veins? Darius had met enough of them to know they enjoyed every luxury and accommodation their wealth and stature granted them. Whether they lived in the United States or Europe, they wrapped themselves in jewels and firs, taking their pleasures more seriously than their business, enjoying the reign of kings no matter the parliament under which they dwelt in the natural sense. To a one, they were free to live their lives however they chose, none suffering a single ill.

If that was hell, Darius wondered what he should consider his own life. And in the next instant, wondered if he should be worried for venturing the thought. Well, to bloody hell with worrying. If his circumstance declined for his mere thoughts, he'd consider it his due and survive. Life and death, misery or blessing . . . all remained in the hands of the specter, looking over his shoulder and haunting the spaces inside his mind. Submission remained his only human right. Not even resignation could fully register. Like a dull-witted ox, he might continue to ram his head against a wall in search of answers or explanations, and even that would give the Baron what he apparently sought—a court jester.

Well, and perhaps, a speck of humanity remained. Darius veered his thoughts toward the luxuries he had enjoyed, the position awarded him in one of the largest companies in the world. Quite a fall from grace. From the second highest in command of an empire, a man who answered to the King himself and carried the voice of the king into every corporate office in the world, to court jester. And by extension, playmate to the prince. The only consolation, shallow as it seemed, Darius knew in a blinding instant, he'd never dreamt of vast riches or fame, had never become entirely comfortable with the deference and homage paid to him when he'd entered a room or a negotiation. He might have enjoyed the business end, he mused darkly. He'd found in himself a talent for playing with numbers and shifting a negotiation in his favor. That he'd believed his life and the life of his clan were intertwined in his success had certainly given him the cutting edge lending new meaning to the term 'ruthless.' He'd never lost a single dollar across a boardroom table, had doused more damaging fires in the economic strategies than he could readily remember. Not once had he ever taken his position or the luxuries of his wealth for granted. Only once . . . only once in eight years had he thrown caution to the wind and spent a little of his alleged wealth on a whim of his own design.

The glitter of diamonds at the edge of the delicate lobes and nestled against that soft, warm neck . . . worth whatever price he'd paid, he considered and forced the threatening image from the surface of his mind. She was a woman designed to wear jewels. If given the choice again and knew in advance, he'd be held to account, he' would gladly repeat that mistake. If in that instant of selfish pleasure, of obsession and frivolity, he'd cast his fate, then so be it. No regrets. Better a court jester with a fine memory in his cache, than a dull-witted ox with a collar around his neck. Diamonds were forever, and on those he could feast his mental eye, feeling a strangeness inside himself to know he'd loved and been loved in return, however briefly—

Life-like, in full color as if a window had smashed open inside his mind, he saw her. . .

Candlelight played across her delicate features and danced in her livid blue eyes; a smile quivered in her lips with the mischief of her wit not well concealed. She sat at a table draped in white lace, fine porcelain plates and crystal goblets, crystal candleholders positioned to either side. Her hand, so smooth and fine-boned, hovered with a silver utensil poised above the plate with a sprig of vegetable on the tines. Intent, her eyes sparkling, she gazed in quiet humor toward another, and Darius heard the male voice, recognized the deep smooth pitch even before his focus turned. Hubert von Hendricks. The wine baron . . . a shrewd calculated bastard who could smile and cut a competitor's throat.

Hugh smiled now, his blue eyes glittering as if feasting even as he spoke. ". . . I can't tell you how glad I am you've decided to stay a while longer, Jenna. I can't imagine sitting down at this table without you here to brighten my evening."

The window snapped shut as swiftly as it had opened and Darius stood as still as stone, his breath lodged behind a wad of thickening rage, His heart hammered a tempo to throb at his temple. Not a hallucination or his imagination playing wicked tricks, not the Baron creating an idle fantasy to torment him. Those moments were real . . . a glimpse into the now. His love . . . his Jenna . . . a guest in the house of Hugh von Hendricks. She was there now. This minute. Sitting with that black-hearted egomaniac, enjoying a splendid candlelight dinner, smiling . . . granting that conniving wretch her warm smile and sparkling eyes!

Rage. Quiet, powerful rage burned through Darius's mind and trembled through his limbs, At his side, the child slipped his hand free, sidled and looked up with a wary shine.

"Darius?"

How long? How many days or weeks had passed? How many minutes had she already spent with this von Hendricks?

She accepted his invitation the day after we departed, the low silky voice imparted, sliding like oil across Darius's inflamed mind. Dark amusement haunted the continuing words. *Of course, he had to tell her that you requested his intervention to see to her safety; after all, you felt responsible for her after the way you used her for your own pleasure. Poor Hubert, the lad's obsessed with her now. I shant think he'll ever let her go, and she seems to be warming to him nicely now. As it appears, I may have a sister-in-law soon, lad.*

"You're lying," Darius heaved softly, his thoughts turned inward, riveted.

Time will tell, lad. Time will tell. Ah, but what do you care, then, eh? You've no love left in your cold heart. No, not love, lad. Jealousy, perhaps. Isn't that so? Hubert, my dear wily brother according to official records, has it all. Wealth. Freedom. Health. Your lover. Hmm, and you have nothing. Quite a fall from grace, I should certainly agree.

"Damn you," Darius breathed in soft rage.

Laughter, low and black, spilled across Darius's mind. *Aye, damn me, my court jester. I so enjoy your company. Now, bring my lad and come join me for dinner. Your blood's flowing hot and I'm not above an appetizer.*

CHAPTER 10

How it happened, Jenna couldn't decide . . . any more than she knew why she didn't just pack her bags and slip out a back door. Christmas was over, here and gone as it was every year, but she remembered sitting in her private room, just staring out the window, which wasn't like other years. She'd thought about her family . . . and Darius . . . and the child, Raphael, who now wore a face, if not the right face. Doubtful the boy Darius had claimed to love would look anything like the ghostly image in that oil painting, but the image stuck.

Two weeks . . . almost three, she realized in a lame moment. Almost three weeks had passed since she'd entered Hugh von Hendricks' home and taken up residence on the second floor. Not exactly a prisoner. Weather providing, she meandered through the surrounding paths and ventured down the back lane to the homestead. Hugh had given her a key and cleared her occasional jaunts with the guards who meandered through the relics as quietly as the ghosts that seemed to linger in the halls. In the homestead, she felt strangely attracted, as if the ancient Algen Brock would step from the study and offer reassuring words. At times, she nearly heard the patter of shoes on the stairs and at least once, turned toward that sound, expecting to see the child flying down the wide staircase.

By sheer luck, Jenna met Emma again. The old woman had been locking up the main house, running a little later than usual. Tour hours began at noon, and ended at three, seven days a week. By five, the last of the visitors were gone. In the summers, Emma had explained, the hours extended, and the tours would run until seven. Daylight only. A few part-time employees would come to take a few groups. "We don't get that many people in the winter," Emma had confided. "I'm surprised we've had as many as we have. Usually, by this time of year, I can count on catching up on my reading list."

Emma lived on the estate, Jenna learned in that first genuine encounter. Behind the collection of log homes, which were mentioned, not shown during the winter months with the cost of heat and the renovations, stood three more modern cottages. The actual curator and his wife occupied one, the chief of security occupied the other. Jenna had met the others, but the curator's wife was nearly deaf and bordering senile. Emma had laughed after the introduction and patted Jenna's arm with a reassuring gesture, "She's a bit much, but don't let her worry you."

By the third visit to Emma's cottage, which had already become a regular stop, Jenna confided the reasons for her present residence, trusting Emma enough to confide the details of the FBI . . . and admitting she knew Darius.

Emma listened. She didn't judge, and she admitted a detail of her own. "I never really met or spoke with Darius Brock. He joined one of my tours one afternoon and I never knew who he was until he'd already gone. One does not forget that face or that smile," she'd said with a conspiring grin that faded as she read Jenna's expression. "I'm sorry, dear. If I've said something—"

"I don't know what I'm doing here, Emma. I should be getting back to my apartment, putting my life back in order . . ."

Instead, she continued haunting the homestead as often as the ghosts on the wind and the image of Darius in her mind. To make matters worse, she felt a routine established between herself and Hugh, and his flirtations were becoming ever more obvious. That she enjoyed his company . . . about the way a shipwrecked woman would enjoy the chatter of a shipwrecked man . . . offered no comfort. Candlelight dinners, wine and chit-chat about everything from new movies to politics. At times, she caught herself in the middle of a near breathless dialogue just for the sake of killing the musing shine in his riveted eyes.

On one such occasion, Hugh slipped out of his usual chair across from her in the living room and settled onto the armchair at her side. The sobriety in his eyes held her from pulling her hand away when he reached across the connecting table and caught her fingers. "Jenna, I think there's something we need to discuss," he said quietly.

The last time he spoke those words, she'd landed in an airplane. Warily, she commented, "Discuss away, Hugh."

"I don't know how to say this gently, nor even tactfully, dear, and I know no matter how I say it, you'll be hurt," he said sorrowfully. "The fact is, dear, Darius isn't coming back for you. I know you care about him and I . . . I think you may have pinned your hopes on him, but you shouldn't have. He's not the type of man to be tied down to a single woman. Honey, I don't know what he told you about himself or what he might have said to have you fall for him . . . I know I may be speaking out of turn, and you may be angry with me. But you need to realize, he truly isn't a man you could depend on. Oh, he talks a smooth line. As your friend—and I do hope you'll regard me as such—I have to admit, it is a line. The only commitment he's ever made is to the von Hendricks fortunes, Jenna, and that won't change. He gave up his own wife and children to work for my brother. I don't know if you know he was married—"

"Yes, I do," she said, certain she'd rather not hear this, but unable to pull away.

"About eight years ago, my brother returned to Europe. Shortly after our father died, we realized grandfather couldn't possibly control the Hendricks Corporation. Amad's always been more business oriented. My father's prodigy, in fact. I wouldn't know where to begin to explain this, but to make a long story short, Amad set out to reorganize certain aspects of the company and if you've heard Emma's spiel, you know the Brocks and von Hendricks have enjoyed a long healthy business relationship.

Amad tracked down several of them in the hopes of finding a few men he could trust . . . or possibly, more clearly," he said with a disgusted note. "Whose loyalty and trust could be bought. Out of those he contacted, Darius was one and there was another fellow who lived here in New York, an attorney with a rather successful office. Both Darius and Kevin now hold key positions in the von Hendricks company. I don't know how much of what I've heard is accurate . . . or possibly I do. My brother's told me this himself," he said with a more disheartened gaze. "He made Darius an offer . . . Amad offered to groom him for the position personally, offered him an incredible amount of money and the position. As I've heard, Darius didn't exactly jump at it. He had the wife, the kids to think about, and Amad needed a man who could be mobile at the drop of a hat, not a family man, if you get my drift."

Jenna nodded.

"Darius him-hawed and held out a while. To hear Amad tell it, the man suffered a little moral dilemma. His marriage wasn't exactly a touch of heaven. He'd been forced into marriage, but he had a sense of responsibility. Fine, Amad said and offered a suggestion and solution. Divorce the wife, give me custody of your son and I'll raise him as my son, and the position's yours for the taking." Hugh paused as if the words left a bitter taste in his mouth, but he continued as if forced, "To Darius's credit, I suppose, he probably weighed the options. He was twenty-two, stuck in a lousy marriage, barely able to support his son. Amad offered him a way out, but my brother's not the easiest man to deal with. He put a twist on it. Once Darius took the position, he wasn't to have anything more to do with his son or the deal would be off, he'd be fired immediately."

Pausing only a breath, Hugh squeezed her fingers gently, smiling sadly. "The same held true for . . . marriage, Jenna. He's not to get himself tangled up in personal relationships. You uhm . . . you might say, my brother owns him, honey, and I . . . I think the past eight years are a pretty good indicator. He's not about to throw away everything my brother's given him and go back to a life of poverty. I . . . as much as I like him, and I must admit, I enjoy his company and respect his business savvy, I don't think too highly of his moral standards. Not that I can truly blame him. He grew up without a father, basically in what we'd consider slums in America. My brother's given him the opportunity to make something of himself and he's done well considering the social obstacles he's overcome." He paused again, appearing only more dismayed.

Whether he was dismayed for her or himself, Jenna couldn't decide. The words rang of truth, but the deliverance carried too many false notes, and the arrogance in those last lines disturbed her.

"As a man, I do respect him, honey, and I can't fault his instincts in business. But . . . well, I'll be perfectly honest, Jenna," he said with a wan grin. "When my brother first asked me to come to your aid and explained the reasons for his concern . . .? Well, my first impression was that you were . . . well, there's no easy way to say this. With your connection to Darius, I thought you might be . . ."

"A hooker?" she guessed with a wry smile, concealing the contempt behind her eyes as she watched him flash embarrassment without denial.

"Not quite that," he admitted with a soulful gaze. "But I did think you . . . I was wrong," he said quietly, losing part of the apology. "I knew the moment I saw you coming toward me, I was wrong, and we've spent enough time together for me to know you truly do care for him regardless how little you knew him. Please, understand, I just don't want to see you hurt, Jenna. These past few weeks . . . I don't know how to say this without sounding like a perfect cad after everything else I've just said, but . . . I'm falling in love with you, Jenna. I couldn't stand by and do nothing when I know you'll just end up hurt by whatever lies he told you to gain your affection. He's not . . . He'll never be a man you could depend on or to love you half as much as I already love you . . ."

CHAPTER 11

The seating arrangements had changed again, which wasn't all that unusual. When Kevin joined them for dinner, he warranted the left-hand chair and Raphael sat on the right. Alongside Kevin, Teddy sat quietly, picking at his meal with his natural aplomb. Directly across from Teddy, Darius sat, likewise picking, without near the grace. Nearly cooked through, the slab of prime ribs lacked even the taste to qualify as a rawhide chew bone . . . though, even if it dripped red, Darius doubted he'd find the energy to be enthusiastic. His limbs were lead; his mind slightly more foggy with the throbbing at his temple. Far away he heard the purely human voice of his older cousin, heard the soft responses from his younger cousin. At the far end of the table, the Baroness, Brian, and Halbrook sat in a separate world, too far away to reach his shallow grasp. On Raphael exclusively, Darius attempted to concentrate, but even that seemed too great a feat.

Sighing, the voice prickled inside and out, and whether Darius moved of his own will or by command, he skidded his elbows more fully to the table and caught his sinking, throbbing head before it landed in his plate.

"Darius?" Kevin's voice came from far away.

"Pappa, may we be excused?" Raphael's voice was closer, laced with a childish reverence.

"No, my lad," the low voice stated.

"Pappa, Darius isn't hoongry now, and I'm due for my reading. He's teaching me aboot space, pappa! Satellites. I sure like learning aboot the stars, pappa! Did you knoow aboot the space shoottles and sooch, pappa?"

"Aye, lad, I've heard a thing or two about shuttles and sooch," Amad played.

"We'll joost be mooving along then," the boy said and started to skid off his chair. "G'day tae you Kevin—"

"Sit down, Raphael," the Baron stated smoothly.

"Pappa! My lessons!" Raphael started with an edge. "I'm learning moore froom Darius than all the time I spent with that fat ox down the table. Aye, a scholar," he said with a snort of derision. "He dinnae huv half the brains of Darius!"

"Lad," the Baron said in a near musing tone. "I'd be tempted to think you're up to something with this newfound enthusiasm for your studies."

"I'm fascinated," the boy said simply. "Aye! He's opened me curiosity circuits, so he has, Pappa. I dinnae even try watching the television for a whole week! Noot even once, Pappa."

"Well, that certainly explains part of your improved mood, lad. Not even a sitcom to have you pining for a large family and friends. I've not known you to abstain from such a pleasure, my lad. Now I know you're up to something."

"I'm behaving, Pappa," Raphael said gravely. "Noot a thing have I done wrong, and you're knowing sooch. Darius says if we keep me mind busy, I willnae be in sooch fixes so often. He's teaching me proper manners, Pappa."

"Is that a fact, Darius?"

Shifting his head enough to see the Baron looking at him, he nodded slightly without raising his weighted skull from his hands. Yes. "Yee-es-suppose so."

"Lad, you're looking a bit . . . puny this eve. If I didn't know better, lad, I'd be tempted to believe you're coming down with a cold."

"C-coold, yes sir," Darius answered catching only the faintest sense of concern from the living spectators. He couldn't even remember greeting Kevin, not that it mattered. If he needed to speak, a voice would tell him what to say.

"Lad, the chance of you catching a cold is very nearly as unfathomable as the universe you're teaching my son to appreciate. Perhaps, you should come here."

Not an actual command, Darius noted, but he pulled his head partway up and dropped his hands to the table. His arms shook, his elbows jellied, his knees threatened to collapse before an internal command firmed his balance.

"Pappa, Darius is always cold," Raphael said in a subtle accusation. "We need to—"

"Silence, Raphael," the Baron warned.

Making his way around the boy's chair, Darius skimmed his hand on the carved back to keep his balance and firmed afoot as he stopped alongside the Baron's chair. With a will of their own, his hands moved, shifting his palms out in front of him. Through a haze, he saw his hands trembling, felt only the awful shifting and swaying inside his head. With an effort, he cleared his focus to see the Baron reach and clasp his right hand, turning it, exposing more than a few inflamed dots. Under the prod and pressure of the Baron's finger, Darius flinched mentally and shuddered uncontrollably at the fiery pulse sliding up his wrist. Not quite catching up to the action, Darius watched in dull fascination as Amad pushed his sweater and shirt sleeve up his arm to expose far more dots and scrapes.

"Lad, I've seen pincushions with fewer holes in them," the Baron mused.

Darius nodded and shrugged, attempting to concentrate. The little lad was hungry . . . the little devil was always hungry. Orders.

"Now's my fix," Amad said in a mildly amused voice. "I don't know on which of you I should vent my current disapproval. Would you have a suggestion, I wonder, Darius?"

In trouble for something, apparently. "T-oss a coin," he managed.

"That might work at that," the Baron said thoughtfully. "Heads, I'll lob yours from its shoulders. Tales, I'll shred my elf's rump."

"Pappa," the boy said in a morose tone. He'd come to his feet and sidled alongside Darius within his father's reach. "I'll . . . ehm. . . well. Tis my fault. Plain and simple. Darius was joost following your own orders, and you were knowing before now. Dinnae be mad at him, pappa. I'm to be taking full blame," he said drearily.

"Aye, you're to blame, there's no doubt," the Baron mused. "Unfortunately, your drained accomplice should have found sense to curb your appetite."

"Pappa, please dinnae blame him," Raphael uttered. "He was obeying your command, tis no more or less you expect of him. I . . . I'm to blame. He cannae tell me no, Pappa, you told him so. If he refused, he'd be in a worse fix. I . . . was fearing you were knowing and joost letting me have my way. Dinnae hurt him o'er this. Please, father? I willnae do sooch a thing again to him."

"Oh, now there's a vow I'd certainly believe were it spoken off the lips of another child—even less than off your own, I'll mention," the Baron mused. "You're incorrigible, my lad"

"I'm knowing sooch," the boy said dismally.

"Tell me then, what was the final step in this grand plot of yours? Er should I guess, You intended to walk him up to the woods and walk him off a cliff? Er do you have a stake up there with his name on it?"

"I ehm . . . I dinnae think he could walk that far, pappa," the boy said with a wry note. "I was hoping mayhap to joost give him a shoove off the main steps. If he dinnae die on the fall, I planned to finish him off with that big oogly vase at the bottom."

Darius turned his gaze to see the boy at his side, waking slowly to the very real danger the boy had planned. "You rotten li'l son of a—"

"Darius," the Baron warned.

Raphael tipped his sparkly, musing eyes to Darius. His brow furrowed, and lips tilted in a glum smile. "I'm trying, me friend. At great risk to the both of us, you'll notice."

His present state was neither an accident nor a natural phenomenon. The boy had been whining for the past several days, hungry at the blasted drop of a hat. On walks, during studies, in the middle of Darius's own sporadic meals. The little imp had been slowly, systematically draining him every chance he got, never taking too much, just enough, and a little more with each of his spontaneous hunger spurts. If Darius could find slightly more energy, he might be inclined to laugh. Instead, he shook his thudding, heavy head and smirked. "To think, I once considered myself a fairly conniving bastard. I don't hold a candle to you, li'l chap."

The boy smiled, appreciating the compliment. "It was working, too! Look at you!"

"I'd l-like to sw-wat your ass," Darius said in a vibrating low voice.

Wariness swept across the brows; the lips scowled. "Aye, that's no way to show your appreciation."

Darius shook his head again and turned his gaze to find the Baron leaned back, watching them with a slightly bemused smirk in his mustache. "S-suppose I deserve whatever I get. Don't bother flipping the coin."

"Hmm, see the error of your ways, do you?"

I'd have seen them sooner if you'd lent a hand, Darius answered silently, his gaze remaining intent as he nodded, *but that's a mere technicality.* "I'll take my due."

"So, you will, lad," the Baron said and motioned with his hand for Darius to drop to his knees, which was becoming an all too familiar position. As Darius lowered, a little clumsily with the sway in his mind, he wondered if he would follow the normal routine and end up slightly more drained for his trouble. Instead, the Baron lifted his own index finger and scored the pad with his own tooth. Dropping his hand, he offered it to Darius not even bothering with a command. Before Darius caught up to his actions, he tasted the rancid liquid and choked a breath as the fire flashed through his mouth. As if engulfed in flames suddenly, he lost his breath and swallowed a gasp as the shudder raced through him. Still coughing, he sank to his shins, shaking his head as the fire-flash quickened to a keen awareness.

"Ahh, pappa," Raphael whined and clasped Darius's shoulder. "Nooo!"

"Aye, lad."

Collecting his breath, the world clearing far more rapidly, Darius lifted his gaze warily to find the boy looking into him with an expression of utter sorrow. Considering how close he'd come to death yet again, the anger sparked in his eyes, and he looked up at the Baron, "How the bloody hell was I to avoid that one, would you mind to tell me?"

"Obviously, you weren't," the Baron said with a subtle amusement. "But it appears you've recovered well enough."

Well enough to pay for letting the lad nearly get away with murder. If not annoyed, Darius might still be amused, and that was certainly a paradox worth notice. The little devil had nearly tricked him through his own total submission. Shaking his head, Darius glanced to the wily little beast, who appeared only slightly more worried than wary. Looking up to the Baron, Darius wondered, "Is it even within reason for me to wonder how I'll avoid a repeat of this particular trick since he most assuredly followed your orders, as did I?"

"Hmm, quite a predicament, I'll grant you," the Baron idled and looked to his son momentarily, then back to Darius. "Unless you're entirely comfortable on your knees, lad, perhaps you'd like to return to your chair, and do turn it sideways to receive this imp across your lap. A few swats might be in proper order for this bit of mischief."

"I—no!" Raphael stated. "I dinnae do nothing wrong, Pappa!"

"My 'lad, you nearly drained your guvnor," the Baron said in mocked surprise. "You don't find that just slightly unorthodox?"

"Well, and look at him!" Raphael said angrily, wrenching his neck to look up as Darius rose smoothly to his feet. "He's too bloody well off for you to be blaming me for a thing!"

"Raphael, I've always been reasonable with you," Amad said in a sighing voice. "Thus, I'll give a choice. The hand of your father or the hand of your governor?"

"Aye, and there's a reasonable choice," the boy said sarcastically and darted his wary gaze up to Darius, who smiled with a trace of honest anticipation. Shivering, Raphael darted his gaze to his father with a far more desperate shine. His finger lifted to his teeth, and he uttered around the nail, "I'm sorry, father. I willnae do sooch a thing again. I willnae, not ever. Dinnae make him beat me." His voice lisped, and the tears gathered. "Y-you d-doo it, all right, then? You, father."

The Baron let out a humph and shifted his hand, availing his lap and looking over to Darius as he sighed, "Appears the lad's denied you retribution, Darius. A pity, I rather thought you'd enjoy this enterprise. Such a reward is not to be yours."

Darius shook his head, seeing the child's hesitation and second thought. Oh, the games these two played, pitting one emotion against the other. The boy inevitably took the brunt of these matches, and this wasn't the exception. Not only would Raphael suffer tremendously under his father's palm, he would undoubtedly feel bad for denying Darius a reward, however slight. Across the table, Kevin and Teddy sat silently, their eyes averted. Obviously, both had been privy to similar exchanges in the past.

Under the first crack and child's gasp, Darius turned his gaze to see the youngster splayed and lurching. Recalling the force of the Baron's slaps and punches, Darius identified with the fierce instant pain that started the child's cries and sputtered sobs. Retribution. The little lad was paying for his tricks . . . and Darius's anger slipped away with each of those cracks. His muscles jumped and gripped in spasms, and it seemed suddenly, the Baron was surely killing him, if not battering him beyond endurance. "Sir,"

Darius snapped, his gaze darting from the lurching child up to the cool blue eyes. "That's . . . ." *Enough! Enough! The boy's paid in full! I'm alive!*

"I wondered," the Baron said as he settled his hand on the boy's back, his gaze still on Darius, and a smile twisted on his lips. *Nothing left, eh? And yet, you scream for me to stop?* "You're quite the fickle beast, Darius."

Raphael scooted and slithered, sobbing in great heaving waves as he slid up his father's chest and buried his face against the collar. In broken syllables, he cried his apologies and sorrow.

With his restored senses, Darius felt the waves of pain and grief flowing off the child as surely as he heard the integrity of sorrow and frustration in the sobs. In a wicked paradox, Raphael honestly believed he needed to carry out his promise no matter how much he dreaded the thought of success. Between his fear of success and his fear of his father's wrath, the child was in a terrible state . . . and it was contagious. If Darius could have taken his own life to calm the little devil, he surely would have. Instead, he felt the hot angry tears gathering in his eyes as he suffered his own paradox. He should not feel! He should feel nothing, least of all *sorrow* for this incorrigible deadly little monster!

"Sons," the baron said with a humph of disgust and turned his gaze to Kevin. "Tell me, Kevin, how have you dealt with two of them underfoot for so long? I've barely had this pair together a few weeks and they're driving me to wits' end."

"It's uh . . . not easy," Kevin said in a low voice.

Sighing, the Baron scuffed the curls at his collar, then nudged the child into motion. "Go warm your brother's chilly heart, lad. He's in a terrible state. Won't be satisfied until he's seen I haven't stricken you dead."

"A-a-ye papa," Raphael heaved and flowed off the chair, sailing to Darius and scooting onto his lap in one motion. Rather than climb and cling to Darius' shoulders, he spread his arms about Darius's chest, burying his head. Whether on his own merit or through the Baron's influence, Darius folded his arms over the boy and clasped the head near his chest. The little one continued to heave muffled sounds and lurch in misery.

"That's enough, lad," Darius uttered, and the words barely escaped when a distant memory sliced from some dark corner of his mind—the same corner where he'd hidden all the memories of his lost son. A nightmare, he remembered. He'd come home late, half asleep, a tad drunk, and he'd found Dylan sobbing, tangled in damp sheets and coated in a chilly sweat. Monsters, Dylan had sobbed, clinging to Darius then as this trembling body clung to him now. Monsters coming to take him . . . to take pappa from him. Inconsolable, Dylan had held onto him and Darius had spoken those words, comforting his son . . . as he comforted one of the monsters now. And he was the monster now.

"Perhaps we should attempt to continue our conversation, Kevin. Eventually, at least one of my lads may cease to wallow in his misery and give us a scant reprieve," the Baron said with a combination of amusement and disgust. "You mentioned we've had more trouble in the United States. Do elaborate, will you?"

"I . . . received a call from Harry Morris this afternoon," Kevin began smoothly. "He's had another visit from those thugs attempting to buy us out of the shipping business. They'd like to set up a meeting. After what happened to Fradden in Pittsburgh, Morris is nervous."

"I assume you've reassured him, and you have names and numbers."

"Right here," Kevin spoke while flipping open a small black leather book alongside his plate. Tearing off the top sheet of a small yellow pad, he slipped it across the corner of the table. "They were allegedly acting for the Ricotti organization, but I put in a few calls to our friends in the Justice Department. They're connected to the Morelli family."

"Know the lads," the Baron said with an idling tone, lifting the paper and breezing his glance over the short list, nodding. "Reminds me, Darius," he commented, knowing Darius's attention had riveted before looking over. A smile playing on his mustached lips, he spoke simply, "Did I mention to you, we located my wine?"

Darius studied him over the curly head shivering at his chest. "May I ask where?"

"Of course you may ask, lad," Amad said as if slightly surprised. "Not that I think you'll appreciate the answer. The cases were returned to the winery rather than delivered to the freighter. All that fuss. and it turns out they were sitting in Hugh's storage. Apparently, it was a simple comedy of errors and a study in dereliction. Hugh's employees never checked the invoices when they accepted the return delivery. They assumed they'd shipped too many cases with another large order that shipped out at the same time. As I recall, I asked Hugh to crate the special delivery as if it were a routine shipment. The lad follows orders rather well occasionally. You might say, almost a little too well, occasionally," he said with a bemused twitch and a glitter in his eyes. "I do despise inefficiency in my ranks, but all's well that ends well, don't you agree?"

An end by no means. "What about the break-ins?"

"Hmm, but you are a bright one," the Baron mused. "Not as easily explained, lad. You're right to assume ordinary means didn't breach the security but nothing appears amiss. I'd imagine that suggests my enemy's still scheming; however, I fail to see why you bother to wonder, lad. You're safe from harm's way."

Jenna . . . the name slid across his mind as swiftly as her lovely image. She remained in harm's way . . . in Hugh's realm. She could be caught by this enemy . . . and it was already too late to push that thought aside or attempt denial. Darius dropped his gaze from the steady shine. But the Baron needed no windows to his soul—the Baron had an open door, a periscope, directly into that tarnished domain. And she was still there. Her wry little smile that seemed to hold some clever secret or comfort; the liquid blue shine of her eyes that had drawn and held him as quick as a warm spring; the rhythm of her voice as they'd chatted over mundane things.

Art and history . . . current trends and childhood antics . . . life. Never in his life had he felt so alive as he'd felt with her in that single day. She was inside of him, a part of him now, and perhaps, he merely needed to preserve that memory, guard it. As dangerous and futile as his thoughts were, he was powerless against them, and he knew at this moment he was still vulnerable. In an eye-blink, the Baron could create the images to stir his blood.

Darius had seen her. Amad had lied when telling him, he would never see her again. Darius had seen her in candlelight . . . had seen her cheeks flushed with laughter and cold as she walked hand in hand with Hugh von Hendricks . . .

Trapped . . . Darius felt the trap snap shut even as the window blasted open inside his mind and he saw them . . .

First Hugh von Hendricks, a softer, more slender and lighter human version of the Baron. Faded sunlight spilled over his clipped dark hair, his stark blue eyes shined with unmistakable desire, his thin lips turned and puckered slightly, as if ready for a meal. Oh, and his hands rested, one touched down within a flow of bronze-tinted silk, the other tentatively alight on a soft porcelain cheek. Jenna. Her deep blue eyes held on Hugh, waxed between uncertainty and wisdom, her lashes dipped beneath faintly troubled brows, her lips quivering as if she meant to speak but could find no words. Only the faintest hint of a smile lingered on those lips . . . and Hugh was moving, gliding closer . . . touching down as if only testing, heating, tipping his head . . . and her hand lifted, lighting on his shoulder—

The window snapped shut, but the scene played over on the surface of Darius's riveted mind. In his chest, his still human heart quickened with the flow of anger and pain that threatened to explode inside of him. Trapped. Locked into that single scene, he saw her again and again, her blue eyes intense, her lips puckering in a quivering smile, her hands sliding and gliding smoothly. Inside himself, he felt that soft caress rising, sinking, the fingers groping for shirt buttons, but it wasn't his image illuminated in his mind, not his chest she caressed and heated, not his lips she locked and held, or his eyes she drew into those liquid pools to wrap in warmth and a contentment as he'd never known.

In his arms, the small body shifted, the face tipping and wet blue eyes searching.

Inside, Darius trembled on the brink of detonation. His body rallied against him to feel the sensations of warm hands as his mind railed against the familiar scent of soft perfume and the fragrance that encompassed Jenna Windrow. He loved her. He hated her. He wanted her warmth wrapped against him . . . knew she rested in the arms of another man. Pain. From the depths of his immortal soul, the pain rose and twined through his physical body, tightening his chest, his stomach, his muscles. As if suffocating, the pressure wrapped around his railing mind and squeezed, immense hands clasping and closing. He wanted it stopped! Physically, mentally, he wanted this stopped and the rage only quickened the images, the sensations. They wrapped together. Hugh's hands gliding over her milky white flesh, his lips tracing paths over those wondrous mounds, vivid in Darius's mind. Her eyes misted, glazed with passion meant only for him! *For himmm! Maaake thiss stop!*

The images were in his head—only in his head! *Not reeealll!* His Jenna . . . the Jenna in his heart, in his soul, wasn't this woman wrapped around Hugh! But he couldn't get out—couldn't stop the vile images. Like a spectator, he witnessed them standing in the center of a vaguely familiar room—the living room in Hugh's mansion . . . then she was there, lying and tumbling in silken sheets, Twisted, he relived the moments in the Chateau Suites—twisting and turning, touching and tasting. Only once, in all his twenty-eight years, had he experienced the connection and burning desire flaming between them.

But here she was now, pouring her love and lust on another man—and that man had become a mortal enemy in Darius's mind. A mortal enemy to be crushed . . . as she should be crushed! But he loved her . . . she was his!

His lover . . . his love! She was inside of him, shredding his mortal heart with her treachery . . . but she was his! She belonged in his arms . . . belonged in his heart . . . he wanted her! Not stopping. His thoughts sailed and raged between the images flashing inside his mind. The hand was fisting, closing out the light, squeezing the life from him, clenching and unclenching as if letting him gasp for air. Dying. Physical death could hurt no worse than this! And his silent cries echoed in an eternal instant, a plea for release from this agony . . .

"Papppaaa, pleeease ssstop!" the child's voice cried, echoing in his pulsing ears. "Pleeease stop! Yerrr hurrrting him! Yerrr killling him, Papppa!"

"Aye, he's hovering on the brink in his mind, there's no doubt," the deep voice mused. "Rather sounds like you a few moments ago, lad. But I suppose we can't leave him there forever, eh?"

Enough!

CHAPTER 12

Under the hammer force of that single word, the images and sensations exploded. Gasping, Darius lurched and ducked his head under the physical impact. His breath wheezed and hissed behind gulps of air and lumps rising in his constricted throat. To his half sobs and pained sounds, his head bowed and lurching against the small shoulder, Darius awoke slowly. Physical . . . as much physical as mental anguish quaked through his shattered muscles, trembling him as he collected a firm hold on the dwarfed body quivering on his lap. Around his head, the small arms circled, and a tiny hand stroked his sweated hair. Against his ear, the soft quivering voice uttered words of comfort and promise.

"There now. . . there's all right . . . hoosh now . . . pappa's done . . . it's all right. Aye, you'll be all right, now."

Further away, a husky tight voice intruded, "Amad, I've never asked anything of you, never questioned an order or command but . . . but what has he done? Why have you taken him from us? Why are you putting him through this? If one of us has done something against you, then let us all suffer for it, but tell us who, sir. Tell us who we need to blame for this. I know he never betrayed you. He's never denied you or rejected you. He's gone against every moral principle inside of him to honor his oath. He's done more for you than any of us in the material world. On his own initiative and authority, he's increased profit margins and found ways to increase your return that even I hadn't considered. How can you do this to him? What could he have possibly done to deserve what you're doing to him?"

"Kevin, my lad," the deep voice lowered to a consoling tone. "Did I ever once promise any of you that I'd limit your human suffering? Were these not my words? Vowed and sealed in blood . . .? All those who live and breathe at this moment are mine to do with as I will."

"But . . . our own oaths, sir? And by your own order, the positions we'd fill?"

"Kevin, wasn't it but a month ago, I had you bring your favorite son to me to enter into the binding covenant?"

"I . . . I knew I'd face that moment from the beginning, sir," Kevin said in a lower voice. "I even knew it would be Allen you'd choose. He would have been my choice to follow in my footsteps. But this . . . even with my occasional participation into our clan's revival . . . It doesn't compare to what Darius has done. By your words, your decree, no others exist who could fill his shoes."

"Ah, well, not quite so," the Baron mused.

Still collecting his breath and trembling in the explosion's wake, Darius heard the words, knew the Baron had shifted his attention toward the far end of the table.

"Brian's pined for years to fill that position, and he believes himself worthy and ready to rise to the challenge, isn't that so, lad?"

From the far end of the table, Brian's voice barely rose to cover the distance. "At your command, sir."

"There, see?" the Baron said contritely, shifting his attention to Kevin. "Not to worry, there's hope for your clan. Brian's a potent substitute who's been waiting in the wings too long. He'll need a bit of coaching to fulfill the business end of the arrangement, I'm sure, but between you and I, Kevin, I'm sure he'll make an able mouthpiece."

"No offense to him . . . or to you, sir," Kevin said carefully. "But I'm not sure that he will. You . . . you chose us for our lineage as well as our uhm . . . temperament? You didn't make any mistake when you determined what shoes we should wear. By my own inherent character to lead and rationalize, to choose between the good of one and the good of all, you slated me for the position I fill, both in your company and in our clan. Darius wasn't the exception or a mistake. You chose him for the morality he could give our children, the integrity and dignity inside of him even when he's forced to make tough decisions. You chose him because he not only wears the title of Father, but it's also a part of him. He would and did risk life and limb to save his son and if he'd met against a lesser opponent, he'd have succeeded. Brian doesn't have those inherent traits, sir. He's not to blame for that, but if even I can see that he doesn't have the sense of morality and commitment to fulfill this post, I know you must."

"I love to hear your arguments, Kevin. Such finesse and refinement is a gift," the Baron said and sighed. "But alas, although you're correct on all counts, I'll grant you, it's a little too late. Rather like making your closing arguments after the verdicts in and executed. Even if I thought I'd like to reverse the decision, which I don't, it would be akin to lifting the lever on the electric chair after the shock's been sent. Your cousin, noble and paternal as he is, wouldn't pass those traits into your clan now without letting a little of something else slide through. I believe, I mentioned the word 'son' at least once in your presence, Kevin. Granted, the lad wouldn't incinerate under a strip of sunlight, but he might yet suffer a horrendous case of sun poisoning should he linger too long." He paused only a moment, sounding almost sorrowful as he continued, "It truly is too late, Kevin. If it makes you feel better, you might consider him elevated rather than condemned. You might even consider your own words and wonder if the lad's integrity has seduced me. I am a self-serving beast, as you well know, lad. Why should I allow your clan to benefit when I could have him entirely to myself, a member of my family?"

Silence.

"Granted, he's not a von Hendricks, but truthfully, Kevin, I've sought an elder lad for years. My own paternal instincts, you might say. So, there you have it then."

"I . . . I'm not sure I have it at all, sir," Kevin said carefully.

"It's really not that difficult to grasp, lad," the Baron said smoothly. "As all creatures gifted with longevity must learn and adapt, so too must I," he spoke as if he were a scholar launching into a complex lecture. "For years, I've nurtured and protected my heirs. Upon a time, most were scattered hither and yon, very few if any, wearing the paternal name to match my own." His gaze shifted toward Darius and Raphael, his gaze settling on the deep blue eyes. "What year was it, lad? Do you recall the year I deemed to correct that malady?"

"N-no, sir," Raphael uttered, listening as intently as Darius now, both turned slightly to have the cobalt gaze lancing them. Darius watched the smile curve the mustached lips, saw the flicker of amusement in Amad's eyes before he feigned enlightenment.

"Ah, I remember," he said and looked back to Kevin. "The year was 1865, the year after the Civil War ended in your own homeland, Kevin. Perhaps that had something to do with my decision—all that brother fighting against brother, north and south," he sighed, amused. "In any case, I decided my family needed new blood. Now, that wasn't as easy as you may think, lad. For years, dear Raphael and I were forced to switch names just to keep a von Hendricks in this castle. The males of my clan have always had a knack for getting themselves into fatal fixes. My own little lad here lost his father to a hangman's noose . . . for the mere act of the little devil's creation. A curse that, to have such virile men cut down for answering nature's call, but so it was with Anton von Hendricks, not too unlike myself upon a time," he paused, catching his tempo. "Had my little lad here cooperated, I might have had a few more living heirs, but alas, he was unruly from the start and fairly poured his blood into me. Thus, by 1865, most of my paternal lines had dried up. Took more months or years than I can readily recall to find a pure von Hendricks. Turned out to be a lass when I did find one, thus, I was reduced to relying on maternal lines . . .Probably where I went wrong, but we'll get to that," he said in a bemused tone, fully enjoying himself now.

"The problem was this, you see. The lass wore the wrong name, and in order to have a proper heir to fulfill a title, one needs to have a degree of integrity. I believe I was wearing the name Raphael, at the time," he pondered and nodded. "Yes, I was. Baron Raphael von Hendricks, in fact," he mused and favored the little boy with a glance.

"As Raphael, I married my ehm . . . thrice removed niece, I believe she was. Corina. Lovely lass. Now, the next problem. How to father a child to this lovely living lass? Simple. Find a randy young nobleman with similar coloring and respectable blood, avail the missus to an affair, and voila! A living heir. Imagine my chagrin when he first fathered a daughter," he mused and again glanced at Raphael, whose brow wrinkled, and lips quivered. "If not for the tiny voice of reason, I might not have a single breathing heir left in this land. Nearly forfeited the entire plan. Ah, but then my li'l voice says, 'Why dinnae we joost try again?' We had the ingredients and the hot-blooded Scot I'd befriended was well up to the challenge. Liam was a splendid lad. He and I had quite a few jolly good times knocking about together. The lad could drink an entire barroom of hooligans under the table and still settle down to a good game of poker.

"If you lads ever take notion, you may find mention of the exploits of Lord Raphael von Hendricks and Lord Liam Donahue." His gaze slid to the deep end of the table and locked on Rebecca. "Ah, and you have, haven't you, lass? Heard that name mentioned a time or two, so you have."

"He was my father's dearest friend," Rebecca said in a quavering tone.

The Baron continued to smile at her, his eyes glittering with dark amusement. "That certainly dates you, dear heart. At times, I forget how old you are. Born, let's see now . . . 1903. Mercy, could it have been thirty years?" His gaze shifted again to Raphael. "Do you recall?"

"I'm thinking that first date was wrong, father," Raphael said thoughtfully. At some point, he'd slid his hands away and settled against Darius's chest. His head bobbed under Darius's chin. "I dinnae think you were even in Europe in 1865, pappa. I dinnae recall too well, joost that you were away for a time and a wee bit mad at me."

"Ahh, so right you are, lad. Was that trouble with Aaron Brock and his brood," the Baron said with a nod and a heated flash. "You were up to your usual mischief and nearly broke the bloody oath right before my own eyes."

"Well, and the lad had it cooming!" Raphael snapped. "They dinnae want no parts of me and you made me nearly into a ghost in me own home."

"Aye, well, you became a shadow of your former self, and you're absolutely right. It wasn't until 1895 I'd begun the quest for a living heir. All your bloody pining over siblings and the like. Well," he said with a lifted glittering flash to Darius then back to Rebecca. "So, it was then, you are the wench I nearly dried up in her crib, and look at you now? Mercy, lass, you'll leave this life as wrinkled as you entered it. The years haven't done you any kindness."

"A malady we all must face in our time," she answered with a subtle edge.

The Baron let out a humph and shifted his gaze to Kevin, who sat in silent commiseration.

"Haven't quite worked this out, have you, lad?"

"I'm listening," Kevin said lightly.

"Yes, so I see. Now where was I . . .? Ah, creation," he mused. "My noble family. A collection of highborn heirs to warm a loving father's heart." His gaze darkened a hue. "After my dear daughter, Rebecca, Liam produced Thaddeus, my pride and joy! What a noble little lad he was. Defender of truth and justice, protector of the weak and illegitimate," he mused and looked at Raphael. "Do you recall the scandal you became?"

"Aye," the boy growled. "Bastard son, born to a barmaid, compliments of Liam Donahue whose good name you chose to protect by taking me under your wing. Aye, I remember well enoough, father. Made me a ghost to watch yer wee brood grow until they'd all risen to a head aboove me own height, then you tossed me into the soup like a sour spice to have me fighting for me life at every turn." And the incident still hurt and disturbed him, if his growl was any indication.

"I'd hardly consider it a fight for your life, lad," the Baron chuckled. "As I recall, I favored you above my own more often than not, treated you quite well in fact."

From the other end of the table, Rebecca commented, "To make my brothers jealous."

"So true," the Baron mused and looked toward her. "But what greater test of a man's mettle, eh? His compassion? Aye, I put a bastard among you and showered him with my affection . . . until he tried to bite your little brother. Ansen always was the more spiteful among you, and a bully from day one. It's no wonder his clan does so well in California. It's a fine haven for the ill-conceived. You, however, fared well in those early years, dear. Took to the little devil like a mother hen with a new chick. A pity you never conceived of your own. It might have kept you looking young longer and given you a better reason to live, dear heart. But alas, the same malady that prohibited you from conceiving has kept you living these many years beyond your prime. A tad too much of your unnatural father's influence," he taunted and winked at her. "Ah, how I love to see your wheels turn, my dear."

"You know I'm not surprised by your mention of Liam, I assume," she said in a lofty, slightly chilly tone. Sitting ramrod straight and prim, she rested in the high-backed chair like a princess surveying her court, her silver hair taking in the light from the chandeliers, giving nothing in return. As dull as a rainy sky, her colors reflected nothing. Even her eyes remained as platinum and opaque as the wool dress she wore. A single string of pearls sagged from her square spindly shoulders, her womanhood an echo of the past to leave her nearly as flat-chested as a child.

The shrew never changed, Darius considered as he took her in, despising her tilted jaw and arrogant posture. From the onset, she rested on a pedestal in her own eyes, looking down at them as if they were peasants in her elegant court. He might mention, the rooms could stand a bit of airing, and the lights could use some improvement. Rather than the remnants of dinner scattered on the plates, he smelled the mildew and must of rooms too-long sealed.

To the motion at his side, Darius riveted his gaze to find the Baron sliding his elbow across the table, nearly ramming Raphael's empty plate. Warily, Darius glimpsed the amused blue eyes even as the Baron motioned him to lean closer, crooking a finger in a physical gesture. By his own will, Darius conceded and leaned slightly closer to accept a conspiratorial whisper.

In a tone rising just enough above a whisper to be heard, the Baron confided, "That's her heart you're smelling, lad. A very musty place, to be sure, too long sealed. Between you and me, lad, I appreciate your observations. A little air never hurts, and simulated light can do wonders to improve an atmosphere."

What the words meant, Darius couldn't quite decide, but sensed the temper behind the blue eyes, enough to be wary even as the Baron drew back and settled leisurely in his armchair.

"You are absolutely right in your assumption, Rebecca, but do let me continue my story, will you, my dear? I rather like this role of expanding my young prodigy's horizons."

She tipped her head as if granting him a privilege.

Young prodigy? Did he mean Kevin? Or was it, as Darius now suspected, yet another lesson directed toward him?

The Baron turned his gaze to Kevin. "So, you see lad, I've always had this paternal desire to raise a family, to perpetuate my family name. Arrogance, pure and simple. As I'm sure you'll recognize the term, we live on in our children? There it is then. I went to great lengths and risks, nearly a century past, to have this legacy wrapped around me. Aye, and what a joy it is!

My pride and joy, Thaddeus, on whom I pinned my greatest aspirations. Ahh, but still you have questions. So, and I shall continue, lad. To be safe, I added a few extra eggs to my basket. Liam, the poor lad, he was kept so busy for a few years, he could barely think to drink, but a fine sport he was. Fathered two more sons, Ansen, whom you never met. Poor lad dropped dead during a tennis match at the ripe age of 60. A pity. I did mention he shouldn't take his heart and health for granted. He never listened to his father," he said in a sighing disgust. "Then we had Cornelius. My, how I hated that name, but for Corina . . .? Anything. Although I was rather pleased that he never passed that moniker into our family tree. The poor lad barely lived long enough to produce a single heir, and that lad had sense to hate the name along with the impotent who fathered him."

Pausing, he ran his gaze about his captive audience and landed his gaze on Halbrook. "Taking note of this, are you, lad?"

"Yes sir," Halbrook uttered.

The Baron smiled and nodded, tilting his gaze toward Kevin. "We had a poor turn after Cornie's arrival. Another lass, and one too many. She was such a fickle beast. Not the courageous daughter you see in our midst now. No, Lucinda was . . . Well? A weakling, for lack of a more definitive term. In every respect, the lass lacked. Mentally, she was nearly daft. Emotionally, a sheet in the wind blowing in every direction. At the jolly age of eighteen, Lucinda fell madly in love with a chap who fell madly in love with her money . . . My money, by extension. Oh, and what a time we had of that," he mused and looked to Raphael. "Do you remember, lad?"

"Aye, pappa, the chap who tumbled from his carriage," Raphael said thoughtfully, his brow wrinkled. "Boot there's something wrong with this telling, Pappa," he said quietly. "I'm thinking may yet, I was wrong before. There's a bit of family missing in this mix. Didn't you hand the title to another in there for a time? Aye, I had a grandfather and grandmother. A fat li'l man with a dull wit and the woman of a lesser make and stouter model. I dinnae remember their names, boot their faces . . .? Aye, they lived with us for a time in these very walls. They were here when that bit of thieving started in the village."

The Baron sighed as if disgusted. "Some things are better forgotten, lad," he said in a dismayed tone. "You're referring to the Baron Carl von Hendricks and his mistress, Thelma."

"Aye! Those are the ones."

"I shad have told this tale without your presence," the Baron mused. "Your honesty is a travesty to behold. Now, and I need to mention my first failed attempt at propagation and rejuvenation. As you may recall, the miscreant Carl was a throwback from the original family tree. A von Hendricks, I suppose I need admit. But probably inbred. He produced only one heir and hadn't sense to realize you took that lad's place at an early age, and I took yours in the years to come. His son, you may recall, we named Raphael, and I sent the bungling little oaf to an orphanage. My indulgence toward bloodline," he mused and returned his gaze to Kevin. "I thought about sending him off a cliff or tripping him into the pond back yonder, but he carried some rendition of my blood. Settled for dropping him in the streets of Strasburg and the orphanage there. You'd be shocked to realize how difficult it was to find a non-secular orphanage in those days. But alas, the mistake was removed. We were stuck with Carl and Thelma for a time, both of whom were still about when I found Corina and started raising my family." His gaze shifted to Raphael, "Now, are you satisfied the facts are in order?"

"Aye, pappa, but it joost seemed a funny thing in my mind. By the time of that carriage accident, we had those lumps doddering about in the halls. Aye, and before that even, I had a time with that ole devil. Was them who nearly sent me . . ."

"Ahh, I see where your confusion lies," Amad said gravely. "You're thinking about your little friend Maxwell. The lad I sent off to a workhouse for a time."

Raphael nodded, his expression dim. "Aye, Maxwell."

"Lad, you've your dates twixt," the Baron said sympathetically. "That experience was close to a dozen years before Carl and Thelma's arrival. I can understand your confusion. We left the castle to run under the Haegars' reign for a time, but alas, lad, they were only servants who treated you rather like a grandson. As I recall, I spent a fair amount of time in the village, and it wasn't too long after I first brought you here. You were in an awful state over the loss of Algen. When you set about finding a friend, I gave you free run for a time."

Amused, Amad turned his gaze toward Kevin who sat rapt. "Sons," he huffed. "The moment you turn your back, they hook up with the wrong crowd. That hasn't changed in centuries. I left the little lad to his own devices for a few months, and the next I'm hearing how my village has a plague of rodents pilfering wallets and snatching coins from purses. Lo and behold, I find my li'l elf running amuck with the leader of that fine band. Imagine the li'l elf's surprise when his comrade slated none but his own pappa for the taking?"

His eyes glittered with amusement and Raphael ducked his head slightly, as if the shame still touched him. The Baron's cobalt eyes lifted and fastened on Darius. "You might appreciate this tale, lad. You and your wee brother share a great deal in common. Rather quick with the hands and a little slight on propriety at a young age. Of course, you needed to survive, whereas your little brother merely needed companionship. He took up with the head thief and wily li'l beast that he is, never bothered to tell his comrade from where he hailed. Poor Maxwell assumed his little comrade was an orphan like himself, tossed from his home at night by a whoring mother."

The words struck the appropriate chord. Darius related that story far too closely with the truth of his own youth. Whether he was angry, or simply annoyed, Darius felt the direct hit as surely as the child who rested on his lap, mortified and filled with regret for spawning this tale. Ducking his head, Darius whispered against the curly head, "I don't believe your father appreciated being corrected or interrupted, lad. For both of our sake, keep your mouth shut."

"Aye, Darius," Raphael uttered.

The Baron huffed a laugh, "Ah, and it warms a man's heart to hear brothers getting along, and what a pleasure to hear such sound advice off the lips of the elder."

More annoyed, Darius lifted his gaze to the Baron and might have voiced his annoyance if not for the mental intrusion. No words needed spoken. The Baron knew his effect at the instant of impact. Futile to counter with words what his mind and body conveyed far more swiftly. Stifled by little else, Darius dropped his gaze away and attempted to quiet his mind.

Instead, he felt Kevin watching him, felt the man's sorrow for him. No longer was he the man who would speak his mind freely or rise to a challenge . . . With a word or a glance, the Baron could silence him. In Kevin and Teddy's combined eyes, Darius was wounded, if not entirely broken. The Darius Brock of yesterday would never drop his gaze in either fear or humiliation. More angry than annoyed, Darius lifted his heated gaze to find Kevin's sorrowful eyes still on him. "You don't know what the fuck this is all about," Darius growled. "Don't pretend otherwise."

Only more troubled, Kevin nodded, "You're right, cousin, I don't. And I'm sorry."

"Ah, and now you're even more sorry, eh?" Darius taunted. "Not the man you thought you knew—"

"Silence."

The word registered inside and out and Darius flinched, closing his mouth on the words and darting his gaze to the Baron. Silence. Silence . . . the only word. Silence inside his head. His gaze held on the Baron as the anger drained from his eyes and mind.

The Baron smiled slowly and lighted the sparkle in his eyes. "You are not the man they knew, lad, and they truly can't fathom what's happened inside of you. If they choose to feel bad for the changes you've undergone, so be it. They are human and they grasp only the reality before them. You are mine, from your shaggy dark head to your toes. You've lost that most precious of all human commodities, son. Your will. That's what they see, what they know. Your every thought, your every emotion and action remains in my hands, and they know me well enough to know you'll suffer at my hands. Rage against their sympathy if you must, son, but realize, they do still have that right . . . and do rage silently, if you will," he said in a more natural, musing tone. "I am trying to explain this to them."

No rage now, only understanding and a sick churning in his stomach. Human rights. Dignity. Human will. His gaze lowered in acquiescence, and he nodded without a conscious thought. He was still half human. Human enough to know he didn't appreciate anyone feeling sorry for him . . . and those feelings came from the past. Came from the distant past when he'd recognized the sorrow in elders' eyes as his mother dragged him about in the daylight. *Poor li'l tike,* those saddened eyes told him, *To have a mother like that . . . To have to live like that. Poor li'l tike . . . Always looks so lost and confused.*

With those very emotions churning inside him now, Darius wanted no further evidence from either of his cousins . . . And on the heels of that revelation, he knew the shame as he'd known shame twenty years ago under those similar gazes. Nothing could he do to escape this circumstance. He could no more punch or kick the presence from his mind than he could have kicked his mother from her own apartment. And how he'd hated her . . . as he hated the Baron now for making him feel this way again. No illusions. Everything churning inside of him was stirred up like soup simmering in a pot, needing only a twist of a ladle at the Baron's hand.

The Baron let out a humph and began again. "All these interruptions, I've fairly forgotten the point of this tale, Kevin."

"Sir, we . . . we are human," Kevin said with a tight rein on his sorrow. "And I think I've gotten the point. For whatever reason, you've taken our cousin and the father of our clan and you've turned him into your . . . son."

"That wasn't the word you considered using, Kevin," the Baron said in a low voice. "I do believe, you meant to say . . .? Slave, wasn't it?"

"Puppet would have been my choice," Kevin said quietly.

"A fine distinction between the two, lad, and I appreciate your honesty. I'll point out, however unkindly, the lad's more like a slave in that, he retains his right to think and feel. Were he a puppet, I'd put the thoughts in his head and send them out his mouth and doubtful, he'd feel a thing. Slave is definitely closer to the word I choose to call him, which is simply, son. Ah, but you still don't fully grasp the method to this madness, and you need justification. Otherwise," he mused. "You may be tempted to forfeit slightly more than your cousin's loss. After all," he paused. "If such a fate can take the father of your clan, why bother to save the children, eh?"

"I've given my word."

"Aye, lad, you have, but what good is your word in the face of hopelessness and despair? How long would you plod along vowing allegiance and obedience to save a dying herd? My lad's given me a great deal of insight into this condition of humanity. Perhaps, he saw too much of the world from an observation point that others in lesser positions couldn't have seen. Poverty, strife, dereliction from duty and morality. Ah, my lad was dying. His heart was no longer in the propagation of your race but rather lost in the desperation of his efforts. Fatalism is the hallmark of such a condition, Kevin. On his honor alone, he's plodded on his course," he paused and in a far more musing tone, commented, "Damn near wore the lad out trying to keep up with the demand. You've a healthy male gland in your clan, Kevin, and I'll mention here, you do have a clan. Granted, the numbers aren't up to the standard I'd hoped at the onset, but the lad's given it his best effort. Fifty-seven males scattered at all points of the globe, that's a commendable high and possibly a record. Should we include the thirty-three lasses he's sired, it's damned near impressive. I think I've been more than fair, Kevin. Considering the first males won't begin to act for at least another five years, we'll see a lull in births, and alas, you were right about your cousin Brian. Wrong about the absence of another to fill the position," he paused only a second. "You may see a little more of the world than you have in the past, Kevin, but we'll try not to tax you too much. A trip here or there, and the world's none the wiser."

"My . . . comeuppance for questioning you," Kevin said heavily.

"Not at all, lad. Merely a necessary extension of your duties regarding an unforeseeable disaster. If the Night Rider craft had ever plummeted, I'd be demanding the same of you, and in a sense, lad, that's exactly what's happened here. Now, as with any tragedy, you've had time to reflect, and you seek an explanation. Justification. What went wrong, eh? How did he tumble from grace? What mistakes could you avoid or who must you blame? Is the covenant still in effect or has it fallen with your sky?"

Good questions, every one of them, Darius found sense to decide and managed to look at the Baron who looked at Kevin with a mere reflective expression.

"The answer to the latter is simply this, Kevin. The covenant is in order, sealed and firm as long as you and yours uphold your vow. Every child born in the past eight years is and will remain free of whatever curse I could put upon them. As I have indulged your cousin's fancy, each of his has received a silver spoon, and thus they will remain gifted so long as the covenant remains sealed. Break it, lad, and I will wreak havoc on your clan, the likes of which you could only begin to imagine. As for your cousin's fall? The justification . . . let me continue my tale, and we shall see what we shall see . . ."

CHAPTER 13

Arms pinned, one at her side, the other folded and mashed between her breast and Hugh's chest, Jenna glimpsed the glare in his vivid blue eyes—crazy eyes. Time stopped somewhere between him clasping her head, wrenching her neck, and her palm landing over his heart to shove him away. What had begun as a tender touch on her cheek had become a vice tangled in her hair and looped about her waist. For a split second, Jenna knew fear before her natural defenses rose and the glare lifted into her own crazy blue eyes. How dare this bastard—

He did dare. His thin mustache curved into a tight smile; his eyes brightened with excitement—as if her instant of fright ignited his passion. Time started with an explosion of motion. His hand wrenched her head sideways and back, his mouth mashed her slightly parted—startled—lips. Like a hot poker, his tongue rammed between her teeth, jabbing her tongue in his apparent rendition of a French kiss.

Instinct overrode fear. Jenna pushed at his chest, gagging on the offensive protrusion and gasping at the fierce clasp on her skull. Against her abdomen, his manhood hardened and throbbed, making an impression as if he meant to show off the length of his desire. Only more outraged, Jenna tried lifting her knee, only to find his knee wedged between her legs, effectively thwarting that female move. This wasn't his first foray into physical force—he anticipated the need. But if she got loose, it might be his last.

A scant five steps away, poised at the entrance to the sitting room, Agent Miller remained as silent as a church mouse, just shy of Jenna's peripheral vision. But she knew he stood in witness—silent witness. She'd barely glimpsed at him before Hugh had stopped her intended departure, clasping her arm, turning her to face him.

She'd understood his intention before his hand ever touched her cheek and she'd started the denial, 'No, Hugh.' For any decent man, that should have been enough. Yet here she stood, overpowered, pinned, with his tongue gagging her. Snarling in the back of her throat, she barely dug at his waist, lifted her foot to slam her heel on his shiny oxford . . . and he withdrew with the speed of a recoiling snake.

Lifting his head, he looked down into her raging eyes, mirroring her glare with a twist. Where she flashed fiery outrage, his eyes glowed with amusement and lofty lust as he continued to hold her pinned. In a musing deep voice, he began simply. "I'm in love with you, Jenna . . . I won't apologize for that or for kissing you. I'm sorry if I've frightened you, darling, or taken you by surprise, but I wanted you to know how much I love you."

Drawing breath, calm despite the anger burning in her eyes and in her mind, she commented, "Get your hands off me and don't ever do this again, Hugh."

As if she were a kitten purring in his arms, rather than a woman prepared to gouge his eyes out, he continued to hold her, his legs stationed strategically between her knees and against her hip to prevent the damage she intended to inflict. Desire flamed his narrow eyes; his spark of dark humor and haughtiness added to her anger. He clearly understood her immobility and enjoyed his dominance, he might enjoy fighting her to the bitter end. "I know you're angry with me, darling," he said, as if addressing a nitwit child, or worse, his addled lover. "But I'll make it up to you, I promise," he added and dipped, brushing another kiss on her lip. In one smooth motion, he released her and stepped back with a speed to stagger her a step . . . and seemed to find that amusing as well, choosing to believe she swooned for him.

Too angry, too stunned to react instantly, Jenna watched his transition, from sly haughty delight to sheepish smile, portraying all the feigned innocence of a little boy caught stealing cookies from the cookie jar.

"Good night, darling. Pleasant dreams," he purred while backing another step. With all the flair of an actual gentleman, he offered a slight bow, and Jenna flashed a thought of plowing her knee into his crotch as he rose.

He was crazy . . . pure and simple crazy, Jenna confirmed with another scathing glance at his arrogant smirk and shining delight. Backing away three wary steps, prepared to slam him if he reached to stop her again, Jenna turned with her dignity intact despite her racing heartbeat and uneven breath.

Miller stood exactly as he'd stood a moment ago; a sentry poised just inside the entrance, appearing somewhat daft with the dull haze in his eyes, the puzzled smirk on his lips.

How much was he being paid to turn a blind eye, she wondered abruptly, sorely tempted to slap the kink off his lips and settling for a scorching glance that didn't faze him. By no means could he have mistaken that assault for anything less than an unwanted advance and yet he hadn't moved, hadn't uttered a sound on her behalf.

Protector—or prisoner?

Maintaining a quick, angry stride up the steps, Jenna refused to buckle to her desire and race up the staircase. Fleeting the memory of Hugh's shiny eyes and sly smirk, she reached the guestroom, and indulged her whim, slamming the door to send the sound careening off the walls throughout the house. Maybe these blasted servants would get the hint, too. Far too often they spied on her and deferred to her to as 'Missus' as though she'd already taken the post and become mistress in the house. Hugh's mistress.

She needed to get the hell out of here! There was something wrong in this house. Something terribly wrong with Hubert von Hendricks!

Not slowing down, Jenna stopped only after gargling and spitting the rancid taste of Hugh from her mouth. She might never drink another sip of wine without tasting that rancid oak-barrel flavor on her tongue.

Standing at the porcelain, Victorian-style vanity, Jenna wiped her mouth on one of the signature-red hand towels with its gold embroidered H . . . and looked into her too-bright eyes. Spooked eyes. Not liking the high shine, not one bit, she considered how she'd likely appeared terrified when facing Hugh. Belatedly, a touch of humiliation surfaced. He'd held her quick and complete . . . but just for a few ticks. She would have fought him to the end. But would she have won if he'd pushed the issue? She'd worn a dress to dinner; indulged the bastard at the onset when he'd sheepishly asked if she'd packed a dress and, 'I know it's silly, but I prefer to dress formally for my evening meals.' No doubt, in keeping with his over-inflated opinion of himself and his adherence to another era, where he believed himself a king to be served in his castle.

Not again, Jenna vowed. Hugh could thrust his bottom lip and pout like a child for all he was worth, but she wouldn't dare wear another dress in his presence. Far too easily, he'd entrapped her, and the blasted dress was too easily accessible if he'd intended to persevere. Bad enough, she'd only brought two dresses . . . and muttered, "What the hell was I thinking?" Of the two, she wore the slightly less conservative style that would have knocked Darius's socks off. And likely inspired her to pack the slinky, clingy, black cocktail dress, hoping beyond hope she'd see him here.

One thought into another, Jenna retired to the bedroom and rifled through the dresser until she found her sweatsuit, the least alluring clothing she'd packed. Even after changing, however, she still shivered and cursed the realization. Another belated reaction to Hugh's unwanted, violent advance. Like the aftershocks of an earthquake, the shivers wracked her system, further evidence of the humiliation.

Tomorrow. Tomorrow—after Hugh left for the winery office—she would demand Agent Aichley arrange for her travel. A safe-house in Timbuktu, or her own apartment, would be preferable to another moment under Hugh's roof.

She'd missed Christmas with her family. For the first time in several years, she'd lived within driving distance of her parents' house, and she'd missed Christmas dinner.

Her eyes stung. Brushing angrily at the tears, she crossed the room and shoved the long curtains aside, searching something, anything, to stop the turmoil. Bright white, the countless dusk-to-dawn lights illuminated the tangle of snow-capped branches beyond the balcony. She hadn't once stepped onto the balcony. Eight inches of snow remained unmarked by human trespass, but birds had lighted on the cast iron rails, leaving black gouges, like bite-marks, on the tops. At the onset, Jenna had decided Hugh feared the dark. At night, his house could likely be spotted from a space shuttle but just beyond the neon glow . . .

Jenna hugged her arms against a quick chill, and for a wicked moment, she thought of Matt Cord, poor shy Matt sprawled on his living room floor. She'd asked about the arrangements for Matt's funeral. Vaguely, she recalled insisting the agents arrange her return to Pittsburgh.

A crease troubled her brow, and not for the first time, she identified the fog affecting her memory. Christmas passed. Matt's funeral passed . . . Reichley had assured her that a lovely floral basket had reached the funeral home in time to offer her personal condolences. Matt had a family. Brothers and sisters, mother and father she'd never met. Would never meet.

Tomorrow she would insist that Agent Reichley arrange her transportation. She was going home, and to hell with a maniac on the loose. The only maniac posing a serious threat lived under this roof—

A prickle lifted the hair follicles at her nape; her attention riveted through the tangled, snowcapped branches just past the glowing driveway. For just an instant, she'd seen movement—controlled movement. Some-one . . . . standing in the vines. Watching her? Spying on her? This wasn't the first time she'd experienced this sensation. At the winery, during that first tour with Hugh's and again with Emma's tour through the main building, she'd suffered the prickling . . . and several times since though the moments were fuzzy.

With a very real sense of someone watching her window, Jenna sidled casually, judged the balcony lock secured and clasped the rod, tugging the heavy drapes closed. Why these damned maids insisted on throwing these drapes open, Jenna couldn't decide, but she'd forfeited any attempt to change them after the fourth or fifth day. In the morning, she didn't mind letting the light in, but these imbeciles opened the drapes every evening when she repaired to the dining room, as if . . . almost as if they invited a peeping tom. The rooms, from this lounging room to her bedroom, carried the flair of a shadow box, and likely enhanced at night with the overhead chandelier and lamps illuminating every corner like a stage spotlight.

Tomorrow, she confirmed again. Tomorrow, she was getting the hell out of here . . . but she still needed to get through the night. And the dizziness, the queasiness that had preceded her attempted retreat from the dining room, struck again with a vengeance. Tomorrow, she would find a way home. Tonight, she needed to vomit.

CHAPTER 14

"I believe we were talking about Maxwell when I was so rudely interrupted," the Baron stated and glanced off Darius with a smirk, landing his gaze on Raphael. "Should we tell this tale, lad? Or would you prefer I return to where I truly left off? The carriage . . . James Ladmen?"

"Dinnae matter," Raphael said glumly, his head still bowed and rested sideways against Darius's chest. "You'll tell them whatever you want."

"True, lad. Very true," Amad mused. "And the tale carries a few interesting turns," he said and looked to Kevin. "You raised sons, Kevin. I'm sure you'll appreciate the humor in this," he commented and just to make sure the arrow struck home, he favored Darius with another glance. "I suppose you could say I'd been a little remiss with my youngster. Neglected him for a time. I'm certain he merely cried out for my attention when he set off on these adventures with his little friend Maxwell.

"Well, by and by, he not only caught my attention, but he and his band of little street urchins caught a great deal of attention in the local citizenry. Our friends and neighbors were being robbed right and left. It became so dreadfully bad, that not even my servants were safe. As I mentioned, I'd left the daily affairs of the castle to the Haegers. They were a pleasantly plump couple, the female of whom attempted to be my lad's governess, though she was a trifle strict with him. Personally, I entertained a great deal more in those days, and why not? I was the most eligible widower around and I had a young son . . . who I believe I called grandson during half that time. A man can stay young only so long in this world without someone wondering where to find the fountain. A touch of gray, a few wrinkles . . .? Child's play," he mused. "I made my regular rounds in town with proper aplomb, although, I should admit, I started becoming far more regular with all the rumors running amuck. Frankly, I've always enjoyed traveling in style, and I need scant reason to flaunt my wealth, as you well know. I correctly assumed eventually, if I waved enough carrots, the little rabbits would bite."

Far more amused, he glanced at Raphael, who ducked a tad lower, then back to Kevin. "Now remember what I mentioned earlier, Kevin. My lad never admitted where he lived, and I should mention, he took to wearing the most desperate ensembles he could lay his hands on. Ill-fitting shirts, dungarees with knees worn thin, coats several sizes too large, boots with the soles flapping . . . a regular little ragamuffin he became before hitting the streets. To his credit, I should also admit, though, it grieves me tremendously . . . after each night of thieving, before returning to my keep, the little devil returned every bobble and coin to its rightful owner." The Baron tipped his gaze to Darius, amused. "He one-upped you, son, but it's not your fault that you weren't so well inclined. Aside from his first ten years, my lad never went to bed hungry. He never needed to pilfer an apple on his way to school just to have a bite for lunch like other boys."

"Jolly glad to hear it," Darius said dryly and nearly bit his own tongue. *Silence.*

The Baron spared him a withering look, then laughed and shook his head, returning his gaze to Kevin with a smile still playing on his lips. "Children. They truly should be seen and not heard," he commented and continued. "So it was, dear little Max, with his grand designs on becoming wealthy and traveling far and wide, had no idea he traveled in the company of a little royal lad who could have handed him a ticket to circle the globe. So it was, as my lad tried convincing Max to stop thieving and can you imagine . . . tried instilling moral consciousness?" he said scathingly. "Little human Max planned his greatest coop. At every opportunity, unbeknownst to his wee friend Raphael, Max trailed after the Baron von Hendricks's carriage in search of the best method to clean the elder lord's pockets. Ah, and what a merry chase that was," he mused. "I'd start a pattern and let the lad get comfortable with a plan, then change my routine at the drop of the hat. Well, and so the ordeal needed to end. My wee lad was far too convincing in his mission. He very nearly converted Max and nearly convinced him to work in the livery," he said in a sighing disgust.

"Ah, but li'l Maxwell didn't let me down. He had a score to settle. One more little cache to set him up for months. After all, he'd wasted a great deal of time stalking his quarry, and he'd seen the gold coins in those deep pockets. Once more, Maxwell promised my wee lad—just once more, than he would quit. So, and it was," he mused. "Max dragged my little lad along on this last night, and much to my wee lad's surprise, he recognized the mark, as they say today, before my carriage ever came into view."

Pausing, he seemed to reflect, then laughed and looked over to Raphael, who'd begun to chew his fingernail. "That's a dirty habit, lad. How many times have I told you? You'll end up biting your finger to the quick?"

"Mmm sorry," Raphael muttered but held his nail in his teeth.

Feeling the little boy's distress, Darius suffered a pang of his own, wishing the Baron would just finish this tale, and damning himself for the thought which could drag it out forever. On his lap, the little body trembled.

"Well, as you might realize," the Baron continued. "My lad was terrified, and I could hear him pleading and begging with his comrade before my carriage ever halted. *Not this one! Do ye know who he is? Dinnae doo this oone! Dinnae steeeal from him!*" the Baron mimed the Scottish accent as well as the childish tone. "Aye, the ragamuffin tried all manner of persuasion except for the most obvious. Had he mentioned his relationship to me, Maxwell might have forfeited. Aye, but then, my lad would have to admit his lies and deceit." Letting the words linger a moment, he continued with a laugh, "At the precise moment when Maxwell launched toward the street to run into me, my lad transformed to his more natural self, caught the boy and slammed him a mean fist in the jaw. Knocked the poor boy out cold, so he did," he said with a hint of pride. "The rest, shall we say, is history. I simply sent my mortified lad home, then delivered the little thief to the authorities. Maxwell traveled," he mused. "Across an entire country to labor in a workhouse for the duration of his youth."

In tears, Raphael dipped his head a little deeper, nearly burrowing under Darius's jacket. By reflex alone, Darius covered the small head in his palm, and an instant later, considered where he might hide his own head as the Baron lanced him inside and out. With the eyes prickling him, he flinched and held the external gaze. Silence.

With a harrumph, the Baron skimmed his gaze to the burrowed child back to Darius, then shook his head and looked toward Kevin, who appeared to study his own hand while moving the remnants of dinner about with his fork. This wasn't the first time Kevin had sat through a tale over the past eight years. Almost as often as Teddy, who was accepted or rejected at whim and whimsy, Kevin had rested at the Baron's right hand, as close to Amadeus von Hendricks as any Brock who'd held the post in the past four hundred years. Kevin was smart enough not to interrupt, merely to listen and await the need to respond, but he wasn't as quick as usual this evening.

"Well, I thought you'd appreciate the humor, Kevin," Amad said smoothly. "But since it appears you're preoccupied, I'll simply add the closure without fanfare. The tale didn't end with Maxwell's departure. Tis a fact, the lad spent fifteen years believing his little friend had hauled him to the authorities. Fifteen years of sweating and plotting revenge can certainly make for an interesting stew. So it was, the lad returned to our little village, an angry man. To his dismay, he found only a child, the child of the child he hated, or so he believed. With a bit of help, he laid a trap, and my wee lad fell into it. Three grown men against one wee vampire," he mused. "They planned to hold him for ransom, then cut his wee bones to pieces and be gone. Instead, my lad was well on his way to enslaving the lot of them by the time I arrived. We had a time with them, didn't we, wee bairn?"

"I dinnae do a thing tae them," Raphael grumbled. "Joost cut the cords and . . . and I dinnae even get myself free. You come into the cave, and you had a time with them. Aye," he said and rousted a little more to look over to the Baron. "They were deserving of it too, Pappa," he said gravely. "What they planned . . . Aye, they were deserving. You saved me life, too, Pappa. They'd have had their way with me."

"Aye, they were giving it a grand effort," the Baron mused.

"You saved me, Pappa," he said smoothly and smiled. "And I brooght the wolf pup, then, too! Remember! We camped out—like in the old days!" His eyes sparking, he lifted his gaze to Darius with a shine of amusement. "Aye! I never told you how Pappa took me camping and the like! He taught me to hunt, too! That was in America! But oh, what a time we had in the forests here. I could take you and show you, Darius! It's a quick jaunt for the likes of us. Do you like to camp out? Have you ever?"

"Uh . . . no, lad. I can't say that I have," he admitted indifferently.

"Ohhh, you dinnae know what you've missed," the boy said gravely. "There's nawt a thing like it to compare! We build the fire and sooch and track the hare. A grand time!" His gaze pivoted to his father. "We huvnae done that for a long time, pappa. We should take Darius and show him. We could visit the auld caves."

Bemused, the Baron locked his gaze on Darius. "I don't suppose you'd enjoy such an adventure, would you, lad?"

The thought irritated him at a gut level, but he held his council. "I wouldn't complain," he said dryly, locking his internal focus on the detail that he couldn't complain if such came to pass.

Amad chuckled and dropped his gaze to Raphael, who appeared slightly disappointed. "Don't lose heart, my lad. Your brother's lack of enthusiasm rears from a different age and era than your own. Truthfully," he said, while lifting his gaze to Darius. "You might enjoy that adventure, though, son.

By no fault of your own, you've never had a pappa to take you camping, but I know for a fact, you enjoy the hunt. It might be interesting to see how you enjoy the kill."

"I'm sure I'll be delighted with the experience," Darius answered carefully.

"Hmm, we'll see then," the Baron said and turned his gaze to Kevin. "Paternal instincts," he said in a lower tone, a more menacing tone. "I've always found myself rather drawn to that most revered of all natural inspirations. Which leads once again to where I left off," he continued in a more natural rhythm. "The children of my dear Corina and my conspirator, Liam Donahue. Liam, by the way, lived out a natural life. My gift to him for his fine service. However, in retrospect, I should have slaughtered him," he mused. "Five healthy offspring in my keep, and what do I have now? A withered wench and a horde of treacherous leches to feed off the fortunes I've accumulated. Well, perhaps, you can see my position now?"

"I am trying," Kevin said carefully and glanced at Darius. His brow furrowed, and he wore a faded expression as he commented, "I'm just not sure I understand where exactly Darius fits into this ehm . . . plan? Or explanation."

Amad sighed and shook his head almost sadly. "Kevin, I think you're getting daft or senile at such a tender age."

"I understand you're not satisfied with your heirs, sir," Kevin said carefully. "And from my perspective, I can see why you'd favor Darius over them. I . . . I'm just having trouble understanding how his present . . . condition can be to your advantage? You've . . . changed the traits you might have found most appealing."

"Have I now?"

Under Darius's steady gaze, Kevin wasn't swift to respond, but he nodded slowly and turned his gaze to collide with Darius. "Forgive me, cousin," he said quietly.

"By your admission, I no longer have that trait inside of me," Darius stated with a touch of anger. "And I'll thank you not to insult me further by reference to our shared bloodline," he stated crossly.

"I wasn't referring to your compassion or nobility, Darius," Kevin said quietly, his gaze unwavering. "Those you have still, as I've seen them turned against you. Truly, my friend, I'm sorry," he said drearily. "I meant your arrogance and defiance."

"Ah, I see," the Baron said. "Even if my son does not, Kevin,"

"I don't doubt that you do, Amad," Kevin said boldly, simply. "I've seen and understood how much you appreciated those traits in my blue-blooded cousin. You've always reveled in his courage to stand strong against whatever trials you've placed before him, and in your way, you've loved the twists he's given you in his quiet defiance. And yet, you've wrapped a chain about his neck. I don't understand, sir. Is this the price he's paid for his arrogance?"

"Ah, now you have offended, my lad, Kevin," Amad said and flashed a bemused gaze toward Darius, who sat stunned by his cousin's words. "He sees you as a simpering slave in my keep, lad. And to think I'm accused of being cruel? This observation, from a man whose word you've always trusted and whose opinion you've valued since you two first met."

A man, Darius considered and turned his gaze away. A purely human man whose opinions and standards had mirrored his own, who rested even now at the left hand of the vampire. A man smart enough to avoid a fatal mistake.

"Ah, so you value his opinion even now, do you?"

"There's no chain about his neck," Darius said in a low tone and turned his gaze to the Baron. "And if he weren't intelligent, he wouldn't hold the position he does. Aside from which, he's right," he said steadily, his gaze locked on the external gaze. "I'll rise and fall at your command, and you'll have me on my knees. What's left of me is whatever you want to make of it.

. . but perhaps I'm smart enough to know you'll never give him the answer he's seeking."

"Sure of that, are you?"

Darius nodded slowly. "Even if you did, he'd be too smart to believe you. I'm the only damned fool who trusted your word and believed in your integrity, your nobility. A fucking contradiction, but I had no choice. I couldn't have done what I've done without respecting the man you were before my fucking clan turned you into a monster."

"Ah, lad. Therein lies the answer you've sought," the Baron mused.

"Liar," Darius stated with his annoyance taking a stronger hold. If only to contradict Kevin's words, the Baron granted him the freedom to speak, but Darius knew he would pay for whatever he said, for whatever he thought. If he cared, if a shred of genuine fear or concern lingered inside of him, not a word could he utter. Infinite misery. That was his single lease on what remained of his life. He could no more control his thoughts than he could hide them, and for those he would be held to account either way.

CHAPTER 15

"You are clever, lad, and I should mention, every bit as apt to defy me as you were before. About that, your cousin's wrong." The Baron continued smoothly. "Even your arrogance remains intact. Unfortunately, you no longer maintain either the right or ability to use them freely . . . and honestly, there's another key to your current condition. But do be quiet now, and let me continue," he stated and looked at Kevin. "Let me tell you about my daughter Lucinda, now, Kevin. You won't enjoy the tale, but you seek understanding. And were I to simply offer you my word, you'd miss the truth.

"Dear Lucinda, meek and weak, the exact opposite of the oldest sibling among us. I mentioned Lucinda fell madly in love with a lecher? My wee bairn intruded at that point. Now let me elaborate."

"Amad," Rebecca intruded in a quavering voice. "Do excuse me for interrupting, but Lucinda was not my sister. If you're referring to the abomination who dwelt in the tower during my youth, I believe you're referring to my father's sister, Aunt Lucy."

"Ah, corrections and intrusions," the Baron sighed and smiled down the table. "But I'll condescend to the truth as you see it . . . if only in appreciation for your firm grasp on memory. Honestly, I'd thought you a tad senile when you failed to correct me sooner."

"Odd, I should have wondered the same of you, dear," she said loftily. "You seem to be having some difficulty rearranging your names and dates in chronological order."

"Ahh, so I have," he mused. "So, would you like the tale of your aunt and the abomination?"

"I've always enjoyed the tales of your exploits," she said with a regal nod. "Please, continue if you will."

"Suppose I must," he said with a wry smile. "Lucinda, my dear sweet daughter, blood sister to the idiot who landed in the orphanage," he said toward Kevin. "She brought the lecher home with every intention of marrying him, and here I was, posing as both her father and her brother. Carl von Hendricks was a dolt I left to his books more often than not. As my wee bairn mentioned, the idiot wore the title for a time." His gaze slid to Rebecca. "Your dear sweet grandfather and grandmother. Are you now satisfied with the chronology?"

"That's more in order."

"Aye, well, I've lost interest in the tale," he idled and looked to Kevin. "To make it short, I learned of my sister's lover's plot to kill the male heir—me, as it were—and to marry my sister for my inheritance. A grand joke he made of my ill-begotten sister, boasting in all the filthy pubs about how he intended to get her with child and marry her money. At the same time, he spent a great deal of his own fortune hiring men to murder me in England, where I was allegedly attending school. By that time, I'd begun a search for a wife and plotted my own marriage. Needless to say, James' plotting intrigued me. Unfortunately, I tired of the game after he married my sister. A horse is an easy animal to spook. James spent the remainder of his days locked in the tower, paralyzed from the neck down. A convenient vessel for my wee lad without even a need to hold him still. Of course, he went mad long before my sister. The pair of them lived in this manse for nearly forty years. Madness," he said with a smile. "It's not as uncommon as you may think, Kevin. We've had a few of them go stark raving lunatic on us."

"I wouldn't doubt it, sir," Kevin commented.

"Have I ever mentioned Thaddeus's wife?"

"I've heard her mentioned," Kevin answered. "I know she suffered madness."

"Truth be told, she was a wicked wench," he mused. "The von Hendricks family has always been rife with plots and conspiracies, and I've not been responsible for as many of them as you may believe," he mused. "Thad's lover was just such another to plot against me and mine. Actually, more mine than me," he said and looked to Raphael. "Don't suppose you've forgotten that one either, have you, my lad?"

"No, sir," he said warily. "She was a wicked one, she was."

"Aye, and you only recently resurrected from the shadow world," he said and looked to Kevin, who listened intently. "From time to time my lad's walked in shadows. After nearly taking a nip of Ansen, I confined the wee lad to a room where he remained a ghost for the next fifteen years. By the time I set him free, Thad had married and created his daughter and two sons. Again, Raphael posed as a bastard child, Thad's own bastard child, in fact. The idea that her husband had an affair to bear fruit bothered Margaret not at all. What disturbed her was that Thad and I doted on the boy a bit. She believed her sons would be left wanting and she would take no chances. Using her husband's money, she paid several miscreants to kidnap my lad. When the lad failed to be trapped in the mountains, she personally caught him, drugged him and delivered him into her helper's hands."

His tone lowered, his temper apparent. "Not bad enough they tied him and planned to kill him once they had the ransom, my lil lad nearly lost his innocence and purity in that den of thieves. Needless to say, I wasn't kind to the lads when I caught up to them, and the wench spent the next several years in hell before we committed her to an asylum and left her to her madness. Now," he said smoothly. "With that bit of history, you have a grasp of what belied the treachery which brought you lads to my attention."

"Thaddeus held you responsible for his wife's demise," Kevin confirmed.

"Aye, and the irony here is simply this, at the time of that treachery, he was as fond of my lad as he was of his own. His guilt and righteous indignation came after years of enjoying every opportunity and luxury that his position afforded him. Ah, the time he and I shared. For years, he and I traded places, burning the candle at both ends, you might say. By day, he was Baron Thaddeus von Hendricks, grand entrepreneur and royal rogue. By night, I filled the same shoes. We shared our wine, our women, and the title with a symbiotic relationship which you may find difficult to believe considering the beast you know me to be. Aye, my heir, my grandson, my son, my father, my grandfather. The lad was as formidable as any opponent I was apt to meet, a quiet and clever wit in negotiations. Ah, and a chilly heart . . . and all of this from a lad who knew me for what I am since the age of fourteen."

The pause came then, a heavy pause, and Darius wasn't the only one to consider the words or the effects of Thad's betrayal. Because of his conspiracy, because of Levine Brock's participation, they were in this room, half their clan depleted.

"Now then," the Baron continued. "What do I have to show for all these years of generosity to my children? The one of greatest promise attempts to destroy me by destroying a helpless child. The others leech the gold from the tills and squander every cent they can. Were I to leave the bank doors open to the clan in California, most would have snorted the vault dry. As it is, they skim the profits from my companies and consider it no more than their due. The females are little more than libidinous harlots who don't have the intelligence or wherewithal to demand payment for their services. Just look down the table at my oldest surviving heir, lads," he said with a scathing glance toward Rebecca. "Nearly ninety-three years old and she'd suck the life from that young lad if I didn't lend him a break now and again. Ah, and the males. Randy illbegots who wouldn't know how to treat a decent woman if they had the sense to meet and recognize one. Quite a few, like the barren lass down the way, couldn't produce a child even if they found a sensible mate.

"So, there you have it, Kevin," the Baron said smoothly. "Now, and I'll ask you again. Why should I allow your clan to reap the only rewards of creation when I have it in my power to harvest that same seed?"

"I . . . ?" Kevin lost his words to his confusion. "I'm still at a loss. If you've made him a son . . . in the sense that I suspect . . . ?"

"Ah, I see your confusion," the Baron mused. "What I've passed into him, you fear he'll pass on to another. Correct?"

"Uhh . . . yes."

"Ahh, and there's the beauty of this current circumstance. The unknown. The toss of the dice and the bated breath to be held," he mused. "And I should mention, this evening's a bit of a celebration on my part," Amad mused. "Not only have I saved my new lad's life, but I've an announcement to make and as you're all related, friends of the family, so to speak, I'd wanted you all present to share our triumph."

Darius studied the sparkling eyes, felt the prickling inside his skull, positive of an internal alarm rising at an incredible speed to have him tense even before the cobalt gaze locked on him.

"Ah, too clever, you are, lad," Amad said. "But I'd not have it any other way. What strikes me as a surprise—although with my intervention early on, I'm not entirely surprised—is that you didn't truly recognize the touch of strangeness in the lass."

Jenna.

"Ah, Jenna. Loved that name from the moment I heard it spoken," Amad said. "And now, possibly I should mention a little known detail," he continued, while holding Darius's gaze. "The mother of my children of yesteryear wasn't an only child. Ah, no, not at all. Corina had a brother, a hearty decent chap by the name of Wilhelm—a direct descendent through the untarnished maternal lines of the von Hendricks clan. Lo and behold, that lad fathered a daughter some years after my own Thad was born. Ah, and after that daughter, another son, who fathered a daughter. That daughter, though she's a bit long in the tooth, fathered a son, and those two my lad, you've had the pleasure to meet. Thus, your beloved is no other than the daughter of that son, Wilhelm, a direct descendent of your new pappa," Amad said with a smile. "A bit mixed, I'll grant you, lad, but the lines run true in that lovely lass. Now, and to clear up another of your misconceptions, lad. I didn't taint the lass," he said simply, honestly. "It would have been rather counterproductive on my part. You may appreciate the amount of restraint I exercised to keep her line pure, as you know how difficult it was to hold rein on your desire for her. I suspected from the onset that you might be attracted by your healthy hormones, and I suppose I should admit, I knew when I put the two of you within reach, I'd need to help you over that last hurdle. You are as good as your word. You wouldn't have broken your vows for love or money."

Darius shook his head slowly, rejecting the words. Not Jenna. Not a von Hendricks. Not possible. But even as he railed silent denials, he saw her deep blue eyes, her smile . . . and he felt the connection when she'd looked into him, through him. A von Hendricks . . . and the Baron had manipulated him . . . arranged the introduction . . . the meeting. But why? "Wh-why did you? Why, if you meant to . . . no!" he snapped with a fleeting instant thought. Creation! A child! He shook his head, his gaze heating with the memory flash of his love in the arms of another man . . . not just any man! Hugh von Hendricks! Jenna von Hendricks! Three . . . four generations removed.

"We needn't worry about incest, lad," the Baron said smoothly. "As I said, this is a celebration, and judging by your normal output, we'll have a fine noble male heir worthy to carry the von Hendricks name in about seven or eight months."

Nooo!

"You're a son worthy of a father's pride, lad, and fortunately, I intend to see that you remain exactly that. Now, why don't you boys run along and play?" he said with a smile and glance to include Raphael. "Your cousin and I have some business matters to discuss."

A slap in the face! An insult added to injury! As if he had neither a mental grasp nor knowledge of the von Hendricks Corporation! Jenna! His Jenna! Moving . . . already in motion by no will of his own, his hand fell into the little boy's hand . . . Jenna in Hugh von Hendricks' arms . . . Jenna carrying his child . . . another of his children . . . to wear the von Hendricks name! Jenna!

"Darius," the deep voice halted him, slicing through his clicking thoughts and turning him to find the cobalt eyes looking into him, through him. "Something you should know, lad, a touch of balm for your injury, perhaps," Amad said with a smile, which suggested just the opposite. "In time, you too shall wear the von Hendricks name. Ten years, lad. In about ten years, the fruit of your loins, my legitimately adopted son, will be ready to pass on the name I've given him. You'll wear the name Dylan von Hendricks."

PART TWO

CHAPTER 16

Coming to Emma was a mistake. Jenna knew the mistake before she reached the neat little cottage a stone's throw from the homestead.

'Trust no one . . .' Those were Darius's words weeks, if not months ago, and this wasn't the first time she heard the silent reminder in her mind or remembered the warnings in other of their brief conversations. After the photo session, alone in the Chateau Suites dining room, Darius had halted her and looked down into her. A stranger still, but she'd suffered the attraction, the heat of his touch, as he'd told her to resign from the company. *To spare him the pain of firing her as a result of her decking the halls of the Chateau Suites.* Had she known in advance of the von Hendricks' agnostic approach to the holidays, she might have refrained—or perhaps not. Vaguely, she recalled asking Hugh about the absence of decorations in his home—along with the homestead. Atheists or not, she'd expect them to capitalize on the holiday to draw the tourist trade at either the hotel or the winery.

On Emma's doorstep, too late to reject the visit for fear of drawing undue attention or giving anyone cause for alarm, Jenna forced an engaging smile and prepared for a short visit. Emma might not be the last person on the estate to offer assistance but she would run a close second. Jenna need only look around her to verify her thought. This old woman owed the von Hendricks company. She depended on the von Hendricks for her life and livelihood, her security in her advancing years. And with the thought, a prickle slid down Jenna's spine. Before she could fully consider the thought, the inside door opened and the little woman smiled, shoving at the screen.

"I was getting a little worried, dear," Emma said pleasantly, her quick blue eyes darting down and up as Jenna caught the door. "When you didn't come by, I was afraid you might have taken ill. You're feeling all right, aren't you?"

The words were natural enough, the concern appeared genuine, but the alarm skittered under Jenna's collar. Did this woman somehow know, or suspect the 'illness' that had begun only four days ago? In self preservation, Jenna hadn't buckled to the nausea or mentioned the possibility of her condition. In fact, she'd made it a point to adhere to her routine beneath the prying eyes of the FBI, the entire staff, and Hugh. "I thought you were probably getting tired of seeing me over here so often," Jenna said lightly, although she wasn't entirely certain of how often she'd visited the matronly little woman—

"Nonsense, dear," Emma said and patted her arm. "I just put on a pot of coffee," she said and gestured toward the arch directly to the right. Any friend of Hugh's was a friend of hers, she might have added.

Asking Emma Chauncy for help was truly out of the question. The tidy kitchen, small and compact, reflected Emma's style and taste from the flowered wallpaper to the knickknacks hanging on the walls. Chair rails circled the room, protecting the paisley-print wallpaper from the antique chairs to circle a Victorian table, one bearing a striking resemblance to the antiques in the main homestead. The entire cottage reflected a utilitarian atmosphere refective of another era, a simplistic design that one might expect of a scullery maid a hundred years past. Aside from the bookshelves in the living room, Emma lived without excess and apparently satisfied. She certainly wouldn't risk her comfort and security for a stranger who she accepted merely through association to a family she adored and idolized.

Trust no one.

Despite the homey atmosphere and the chatter that began as Emma collected cups and saucers, Jenna suffered a chill. Something was wrong with this place, with these people. From Emma, who concealed her loyalty behind her enthusiasm for the history of the von Hendricks, to the maids and butlers catering to Hugh's every whim, to the security men who walked the grounds bundled against the weather—something terribly wrong hovered beneath the shiny veneer. And Jenna knew abruptly what it felt like. Listening to Emma relating an anecdote from the afternoon tour, smiling and laughing in all the right places, Jenna realized exactly what she was feeling . . . The same thing she would feel if she walked into the headquarters of a religious cult. Brainwashed. Even Emma with her smiles and humor . . . the woman's life, her thoughts, her loyalty revolved around the von Hendricks family. More than once in the past six or seven weeks, Jenna had listened as Emma had talked about 'poor Hugh' and how he was such a 'dear man.' More than once, Emma had implied that she wouldn't blame any young woman for falling in love with Hugh. He had it all . . . money, looks, character.

Having stood on the receiving end of Hugh's character, Jenna confirmed her belief. Either the little woman was brainwashed or blinded by gratitude. Unfortunately, with the way the house staff hustled and beckoned at his command, never needing or receiving a kind word for their adoration, brainwashed remained the only viable conclusion. By what manner Hugh had programmed his following, Jenna couldn't decide. The man treated anyone below him as though they walked the earth merely to pour his wine and deliver his meals . . . and these assholes accepted it like trained monkeys.

"I'd invite you for dinner, dear," Emma said as the shadows thickened outside the lace swags. "But I'm sure you'd rather dine with Hugh," she said with a cagey smile, honestly believing those words and approving wholeheartedly.

Jenna smiled and refrained from mentioning, she'd rather dine with a boa constrictor. Emma was out of the question. Jenna needed a new plan, and as she thanked the woman and returned to the car with Reichley on her heels, she suffered a renewed urgency. Time was running out. She needed to get out of here before Hugh either squeezed the life out of her as he had all these others, or he lost his patience and did something for which she'd need to kill him. She needed a plan.

"That woman certainly didn't miss her calling," Reichley said in an almost natural tone as he sped along the back lanes that trailed through the von Hendricks vineyards and forests. With the onset of dusk, he'd turned on the headlights and the dashboard lights reflected on his face to cast his expression in deeper shadows. If he'd meant the words as a joke, his manikin-curved lips betrayed him. His gaze fleeted over with an oddly blank stare then returned to the lane. "I don't think she shut up for five seconds."

The words, the expression, somehow neither were in sync and she'd noted this strangeness more than a time or two. FBI. Perhaps they were trained to think one thing and say another, their faces emitting nothing. She'd witnessed the same thing on Miller . . . Right before both men had assured her that the danger hadn't passed in Pittsburgh, and they had orders to keep her in hiding. Temporary witness protection, Reichley had stated, and Miller had confirmed the status, promising he'd intervene if Hugh stepped out of line. At least the fellow had kept his word in that regard, but for how long? Those blank expressions and foggy gazes worried her.

Internalizing the shiver, Jenna commented belatedly, "She's a natural storyteller."

The subject dropped, and too soon, they pulled into the parking corral at the rear of the house. The spotlights had already ignited, highlighting the white aluminum siding and stone facing. Spikes of white light shot into the thick forest perimeter, creating a spider-web funhouse effect in reflection of Jenna's thoughts. She felt like a fly snared in a spider's web, and the Las Vegas flair of neon light offered little comfort. In simulated light, the house lingered in perpetual surrealistic daylight, made ten times brighter by the reflection of snow draped over bushes and shrubs, across the lawns. Meticulously, undoubtedly at Hugh's command, the stone walks and patio remained clear; stone benches highlighted under coach lights added to the showplace ambience.

From her suite, Jenna had watched the grounds keepers tending to the lawns, fascinated and mildly disoriented as the two-man teams shoveled new-fallen snow into a small wagon on the back of a garden tractor. With Hugh's wealth, he could certainly afford a snow blower or a plow. With either, however, the snow would mound at the edges of walkways or blow across the lawn marring the pristine white surface. Obsessive-compulsive, she considered. The result of this meticulous, tedious exercise in human labor bespoke of that mental disorder. Unblemished, the snowy landscape reached to the very edge of every sidewalk and trimmed the driveway around the house, creating an ice wall. If Hugh could find a means to dry the walks where afternoon sunlight melted the sharp edges, he probably would.

As Jenna walked between the foot high walls of snow, cut down sharply with shovels to meet the edges of the walkway as meticulously as stone or wood, she considered suggesting using hair dryers, then countered the thought. This asshole was probably mean enough and crazy enough to outfit his entire house staff with battery operated blow dryers and enlist them to dry the sidewalks so he could avoid wetting the soles of his Italian shoes on his return from the main winery.

Depressed and slightly angry, Jenna strode through the back door, held open by a blank-faced scullery maid. If the stubby woman wore a name, Jenna had never heard it. Passing her without a glance, Jenna continued to the main stairway. No getting around it. She would need to sit down to another meal with this snake and plaster another smile on her face, feigning to enjoy his company. Ever since that kiss, the bastard had walked around with a smug look on his face, slicing her with the occasional leer, leaving no doubt of his thoughts. That he intended for her to know was no surprise or mystery. He appeared only more deeply amused when she refused to acknowledge him. If he thought for one damned minute this cat-and-mouse game would win her affection, he had another thought coming.

Angrier than she cared to consider, Jenna pulled a dress from the closet, then changed her mind and pulled her wool suit from the rack. When exactly he'd begun filling her closet with dresses, she couldn't even recall, but she had no intention of indulging him yet again. Out of necessity, she'd worn some of those dresses, although she recalled wearing her jeans a time or two.

A wry smirk curling her lips, she continued into the bathroom where she'd begun changing at the onset with a sense of someone spying her through the balcony windows. Recalling the anger in Hugh's eyes when she'd arrived at his table wearing jeans, her smirk faded. He might as well have shouted, 'No woman under my roof will wear pants at my table!' He'd pouted throughout that meal, barely speaking, avoiding eye contact. For that alone, she'd considered wearing jeans for all time—but her closet had begun filling with dresses.

He was a snake, one of those colorful snakes that wore a thin line of a mouth always turned up in a smile.

She dressed without her usual flair . . . but the suit provided the intended effect on her psyche. For some reason, the suit made her think of Darius and lifted her flagging mood. Maybe the wool, a soft English wool similar to the jackets and slacks he'd worn most often in her company. Whatever the reason, between her executive image and the feeling that he wrapped his arms about her, she felt a strange comfort and strength as she checked her reflection in the mirror. Now, if she only had a weapon of some kind.

Something heavy she could slip into her pocket and slam across Hugh's jaw if he attempted to take any more liberties. A gun would be nice.

"Good grief," she uttered and settled for lifting the set of house keys off the dresser. Hugh might be a snake, but she doubted she could shoot him even if she had a gun. Ramifications. She could just imagine trying to explain putting a bullet in her host.

Jenna wondered what would happen if she simply demanded to leave, but even before she reached the door, she knew the futility of that idea. Between Hugh and the agents who were apparently on his payroll, they would either talk her out of her decision or simply refuse her again. She would rather not know to what lengths Hugh would go in order to keep her here, but the mere thought sent a tiny prickle down her spine.

On the surface, nothing appeared out of place inside the house. No one stood outside her door to stop her from walking room to room. She reached the first floor before Holter, lank and somber, stepped from an alcove where he'd likely been waiting. Nightly, he escorted her to the sitting room, where Hugh joined her every evening.

Already, Hugh waited. Dressed in his normal suit and tie, he appeared freshly changed, although she knew differently. How ever he occupied his time during the day at the winery, manual labor wasn't part of it. Creasing his newspaper, he set it aside the instant she entered and rose, his normal smile faltered as he slid his gaze down her attire as if appraising a side of beef. His smile halted as his focus rose, and something akin to dismay creased his brow before a smile twisted into a more engaging curve. "As much as I love that outfit, darling, I truly would have preferred seeing you in that dress I bought you," he said with a pouting tone which no longer disguised his genuine disapproval.

He wanted her to change, she could tell. "It's much too lovely to wear without a special occasion, Hugh," she said with a catty smile of her own. "I thought I might wear it on Sunday—" *Or when hell freezes*, she considered as she veered deliberately toward a separate chair, avoiding him by an arm's length. With a thought of the latest dress he'd delivered last evening—and she'd almost donned—her anger hiked behind her eyes. The flimsy blue cloth fell too low at the bust and rose too high at the thigh for her taste; it wouldn't even pass for a decent nightgown or negligee and the day she dressed like a hooker to please some spoiled rich asshole, was the day hell would definitely freeze.

"Really, Jenna, I've looked forward to seeing that dress on you since I first saw it," he said with another subtle pout, a hint of anger in his eyes as he moved to his chair. "We have time. I'm sure we could hold dinner for a few moments—"

"Don't be silly, Hugh," Jenna interrupted with a playful, chastising tone. "I wouldn't dream of forcing you to eat a cold dinner, and it would take far too long for me to change. Besides which, I've always believed anticipation makes life sweeter."

Slightly more annoyed, he held her gaze a moment without losing his smile, then submitted loftily, "I've always believed just the opposite." He spoke in a teasing tone, but his eyes betrayed him. "I've never believed in self-sacrifice or self-denial. If you have the means and you want something, you should have it. Please. Wear that dress tomorrow, Jenna. If you'd like something special to wear on Sunday, I'm sure I can arrange that."

"Hugh, you're taking all the fun out of receiving that gift," she said with a mocked pout of her own. "With a dress like that, I couldn't simply waltz in here with my hair hanging in my face. It'll need a certain hairstyle . . . and the right jewelry."

"You'll have all day tomorrow to work out the details, darling," he said and waved off the butler, pushing from his chair and leaving no doubt the subject was closed, discussion ended. Coming to her, he offered his hand. "I'm sure dinner's ready. You've come down a little late this evening. You are feeling all right, aren't you?"

Twice in less than two hours? "Fine, Hugh," she said while rising without his hand. When he offered his arm, his eyes glittering, she reached a singular decision. This was the last time she would accept his arm to walk a distance of twenty paces, his proper rearing and etiquette bedamned. Slipping her hand about his forearm, she managed not to cringe when he covered her fingers in his other hand.

From the first time she'd entered his dining room, she'd accepted the chair at the far end of the table, which wasn't quite far enough. Compact, the table would seat only six, with elbows touching between the side chairs. Candles flickered in the center of the table, already lit when they sat down. The first course, generally a garden salad or soup, arrived almost instantly. They ate alone with Miller or Reichley undoubtedly consigned to the kitchen. Maids shuffled back and forth through a swinging door behind Hugh, arriving and disappearing like phantoms, delivering plates, pouring wine or coffee. Coffee, Hugh had said, should be poured after the meal and enjoyed in the living room with quiet conversation. Throughout that first week, he'd indulged her, ordering a maid to bring a cup and keep her coffee filled regularly, but by the second week, he'd insisted she drank too much caffeine. 'For him,' would she wait until they retired to the living room? Wine was served with every dinner, and most lunches. Hot tea remained the acceptable breakfast drink, although after she'd snapped at him on the third coffee-free morning, he'd relented. Coffee arrived with her breakfast, generally delivered to her room by one of the maids unless Hugh requested her presence. For the past four mornings, Jenna had disposed of the poached eggs and toast, sending the entire ordeal down the commode to dispense with the smell that had threatened her equilibrium.

Dinner was quiet. Hugh appeared preoccupied, but he was probably still pouting over the dress. His answers to her attempt at conversation were short, his gazes long. Having passed up breakfast and ate sparingly for lunch, Jenna turned her full attention to the meal, grateful for the silence and avoiding his eyes. She knew when he studied her, felt the oily prickle of his heated gaze without the need for a glance. His descended, descending mood, enhanced in the ensuing silence, as unsettling now as on countless other occasions when she'd sensed him brooding. The dress, her refusal to change into that dress, had upset him. He was accustomed to getting what he wanted, and when she denied him, he reacted like any spoiled child, prepared to throw a tantrum. Presently, she was sitting on a powder keg, and that realization only confirmed her decision. With or without assistance, she was leaving this nuthouse. If not tonight, then first thing in the morning.

This was absolutely the last dinner she would share with this snake, and God pity him if he tried anything untoward this evening. Silently, she vowed to send a knee skyward or rake racing stripes down his face.

But at her nape, doubt niggled, lifting the hair follicles under her draped locks. This wasn't the first time, she'd made that silent vow. At the edges of her mind, she knew she'd attempted to depart . . . and the struggle to remember the details sparked her anger to simmer even before she glimpsed any of his dark glances and long leers.

Like a living entity, his mood shifting, darkening, pulsed in the air, building with the essence of a powder keg brewing. When the stout maid wheeled the dessert cart through the door and he waved her away, Jenna knew the explosion advancing.

Annoyed, Jenna watched the maid's reverse course, but refrained from comment although she might have enjoyed a slice of that three-layered—likely decadent—chocolate cake. Never just one dessert on that cart. The immense chocolate cake, two different pies, a cherry-topped cheesecake and separate servings of crème brulee had decked that lovely silver server, likely worthy of a five star rating in any grand hotel . . . and this idiot had waved it away without a first or second glance.

Ignoring the retreating maid altogether, Hugh lanced her across the table, deciding shortly, "We'll have coffee in the living room, darling." Smoothly, he rose from his chair and started around the table toward her.

Setting her napkin aside, Jenna rose as well, ignoring his advance until he reached her, offering his hand. Rejecting his touch, she looked into the more angry dark shine. "Hugh," she spoke on a sigh, enlisting a deliberately calming voice reserved for hotel guests' unruly children. "If I've done something to upset you, I apologize."

"Whatever gives you that idea?" he asked while holding out his arm, nearly daring her to reject his escort.

Defusing him took precedence over her hostility. She landed her hand on his arm, more in a consoling gesture than accepting the touch of his silk suit. "You've been so quiet," she said lightly. "I hope everything's all right at the winery."

He patted her hand in reassurance, but again, his eyes betrayed him. "Nothing you need to worry about, darling," he said confidently, and led her into the hallway. "Actually, I just have something else on my mind," he said while giving her a lopsided gaze, a cagey smile.

She knew exactly what that 'something' was. His fingers locked a little more firmly over her own and his forearm held her wrist a little tighter to his side. "Oh, and what would that be?" she asked, as if she were as dumb as dirt.

"Oh, just a little something," he said in a more teasing tone, not even glancing toward Miller, who sat in one of the receiving chairs at the front entry.

Jenna wondered if Miller would even run to her rescue if she bothered to scream. In a half glance she saw his dull gaze and nearly imperceptible smile, a touch of curiosity at his brow.

No way out of this. She was on her own for the evening.

Undoubtedly, if she begged off with a headache or a need to turn in early, Hugh would recognize the excuse and spin out of control. Denied twice in an hour, he wouldn't take her rejection well . . . although, fighting with him could work in her favor. He wouldn't expect her company for breakfast, and she could be halfway to the nearest bus station before anyone discovered her absence. If she played this right . . .

Rather than break his hold and grant Jenna a choice of the early American chairs scattered about the room, Hugh led her directly to the couch and lowered with her, without releasing his firm clasp. Settling onto the cushion alongside her, he continued to leer at her, making no attempt to be catty now. Behind them, the butler had trailed, and with a wave of Hugh's hand the man started to retreat. On second thought, Hugh stated, "Bring us a bottle of wine, Holter. We'll skip the coffee this evening."

"Hugh, as much as I enjoy your wine, I've had enough for one evening," Jenna said lightly. "I'd rather like a cup of coffee."

"Indulge me, darling," he said and flagged his hand to have Holter hustling out, closing the door behind him. Alone, Hugh turned his full gaze on her and lost the smile in slow stages. "I've decided, Jenna. I've been more than patient with you, and I've given you ample time. I really don't believe we need to play these games anymore," he said smoothly. "I planned this evening a little differently. I bought you that dress so you'd have something nice to wear for this occasion, but you are a stubborn little minx."

"Yes, I am, Hugh," she said smoothly, her gaze losing the soft edges, heating. "As much as I appreciate your hospitality and your gifts, I've told you several times, I'd prefer you don't give me anything else."

"Don't be ridiculous," he said, dismissively, huffing with a wry smirk. "There's not a woman alive who doesn't love to receive gifts. You may pretend all you like, darling, but I know better. The same way I know you're just being coy with me," he said, with the shine darkening his eyes. "I truly don't like the games, darling, and we'll address those in further detail in the future. I don't like starting this evening out on a sour note."

He was crazy, Jenna decided at that instant and started to slide her hand free. His fingers clamped firmly, locking her hand to his arm, and for a split second, she considered slapping him. She wasn't about to engage him in a wrestling match on this couch, though. Locking her cool gaze on him, she stated, "Let go of my hand, Hugh."

Anger chilled his blue eyes despite the expression of dumbfound creeping onto his sculpted face. He should be a handsome man. All the right ingredients existed. High intelligent brow, a lovely shade of blue eyes, a firm jaw and strong cheekbone structure. Even his hair fell in a stylish wave to loop over his temple and sweep past his ear. The hair was a little short, buzzed and cropped about the ear . . . just shy of a new-wave cut. Separately, the components of his face were handsome, but put together, the artist had failed to find symmetry. His eyes too close, his cheeks too high, his lips too thin. The smile and manic shine made the effect more gruesome in the blue orbs. "I like having your hand on me," he said in a playful tone—the sheepish little-boy tone that grated Jenna's nerves. "In fact, I'd like having both of your hands on me, darling."

The butler knocked then, and Hugh distracted, snapping a command, flashing an annoyed glance as Jenna slid her hand free. As the butler presented the wine, Hugh fell into a sophisticated role, checking the year, returning the bottle for the elder man to open.

Jenna seized the opportunity, sliding across the cushion and rising smoothly, looking at Hugh from the opposite end of the low coffee table. Her temper had arisen and his catty, somewhat bemused shine tipped her shallow hold. "You were right, Hugh," she stated. "The games are over. And that's not a subject we'll discuss later. We will address the issue right here, right now."

"Darling, please, come back and sit down. There's something I'd like to ask you—"

"I have asked to leave this house several times, Hugh. When I came here, as the FBI suggested, it wasn't with the understanding that I'd be held prisoner. Furthermore, I didn't agree to come here to become your mistress or whatever the hell you have in mind. I don't know what kind of fantasies you've been dreaming, sir, but this has gone far enough. We are not romantically involved. I am not in this house to entertain you or your fantasies. I will not be told what to wear, what to eat or drink, when to go to the toilet—not by you nor any other of your gender, not today, not tomorrow, not in the hereafter. Do I make myself perfectly clear?"

"You will not raise your voice to me in this house again, Jenna," Hugh said in a lower tone as he rose slowly. His gaze heated, his smile gone, he started through the space between the table and the couch. "You have toyed with me from the moment you entered my house. I am willing to forgive and forget, Jenna. I'm in love with you and I fully intend to make an honest woman of you. There will be rules you'll need to follow, but I'm sure in time, you'll get used to behaving like a proper lady—"

"Good God, you are insane," she stated while sidestepping toward the door, noting the butler's near startled gaze without losing sight of Hugh stalking her around the table. "I have no intention of marrying you, Hugh. In fact, I wouldn't marry you for all the gold in China. Is that at all clear to you? Or are you too far gone to understand plain and simple English?"

"Oh, you're going to marry me, darling," he chided as if he hadn't heard a single word. He continued past the table.

Jenna backed toward the door, not needing a glance to judge the distance to the reading lamp that stood three easy steps away. When she was within grabbing range, she stopped and held his chilled gaze.

"I really didn't intend to squabble, darling. This should be the happiest night of your life. I'd hoped to have a glass of wine, maybe turn the lights low and enjoy the fireplace and lighted candles. I know you don't expect all of that, but I intend to introduce you to a better life, darling. There'll be no more laboring in some silly hotel, not for the wife of Hubert von Hendricks. Besides which," he said, stopped within arm's reach. His gaze dipped down toward her middle and rose with a cocky smile, a nearly cynical shine. "You'll have plenty to keep you busy for a while. Of course, I'll insist no one outside this house knows that you're carrying another man's child. I assume it's Darius's child, and if not, I'd rather not know, darling. As for the child, it will wear the von Hendricks name, and you shall never tell it any differently. There's no reason the child need pay for your indiscretion for the rest of its life. Better it has all the advantages of class, and I will see that it has those, darling."

Recovering from the initial shock of his knowledge, she verified many a fleeting thought to realize . . . cameras! By no mistake or coincidence, the butler and maids arrived, timing their appearance to coincide with her rituals, morning and night. What outraged her more, his words or the thought of cameras inside her bedroom, she couldn't decide, but his smile enhanced her flow of adrenalin.

"Now, darling, why don't we return to the couch, and we'll try to repair the shambles you've made of this evening and make the best of it. Under the circumstances," he said with another wry glance toward her waist. "I don't see any reason we need to wait for the marriage vows to enjoy each other's company—"

Not a single clear thought touched her mind. Her hand flew with a speed and accuracy, hitting him square in the dimpled cheek and snapping his head a half turn. In another half second, she stepped a single pace back and latched the lamp pole, pivoting with a speed and force to snap the plug from the wall socket. The shade flew from the top of the brass pole as she wielded the post like a baseball bat, prepared to strike a home run. She was already in position when he snapped his head back, a hand to his cheek, his eyes wide with outrage and an insane shine. "You take even one step closer or make even one more lewd remark, Mr. von Hendricks, and I will knock your fucking head off, I swear before God," she hissed in a low, lethal tone.

His eyes blinked, his hand started to lower, and he looked as if he might truly engage her in hand-to-hand. Instead, he flashed his eyes off his butler then toward the open hallway, stating, "Escort my fiancée back to her room.'

Jenna pivoted a half turn, putting her back toward the inside of the door and darting her gaze to find Miller poised, his expression uncertain. "Agent Miller, you have two fucking choices here. You and your partner can help me get the hell out of here, or you can shoot me, here and now. I am not staying in this house another Goddamn night. Do you understand me?"

"The woman's obviously insane," Hugh said in a lofty voice. "I'm sure between her condition and the—"

"Mister," Jenna snapped and lanced him with a glare to ignite kindling. "If you say even one more word, you will be picking your head off the floor. I have had it with your arrogance, your snobbish mouth, your lord of the manor bullshit. You are the most spineless piece of work I've ever had the displeasure to meet and if you so much as breathe on me again, so help me God, I'll rip your skinny lips off your face."

The insanity of her position or the impotency of her threat didn't sink in, not until Hugh started a near inhumane snarl and his voice elevated to rage, "Getttt thatttt bbbbitch to herrr rooom!" In the next instant, he lunged, and Jenna swung. He came in high, arms outstretched, and she came up low, landing the heavy brass base against his ribs. Howling, he reeled away. In the next instant, Miller grabbed her from behind, almost gently wrapping his arms about her as she brought the lamp post over her own head and landed the shaft against his ducking head with a thud. Gasping over her shoulder, the agent barely drew breath before Jenna slammed her heel on his foot and his arm-hold broke. Not thinking. Without a single thought, she pivoted, and her hand slid almost of its own accord, latching onto the gun, yanking it with a force to break the Velcro strap lock. She had the gun and for whatever reason one retains information, she knew exactly how to use it, snapping the safety off even as she spun from the scattering arms. It wasn't a learned skill, not an art or a course she'd taken to put her back against the wall, the gun cocked to fire. A ten-minute fascination with a new pistol one of the security guards in Chicago had showed her, and about that long with a policeman, who'd suggested she might consider carrying a weapon if she made the bank drops often.

'. . . It's not that hard to use. You just flip this lever . . . You should take lessons and a safety course . . .'

She held the gun. Hugh von Hendricks rested on his shins, heaving and coughing, sputtering like a dog with a bone stuck crosswise in its throat, both arms about his waist. He had a broken rib or two, she could tell. Miller had backed off. He stood between her and Hugh, his arms outstretched to either side like an evangelist preacher besieging God. His face had paled, and his eyes had turned rather pasty—not likely being struck by the holy spirit. He might have a concussion, she couldn't tell. He was still on his feet. "All right, sir. I believe you have a set of car keys in your pocket. Is that right?"

"Y-yes, miss," he managed and glanced toward the fallen tycoon whose butler had hurried and knelt beside him. Miller looked back at her and several others had come running, now gathered and huddled just beyond Jenna's sight. She could hear them whispering, nearly whimpering in fright. "Why don't we talk about this, miss. Give me the—"

She needed only to raise the gun a notch for him to realize she meant business. "You and I are going to leave, now, Agent Miller. We are going to find a telephone and I will speak with your superior," she said calmly. "If you don't agree, I will blow your kneecap from its socket, if not your head from your shoulders. I'm not a nice woman when I am angry, sir, and right now, I am genuinely pissed."

"Uh . . . uh, all right, miss," Miller stated and started backing from the doorway.

"Halt right there and turn around, sir," she said with a thought of how fast he might dive clear. Taking Hugh von Hendricks hostage wasn't a welcome thought or an option. As Miller turned, Jenna closed the distance quick, surprised at her own calm as she shoved the barrel against his spine and caught his coat as he stiffened. "Now, I suggest you tell everyone to get out of our way, sir. I really don't want to explain why I was forced to shoot you . . ."

CHAPTER 17

Misery had a name now . . . it was Jenna Windrow, and with every passing moment of the night, Darius knew her with a greater intimacy. Over and over, the scenes and words played inside his head, distracting him from the most mundane tasks, halting him in mid sentences. By the Baron's will, Darius heard and responded to Raphael, but his thoughts remained locked, spiraling between the torrent of emotions set off inside of him. Misery. To think of her in Hugh von Hendricks' arms, to think of her standing at the man's side . . . To remember Hubert von Hendricks as the privileged, sneaky wine merchant who'd probably deliberately kept the shipment from reaching the ship, and thus, his alleged brother. Hubert, the bastard who'd once confided, he liked to play rough in bed, claimed women enjoyed getting slapped around a little. If he touched her . . . If he hurt even a single hair on her head . . . If she loved him . . . She'd kissed him . . . She would marry him . . .

Around and around, the torment chased him. Heat spiraled through his trapped limbs; waves of pain drove short, gasped breaths off his lips. He would go mad. Had already gone mad. Mad as a hatter. Nothing he could do. No battle he could win. She was killing him over and over again, rising before his eyes to look up into him with all the warmth and love a woman could offer. He held her on the overlook on Mount Washington, her body warm and right against him, offering him the strength to stand firm, enjoying the bird's-eye view of the city of Pittsburgh, and watching a barge navigating the three-rivers' point to troll down the Ohio River. She'd pointed out the rivers in her lyrical voice, speaking the names as if reciting a sonnet—the Monongahela, the Allegheny and the Ohio . . .

He'd seen hundreds of cities, visited a hundred towns, villages . . . Pittsburgh would haunt him. There, he'd lived a lifetime in a single day with the woman he loved . . . and in odd moments, he could believe himself back there with her, holding her hand, enjoying the sparkle in her eyes and the soft smile on her lips. Then she stood in Hugh's arms, kissed him, laid with him . . .

With so much talk of madness within that dining room, Darius caught himself stopped, frozen within the shadows of the hallway on the first floor, wondering if he would end up like all others who crossed the Baron. Would he be chained in a dungeon room, forced to survive on rats and spiders? Would he live in the tower, an available meal to the child who'd stolen a little piece of his heart? Would he end his days strapped to a bed in an asylum like the wife of Thaddeus von Hendricks . . . or end his days slaughtered like the miscreant Maxwell whose madness brought him to ruin?

In every case, in every tale, those chaps, lads and lasses alike, had done something to deserve their condemnation, but Darius couldn't recall a single act of treachery in his own regard. He'd never plotted an ill against the Baron or Raphael. He'd never once pilfered a coin or stolen a pleasure unsanctioned by the Baron. Games. Mere games and illusions. No matter how often he'd feigned his defiance, he'd never betrayed the Baron.

Moving again, his thoughts turning, his madness raging anew with more visions, Darius passed through the back gates.

The little lad had retired to his room, and Darius knew the boy suffered another of his moods. Raphael took spells. As weary and worn as any old man, the boy had trudged to his room and crawled behind his curtain, refusing to acknowledge a word. He wanted to be 'alooone.' Aimlessly, Darius had left him, his own sense of direction lost. A walk. When the world seemed too large, his moods too rampant, he'd always walked or driven, and even as a child, purely human, Darius had enjoyed the night. The night was the best time to indulge his needs, the only time he'd ever had in life. As a free man he'd walked, as a man half chained to a monster, he had driven. Fully bound, his feet carried him now, to pass through the rear doors, his mind raging anew in circles of misery.

He felt it then . . . the silence inside his mind. By no mistake could he believe himself alone, but for the first time in the past hours of misery, he couldn't feel the presence at his shoulder, couldn't hear the Baron's silent speculation and enjoyment. That he might live a long and hellish life, feeding the Baron with his own rages and misery, Darius had no doubts. For whatever reason, the Baron would feed off him, as he fed off the misery he instilled in others. Not just blood. Oh, the Baron needed that to survive, to keep his flesh and bone malleable, but it was misery and pain, the human emotions, to spice those meals. Half human, half monster . . . every human sense enhanced by the Baron's own taint. Soup. A whole kettle of soup boiling with all the spice the Baron could hope for. The emotions that would have driven Darius to madness or destruction if he remained fully human, resided inside him still. No escape into madness. No buckling to the futility of his existence and ending it. He was sane, could remain sane until the Baron tired of him in a few years. A few decades.

Misery. To live with the memories and to catch these glimpses of his love in another's arms for even another day . . . madness and misery.

The chill in the night air touched him, sinking into his bones, but Darius lent only a fleeting thought to his physical misery. Aimless, he walked within the high hedges, losing himself in the maze as easily as he lost himself in his mind. The silence and stillness offered a relief, a reprieve. He could feel, if only for a moment, as if he were alone inside this shell that no longer belonged to him—if it ever had. Misery. Around and around, his thoughts continued to sail, but his mind cleared. He saw her as he'd seen her that first evening, standing at the French doors in the Chateau Suites banquet hall, her face cast in soft light from the chandeliers. Never had another captured his attention on the instant, halting him, suspending him. Frozen, riveted, he'd taken his fill from the flow of her long black dress, silhouetting her incredibly sleek form, to the lift of her bronze-hued hair in a Victorian style. She'd appeared to step from the photo of another era, another time when kings and queens resided in wondrous castles from which the Chateau had taken its design.

On dual planes, he suffered the prickling sensations, the tension she inspired inside his mind . . . and a warning. Not the Baron's warning. This was different, and he understood the difference even as he noted the shadows thinning at the bases of hedges. Walking. He needed to walk. Think. Remember. Her picture. He had it with him still. A photograph to kindle his misery. For no other reason had the Baron allowed him to keep that photograph.

This is what you had. This is what you lost.

Bringing the photograph from his breast pocket, Darius veered without a thought, settled onto the nearest bench and rested. The chill had become a part of him. He stripped off the gloves and let them drop between his knees, settled onto his forearms and held the picture between his trembling hands. She was beautiful. Resting poised like a fairy princess, she needed only a white dress to carry him into a childhood fantasy. She wore black, long and slinky, sitting primly on the hearthstone, her hair capturing the light and sending off bronze sparks. Never in his life, not on another woman anywhere, had he seen that incredible kaleidoscope of color. The fire crackling on the hearth warmed him even as he studied the sparks caught at the edges of her copper-colored hair. A new minted penny, the curls slipping over her brow, wispy about her neck and twining over the collar of that elegant jacket. Had she removed that jacket, he might have incinerated before her very eyes. Oh, and how those eyes looked into him even now. Lifted at an angle, her face evoked the elegance of her class, the nobility he'd recognized. She seemed to mock him, smirking just a tad; the sparkle of her eyes transcended the photograph to touch inside his mind.

Oh, and he was feeding the Baron. Darius could feel the heat rising inside of him, his physical human anatomy gripping with the tension as he'd gripped while spying her through the lens as if looking through a telescope. His vow. His oath. The fate of his clan had stopped him from lowering that camera and taking her in his arms. Had he known then what he knew now, he never would have held that camera so still. He wouldn't have wasted an instant.

Trembling, he watched as the picture enhanced, brightening as if imbibed with an internal light that could only come from her eyes. He held her eyes, entranced, even as he felt the heat rising. Hot . . . he was getting hot just looking at her. The firelight dancing on her hair, sparks flying from her eyes, mocking him, daring him. Nothing of the weariness of that late hour touched him now. Cool darkness. Night. He could have laid with her that entire night, should have stayed in her arms and welcomed the last daylight of his life. Ah, how he remembered the sun drenching him, blinding him on that sidewalk. Only his eyes had hurt, stung from the sudden glare. And he remembered that sting, felt it now threatening to wash the tears over his eyes and blur the picture trembling in his hands.

The photograph . . . he needed to look at the photograph, needed to feel the misery. And he began to feel it. His hands trembled. His head ducked by sheer instinct as the light brightened, reflecting off the glossy print. "You . . . are killing me, luv," he uttered aloud, his breath quickening with the pains stabbing deeper, sinking into him. "Ah, sunlight . . ." *She is the sunlight. The warmth. The life* . . . "And the death," he added in a soft breath. "Life and death . . . love and hatred . . . misery and salvation," he heaved softly and suffered the eyes prickling the edges of his mind. "I'm sorry, master," he uttered as he closed his eyes against the sting of tears and the physical fires sinking into him, through him. "Sorry, father," he heaved. "I gave you . . . everything I had," he uttered and the internal eyes riveted, intrigued. "I am sorry . . . I gave my word . . ."

Talking was becoming too difficult. Pain. Heat. He flashed the image from the photograph into his mind and clung to the stark blue eyes, his attention riveted. *I'm sorry, my love,* he spoke only in his mind. *I gave you my word . . . I never should have given you my word. I couldn't protect you. I wouldn't have even tried protecting you against Amad . . . my word . . . my clan . . . the children. They are mine. Forgive me . . . God, forgive me. Misery is my only salvation . . . Don't let me wake. My vow. My oath. I've never broken the covenant. I'd never have broken that covenant . . . I gave you my word, master. That's all I had left . . . and even that wasn't left to me . . . no honor . . . no integrity . . . you've taken my son . . . made me hurt your own son that we should both be hurt . . . you've taken me . . . my clan . . . my pride . . . my love. You have it all, Baron . . . and I will see you in hell . . . but I pray I never see her there beside me. If there is a God . . . if there is a heaven . . . let Him help her find it.*

He was moving. Not on his own power, but the vertigo sent him stumbling. Spikes pierced his flash, driving gasps wheezing from his lips. Stabbing, the knives drove into his limbs, worse now than that first evening of his change, the race through an icy forest. Hot or cold, he couldn't decide, wasted little time wondering. As if he had stepped into an icy shower or a scalding spray, his breath caught in gulps and the tears spilled from under his closed lids. Daylight! He was moving through sunlight! Through the rear gardens—he tasted the hedges and dirt, familiar. Only once in his life had he looked upon the maze under full sunlight, caught in a disorienting moment to wonder how the sun could shine in such a place as bleak as this.

Daylight. Sunlight. Hot spikes, like razor edges, cut into him, slicing through to the bones within his melting flesh. No clear thoughts remained. His short cries, his rising panic drove him faster, running, stumbling. Lost. He was lost in the maze, and his eyes were useless in the brightening light. Tears blinded him as surely as the fires raging over his smoldering flesh. His gasps became cries, his breath lost behind a scream as he rammed a hedge and ripped his blistering flesh on the branches.

Catching fire. Incinerating. No other thought remained. He knew only the agony as he stumbled and splattered on the stone walk. By animal instinct, his body curled into itself, his face tucked against his knees and arms locked around his shins. Rocking within the flames, he entered hell and welcomed the fires with a scream of agony to sate the Baron von Hendricks for an eternity.

CHAPTER 18

Sitting in the passenger seat of the von Hendricks' company car, Jenna held the gun steady on the agent, only half-heartedly listening to his careful prediction for the future and his reasonable attempt to recover his gun. She'd escaped the house, but undoubtedly, Hugh had enlisted his entire security force along with the local law enforcement agencies to capture her. He was crazy. Far crazier than she had first imagined . . . and he had money. Those were two extremely bad bedfellows. If he could buy the loyalty of two Federal Agents, it was reasonable to assume, the man could buy every law official in the damned state!

She needed another car. She needed to ditch Miller and hope that Reichley found some grain of loyalty to his agency and placed the call to rescue his partner. She would be extremely lucky if the FBI didn't issue an APB and list her as an accomplice to Lisa Blythe. All because of a damned marriage proposal from a maniac!

Well, twenty-twenty hindsight. If Hugh hadn't advanced like a damned lunatic snake, she might have handled things differently.

Her attention split between watching Miller, the road and searching her options, Jenna snapped an order to send the agent careening off the mile lane to the highway onto another dirt road.

'Thank you, Emma,' she nearly spoke aloud, remembering the score of material the old woman had shared with her. History. For the sake of history, Emma had collected the current maps to show the stages of the estate's expansion. The original forests and hills consisted of a few hundred acres . . .

'Today,' Emma had boasted a week—a few weeks ago. 'The estate covers more than a thousand acres.'

Hopefully, the lane she'd chosen was the route she wanted. Jenna remembered looking at Emma's map, thinking the road must be a creek. The line had cut diagonally through the entire estate, passing through the new and old vineyards, crisscrossing other lanes. Choices. She had no damned choices. Regardless of which lane she chose, she'd land on a main highway and the state patrol or some other local official would track her down. Only one real choice remained.

"Do you have handcuffs?" she asked, then countered. "I know you do, Miller. Hand them over, real careful like." God. She sounded like some poor rendition of Ma Barker! 'I'm an assistant hotel manager!' she screamed silently as Miller obeyed carefully, presenting the cuffs. "The keys too, sir," she said in a gentle tone.

When she held the keys, she concentrated on the lane. "There should be another lane on the left . . .There. Turn," she stated, and he slammed on the brakes. Hugh's obsession with snow muck on his roads had paid off. Even the secondary lanes were clear, although the snow piled on either side, nearly higher than the door window in a few places. Her options were limited. Choices few. "Stop here," she stated.

"Miss, if you'll let me help you," Miller said quietly as he obeyed. Looking over to her with a near pained expression, he continued carefully, "You have every right to be upset. That fellow's crazy. But this . . . this isn't the answer, miss—"

"I asked for your help, Miller. I've wanted off this estate for weeks, but you and your cohort refused to help. It's too late. You should have stuck to being a federal agent instead of jumping onto that bastard's payroll. Get out of the car."

"Miss, I'm a federal agent," he stated. "That's the only payroll—"

"You can take it up with your superiors. Now, get out," she snapped.

He uttered a few words and opened the door, sliding out and climbing afoot as Jenna followed his path, settling behind the wheel and stating, "Step back."

"Miss, it's freezing out here."

"It's about a mile back to the house," she stated. "If you're in good shape, you can make it in twenty minutes. By then, I should be out of the state, and I intend to phone your superior, Agent Miller. You better have a damn good explanation for letting that bastard attack me."

Reaching, she pulled the door shut and hit the gas before he lunged for the door handle. She wouldn't be out of the state, but lying to a federal agent was likely the least of her worries after holding him hostage. If she remained on this lane, she'd find the highway headed toward the nearest border, but she wasn't headed for the blasted border . . . neither a state line, nor the Canadian line.

Skidding the car sideways onto a connecting lane, she doubled back toward the estate.

As she neared the grove, she snapped off the lights and slowed. Moonlight reflecting off the snow offered enough light to slide the car into an inlet made by the plow; pure adrenalin would keep her from freezing to death on the short hike to the homestead. Vaguely, she recalled lifting the keychain from her dresser—thinking more about a weapon than escape. She couldn't readily recall how she'd garnered a key for the Homestead from Emma. Another of those blasted fogs. The house had a phone. If she could stay out of sight and avoid running into the security guards, she would gain a single chance to escape this mess without a prison sentence. Bedamned if she would bring a child into this world behind bars! Any more than she would give her child the von Hendricks name! To hell with Hugh von Hendricks.

Anger helped. She slid out of the car and launched into a trot, staying close to the embankment. On dual planes, she listened for engine sounds and watched for even a flicker of headlights. Hopefully, by the time they found the car, she'd already have placed her call and Agent Wharton would have dispatched a rescue team. Hope. Hope and a lot of luck, she added silently as she passed through the wooded grove. The lights glowed behind windows of all three cottages. She wondered about the crazy old woman that Emma had mentioned, senile and deaf; then thought of the other crazy little woman who loved a two-hundred-year-old ghost and his more ghostly son. Emma loved them. In her tales and stories, she animated, speaking as if those ghosts were old friends whose lives she knew intimately.

Even before Jenna had heard the stories, the house had captivated her, and as she ducked silently down the garden path, she considered the strangeness to feel as if she ran toward safety. Perhaps Emma wasn't so crazy. That powerful image over the fireplace held a place in her own heart. If the Baron Amadeus von Hendricks were alive, doubtful he would condone an asshole like Hugh. If the old ghost had carried half the nobility and strength as his picture portrayed, he would have been a fellow to reckon with.

Shivering with as much fear as cold, Jenna collected the keys as she trotted into the cove at the homestead's back door. She knew how to shut off the alarm system, an outdated system considering the wealth of antiques inside the house. Inserting the alarm key and disengaging the system, she shivered and nearly lost hold of the keyring as she fumbled the second key into the main door. If she didn't step inside and enter the five-digit code to disarm the alarm within thirty seconds, according to Emma, an ear-piercing siren would blare from one end of the winery to the other. Counting the seconds silently, she concentrated, passing through the door in ten seconds, already punching buttons on the inside panel. In the soft glow of nightlights throughout the main entrance, she struck the last number and held her breath for a split second before the lights flashed from read to green. According to Emma, the external fire-alarm was the first line of defense. If that light hadn't turned green, the house would have lit up like a Christmas tree and the system would have sent automatic calls directly to the police station, Hugh's house, and the winery's security room a mile away. Breathing a sigh, she leaned against the wall and reached sideways, locking the door from the inside. Safe.

But not entirely safe. First things first! She needed to place some calls. Ducking below window sight line, she passed through the receiving room and crept across the foyer, holding her breath against the creaking and cracking of her footfalls on the old wood. Behind the counter of the tour guide station, she rested in a stooped pose and lifted only enough to collect the phone off the counter near the register. In shadows, she settled onto her shins, and still huffing, began dialing the long-distance number. First things first.

Trust no one.

Huffing softly, she listened as the phone began ringing and when the familiar female voice erupted, Jenna breathed a sigh. "Mom. It's me."

"Jenna!"

"Listen!" she said just above a whisper, her senses alert for any outside sounds. "I don't have much time. I need you to do something for me."

"Honey, where are you—"

"I'm on the estate of Hubert von Hendricks, Mom. It's the winery in upstate New York, and I'm probably in a great deal of trouble. If I can't, I need you to find Agent Wharton with the FBI. Tell him, no matter what he's heard, it's not what it sounds like. I need him to get me out of here. If he doesn't. If he won't and you don't hear from me again in the next twenty-four hours, I need you to find Darius. Call every branch office, call the main offices in London. Don't quit until you talk to him, Mom. Tell him I'm in trouble and I don't know who to trust."

"Honey, my God! What's going on there? What's happened? Are you hurt?"

"I'm all right at the moment, Mom, but I honest to God don't know how long I'll remain that way unless Agent Wharton arrives here very quickly. You have to tell him, his agents are working for von Hendricks now. I don't know how or why, but I know they're on this asshole's payroll. They haven't let me near a phone to call him. I haven't been allowed off this estate. When you get him, tell him he'll find me in the homestead. I'm hanging up now. I'll try to get Agent Wharton . . . and mom? If uh . . . if anything happens to me . . . I love you. Tell dad, I love him too."

"Oh g-God, Jenna! Don't hang up—"

"Gotta go, mom. Please make those calls right away. Find Wharton or Darius . . . or anybody in the FBI. At this point, I don't care who. Love you." She hung up before her voice could break, but hot tears dripped down her cheeks. Speaking her fears aloud had taken a toll. Short hairs lifted at her nape; spiders tap-danced on her scalp lifting her hair follicles. Something could most definitely happen to her, and a jail cell with iron bars seemed far safer than sitting behind an old counter in the heart of von Hendricks wine country. Muttering a curse, she drew a breath and picked up the phone, dialing the second number which Wharton had given her, 'in the event of an emergency.'

Three rings later, a deep voice answered with a simple, "Hello, Jenna . . ."

"Do not attempt to move, son."

The words cut through the agony like a sword through butter and Darius moved in pain, shuddering uncontrollably and gasping a thin breath. "Well, I did warn you, lad. For your own comfort, you should lie very still, but as you may realize by now, I won't assist you with that undertaking . . ."

In hell . . . he had found hell. Waves of fire spilled over him, shuddering him and driving the air from his singed lungs. He heard his shallow breath wheezing as surely as the fuzzy images swirled in the slits of his eyes. He wasn't alone in hell. By sense, by sound, by the sheer force of the pain wracking his splayed body, he knew the Baron stood physically, hovering over him. Others stood about here, too. Even in his misery, he caught the human scents within the bitter aroma of burning flesh . . . his own burning flesh and a mix of tangy odors.

"Foolish, lad, a very foolish stunt," the low voice sighed. "But alas, boys will be boys. What is it, I wonder, that makes a son ignore the wisdom of his father?"

"Paa-ppa," the soft, shaky voice pleaded. "Dinnae torment him noow, plllease?"

"A mere question, elf. An age-old question, I shan't wonder. You'd think I'd have found the answer by now with you in my tow for so long."

"Heeelllp himm, pappa. You cooould help him."

"Ah, my lad, you know me better than that," Amad said in a low growl. "I gave him the wisdom of my years, and what does he do with it? Reaches from the frying pan into the fire with no more sense than a toddler clasping a hot kettle."

The sighing voice came an instant before the pain exploded in Darius's jaw and ran the length of him. Held on the apex of agony, nothing touched him for an eternity or an instant. Too soon, Darius understood a body jostling the mattress beneath his melted limbs and the firm encompassing clasp on his jaw. If he had eyelids still, the flesh had melted into a thin sheen. He could see the silhouette of the Baron; tasted the musty scent on his grunted breaths and gasps.

"Ah, my lad, you've made a mess of yourself, so you have," the Baron said in a low, sighing voice. "What? No cries for mercy? No pleas for a release from this hellish corpse you've made of yourself? You would rather lie here in a vat of boiling mush than call out to me for salvation?"

Salvation . . . in misery. Whatever that dark place beyond the fires of physical hell, Darius knew he'd dwelt alone there. No thought. Beyond the conscious realm of misery, no thought followed him. White hot pain . . .

but no conscious ability to grasp the pain. Nothingness. A nebulous. True salvation. Salvation in misery . . . He would boil in the vat! Freedom! A place without dreams—or darkness—or thought—or memory—or misery. No life. No death. No pain existed in unharnessed agony—

"Lad, you are tempting fate and testing my patience sorely," the Baron warned.

An epiphany sped across his boiling mind. *Misery is light . . . and I am the miller.*

"Ah," the Baron let out a humph. "So, you liken yourself to a blind bug seeking salvation, do you?" the Baron mused. "I wonder if you would feel the same if I stood you in the dawn light each morning and healed you each night? Eh, blind bug? How many times would you walk this fiery path toward redemption if we repeated the process daily?"

His eyes clearing enough to see the blue orbs; his breath wheezing and body quivered on the brink of agony. Only in his mind, Darius spoke his mind, *I would welcome the light.*

"If you were another man, Darius, I would believe you a brave idiot or a raving fool," Amad idled. "Do you see your precious lover in this place of nothing, lad? Does she dwell in that realm of darkness with you?"

Did she? Was she there with him beyond the wall of fire? He wanted to return to that place of dire agony. She must be there—

The pain exploded at his chest, spiraling outward until he felt his fingernails and toenails incinerating. His cry of agony followed him into the nebulous . . . but he heaved sips of air, half cries escaping through parted lips as he returned. The Baron's hand rested at his chest; an immense weight submersed in the vat of boiling flesh. Subtle flutters of motion burst blisters, spilling fetid juices, flashing flames through his limbs. Fear tinged the edges of his waking mind, but he longed to feel that hand move more quickly, roughly. Salvation. Freedom lay just beyond the first seconds of agony. As if he jumped through fire, jumped through the physical realm into freedom, he needed only to endure the first moments of hell. Freedom.

Freedom from pain—from the eyes which darted like illusive shadows at the corner of his vision. Freedom from humiliation—and regret . . . from commands to strip him of his human dignity and honor—freedom from damnation.

With a humph, the Baron commented, "You're the devil's own disciple, lad. I'm tempted to believe you truly welcome this physical hell—that you'd revel in that daily exercise and run into the light laughing."

Peaceful oblivion, Darius agreed silently, still sipping heated breaths.

"Lad, you've bought yourself a walk through hell," the Baron said sadly. "But we may have you up and about in time for the wedding. This lass of ours, by the way . . .? You'll be happy to know, she's giving me a time," the deep voice continued outside, and inside now, cutting through conscious thought, holding Darius rapt. "I can't for the life of me understand why, but she seems entirely put off by the thought of marrying my dear sweet brother. Of course, I had a chat with her and managed to smooth her ruffled feathers. No more than a lover's spat, I assure you, lad . . . She doesn't seem to appreciate Hugh's idea of romantic pursuit, but I feel for the lad, you know? He can't seem to get the ole pecker up unless he's slapping or bruising. Some latent Oedipus complex, I suppose," the Baron sighed. "In time, I'm sure she'll get accustomed to his style and learn to enjoy his methods. She has such a loving heart; she may yet beg for him to slap her around just to make him feel good.

"Of course, I've told him he must temper his affections for a time. We wouldn't want to damage our infant, but after the birth . . .? Well, if the lass is still not adjusting, I might lend a hand. I certainly couldn't expect Hugh to restrain himself indefinitely, not with such a bonny lass living under the same roof. After all, he'll have the responsibility to raise and nurture the child. Without a doubt, he'll need some reward and return on his investment of time and love.

"Oh, I know what you're thinking, lad. I had the same thought. I wouldn't want to see that lovely face bloated and broken, but rest assured,

Hugh's a careful lad as I'm sure he's told you, son. It wouldn't look good to have the wife of such a nobleman running about with black eyes or broken lips. A few bites and welts, a few bruises on the unmentionables won't catch the public eye or lend the von Hendricks name to scandal . . ." The voice sighed. "Peaceful oblivion? Aye, lad, she'll have that from time to time. Ah, but that's no concern of yours. You seek your own peaceful oblivion . . . and who am I to deny you, eh? As you wish."

White hot, the pain took his breath and his mind away behind a scream of agony . . . but he wasn't gone long enough, never gone long enough. Far too soon he awoke to the soft voice, careful touches, to the sight of Teddy Brock hovering over him in every conscious moment. The lad was gentle, never jostling the bed or yanking the oil-soaked cloths away too swiftly, and for that, Darius hated him. In hell, he listened to the soft cooing voices, his misery made worse by the human scent that mixed like sweet perfume in the rancid odors of burnt flesh and festering infection. In a quivering voice, the boy fretted and soothed. His scent and touch mirrored his voice, reflective of a woman in Darius's boiling mind.

So many faces in his mind. Time eternal, he lay watching the faces of all shades and shapes. All color of lifeless eyes stared up at him, through him. In shame and sorrow, he moaned and in misery he lay rapt, the nightmares less natural in his mind, more powerful for the awareness to rise when the images came. The Baron visited him, physically, mentally, taunting and chiding, or cooing sympathy and sorrow for the sake of the child he held at his side. Raphael never came alone, but Darius knew when the child hovered at his side. Awake to the cool gentle hand holding his inflamed fingers, to find the ashen face through slits of swollen lids. A well of sorrow swelled from the very depths of the child's tarnished soul, touching Darius in those moments, and he forced his fingers to clasp those tiny digits. The boy understood, with the wisdom of an ancient, the child understood and through Raphael, Darius found salvation often, feeling the slap upon his burning flesh and welcoming the agony that sent him away.

Never long enough, never long enough, were those moments of peaceful oblivion where he lingered beyond the charred bones and melted flesh, beyond the new flesh emerging from the boils to expose his nerve endings to every touch. Too soon he awoke to the images the Baron provided or the natural delirium and nightmares to roust him in moaning fits and seizures.

Far too conscious, he lay watching the images scrolling through his mind. Jenna, his love, seated at Hugh von Hendricks' table, staring down at an etched dinner plate with a troubled brow . . . or resting on a couch, accepting the pawing hands and bruising kisses the lecher planted on her soft lips. Oh, and he saw her futile struggles and her heated flashes between those kisses. Vulnerability and confusion flickered in her eyes as she lost to the greater power and panted, inciting Hugh toward greater excitement and lust. Rage boiled in Darius's heating flesh as surely as his mind taking turns and twists to see Hugh von Hendricks face bloated, to feel the neck clenched in his fists, imagining the deep blue eyes bulging in terror and confusion. No punishment was too slight, and death was too final and quick for the rage boiling in Darius's trapped mind. In twists and turns, Darius imagined wrenching the arms as this lecher wrenched and squeezed the arms of his love. Bones snapped, howls of pain and shrieks of terror resounded like music to his ears, as he snapped the spindly fingers one by one and rained blows on the thin lips. In misery, there was salvation . . . but for endless hours, Darius reveled in the damage and devastation he wreaked upon the body of Hugh von Hendricks, killed him and revived him a thousand times, if only in his mind.

The deep voice intruded, sighing, slicing through the rages, pointing out the obvious reality and finding fault in the fantasies. No answering cries of denial or painful wells of misery erupted in those moments. Darius waited, listened, opened his mind to the images that inevitably came to torment, and reveled anew in his rages as he viewed her plight through the windows of other souls.

The Baron held no firm grasp on her, nor Hugh, Darius knew. The visions came from others in that wicked living realm, from butlers forced to watch and maids who delivered hot tea and cool cloths. His love lay in a vat of misery, and he could see her life force ebbing, felt her spirit sinking. She wore the ring, now, a tremendous diamond ring slipped onto her finger under candlelight as her eyes clouded with doubt and confusion, a worried frown touching the lips which had smiled so warmly upon a time.

"There's bound to be a scandal," the Baron said lightly. "What with the child coming so soon after the vows, but we'll handle those . . . With a few loose words to reporters, a few hints, the public will believe Hugh and the lass were married months ago by quiet private ceremony. Ah, to turn such a grand scheme to the advantage . . . the tabloids and social columns will do wonders with this romantic tale. Bachelor tycoon falls madly in love at first sight . . . a story to warm the hearts of people everywhere. Jenna Windrow . . . a pauper princess showered with love and gifts from a man who could have any woman alive . . . can you imagine it, lad? She'll be a heroine for every young girl in America! If not the world. Living proof that dreams can come true . . . and Hugh will be the hero, a handsome knight fighting the trappings of his class to bring his lover to his own noble status . . ."

The whimsical tone dropped to a more conversational pitch to wonder, "Did you see her try to slap him for calling her a whore? I think that was a mistake on her part. The lad's made a habit of it, now. She's a fighter this lass of ours, my lad. She's going to keep Hugh sated for years. He might actually give up his keys to the local slut houses and concentrate all his efforts on that lass. A pity, I rather liked the lad's taste for variety. Nothing's too far afield for that boy." A laugh in the low voice, the Baron mused, "I sent him an early wedding gift, lad, from both of us, I'll mention. His own subscription to that new publication dedicated to the thrill and adventure of voyeurism. He'll enjoy hours of pleasure and undoubtedly give us a few in the process . . .

"Between you and I, lad, this boy's always been my favorite. A real chip off the old block, you might say . . . only fitting he reaps the rewards . . ."

On and on the voices and images, the waves of pain, the soft gentle voices and careful ministrations.

Physically, Darius had gained a new layer of flesh, shedding the blackened flakes like scales off a snake's hide. Sensitive and thin, stretched and burning, the skin turned an unhealthy shade and offered no comfort against the elements. He could move, could rise from the fetid mattress and walk about the small room with Teddy's help, and Darius welcomed the pain of that endeavor. Inevitably, he fell into oblivion time and again, free of the chains and voices, the images and memories. Salvation was still misery, and in his way, he knew his body had ceased to heal, would get no better. Half dead, half alive, he retained neither enough of his humanness to weight his flesh, nor enough of the vampire to improve his condition. He was a walking abomination. A gray living visage of a monster with eyes never quite closing and hair scattered in patches on a smooth bulbous head, that never ceased to bob like a buoy on a rolling sea. With every step, his lips drew back in a ghastly smile to send flutters of fear through his companion of weaker construction. Teddy shivered at the sight of him and dripped tears under a mere glance. A monstrous rendition of what had been a human form, and in his way, Darius found the humor and satisfaction. He had made a mess of the Baron's possession. Whether he'd set out toward this end was of no consequence. No more than twenty paces could he walk without falling into a vat of hell and crossing over the fire-line into salvation.

Half man, half monster and only half chained once again . . . he could live with that.

CHAPTER 19

To the Baron's image hovering in the shadows above the bed, Darius awoke slowly from the pit of darkness. His sight had improved. Clearly, he identified the purely human form, the cobalt eyes and knitted brow, the pensive smile on the black mustached lips. Always the epitome of fashion, Amad wore a black sports jacket over a gray jersey, his thumbs hooked almost naturally in the hip pockets of designer black jeans. Almost amused, Darius recognized his influence in the current ensemble, a reflection of the style he'd adopted for himself upon a time. At the moment, he could wear nothing more than soft baggy linens to hang loose off his shoulders and hips. He'd tried heavier cloth at the Baron's command and walked only ten paces before the material grated his raw nerves and pitched him into blackness. Ah, but Amad was a handsome chap, appealing to men and women alike, as much by the strength in his size as his innate talent for seduction.

"This," Amad said in a heavy sigh. "Will never do, my lad. You truly have made a mess of yourself. Granted, I didn't give you the form you were born with, couldn't claim that grand design . . ." Shaking his head, he moved his hands and sidestepped, settling onto the end of the mattress and awaiting the flinch to pass, watching with a smile. "What am I to do with you, son?" he asked in another sighing tone and slid his hand to clasp Darius's jaw in a near gentle grip, letting his wrist sink carefully to rest on Darius's chest. Smiling, Amad ran his thumb over the edges of stretched lips and cheek, watching his effect.

This, too, would pass. Physical pain, the prickly needles of fire under the touch, became no more or less offensive than the cold that saturated his living flesh before the fires consumed him. When the pain increased beyond endurance, Darius would know relief. His eyes held steady, unable to close enough to squint or physically flinch. Tears welled and dripped by natural consequence, and he'd acclimated to the well of tears watering the images in his sight.

"You are correct, you know, lad. You can't heal beyond this point. If you were fully human, you might undergo enough surgery and live long enough to reach a degree of lesser discomfort. You'd never be pretty, but you'd be alive. On the other hand, were you entirely human, you wouldn't have boiled so severely, and if you had, you wouldn't have survived. And on the entirely other hand, lad, were you fully not human, you'd never have lingered in that heat long enough to reach your present state. You'd be dust in my garden. An uncomfortable state of affairs, this paradox of living tissue. Frankly," he mused. "I'd not mind taking you out for a stroll just to watch the reactions. My lad, we'd have a rush on the morgues, the likes I've not seen since the Black Death. Ah, but you've stolen that pleasure from me. You're an incorrigible son, so you are. A regular ole ingrate."

Only in his mind could he voice words, and he did so now, to wager, *You still love me.* Loved to torment . . . loved to feel the misery of human suffering . . . and rages.

"So, true. So true, my lad," Amad mused. "But alas, I liked you better when you could rant and rage afoot. And I have to tell you, lad . . . that smile's enough to give even *me* the willies."

You love that too, Darius responded, grimacing under the flutter of motion and spikes in his lips.

"True again," Amad mused. "I do have a knack for reaping benefits even from the most ridiculous turns and you, my lad, seem to have a knack for pleasing me immensely at every twist."

Glad to be of some service, then.

"Smartass child," Amad idled in mocked disgust. "I truly am cursed. Ah, but what's the sense to battle against damnation, eh, lad? We butt against forces beyond our control. Just look at you," he said as if to make a point. "As a fully mortal man, you buckled to those forces, knowing yourself to be the lesser of two evils, and adapting. You land in a vat of hellish proportions, no longer entirely mortal, and you battle still . . . adapting. Huh, and you think yourself so different from me? The irony is the likeness between us. Even in your own helplessness and vulnerability, you found a means to reap reward and seek the benefits. I can play inside your head, aye. I could tamper with your mind from now until the end of time, and you'd remain helpless. But you, you ingrate, you find a means to escape the chains regularly, convinced yourself that every minute of nothingness is a reward and a reprieve from the madness you endure in the waking realm. Damned ungrateful, lad, and downright clever. But alas, I'm not a merciful father. Not your friend, though in another time, I might have been . . .

"The Brocks, even in ages of old, always held a certain kindred spirit to my own. Many of them I did call friends when I dwelt in the living realm. Servants, aye, but no matter the station they held, a noble spirit shined through. Thus, when the time came, for those of you who couldn't be twisted and drawn into the plot, I deemed to remain half sated. And there were a few, lad," Amad said quietly.

"One was the Castellan's son, a boy slightly older than myself at the time. His name was Kenneth. Ah, and the times he and I shared. We were more like brothers. I was closer to him than to my own brothers, truth be told. We hunted, we caroused, we learned to ride on the same steed, and learned to hunt with the same bows and arrows. For two years, as I stood in my own chains, enthralled to a beast you've only to imagine, my hatred for Kenneth festered. Oh, and I hated that lad, convinced of his betrayal and his hand in my damnation. Aye, and upon my return, I wanted to mete my wrath on him. You've only half sense to realize the extent of my rage and hatred. Kenneth, I found in his hut, abed with a wife he'd taken in my absence. He turned his back on me, left me to his clan, and naught but red could I see as I laid eyes on him.

"Ah, and imagine my shock as I took the blood from his neck, the life from his loins, and learned his innocence. He never knew, lad. Not what his clan had done to me, not the plot against me. Between the elders of your clan, they decided he should never be told lest he turn against them and bring their entire clan to ruin. He alone had stood firm and rose his voice against the ugly rumors surrounding my absence. He alone had gone to my own father to offer comfort and assurance, to plead my case that I had neither raped his cousin nor left the castle in shame . . .

"Months . . . for months, the lad had gone in search of my bones, fearing I'd tumbled from my steed during that day's hunt. Naught of the lies or rumors did he believe, and he mourned for me as one nobleman and brother would grieve the loss of another. By the time I learned my mistake, lad, it was too late, and I was too new to my transformations to correct the injustice. Frankly, lad, had I known my talents in full, I might have damned him eternal. Thus, in fate's decree, the lad slid smoothly from this life to the next, his reward for his love and loyalty.

"Because of him, lad, and only him, your clan survived that night, and you are alive to hear this tale."

Should I hate him?

The Baron huffed a sound, his smile quick again. "Enough of the ancient past, my lad. Nobility and honor bear no merit on what's in store for your future. In fact, son," he said grievously. "You shan't be a bit happy with this turn, I'm near certain. A pity, Darius, but I won't stand for your impudence nor this half state of freedom you've embraced." With a smile, he lifted his other hand, and Darius watched the incisors stretching beneath the black mustache, elongated like the fangs of a canine. The eyes flickered red as the index finger slid between the yawning lips, and Darius couldn't help but think of Raphael's nasty habit of nail biting. It looked as if Amad would chew his nail, but that was not to be.

Shaking his head in quick jerks, igniting the fires in his clamped jaw, Darius struggled. Lifting his enflamed, club hands, ramming the Baron's arm, the fires exploded inside his skull before the lanced finger touched his lips.

Heaving, half sobbing, he curled on his side on the mattress for the first time in weeks, his limbs folded in too natural pose. Physically, the fires ebbed, and his sobs stifled, but awareness offered no salvation. He was back. His own hair matted, sweated on his temples and forehead. His own breath heated the thin damp cloth clinging to his repaired flesh. The Baron had left him to his own devices, hadn't needed to stand in physical witness to enjoy the misery of healing and renovation that Darius had no power to escape. Whether he'd lost more or less of his humanity, Darius couldn't decide. He was alive inside the fully chained shell and the Baron's speculating gaze only confirmed his knowledge. His sobs and heaves turned to growls of protest and frustration, increasing as he rose to another power and walked within the room. The fires had cooled. No sparks lifted from the pads of his feet or flashed from his bending limbs and flesh. Repaired. Fully repaired. Within the shadows of his compact room, he stood before the mirror, scanning his phantom image cast within the silver shine, the same image he'd viewed in mirrors throughout his life.

His knees buckled to a new pain, a greater agony. On his shins, he folded. His hands lifted to cover his face and he bowed, dropping his head to the floor between his knees. No end. No salvation. Only misery. Endless, eternal, misery. And she had a name, a face like an angel, the smile of an imp.

Enough, now, lad. Your little brother's waiting for you. Missed you terribly, so he has, the voice taunted, and Darius retained no will to resist the internal impulses lifting him off his knees. *You've seduced my elf, lad. In every moment, he's idled the hours thinking up ways to warm your chilly heart and comfort you in your misery. Ah, and he has a surprise for you, so he does. Hmm, but you shan't traipse through my house looking and smelling like a raging beast fresh from hell's fires. Shower. Dress properly. You'll find him in the study when you're finished.*

The healing process had finished, but the heaviness remained leaden in his limbs, his system drained. Sluggish, Darius obeyed the command, moving through the natural ministrations and tending to his needs personally for the first time in weeks. Without a need for further command, Darius dressed in his own style, his thoughts as slow as his motion, with a single thought playing like a mantra inside his head . . . *no end . . . no end . . . only endless misery. No end . . .*

Still chanting the oath inside his head, determined to hold any other thoughts at bay, Darius meandered through the halls, sensing, not seeing the shock in his young cousin's face as he passed the boy in the hall. Miraculous recovery. Repaired. Salvaged for the single purpose of feeding the monster. No end to his misery . . . and she had a name, a face. Eyes like liquid pools under the summer sky. He loved her still, would love her forever, and therein lay the misery.

As the Baron promised, Raphael waited for him, and Darius registered the boy's delight as the lad jumped off a chair at the far end of the room. For a moment, Darius couldn't decide what exactly he saw. In the lamplight, the child appeared as though he stood in some strange photograph . . . or lingered in the half-light of a camera lens. Rising to his curiosity and doubt, Darius stopped and took in the image, from the cowboy hat tipped back on the black curls, to the western boots. The heels clicked with the child's bouncing. When the devil child was excited, he bounced, rising on his toes, dropping to his heels. Up and down, he rose and fell as if on springs, spurs jangling, hat bobbing threatening to tip off his tilted head. The elf hadn't missed a single trick, had apparently plied his father's indulgent nature to adorn himself fully from blue jeans to a checkered shirt, to a handkerchief tied at his neck. A tooled leather gun belt held low on his hip, tied off at the knee, and for a moment, Darius wondered if the imp would draw his tiny weapons and fire a genuine bullet. His hands were behind his back, his blue eyes danced bright with excitement, quivering his lips, lifting natural color in his soft round cheeks.

"I'm a cowboy!" Raphael huffed.

"I uhm . . . see that," Darius admitted, watching the imp bounce. At the sturdy heels clicking on the shined marble floor at the edges of the room, spurs jangled like tiny bells enhanced in the empty parlor.

"Joost like on the TV!" the damned child huffed excitedly. "Joost like the ones who romped aboot, heading west in the American history books! D'ya see then? I can ride, too! Pappa said we can get horses again! I've knoown how to ride forever! I learnt in America! With Pappa and Algen! I raced me own poony on the winery, I did! I can ride as good as any cowboy! And you know what else I can do . . .?"

Shoot a pistol? "Uh . . . no, lad," Darius said warily, feeling the bemused internal eyes watching this exchange and apparently enjoying every minute.

"Ahhh, coome oon, Darius! Dinnae be sad!" the boy huffed as if annoyed. "I wanted to make you happy! I practiced and practiced soo I could make you smile! I have a surprise! Aye! And I loove surprises! Dinnae ye too?"

"Uh . . . suppose I do, lad," Darius conceded, managing a slight smile. When Raphael deemed to be a child, to be a happy child, no one remained immune to his seduction. Looking at him spruced up in his classic cowboy style, miming any natural child with a talent for make believe and an indulgent wealthy father, the little lad could pass for a child of the natural realm. "I do appreciate your eye for detail, lad."

The hat strings jostled, and the black felt hat nearly tipped off his head as he giggled. "Aye, for you, Darius! I knew you'd be well! Pappa's mad at me for wanting to make you smile," he confided. "Yesah, but the ole cowpoke's always a'fuming at me for soomething," he said in a mocked cowboy drawl which combined in calamity with his Scottish brogue.

Amused, Darius studied the sparkling blue eyes. How a little creature of such dark persuasion could bring a smile to his lips, Darius couldn't decide. His own need, perhaps. Something in his dark nature to take his pleasure where he could and welcome whatever small indulgence the baron granted to him.

Bouncing again, jingling and giggling, Raphael huffed, "Want to see now? Want to see what I can doo, Darius? I've practiced every day! Want to see?"

"Love to, lil chap," Darius conceded and watched as the boy turned in a half step, bringing his hands from behind his back and producing none other than a coil of rawhide rope.

His eyes flashed sparks of excitement from beneath his tussled black curls, his lips pursed in concentration as he manipulated the large coil in his hand, a child determined to show off for an adult. He smiled and looked over, flashing a glance at the reading lamp standing near the chairs where they'd spent many a night sitting, reading. "Noow, watch the lamp! Aye, and think ooov a cow! Sure and it won't move, but I'll be doggin a cow soon's spring drops me a calf in the barnyard. I'm joost practicing with the lamp, now," he said gravely and sobered a tad as he looked up at Darius. "I was thinking to try on the deer, boot they're a sight faster than me. Pappa says we've cows on the way."

"I'm sure you do then, lad, And until then, the lamp's a worthy substitute," Darius mused.

"Aye! Watch now!" he stated and bounced, swinging the rope, looping it and letting it lengthen like a pro to whip from his side to rise, expanding above his head. "Watch the lamp!" Raphael demanded and Darius flashed his glance toward the lamp.

With the speed and agility gifted to him by his nature, the child lashed the rope across the distance, and an instant too late, Darius felt the loop dropping over his head. By reflex, he lifted his hands, waking to the shock as the rope snugged at his elbow joints and slammed his arms against his ribs. His senses waking, he felt the swirl of unnatural air, the child's essence whizzing around him . . . and the rope twining, snugging. Growling rage and shock, Darius started a step only to find his feet tangled in the coil of rope wrapping, binding his legs. A second—only for a split second, Darius saw the red feral glow and felt the impact as the child rammed him in full flight, sending them both to the floor in an echoing thud.

"Nooo!" Darius demanded, but already the small chilly fingers tugged at his collar. Twisting his head, he tried ramming the small head, glimpsed the fangs flashing, and heard the animal growl, "I looove youuu, Darrriusss!"

Twisting, struggling, Darius gasped at the sudden wicked pain in his neck. In an instant, he returned to the fires of hell, the flames singing his neck, his collarbone. He felt it. On every level, he suffered the physical pain and the knowledge, the reality. With that first sinking bite, the child held him, froze him. His struggle ceased only in his physical limbs. His mind raged as the chilled fingers touched his face, as the burn of the small fangs sank through his kinked neck and his head flopped sideways under the child's push. Blood. His blood. With the first quick draw, his heart staggered a beat. Trussed like a calf to be butchered, if not branded, he grasped the reality. The child was taking his life. And in an odd moment, he smiled, if only in his mind.

The seconds dragged into an infinity; the pain unyielding as what remained of his human blood raced to the unnatural pull at his neck. He'd seen them feed, had watched them sip from arms and hands, had stood helpless time and again as others had stood feeding the Baron and his son. Darius had endured the pain of that bite and retained the conscious ability to feel like a goat to be milked. Not once had he seen them take a life fully, not once had he imagined the sensation of a quick bond to hear the child's voice crying sorrow and misery even as he continued to fulfill his promise.

The imp would set him free . . . and how he reveled in that freedom already, feeling the chains breaking from his flesh and bone as his blood soared toward the child's command. At the edges of his mind, Darius heard the Baron's rage, but even with that lord's great speed, there was no time. No time left to stop the child. A main artery had severed. Darius felt his blood pumping, racing toward that leak as much by natural order as unnatural dominion. He was as helpless as the Baron von Hendricks who swept through the door several paces away. Finished. His heart slowed with the race ending. He felt himself slipping away, his muscles and bone falling into oblivion behind the emptiness. If he could voice his thanks, he would. Only sips of breath remained inside of him and those were nearly gone now, a silence sweeping through him.

On the brink of consciousness, Darius recognized the faded image of a child's face lifting in front of him, felt nothing under the hand that stroked his cheek. But he heard the sobbing breaths, the words, "Gooo nooow, Darrrius. Gooo too sllleeep, mmmeee friend. It'sss aaalll rrright . . . llleet gooo . . . Yerrr freee tooo gooo. Sllleeep. Jooost sssleeep . . ."

CHAPTER 20

"**B**it of a problem here, eh, my lad?"

"Pppaaapppa! Why willnae he gooo?" the child whined miserably, and Darius felt the jostling through his dead limbs as the hands tugged and pummeled at his chest. "Whhy willnae he joost gooo? Heee's noo life leffft to himm!"

"Appears, he's not in total agreement with you, elf," the deep voice mused. "Something of a curiosity, isn't it? You've drained the last of his living vestiges, taken his life, so you have, my lad," the deep voice said almost playfully. "Ah, but he clings to that last thread. Aye, and truth be told, elf, he might linger like this for quite a while. A tad too much of my own blood in him, and him just recently gorged."

"Nnnooo, pppapa! Pleeease. Finnnish himmm! Pleeease! Let him gooo! Heee's des-serving, pappa," the child hiccupped. "He is, pappa. Finnish him! Let himmm goo."

"Lad, as much as I hate to disappoint you, you've not left enough inside of him for me to finish what you've set into motion. Technically, son," the baron said grimly. "The lad's dead as dirt. A few more ticks of his heart, a few spasms, he'll be still as stone in this life. Not a damned thing I could do to change that. You've kept your promise. Killed him dead."

"I dddinnae Pappa! He's noot dead! I can still feel the life to him! Hear him! Pappa he's lissstening! You huvtae help him! Dinnae let him sooffer any looonger. He was a goood man! The best, pappa!" the boy heaved and sobbed, dropping his head to brush the curls at Darius's chin. "Gooo, Darrriusss! Leeet gooo!"

"He has nowhere to go, elf," the deep voice sighed.

Through a haze, Darius saw the shadow fall over him, felt the small body lifted and heard the sobs breaking, then muffled in more desperate pleas.

"I can't kill a man who's already dead, lad, that's a fact," the low voice consoled. "And this one's turned under. There's no doubt. He hasn't enough drops left inside of him to keep a heartbeat or breath inside of him. We could bury him, perhaps, and leave him for time and natural decay. Eventually he'd fade. Or we could carry him up to the mount and stake him to the ground. A few days' time, the predators would strip his bones and the daylight would char whatever remained. Aye, but that's a hellish end to a good man, don't you think? I'd not think twice were he an enemy and deserving, but alas, tis no fitting end for a lad who gave himself freely into our service and honored his word with uncommon valor. A predicament you've gotten us into with your mischief, lad."

"Let him gooo, Pa-ppa," the child heaved. "Ma-ake him gooo!"

"Lad, I'm not the only one to hold him here," the deep voice idled. "I hold a part of him, aye, but only part. He's bound himself to another and woven that thread tight."

"I-I dinnae understand."

"No, I don't suppose you do, elf," the Baron mused. "And perhaps you never will in your childish nature, but tis a fact, your brother's a man. Aye, and this is a mess, my lad. Not only is he a man with whom I've entered freely into a covenant, but I've made him a son . . . Humph," the Baron idled. "And the devil's had the poor luck to fall in love with a daughter of my own clan. Aye, four hundred bloody years, and it's come down to this. Brock and von Hendricks blood mixed and bound by a force greater even than the bloody covenant. I should leave this devil to the wolves on bloody principle . . ."

The silence dropped, an ethereal silence without a heartbeat or living breath to intrude. If others moved within the stone walls, the sounds were too far away to hear. Lingering in the stillness, his body as still as stone, Darius could see them still, hazy shadows cast in the dull light, their features indistinguishable in his faded vision.

"Ahh, to bloody hell with it," Amad muttered. "Stand aside, elf."

Only the shadows thickened over his dead eyes as the sleeve yanked off the arm above his face. Darius knew only by the feral sparks and growl, the vampire would feed. He felt nothing. Merely hovered on the brink of sleep as he watched the fangs raked across that lifted arm. His head jostled under a firm grip on his jaw, and he knew when the first drops splattered inside his gaping mouth. Something . . . he felt something.

Abruptly, his body shuddered and convulsed. His insides exploded. His awareness shattered.

To a feeding frenzy, his senses quickened, a need greater than any he'd ever known, and he was filling! Bitter, tangy fluids spilled through him, flashing through every dead crevice, waking him more in every flashing instant. Ah! And he wanted it all! His fire-lanced eyes flashed upward, locking on the feral eyes above him and his body moved, sucking from the limb as easily as he would guzzle from a bottle of rich wine. He felt the reverse pull, the wrenching tug and a growl slid from his throat, joining this second beast's snarl.

Hunnggrrry! Only that thought held as he tried keeping the offering in his locked jaw, drinking and filling. As the arm yanked away, he lunged and collided with the backhand, slamming him back to the floor. Pain ripped across his lips as naturally as any fist and he shook his head, reaching naturally to clasp his jaw as he shook the spots from his eyes. Splayed on his side, he climbed only as far as his elbow. His entire body shuddered and shook with a strangeness to lend him pause. Heaving breaths, rubbing the ebbing prickles from his jaw, Darius lifted his gaze warily to find Amad resting an arm's length away.

Resting on his hip, sitting on the floor with one knee drawn and his hand dropped to the floor, the Baron glared down at him, studying him with a quirked brow and a smirk. "Hungry little bastard, so you are, son."

In rapid glances, Darius took in the bare forearm extended to the floor, saw the smears and trails, the ebbing holes. His head shook, waking his mind.

"Don't even think about it," Amad said in a mocking rendition of American slang, a more amused shine in his cobalt blue eyes. "You've had more than enough to tide you over."

Dead. He had died. He remembered the ropes. And in more rapid glances, he glimpsed at the remnants of snapped and frayed twine scattered on the carpet around him. To the sense of fright, and his own memory, he followed the scent and found the child peeking around his father, undoubtedly stooped within the shadows of the elder. Dead. The child had killed him. He should not have life or breath to pick himself up, to rest on his hip.

Far more warily, Darius lifted his gaze to the piercing blue eyes and his thoughts halted under the red darts, feeling a swell of hatred and heat flashing through his system. Wariness and alarm haunted every edge of his mind under the intensity of that gaze, but he'd never backed away in fear. This wasn't the exception. His muscles coiled and prepared to react, he rested in a similar pose, at a near equal height . . . and listened to his own thoughts, his own mind racing and searching. No prying at the edges. He felt a prodding, the prickling of an external force and remembered a footrace through a snowy nightscape not long ago. Probing. An external probing no different than what he felt under the searching eyes. Almost patiently, Amad continued to study him in silence, the wariness in his blue eyes and mustached smile visible.

Dead. He had died . . . but he was not dead now. All too alive, he breathed in the familiar scents of the man and child across from him . . . as surely as he caught the scent of fully human essence lingering in the room. And he knew abruptly, this keening awareness, the sounds coming to him, a lull of voices which reached him more like the sound of the Baron's words inside his head. No pain now. An unnatural emptiness lingered inside of him, a pulse like an echo beat inside his head and his breath seemed more a vapor of thought than air. He knew . . . knew without a single doubt, he was now—fully—a son to the Baron von Hendricks. "Youuu bassstard," he hissed.

"Ah, should I have expected otherwise?" Amad mused and shook his head as if in disappointment, his eyes glittering with menace. "You're an ungrateful one, son. Been that way from the moment I set eyes on you."

"You've damned me to hell," he growled.

"You've been damned since conception, lad," Amad said idly. "And you're not fool enough to doubt it."

"I should have bloody killed you when I had the chance," Darius hissed.

"My lad, you never had that chance," the Baron said smoothly, simply. "And you don't have it, now, I'll mention."

"Is that a fact," Darius idled as his thoughts twined with the option laid before him. He was the monster, not by metaphor, not by half. Full-blooded, or bloodless, he was the Baron's equal in damnation, and in his way, he knew it. If they fought now, it would be a bloody battle to the end, and his blood rose quickly toward that challenge.

The Baron sighed and shook his head, a more natural amusement in his dark blue eyes. "Were you a lesser man, lad, you'd not be sitting before me," he commented. "I make mistakes from time to time, I'll grant you, but this isn't one of those times. You won't take the life of your father, nor your little brother, though I'd not wonder if you felt the need. Ah, and you'd like to, my own, but on your honor, you'll stand down. You are bound, as am I, infinitely more now than when I brought you into this manse eight years in the past. I watched you then, my lad, a mere stripling at twenty-two, a wild spirit with an unruly temper . . . Ahh, but you were a joy to behold. A nobleman to rank among the best I've seen of your clan and there were a few, lad. A few I'd not have thought twice to claim as sons, save for the vow that stayed my bite," he appeared amused and shrugged. "You, lad, had the poor lot to become fair game. Did you honestly believe I'd chosen you merely for your looks?" Amad mused.

"That thought never entered my mind," Darius said dryly.

"Aye, you are bright, Darius. That in itself can be a curse. Were you a fool, you'd have been turned to fodder long ago. Ah, but you sit before me now. A fine lad, made no less fine by the gift I've given you."

"Call it what it is," Darius snapped. "As you were once condemned by my clan, so too, you've damned me, to live what . . .? An eternity of hell? To become a plague on mortal man? Nobility bedamned, you've cursed me worse than I could have dreamed possible and I'm no mortal man to be fooled or even seduced by your words or lies. You've stripped me of the decency and integrity I once had. Of the compassion, no differently than Kevin observed. And you're not fool enough to think I'll thank you for this."

"Would you have preferred to be bound in mortal chains, lad?"

In a paradox, he knew only one answer, and hated himself for that single truth. He preferred damnation—eternal damnation—over the chains. A growl slid off his lips, and he tore his gaze away to glare across the carpet. Inside him, the anger burned, but his mind was his own . . . his body returned to him. His gaze snapped back, lancing the bemused eyes. "I won't bow to you, sir. Not again. Damn me. Damn my clan. I will not drop before you or bend to your every fucking whim. Fuck you and fuck the oath I've vowed to you. Your covenant bedamned as eternally as myself," he finished and rose smoothly, turning, pacing away and still aware of the Baron rising behind him.

"We no longer need the covenant."

At the calm, almost quiet words, Darius pivoted and met the gaze at equal height. "Then I am free to kill you," he mused.

Amad huffed a sound and shook his head. "Ah, how I do enjoy your youth, lad. Foolhardy as it is. You may try, if you think you have the need, but I should think you've another greater concern, and a question in your mind."

Jenna! His eyes darkened, turning the color of charcoal. "I'll—"

"You'll listen," the Baron said smoothly, and held Darius from an advance by the force of his calm gaze. "We are bound. Curse the covenant if you will, my lad, but that which you've put inside the daughter of my clan binds you more thoroughly than your blood ever will. You, you unruly ingrate, I've chosen as a son and made you the father of my own clan, as you are to your own."

"I really should kill you," Darius decided, but held his ground.

"Humph," Amad uttered and reached smoothly as Raphael leapt toward him. On the young face still streaked with a gray sheen of tears, the fear and wariness glowed neon. He still wore the cowboy hat, though it dangled at his back from the rawhide sting about his neck. Clinging to the elder's hip and neck, he darted his shimmering blue eyes off Darius up to the Baron, who studied him with a firm gaze. "See the error of your ways, eh, elf?"

"I w-wanted to helllp him, pappa . . . noot this. Noot ever this," the child uttered and lifted his finger, biting his nail as he looked at Darius with his fright unmasked. "Aye, and you've r-reason to hate me, now."

For a moment, Darius considered the words and realized, "I've only myself to blame, Raphael. It's a damned desperate fool who would trust his well-being to a child, much less a child of your damned dominion."

"Aye . . . boot I tried, Darius. I tried to help you," the boy said morosely and dropped his gaze momentarily in shame. "Ye'll drink me bloood now . . . er beat me at every turn. It's the way of it. Aye," he said morosely and lifted his desperate gaze to his father. "Ye'll make him too, huh, pappa? Joost like Jooseph. He'll be Jooseph all o'er again."

Curious, Darius noted the flicker of thought in the black brows . . . and for the first time since meeting this pair, he felt the connection, a weird, tangled connection between father and son. The child's pain and fear touched the elder at a level to shrink whatever hatred. At a gut level, Darius felt it too. A well of sorrow and desperation he'd felt only in human form . . . a human pain so pure and natural not even his enhanced nature could distinguish where the child ended, and vampire began within that tiny living form. More curious, troubled, Darius watched the Baron battle his black nature just to raise his hand and scuff the head in a gesture of comfort. His own damned essence would have done the same, and Darius fought a private battle to keep from moving forward to comfort the damned child. "Who the bloody hell is Joseph?" he growled instead.

Amad looked over with a flicker of dark amusement. "You would rise him to a challenge, aye? Call him out for a duel for the pain and fear you sense in my wee lad?"

"Merely a question," Darius stated, committing himself neither by tone nor greater interest.

"Liar," the Baron mused. "Battle against it, aye, but you won't win. Bloody hell knows I've tried ridding myself of this elf's hold more than once in the past. Left him to dungeons, to thieves, to all manner of ill . . . Aye, and I find myself racing to his bloody rescue and meting revenge as if I'd fathered the lad by my own loins. Spare yourself two hundred years of grief, Darius, accept that he's weaseled his way into your chilled heart and attempt not to deny him. You'll do yourself a grave injustice if you hold him at arm's length."

Not trusting the words, Darius watched as the Baron leaned over and slid the worried child to the floor, turning him and sending him forward with a swat on his rump. "Go see your brother."

Spurs rattling, his wide eyes flooded and lips quivering, the little boy sidled. One hand covered his rump and the other shot to his mouth to gnaw his nail. He shook his head, darting his gaze between the Baron's firm glare and Darius's more wary shine. The imp had tricked him often enough in the past with that innocence and wariness. When the body charged, Darius reached, rather than struck, and caught the lad smoothly, bringing him to his hip. At far closer range, Darius looked into the moist blue eyes, and it was not an anomaly of nature he saw in those depths, not a rancid scent of corruption or deceit.

With a sob of relentless sorrow, the child buried his face at Darius's neck and heaved apologies.

By whatever this strange nature, this privilege or curse, Darius knew the child no longer posed a threat, if at all he ever had. On his own feet, Darius stood firm, having heart enough to cover the head in his hand and duck to breathe the confounding scent wafting off this child as quick and pure as any human condition. For a half second or less, Darius suffered a pang of desire to drink in the scents by whatever means. In the next second, he shuddered and knew he would never sate himself on this innocent's blood, nor his misery. The child could be no safer than if he rested in his natural father's arms, and with his revelation, Darius found a weird comfort. A monster. Aye, he was that. But he'd slay this devil Joseph in a heartbeat for whatever wrong he'd done this child. His thoughts turning in rapid clicks, he thought again of Jenna . . . and the child she carried in her womb . . . and his temper rose accordingly to find the Baron hovering at closer range, watching him with a menacing glare.

A test, Darius knew at that instant. The baron had sent this child to him to test him, and the dwindling rage in the cobalt eyes salved nothing of his hostility. "You've created a monster in me, Amad, and I will wreak havoc on your clan."

The smile slid into the lips. "Ah, lad. I'd have it no other way . . . But there's another little matter we need discuss first. A business proposition, as it were."

"Oh?"

"But even that's ahead of itself, son. A celebration's in order for your restoration. I do believe we'll invite your cousins over for dinner."

Doubt and outrage flashed hot in Darius's eyes before the Baron chuckled.

"Not as the main course, ya bloomin' idiot. As our guests."

Even Raphael giggled as he lifted. His wet eyes flickered mischief as he spoke with a dramatic huff, "If we had our guests for dinner, my friend, we'd have noo company a'tall."

CHAPTER 21

Nothing had changed in the others. The changes were inside him, and as Darius watched his cousins settling into the chairs, he knew the difference between them. They were human. From Kevin, who appeared slightly surprised then grimmer and dreading to Brian, who appeared only disgusted. Because it amused him to do so, Darius merely sat back in his chair, watching them with a mocked expression of confusion. Oh, they were human, and Teddy was the most innocent among them. Remembering how gently the boy had taken care of him, Darius suffered a slight change in his feelings toward his younger cousin. Given the situation, the lad had shown an uncommon courage and strength to tend to the grotesque form in which Darius had lingered. The lad hadn't even retched that Darius could recall. In every minute, the boy had attempted to make him comfortable, and Darius couldn't exactly blame the lad for not understanding the basics of true misery . . . That there truly was only so much a human body could endure before oblivion enveloped the mind.

What were the rules of his new condition? Darius wondered as he leaned forward and collected the wineglass in front of him. Something so simple, to respond to an impulse and attempt to quench his appetite or thirst, shouldn't seem so strange. But the wine didn't help. The taste barely touched his lips before he knew it wasn't what he wanted or needed. If the smells and scents in this collection had bothered him in his prior state, the aromas threatened to snap his resolve now. He was hungry. And his gaze trailed slowly down the table, lingering on his cousin Brian momentarily, watching the young man drop his gaze away as if to hide his thoughts. His thoughts were wide open without a need for a glimpse through the windows of his soul. The boy harbored only disgust at the sight of his older cousin, and remained as envious as ever, still convinced he would take his rightful place to propagate the Brock clan.

Darius's mind drifted, remembering that evening, recalling the Baron approaching the dark-haired haughty boy. Amad had moved between them, had walked through them, sniffing and scanning, looking into them. Brian. In front of Brian, one of the youngest and apparently most virile by his posture, the Baron had stood for a long moment. In word games and jibes, the Baron had broken through the lad's arrogance. Oh, the child had believed himself a Casanova, a gift to all women. By no fault of his own, he hadn't hidden his disgust for Teddy, who the Baron had called toward the front of the collection, the only virgin in the group. Rather than compassion for the mortified seventeen-year-old, who the Baron had openly humiliated in front of them, Brian had held his slightly younger cousin in contempt. Well, and Brian had paid. Buckling to the words and taunting, to the Baron's seduction, Brian had gone against his every base instinct and belief in himself and kissed the Baron . . . and before long, with the Baron wrapped in his arms, Brian had awoken fully to realize it wasn't a woman he held, but instead, another man.

His own test had come shortly thereafter, Darius remembered. Having seen one after another of his clansman taunted and teased, humiliated, he'd prepared for the worst as best he could. Oh, and it had been a test. He couldn't even recall all the tricks or words the Baron had used on him to drive him to a fine rage. A rage it had been, though. Without shame or humiliation, he'd stood his ground against the tirade of verbal slaughter. At one point, Darius remembered the Baron clasping his jaw, tilting his head back and looking into him, and with a smile Amad had asked, 'Afraid of me, now, is that so, lad?' 'Scared to bloody hell and back,' he had answered without an ounce of sarcasm or shame. 'But I'll fight you to the bloody end to rescue my son, sir. . .'

His son. Dylan. The child had already been lost; the lad's fate sealed before Darius had ever received the invitation to visit this castle. With his thought, his gaze drifted off Brian and fell on Halbrook, who forever sat at the Baroness's end of the table. Hatred. Undefined hatred slid over Darius's mind and coursed through veins, and as he drew the scents from that corrupt little man, his anger heated. No longer chained. No longer confined to the Baron's whim, Darius slid off his chair and onto his feet, already halfway to Halbrook.

Manic, the quick, beady eyes darted behind magnified glasses.

The Baron cleared his throat and commented, "Patience, Darius."

On nothing more than his impulse, Darius had acted, and he drew up short. His gaze spiraled toward Amad at the end of the table, then glanced at Kevin and Teddy, both of whom watched him with a tad too much sympathy for his liking. His gaze sped to Amad. "I've been patient for eight bloody years."

"Ah, the peccadilloes of youth," the Baron sighed and shook his head as if disappointed. "Lad, you're suffering the malady of today's moral decline. Restraint and discipline are no part of your vocabulary."

"I've restrained," Darius stated. "I've been sitting at least five minutes."

Amad studied him, then rolled his eyes and flagged his hand. "Oh, have at it then," he said as if in disgust. "I've had my fun with the flabby old goat. His accolades and feigned adoration's gotten downright boring over the years."

Smirking, Darius turned his attention to Halbrook. The magnified eyes widened as round as saucers and darted toward the Baron, to Darius, back to the Baron. Striding toward him, his gaze locked on the ruddy cheeks, the moistening eyes and quivering lips, Darius felt his tides rising, his senses swimming with the promise of a fulfilled oath within his grasp. "Ahhh,

George, how I've longed for this day. You don't know what a pleasure it is to find you here, waiting like a ripe melon to be bloody plucked off a vine."

"D-D-Darius—please!" George huffed worriedly, his gaze shooting toward the Baron. "Sire! Milord, Please! What's this about! What have i-i-I done? I d-d-don't understand!" he whined and sputtered. "I'll d-do anything you ask! Pleeease!"

"George, really," Amad said in a chastening tone. "Don't be such a bore. I'm not the one you've offended or wronged. First, there's the little matter of hundreds of lives lost before you bothered to take notice. As the lad's met many of those affected by your dereliction, he's every right to feel a tad invested in those losses. Ah, then let's see . . .? There's the matter of his only son at the time—a little lad you chose because of his background. Aye, and as I recall, you offered to slit the li'l chap's throat if I so much as blinked. Well, and we've the past eight years to consider," Amad paused thoughtfully. "Seems to me, little man, it's your voice he's heard time and again as he made the sacrifices to repair your mistake. Having his healthy male appetites reduced to the service of a stallion certainly didn't fare well on his psyche, and you are the fellow who provided his orders. All told, George, I think it's only fitting I let my lad stretch his legs a little with you."

Standing over him, Darius smiled down into the wide, terrified eyes. His mahogany orbs shined in quiet rage as he breathed the scents wafting off the trembling mass. "Damn, but I'm hungry, George," he commented lightly and reached a hand, touching the sweat lifting on the balding pate, hearing the whimper and feeling the cringe under his touch. Oh, this was different, and somehow thrilling. However, he felt slightly uncomfortable, as if he should wait, as if acting too soon would rob him of the greatest pleasure. Already, he vibrated with need, his body heating as images began rising through his mind. A connection . . . a weird connection as he looked down into these soggy, wide orbs. All the reasons why he should take the fellow's life zoomed to the foreground . . . but other images assailed him as well. The Baroness watching with a wicked interest and curiosity; his cousin across the table, considering him no more than a puppet; Kevin and Teddy watching worriedly, fearing as much for him, his immortal soul, as for Halbrook's life. Neither doubted that he could take this lad's life . . . but both believed the Baron held the strings on this charade. And therein lay their sorrow.

Growling his disgust, Darius broke the connection and peered the length of the table to the Baron. "I'll lose control, won't I?" he asked simply.

"Probably," Amad said, indifferently.

Frustrated by his restraint, Darius looked down into the still drowning eyes and smiled more darkly. "Soon, chap. Very soon. You have my word," he said and, on a whim, leaned and brushed a kiss on the sweated head, taking an undeniable delight from the shudder. Stroking the balding, bobbing head, Darius rose and sped his gaze across the table to Brian, who still held him in contempt. Only more amused, Darius strode around the table, catching the wary eyes. "How've you been, cousin? Haven't seen you in a while, have I?" he said amiably and held out his hand.

"You're looking well," Brian condescended and accepted the handshake, positive the Baron controlled this enterprise. The lad had learned, at least enough to know, he would rather not offend the master or draw undue attention to himself.

Darius held the hand firmly against extraction and, looking down into the more wary eyes, Darius read the subtle alarm. "You and I," Darius began conversationally and glanced off the Baroness, who watched him with unmasked interest. "We've shared a similar trade, haven't we, lad? And it's no surprise I feel a special bond between us. You alone can understand the burden I've had to bear. You understand, I'm sure, what a grievous responsibility it is to pleasure a woman. Ah, what a burden. So many and so little time," he said with a sigh and leaned a little, flashing a sly glance off the old woman, back to his cousin's slightly angry eyes. "There's something to be said for experience, cousin. I bet she's taught you a score of jolly good tricks. Any chance, you'd share a few with me?"

"Darius," Brian said in a near whisper. "I don't think—"

"Lad, please," Darius said with a mocked hurt shine, another fleeting glance, this one toward Amad who watched with a quirky grin. Dropping his gaze to Brian, Darius adopted a more hurt and dreading glance, waking to an unbeknownst thespian talent. "We've no choices, lad. You'll have to kiss me. And believe me, lad, I'm feeling no better about it than you."

"Darius—"

Dropping his head in a bow, Darius brushed a kiss on his cousin's startled lips then lifted and flashed a sour glance, a heated shine. "Lad, you've spent far too much time locking lips with that hag. I'm sorry to tell you, boy, you'd not win a lass's heart with that rancid breath." Under the heated rage in Brian's eyes, Darius chuckled and released the hand, watching as the boy wiped his mouth on his sleeve. "Taste of something dead, isn't it, lad? Or is more the taste of something more alive than what you've been bedding for a time?"

"Amad," the Baroness huffed in quiet indignation and dry disgust. "I do wish you'd restrain your child and spare us this morbid live entertainment until after we've partaken."

"Ah, lass, forbid me my own appetizer, would you?" Amad mused.

"As you wish, Amad," she conceded in a quavering disgust and flashed a platinum glance to Darius, all too apparently, expecting him to be turned against her, or on her.

"Madame, I'd not kiss you again for love nor money," Darius mused. "My young impressionable cousin wasn't the most together lad before you sucked the life from his lungs. You're a shriveled shrew," he commented and leaned confidentially toward her. Smiling and half whispering, he commented, "I don't think you'd want to tumble me, madame. I'd snap your bones for the bloody hell of it, and I'll tell you, lass, if you slap my own little brother about again or work your wicked whiles against him, I'll be tempted to show you a few tricks of my own."

"Darius, as I know who controls these fits of your fancy, I won't take offense," she said and reached as if she might take his hand and offer comfort.

From some darker place, a heated flash rose and glittered briefly in his eyes, his smile less kind than menacing. Withdrawing with a bow as her eyes locked in surprise, Darius turned from her and continued up the opposite side of the table, drawn as much by his younger cousin's scent as his need for a clear breath. "Ah lad," Darius idled as he reached Teddy and looked down into the pale blue eyes filled with such sorrow. "You'd likely break my heart with that look . . . if you didn't smell so blasted good," he mused and touched the shoulder, leaning and breathing in the scents near the boy's ear. He felt it then, his cousin's quickened pulse, his deep well of affection. No wonder at all the boy had been hurt so easily by Darius's harsh words. The young lad was half in love with him, and the other half afraid for him. Toss in spicy flavors of admiration and a pining desire to be just a tad more masculine and fiercer like his older cousin, and the boy was a simmering pot of stew. Under the touch on his shoulder to hold him stiff and uncertain, the boy flushed with subtle excitement, a trifle like a maiden receiving the flirtations of a secret love, with her other secret love watching. Only the thought of Darius acting on the Baron's order, lent the lad a more troubled disposition. "Ah, Theodore," Darius whispered against the boy's slightly canted ear. "You've a heart of pure gold and you think yourself such a disgrace," he said kindly.

"*Par-ardon moi* . . . I'm sorry, Darius," the boy uttered. Not lifting his head, his cheeks flushed with shame now.

Sighing, Darius slipped his hand under the soft chin and drew the flushed cheeks from the bow, looking down into the soulful eyes. Not quite twenty-five, but the boy remained trapped in his adolescence. He held no clear grasp of adulthood, knew only there were things he missed and felt, things not quite like all others around him. Fate had played an unkind trick on him long before the Baron had caught him. Teddy would have been a beautiful woman with men dropping at her feet. Instead, he was a beautiful boy. Darius stroked a thumb over the quivering lips, feeling the boy's sorrow . . . for him. The boy fully believed the real Darius would be mortified with what the Baron forced him to do at this moment. For Darius, Teddy was heartsick; and for himself, that he should take a secret pleasure from this touch. Smiling slowly, holding the blue eyes, Darius leaned down again and locked his lips over the boy's startled breath. Ah, and he tasted as good as he smelled. All the warmth and flavors . . . like another . . . like his misery.

With a gentleness to defy his past disgust, Darius tilted the head more and deepened the kiss, his thoughts sailing in quin-eccentric directions to be taking this liberty, drawing something from the boy who heated and melted under his touch. His own seduction . . . he felt it then. This strange power inside of him taking control, drawing the boy toward him, rising the images through the lad's mind to start his heart beating faster, his blood pumping—

Pulling up sharply, Darius looked down into the dazed eyes, watching the boy recover in slow degrees. His mind woke slowly to the shock and horror of what he'd done, how he'd reacted. He was heated. For what, the lad had only a wild imagination and unrequited desire to grasp.

Smiling a little sadly, Darius stroked the red cheek and wiped a tear away with his thumb, shaking his head. "You're a beautiful boy, Teddy," he said quietly and lifted his gaze to find Amad watching with a subtle shine. "He's in love with you, Amad. It's not a lie nor a deception, not a wily defense to keep his health or ensure his safety. You've not stolen his soul, but you hold his heart in your palm. He among us, has walked through the fires of hell for you, out of love, not hate or desperation. Perhaps, in that, he's stronger than the lot of us despite how fragile he appears in our midst. Take the doubts and insecurities from his mind, or I will in the coming nights. Such gentleness and kindness should not be wasted."

"Lad, you've not the stomach to carry out your threat," Amad mused. "You're too accustomed to the path you've traveled."

"I'll make exception if only to repay the kindness he's shown me, Amad. Knowing me as you do, you know my word will stand regardless of how I'd feel in the carry through. I'd not let the lad feel what I'd feel, and I'm not a naive child. Lift this curse and fear of the unknown from him and suffer to be kind about it, or I will."

"Giving me orders, now, are you, son?"

"Ultimatums, father, as you've given me in the past. The choice is yours."

Under his hand, Teddy trembled slightly, and his hand lifted, clasping Darius's fingers and drawing his gaze to see the fright and fear in the eyes. "Darius—"

"You've given yourself freely, lad, by no real choice, but without reservations. You are his. I can't change that, and I doubt you'd want me to. When the time comes, lad, whichever of us awakens you to the world you seek to know, don't be afraid. You've the scent of a pure loving heart no matter the strangeness of your desire and it's a seduction in itself."

"Ohhh, Darius," he uttered, seeming to seize what the others had missed. The tears gathered quick in his eyes. "Ohhh," he uttered and ducked his head sideways, resting his cheek against their combined hands, squeezing his fingers more firmly.

Stroking the silky blond waves, Darius shook his head slightly. "Ah, my fickle cousin," he sighed and looked over to Kevin, who understood as well, his dark eyes tense.

"Darius," Kevin said in a low voice.

"I still hate you," Darius said smoothly, and moisture rose in his older cousin's eyes. Smiling slightly, Darius commented, "Don't mourn for me, Kevin. Mourn for those who have brought me to this," he said simply and turned slowly, his gaze sliding down the table to land on the old woman who rested so prim and proper in her throne chair. His voice unchanged, he continued speaking as he started toward her, his gaze heating. "Mourn for those who used me in an evil plot toward their own gain."

The woman tore her gaze away from him and sent a disgusted glance toward the Baron. "Have you finished, now, Amad?"

"Lass, you'll notice, I've begun nothing to be finished with. My lad's feeling his oats a bit. Let's give him a moment and see where he leads."

She sighed, more disgusted, and slumped back in her chair, lifting her gaze as Darius again passed behind his dumbstruck cousin. Brian had caught on, but this shrew had yet to realize the integrity of her sight. "Such is the way with evil, eh, madame? You are so blinded by your vileness, so secure in this realm, wrapped within your cocoon of evil . . .? You have yet to see what stares you in the face, eh? And so I'll point it out to you, lass. The culmination of your grand design. Evil personified, eh?" he said with a smile. "This is what you sought, isn't it? Immortality. Ahh, to live a thousand years with your wealth and riches, your title. You've lived ninety-plus years within the shadow of a vampire." In a more musing, nearly whimsical tone, he commented, "It must have truly pissed you off to see those wrinkles sprouting and to watch your breasts sagging. Ah, and to know, eternal youth stood before you, just shy of your grasp. Had to look elsewhere, eh?" he said playfully and winked.

"This is all very fascinating," she said dryly and looked toward the Baron with a steely glance. "But I should think you'd have the courtesy to put an end to these theatrics. Regardless of your nature, you've maintained your social graces, Amad."

"A pity you're not appreciating this show, dear heart. From where I sit, it's rather intriguing and vastly entertaining. My lad has a talent for drama, and he's developed a rather latent fondness for the spotlight. Aye, he's making his pappa proud here, and I'd not be the one to stifle his wild thrill."

"Oh, very well," she said in condescension, and lifted her gaze to Darius. "Do continue, by all means, child."

Amused, he stepped closer, sidling, holding her gray eyes as he moved nearer her chair. "I've said it before, madame, and I'll say it again. You've the smell of something dead to you. Something decayed and left to rot. Fortunately," he said as he came within reach to slide his fingers over her crinkled chin. "I'm no longer of a nature to mind that scent. In fact, it's a flavor of its own," he said while standing above her and looking down into her emotionless eyes.

"When this began, madame, I believed the Baron stood behind my trials, and that's how you knew it would be for me, didn't you? I had a single purpose and no way to avoid calamity. You, sitting behind this mountain of stone, you secured access to it all, from my schedules through George to the Baron's manipulations via his words and my cousins. I was trapped. Confined to my own human nature and my limited knowledge, bound by my oath that even if I suspected the Baron, not a move could I make to retaliate. I was a dispensable pawn in this game, though I likened myself to a knight of sorts since I held one of the higher positions in the company. Even when he mentioned an enemy, I doubted one existed, assumed he was playing a game with no regard for the human lives lost. Fradden, I assumed, paid for the mistake with the wine. I remained oblivious. Too often moving even to hear the news of the lives lost in my wake, but the Baron knew, eh? Those deaths were for his benefit alone, and when I learned of them, I grasped the integrity of the enemy. Not that it offered any bloody way out for me. I was bloody doomed from the start, and you knew it."

"Darius," she began temperately, and sighed. "I feel for you, child. You and all of your cousins who were lost in this age-old wickedness, and yes, I have known. You were all doomed when he brought you here. There's nothing I can do about that, dear. I couldn't then—"

"How old is this plot, madame?" Darius asked smoothly. "Were you wicked in your youth? Did you, by some slight chance, work your wiles on your brother's wife long ago, convince her that she must destroy Raphael? Did you convince her he was a threat to her children's inheritance? That she needed to destroy him to secure her own future and thus sealed her fate? Was that your plot at the onset?"

She sighed and shook her head, turning her prim gray head toward the Baron. "What is this all about, Amad? Is there somewhere it's leading?"

"He's a child prodigy," Amad mused. "Do let's hear him out. I'd not want to crush his confidence when he's on a fine roll."

"Amad, I have no desire to play into this fantasy or condescend to your black humor. I'm too old to worry about offending you, and I believe I've earned the right to dine at this table without being drawn into another of your wicked games."

"Madame," Darius said in a low voice, and drew her lofty gaze up to him. "The Baron Amadeus von Hendricks is no part of the game we're playing here. By his nature, he'd not destroy the wickedness he created or destroy his own clan for revenge. Blood is the lifeline that's protected you these many years, that and his nature to enjoy your wiles. You are wicked. A bitter human tribute to his curse. And he knows it, madame. You are human, but you are his. Knowing his arrogance and his belief in his noble lines, you have been secure. And now, madame, you see before you, one who hasn't that same attachment to you or yours. Oh, I'm bound, there's no doubt. But on my honor, the need for revenge against my sworn enemies now comes first in my mind, and you are that, Madame Baroness. As the Baron Amadeus von Hendricks once swore vengeance against those who condemned him, so too, have I. Now, you see my fix, perhaps?" he asked lightly and smiled, shrugging. "I can't well destroy Amad von Hendricks, as I've sworn on my clan to protect him and all that is his. Fortunately, that means I'm also bound to mete justice against those who would act against him, and you, madame, are that."

She shook her head, again posing an air of disgust and turning her gaze toward Amad. "Has he finished with this charade now, I ask you?"

"Oh, dear heart, you truly are blinded by your darkness," Amad said in sighing tone, but his voice darkened considerably as he continued, "Thus, let me clear this up for you, dear. Although the lines of von Hendricks, the blood of kings, runs in your veins, yours is a distant attachment whereas, the lad who stands hovering over you, poised I might add, for attack, is bound to me by my very own blood running thick through his veins. My son, Rebecca," Amad mused in a low tone. "And it's rather ironic, dear. He's not at all pleased with the gift of eternal youth I've bestowed on him. Too blasted clever right from the start."

Her eyes still carried doubt, but a hint of curiosity lit her gray orbs as her gaze lifted to Darius, rejecting belief even now.

Darius studied her only an instant more, drawing her into his spell and without more than a passing thought, reached and brought her spindly arm from the armrest, drawing it up as another strangeness passed over him, through him. He held her with his eyes, hearing her silent cry of fright, then pain as he sank his incisors into her flesh. With the first rancid taste hitting his system, he pulled away and spat, but he could still hear her cries of doubt inside his mind, an echo to hold him poised and gazing down at her. Her eyes emitted nothing of the sounds he heard . . . not entirely unpleasant sounds. Far better than his own silent screams that had rung inside his head too long. Curious, he listened and understood her railing oaths, canting his head as if he needed to listen more closely. She doubted the reality even now, refusing to believe he'd bit her physically.

"Well," he said absently, and slid his attention down the table. Amad watched him with a subtle amusement; Raphael rested, only curious and impressed. "That went . . . well, I suppose."

Amad huffed a laugh and settled more fully in his chair. "Not certain, are you?"

Darius looked down at the motionless woman, wondering absently what he should do with her now. He understood the basics, he supposed. By whatever means, he held her captive inside his head, or at least, her voice.

Considering his personal experience, he wondered more about this strange power, to have an extension of himself, and decided, he would rather not hear this shrew echoing inside his skull through all eternity. He needed answers, though, and this seemed a reasonable time to seek enlightenment. On a whim, he asked aloud, "Did you design this plot against me?"

Instead of an answer, she wrapped herself tighter in denial, convinced he would never learn the truth, secure in her belief, he was nothing more than a dog chained to the Baron who would never harm her. *Not her—his daughter—his heiress.* In her mind, she remained the epitome of his creation. Only right and just that she would take the Baron's place and inherit the legacy. She was smarter, wiser than any of them! She should have been her father's favorite. She was so much smarter than Thaddeus!

Huh! Thaddeus had gotten what he deserved for being such a fool. If he'd kept his mouth shut, only the Brocks would have paid, and they were nothing! Mere servants to the von Hendricks! A disloyal band of cutthroats and thieves! Misfits and weaklings, the lot of them, and this mere boy was not the exception! The son of a derelict and a whore! A pauper! Amad had only chosen him for a prominent position in the company as a joke! Huh! And Amad expected her to believe he'd made this mere servant boy a vampire! A joke! Amad would never have given this peon eternal life!

He cherished his bloodlines too much for that. Eternal life was their legacy! Her legacy! Either she would stand at Amad's side, or she would stand alone after he fell under the army she'd helped to create! Her time was coming! He so loved his games! His tricks! Well, it will not be long now. The wedding. That joke of a wedding! She had only to wait and bide her time a little longer, keep her council. Amad would never touch her—not the Baroness von Hendricks! If anything, he would revel in the sport and know, alas, she was the woman he had sought—

"Lad," Amad intruded carefully. "I'm beginning to wonder which of you is in thrall. Are you having a problem or is she such an intrigue?"

Darius waved off the interruption, studying her lined expressionless face, her blank eyes. None of her thoughts appeared on her face, but he heard her still. Intruding as she fell into visions of her grand ascension into royal status, he asked, "What do you know about the wedding?"

As if she would tell him! She would tell him nothing! Amad considered her a harmless old fool, another of his loyal subjects, and she would not enlighten him just yet. She would accept his slander and chiding, his taunting through this peon. Huh! But he would learn differently soon enough! For him, it might be too late! The army—her army stood in place! And how she reveled in the beauty of her plan!

Hugh—dear Hugh! What a joy this great nephew was! Hugh had made all this possible! His greed, his quest for treasure! When this was finished! If he were the victor in this game, she would ascend him! She would change him personally! That was the reward he deserved for his loyalty! Not some stupid slut carrying a bastard child to a servant! An abomination! A sacrilege and slander to their name! That, she would not tolerate! Hugh would keep his council, play along! But that slut would never wear the von Hendricks name!

Let him have his fun at her expense! Let him work his stupid wiles! She would survive this servant's taunting and when it was through, she would have him in chains! Whether Amad survived or not, she would have this handsome boy in chains, her servant, her concubine! He would take the place of his cousin!

"How do you plan to ascend, madame?" he asked in a lower tone.

Huh! The fool! Such a polite little idiot, but then how could it be any other way? The words were not his. He was no more than a puppet in Amad's little charade! How would she ascend? Foolproof! No matter who won in this game, her rise was imminent! She had the child, and the little idiot would have no choice! She could manipulate him. She'd done so often enough. With Amad gone, he would need a mother. She knew how the boy pined for a mother! Oh, and she would give him a mother. She didn't need Amad or that other one! If Amad killed him, it would be no loss. Regardless of the outcome, he would not survive. He was just another loose end that she'd tidy up after this battle ended.

Reform! Renovation! She had plans for the future! Her family—the von Hendricks would rise and take their rightful place! Huh! Amad was obsessed by the past! So obsessed with revenge for the loss of his inheritance, he failed to see the total picture, the potential of his gift! She would not be stuck inside this castle! The world! She could rule the world!

"Who is this other one?" Darius asked and alarm glitched the rambling. "Whoo iss this other one?" he growled with his temper ascending.

Huh! They thought they had this figured out! Thought they could frighten her or trick her into an admission because she was old! Amad probably knew by now, probably guessed she was involved in this plot! But he would never know for sure, and he would never take her, not unless she gave him a reason as Thaddeus had. She knew him, knew how much he prided his family! She would never admit her involvement, never be drawn into his tricks or rise to the bait he sent through this peon—

"Well?" Amad intruded again. "And what was her answer, then?"

Annoyed, Darius shot his gaze down the table. "If you'd stop interrupting, I might find out."

"I might have eternity, lad, but I'd rather not spend the bulk of it sitting here watching you poised like a priest awaiting her confession. Just have her answer and let's move on with it."

"I'd like nothing better," Darius growled. "But she's not exactly cooperating."

Amad studied him, then smirked. "The chances of that are extremely slim, lad," he commented. "And I'll mention, you needn't stand there studying her as if she's a fine piece of art."

From experience, Darius knew the words were true. Amad had never needed to stand over him, not to manipulate or eavesdrop. This should be easier. Faster. She should have simply answered him. Unfortunately, it might take more time to work out this weird talent and learn the techniques. Biting her hadn't exactly provided the intended results.

CHAPTER 22

Turning, pacing away, he heard her still, and his gaze listed to her. She was aware of him, still. She found his frustration amusing, positive she stood up to the Baron's test of wills. Damn it! He was wasting time, time he might have in excess, providing he learned the details from this shrew! The wedding . . . a trap of some kind. Jenna—

That slut would be lost. If not already, she would be soon. The other wanted her and he would have her, though he might not want her as badly when Hugh finished with her. Or then, possibly, he would. His taste was simple. Another ill-bred fool! A servant! With the power to rule the world, he was still only a pauper! But what a joy to have found him! Hugh—such a grand child! She'd known Amad would choose him even before she learned the plan. Hugh, such a wily child, such vices! She knew when Amad took his namesake's place in the family line, Hugh would be spared. Hugh was destined for greatness. Becoming his favorite old aunt, his confidant despite the miles between them . . . her own foresight was another measure of her superiority. Her destiny—

"Ennnough," Darius growled and focused his gaze exclusively on her prim silver head. "You will tell me now. Who is this other and from where did he come?" As her thoughts started, he snapped, "Answer me aloud!"

"A stable boy," the quavering voice fell off the thin lips with a huffed breath. "His name was Joseph Chauncy . . . a stable boy," she wheezed with an echo of scathing sarcasm, but her thoughts reeled at the sound of her own voice, at the strangeness inside her mind. "A mere stable boy . . . but a vampire."

"Ah, shit," Amad muttered, sounding all too human and disgusted.

Pivoting his gaze to see Amad looking toward Raphael, Darius followed the gaze and saw the youngster's riveted wide eyes focused on the old woman. Joseph. For the second time in a few hours, someone spoke that name, and Darius sensed Amad anticipated that information.

The child appeared mortified suddenly, his eyes filling and turning toward the Baron. "Joseph, pappa?" he uttered. "He is still alive? Is it true?"

"Aye, suppose it is, lad," Amad said, and slid his gaze to Darius, not amused. "Poke at her a bit more, lad. The chap's not wearing the name Chauncy now."

"Seems to me, that's cutting corners, Amad," Darius said idly. "I think I'd like to hear a bit more about this chap. Who he was. How he came to be what he is, and what exactly he might hold against you. Those answers would do for a start."

"You don't need her for those, lad," the Baron said smoothly. "As she said, he was a stable boy. Not the brightest boy about, nor the most honest. My lad was still a mere boy when the two of them met. Nearly the same age, so they were," he said and tipped his gaze to Raphael, who had bowed his head more deeply, his curls trembling at the edge of the table. "Would you like to tell this tale, my lad?"

The head shook in a quick jerk. "Noo, pappa," he whispered gravely.

"Very well then," Amad sighed and looked toward Darius, his gaze indifferent. "As I probably mentioned before, I hadn't intended to taint my lad to the extent he is. More to the point, he was my first attempt to secure the family's untainted blood. Mistakes happen," he mused and glanced off the child. "Suppose I don't suffer any regrets. At the time of Joseph, though," he continued smoothly. "My lad was still a child. Young, impressionable, vulnerable to some extent. He was desperately alone in a strange land with barely a grasp for language and a raging desire for friendship. He turned to Joseph. Oh, and for a time, the lad played along, but I'll mention, the word is *played*. By all manner of deception, the boy offered friendship, warming to my lad but always a tad sneakily. The complexity of class structure, mind you, lad.

"Joseph was the son of a mere farmer on my land, but he harbored tiny visions of grandeur. He could have done worse than to accommodate the son of a Baron. Oh, he treated my lad with deference, at least for the sake of the others in my employ. Away from prying eyes, Joseph was my lad's best of friend, and I'll give the boy credit. He possessed an innate talent for such a task. I remember my little lad crying in great wracking sobs the day Joseph refused to come to the house for a meal. 'Wouldn't be proper,' Joseph had explained, and this to a little boy who still, at that time, was merely an indentured servant in my keep. How my lad suffered over that excuse, and he was still, as I said, predominantly human. He gave Algen a time of it. The poor man nearly stood beside himself trying to explain Raphael's new station in words the lad could understand. No getting through to my stubborn elf. He was convinced he would be tossed into the livery after I had my fun with him." Amused, Amad commented offhandedly, "The lil lad had a child's natural perception. As much as he idolized me, he knew better than to trust me entirely. Unfortunately, as time certainly mandated, the lad's love for me outweighed his fear and good sense . . .

"Ah, but we were discussing Joseph, weren't we?" he mused. "Well, in due time, my wee lad ceased to grow, while Joseph grew like a bad weed. In retrospect, I believe therein lay the crux of the events to unfold. Here on the one hand, we had a fully human boy, a servant, sprouting into adulthood as if on a fast train, and my wee lad, no longer human, stopped short. Add the enhanced senses of his inhuman child nature, which I'm sure you're beginning to grasp, Darius, and a recipe for disaster kindled into a fine stew. For a time, my wee lad developed a talent for presenting himself as a tall strapping teenager, lending new meaning to the term, 'in the eyes of the beholder.' He managed even to fool Joseph. And for my new lad, I relented, allowing the farce to continue. Even went so far as to keep the lad in a new wardrobe regularly, which helped a great deal toward his self-image. Upon a time, however, the wee lad faced his own illusion. We'd been traveling for a time. Nearly two years in that stretch, I believe," he said reflectively. "Aye, and when we returned, lo and behold, Joseph stood a solid six foot, had graduated to the livery position and passed his eighteenth birthday in our absence. My lad saw red. He'd had a taste of other teens, mind you, and he'd seen enough other boys of the ton taking mistresses. Thus, to him, it seemed like a natural progression. My lad was determined to catch up with his age. Believe I mentioned to you, Darius, his single attempt to become a man in the carnal sense?"

Darius recalled the mention and nodded, watching the shiny black curls sink a little lower, the small head nearly even with the table. How much more Darius understood that child's plight, his frustration and moods. To be trapped forever as a child, as vulnerable and ill-prepared for the world as any natural child.

"Aye," the Baron idled, perhaps sharing the thought. "But he made a grand attempt and out of pure spite for his old friend who'd outgrown him by leaps, the wee lad chose the boy's older sister for the taking. Needless to say, that event never fully came to pass, and in his frustration, my lad fled to the stable to visit his favorite and only friend at the time—the little black pony I'd given him for his final birthday. Joseph was there, still grooming the carriage horses behind which we'd just returned. In my lad's confusion and pain, aye, and he was in pain that eve—he lost rein on his own illusion. Joseph saw him for his natural size. Whether the wee lad acted in fright or frenzy, I've never decided—"

"I dinnae wa-ant him in y-your keep," Raphael uttered. "W-wanted him to l-live his life a-a free man, pappa. H-he was my friend."

"Aye, you believed so even then, elf. But you learned differently before too long," Amad said and sighed, turning his gaze to Darius, oblivious of the others at the table between them. "The wee lad tranced him without a bite. It's a talent you'll understand if not already, lad. Not a firm hold, but it suffices for a short time and lends a moment or two for a second thought. Upon this scene, I arrived. Raphael standing, Joseph kneeling in a shallow trance. Aye, and it was shallow. My wee lad was a fledgling still in every sense of the word. Already, the taller lad began to rise, and he knew he faced something of a strangeness to defy nature. To make thus short, Darius, I strengthened the trance and took the lad into my keep. My wee lad's misery knew no bounds. His friend, now fully under my reign, the boy's future in my hands. Joseph continued to see him as a child, though the lad had no free will to create any problems for us over that knowledge.

"Eventually, Raphael pulled a stunt rather similar to this evening's earlier transgressions. The elf meant well, as he did with you, Darius. A paradox, and a parallel, perhaps. For you, he meant to keep his promise and release you fully from the misery he felt inside of you. Taking your life, he meant to set you free, not to damn you with the curse of time which he's come to know too well. Back then, though, lad, he saw only a means to set his young friend free without taking his life. He did so. Thus, by the time I reached them, I barely had time to yank my wee lad from Joseph's jaws. Therein lies a lesson, my lad may never forget, and a consolation it's been. As you came awake hungry, Darius, Joseph came awake starved. He was well on his way to draining my lad and would have killed him.

"Thus, we had a grandson in our midst," Amad mused. "And not one of a nature to be kind or even grateful for the sacrifice my elf made for him. In fact, the man's nature that he concealed behind his amiable smiles became fully realized. The ill-begot never missed a chance to slice a ribbon across my elf's back or cheek and drink the spill. By a thin thread, I held him in check with a promise to take his life if he ever acted on his desire to drain my lad fully."

Recalling those seconds in the study as he'd held the boy, remembering the deadly shine in the Baron's eyes when he'd looked up, Darius had no doubts the Baron's promise had thwarted Joseph. "Obviously, the chap survived," Darius commented. "Where's he been and what grudge does he bear . . .? Assuming it's not merely eternal youth to outrage him," he added with a smirk.

"Ah, you're too clever, lad," Amad mused. "And I suppose there's no point in lying," he said with a glance to the old woman. "You'd reach your own accurate conclusions. The fact is, when the wee lad and I ventured back across the ocean, I knew I couldn't trust the ill-begot, and I probably should have recognized his signature months passed when you encountered his soldier. The problem was simple . . . Joseph had no restraint and no mind to fully grasp the complexities or delicacies of our circumstance. Unlike yourself, lad, he had little regard for discretion or moderation, no sound moral foundations or compassion. Frankly, I was forever cleaning up after him. He couldn't bed a lass without biting and generally left them half, if not fully, asunder." He paused and, perhaps, only Darius felt the heat of whatever held his cobalt gaze in a quick of thought.

"Alas," he began again smoothly. "I couldn't leave the beast to run amuck. I'd had my fill of the new frontier and pioneering and laid enough foundations should I decide to return. To be specific, I left the lad chained and sealed in a chamber on my property, and frankly, I assumed he'd be dust by now. For years, I heard his rages, but eventually those quieted and died. Thus, the story of Joseph, lad. Not pretty, but who in his life has no skeletons in the closet?"

With a humph, Darius bounced a glance off the shivering child and shook his head as he looked toward the still tranced woman. She hadn't fallen silent. In the back of his mind, he heard her scheming and plotting between fits of confusion when she thought her limbs weren't responding as she hoped. With her near sightless eyes still turned in his direction, she'd convinced herself that she stood her ground against the Baron's game. Slightly amused, Darius let his smile enhance and heard her scathing remark—

I'll wipe that handsome smile away soon enough. And in her mind, she believed herself returning his smile.

Ignoring the remark, he considered the facts thus far and understood. Hugh probably had been seeking treasure when he stumbled upon Joseph in the lost tunnels.

Without a word, his gaze still locked on her, Darius drew the details from her mind, somewhat startled by his success. As if drinking from a fountain, he merely listened, and the images flowed into him. As much as ten years ago, Amad replaced his namesake, his living heir, Hugh's older brother—a fellow who'd met his natural end in a skiing accident while visiting his family dwelling in the Carpathians. Rebecca hadn't much cared for her great nephew's arrogance; hence, she'd taken it upon herself to assist with the Baron's transition.

By then, Hugh lived on the vineyard, unaware of his living brother's demise, not that he would have cared one way or another. He'd broken ground for his own home and set his sights on his future. By his greed, he'd determined to capitalize on the family history, but there were places under the homestead that had been sealed for years. He suspected treasure. If not gold and silver, then tunnels of wine fermented a hundred years or more in the past.

Instead, the workers he sent into the caverns began to disappear, and unbeknownst to Hugh, a pair of workers found the crypt, along with an ancient cache of wine in the catacombs.

Strange times then. Young women vanishing from nearby towns and cities, some as far away as Buffalo, last seen near the winery. Hugh had begun to panic, fearing the authorities would suspect him, and naturally, confided in his dear sweet old auntie in another country. Clever as she was, Rebecca suspected another of the baron's ilk lurking . . . and through Hugh, she'd discovered Joseph and his growing band of minions.

Clever indeed. She'd gambled with Hugh's life, forcing him to confront one of the thralls working in his winery, and together they'd nurtured the monstrosity, a two hundred-year-old skeleton hanging in chains within the catacombs.

Slightly more surprised, not entirely sure what to make of his knowledge, Darius collected the facts more swiftly. Joseph Chauncy had no memories left to him. Time had deteriorated whatever memories had existed. Rebecca had known him, however. She'd identified him through her vast store of knowledge of family history. Joseph Chauncy, the stable boy at the vineyard who'd never arrived in Europe. Joseph Chauncy, a beast who she'd fed, through Hugh, only enough knowledge of the past to rekindle his hatred for Amad von Hendricks. And the poor bastard still lived in the tunnels, a prisoner, though Hugh kept him sated. They'd sacrificed Lisa Blythe, sending her into that tunnel . . . and letting her return with the plague to The Chateau Suites.

Darius found the Baron watching him still, while he recalled those moments in Jenna's kitchen, the Baron's bite, his control. Annoyed, far more annoyed than he cared to consider, he realized the Baron had known . . . had known this plot, the key players, had known about Joseph, as much as two months ago.

With his temper rising, Darius continued drawing from the old woman who sat as still as stone, her conscious thoughts waking to the reality of the intrusion inside her head. She'd seen it done . . . had never believed or fully understood the concept. Pacing, Darius concentrated on this Joseph . . . a beast. Apparently, the fellow hadn't awakened in any fair condition, but the Baroness had only Hugh's words about the ghastly appearance . . . 'A walking abomination,' Hugh had told her over the telephone. 'But it doesn't matter, he's cooperating. As long as we keep him fed . . .'

Stopped, Darius stood a moment, his attention divided between the old woman's plot, the Baron's deception and conspiring, and the more immediate, scattered thoughts of his human cousins. He was no longer one of them. Fully changed. But into what, he couldn't quite decide. He wouldn't have chosen this turn . . . but his thoughts were his own, his actions entirely under his own devices.

And he was hungry!

Uncontrollably, his gaze drifted and fell, distracted to see the little man quivering like a derelict rendition of a jolly fat man. Halbrook was scared, and his fear wafted like a sizzling steak, more enticing than the revenge Darius had sought earlier. The shaking stopped, the flushed face waxed into a dull-witted expression and the eyes glazed. His gaze turning yet again, Darius sensed the talent at work and landed his wary focus on the Baron. "How much of what I've just learned have you known for years?"

"Do you expect or need an answer?" Amad asked in a whimsical tone.

"Did you send Hugh to the tunnels?"

"Ah, lad, the credit you give me. I don't know whether to be flattered or dismayed by the implications."

"You're flattered," Darius stated crossly, passing Halbrook without a glance and advancing, returning to his place at the table without losing eye contact. "Where did it begin? I asked the old woman. Now I'm asking you," he stated simply. "Did you nurture the shrew from birth to enter into this game? Did you force Thaddeus into the plot—"

"Did I know Levine would break the Covenant and did I plan to have your clan destroyed?"

"Did you?" Darius asked, reaching for the wine, changing his mind. The taste did nothing for him. What he wanted rested at the far end of the table, presently held as deeply tranced as the old woman who'd begun struggling against his hold. On different planes, he collected the sensations and sounds around him, the thoughts and smells. And still, he held his attention and gaze on the Baron, who studied him in return with a bemused smirk.

"Think, lad," Amad said quietly, nothing in his eyes. "And use the talents I've willed to you. We . . . none of us have such a firm grasp on the future. Oh, we can plan, and we can plot, and we can dwell on what we know to be human nature. Without our personal investment, we can anticipate what courses our plots will take. Now, answer your own question and let's move along."

Levine Brock had destroyed their clan, broke the covenant. Fully human, the man had made a choice, just as Thaddeus von Hendricks had chosen to plot and the Baroness, seeking her visions of grandeur and her legacy . . . to drink from the fountain of youth. "And the shrew called me an idiot," he muttered and found the wine glass already in his hand. She had the fountain in her grip. Joseph could have given her what she sought from the Baron. But in her vile nature, she'd trapped herself. The blood of a stable boy hadn't been good enough for her. She wanted the Baron or the child to pass on their legacy. Royal blood. Shaking his head, Darius sipped the wine and soured with the first taste on his tongue. He was hungry . . . or thirsty . . . and he felt as if he stood in the center of a smorgasbord. None of which he could taste. His gaze ventured back toward the old woman. On dual planes, his thoughts sickened him, his memory of that bite and the incredible flavors—

"Darius," Amad intruded, his gaze animated to appear human. "I won't give the sniveling old fat man to you fully, but you need more than you've had. You've dined in my company often enough to know, I am generous with my guests."

His senses keening, he watched the hefty man struggle off his chair and waddle toward him. With a fierce determination, Darius returned his gaze to the Baron, a man with whom he had entered into a proposition . . . a business proposition. A partnership. "Call forth the banquet you generally lay before your human guests, Amad. When the feast is laid, I'll consider the offer."

Halbrook settled into the chair at Darius's side and stared at the table.

"As you wish," Amad stated and within seconds, the carts arrived through the arch, with four plump maids hustling to deliver the soups and salads, entrees. Deceptively formal and elegant, the banquet feasts had always struck Darius as odd, but never more so than now. He watched with faint amusement as his cousins received their meals, each one refusing to meet his eye or look at the Baron. They were human, fully, but they rested in the company of aliens, deeming to accept their circumstance with a bravery and courage few men could duplicate. They had no choice . . . other than madness, and the situation was madness enough. Made worse, as Darius looked at the plate in front of him. Oh, the eye appeal touched him. He'd loved food, most any kind of food. Undoubtedly, a result of his early years of depravation when meals were scarce and far between. As much as he wanted to inhale the cuisine in front of him, he knew neither the thick broth nor mutton would sate him. What he wanted, what he needed, stood beside him, and it sickened him more to realize his pulse quickening with the smell of the plump maid. He no longer retained the luxury even to consider himself civilized. Ordinary means would sate nor appease the forces rising inside of him, taking control of him. He was hungry—if not starved—and he needed every ounce of his willpower to hold himself steady as his cousins indulged directly across from him. Eyes downcast, faces grim . . . neither could look at him and he felt their determination to avoid eye-contact as if he were disgusting, or they were ashamed to meet his gaze.

Suddenly, Darius felt as if he were the lamb sent to be slaughtered? Perhaps, from the onset when Halbrook had taken Dylan from their flat in London.

With the thought, his temper ascended on par with his frustration—on an even keel with his starvation. A sacrifice! Had Kevin known? Had Halbrook? Who? Who among their clan had marked him to be the sacrificial lamb? To be the one among them to suffer eternal damnation?

His gaze heated. Darius suffered the shine rising in his eyes, the physical changes threatening to manifest as his gaze locked with the Baron. "Why me?" he asked in a low growl. "Is it truly as it feels? Was I the lamb to be slaughtered at the onset? Was that why they brought my son to you? Have I been the only fool these many years to believe . . .? To cling to the hope that I would survive if I upheld the oath? Was it a given from the start that I'd be damned as well as condemned?"

Rather than answer, Amad turned his dark gaze toward Kevin. "Shall I tell him, lad, or will you?"

For a long moment, Kevin's focus hovered on his spoon, but lifted slowly, tilting toward Halbrook before meeting Darius's gaze and appearing more disheartened by whatever he saw. "Only two in this room knew what I know now, Darius," he said drearily. "You, I, none of the twelve of us knew the extent of the curse upon our clan. I doubt I know all of it even now. What I know is that only after the Covenant was broken could the curse be lifted . . . but to lift the curse, one of us would be sacrificed. There were conditions, cousin, certain criteria to be met. I didn't know what those were, Darius, but I knew one of us within this room would be forfeit . . . and I feared nearly from the start that you or I would make the sacrifice—"

"Your cousin has the gift of gab, lad," Amad intruded with a sigh. "But alas, he has no talent for a fine tale. Do pardon me, Kevin, but I suppose the truth should be told off my lips. No offense, lad, but your emotional investment will only outrage your cousin now."

The truth of the words drew Darius's heated gaze to the Baron, who met his hostility with cool indifference.

"You were no more or less a sacrifice than the others when you received my invitation," Amad said directly. "In fact, you were less," he said with an ironic smirk. "There was . . . criteria, as your cousin eloquently mentioned, and truthfully, lad, on the surface, you didn't qualify. I had . . . shall we say, certain qualities in mind when choosing the twelve." His gaze listed toward Kevin. "I sought integrity," he commented then toward Teddy. "Purity." Toward Brian, "Virility." Returning to Darius, he continued, "In that room, we had a collection of human volition. From a man burning with love for his new wife. Another devoted to divine power and righteous to the end. We had innocence, as I'm sure you remember your cousin, Sam. We had morality . . . and even piety," he said with a scathing glance toward Halbrook. "And contrition . . .

"Frankly, lad, I had my twelve, twelve fine men worthy to stand before me. Each hailed from decent loving homes, none too rich or too poor. None, and I do mean *none* of questionable character or lineage. You weren't the second lad, or the third, or even the twelfth. You were the thirteenth man on my list, brought into this room merely because it amused me to have a thirteenth. My own dark nature, my curse, my lad. You were the black sheep. No real son to any Brock, raised a pauper by any standard. A man without sound morals. Integrity . . . ? Hah! You were a liar, a thief, a con man . . . and to be entirely honest, I wanted to meet the man who fathered a child for whom such little regard was paid . . .

"It's a sad fact, lad, but even the pious and righteous weigh their losses. I knew why your ancestors brought me such a disgusting little beast for their first sacrifice to lift the curse four hundred years ago. That child posed an abomination, mentally, physically. Ghastly," he said with a mimed shudder. "But here was a handsome little lad, delivered to my doorstep, determined by the scribes and scholars of your clan to be the least likely missed. He was innocent, that was true, and they decided—correctly, I'll mention—that I needed innocent blood for the sacrifice they meant to offer me. He was a Brock, that much I knew before I ever nipped him," he paused, apparently enjoying the spark of anger in Darius's gaze. "With all your other vices and avarice, I knew you'd take offense by the loss of your child merely on principle. Thieves don't like to lose what belongs to them. Fact of life. Anger, Darius . . . anger brought you here. A touch of blackmail," he mused. "For my black sheep. You didn't love the boy. Liked him, possibly, but you resented him from the start. If not for the entrapment into a marriage with a woman you didn't particularly love, then for the added expense and responsibility. I suppose I should have taken closer heed to that first sign," he said with a sigh.

"Against your every desire, you did the honorable thing and married the mother of your child. I—being who I am—looked at the string of affairs, your lack of commitment, your disregard for the vows you spoke freely.

Aye, you were my Ace. No man of your word, lad," Amad said with a wink. "A kindred spirit right from the start, that's what you were to me, and that should have been my second warning. You were a damn deceiving little bastard from the onset, and it grieves me to wonder if there is another on this earth more wily than myself."

He paused as if to reflect, then shook his head and sighed, "I did see you as a kindred spirit and it amused me immensely to rise such a study in avarice to the position of prince in the great Brock clan. Thus, the game fate played on both of us, sneaking you into my house under false pretenses, fooling even me by the cloak you wore around your heart. Had I looked closely, I might have recognized you, as well as my attraction." His gaze slipped to Raphael. A smile played on his lips when his attention returned. "Innocence in its purest form has always attracted me and beneath that angry mask, lad, you were as innocent as my wee lad, your every act governed by the simplest of all vices . . . you never knew what it was like to be loved. And therein should have been my third and final clue. An insatiable lust never governed your affairs for carnal pleasure, nor a retaliation against wedding vows and the woman you married. You, you damned fool, were looking for love, whether the love of a parent, a woman, a friend, a child. Love is blind," he mused and shook his head almost sadly, his blue eyes glittering.

"By the time I realized the deceit in your charade, it was too late. I'm a man of my word, one of my worst traits by my standards. Were I less, I'd have killed you outright. Instead, I allowed you to father your clan, hoping, I'll mention, that you would buckle to another vice. Ah, but not you, you rotten devil. As fate would have it, misery strengthened you. Instead of breaking, you rose fully to the challenges I laid before you and became the epitome of human volition, the compilation of every trait I found decent in your clan. Thus, lad, you sealed your fate.

"A lamb to be slaughtered? Humph. Nothing as simple as that, Darius, but let me explain what your cousin failed to convey," the Baron chided.

"He mentioned lifting the curse, lad, not merely repairing or halting the effects on your clan. He said *lifting* the curse, lad. And I am the curse that you've lifted from the backs of your clan. After four hundred years in service, the Brocks are now free to do as they damned well please, save for those I've already taken under my wing or bound to me through their spoken vows and blood."

"Now, you have lost me," Darius admitted, studying the bemused shine.

A sparkle of unnatural amusement lifted in the cobalt eyes. "About two hundred years ago, Darius, one of your ancestors attempted to lift the curse. He was a good man, an honorable man, as decent as any I'd ever met, as my wee lad mentioned to you. Unfortunately, by my own curse, my word and my vows, I couldn't change him fully and accept the sacrifice he offered freely. Oh, the criteria was met, by no uncertain terms. He was everything you are, and he loved a von Hendricks as much as I once loved a Brock," his gaze slid toward the bright-eyed child at his side, then returned to Darius. "I'm referring to Algen Brock, lad. For nearly twenty years, the man begged me to make of him what I would, that he would live eternally with the misery of loving a von Hendricks. He loved my wee lad enough that he would have forfeited his immortal soul to nurture the child for all time, and he knew the misery of that sentence. Unfortunately, I couldn't take Algen's blood. The covenant remained intact. Not even with his pleading could I have damned him into eternity, and that, lad, is the vengeance I swore upon my damnation.

"When I could damn another Brock, one as innocent, as noble and as in love as deeply with a von Hendricks as I had been with a Brock upon my death from humanity, only then would I have retribution and forgive the injustice against me. Only then would I set your clan free. That, Darius, is the criteria you have met."

"Jenna," he realized.

"Aye, Jenna, a direct descendant," Amad said idly. "And there again, fate played a hand in your damnation, lad. In my confounding arrogance, I chose a young woman free of my physical taint, one who might well reap the reward of your seed and pass something of your apparent nobility back into my lines. Looking at the misfits I'd reared and considering the vow I made on my eldest living heir, those alive now are damned. A lesson for you, lad, take care in what you say to your clan. Can be a hellish mess to straighten out when you fully intend to destroy your own bloodlines. Before I could fulfill my oath to my own . . .

"Well, let's just say, I played the odds, and lost, as it appears. You, unfortunately, stood up to the test. And a shame, you lost as well. Had you forced me to drag you across that carpet to receive my bite, you'd be peacefully oblivious and mortal still. You are not," he mused. "Damned eternal, so you are. Ah, and the final coupe, for which I'm fairly pleased. My living clan is now your mortal enemy. You, son, are the wrath I've wrought upon them. Hmm, and I've a great-great-great grand heir in the making. I do like this turn, lad. A pity you shan't know the peace you've given me. For you, damnation's just begun, but perhaps you can take heart in your accomplishment.

"With your damnation, you've released, revived and restored your clan. None again to suffer the threat I have been and the games I've played. They are free, lad. Save for the twelve, I've released all others from my keep, and I'll mention, that includes your cousin Adam, whose will I've held since taking our enemy's soldier. He will live his life naturally, and who's to say . . .? Perhaps in time, he'll father his own natural child. Now, indulge and sate your appetite, lad. We have a wedding to attend and I've a thought, you may need your strength . . ."

CHAPTER 23

At times Jenna felt as though she walked in quicksand or curled beneath a heavy blanket that offered neither warmth nor comfort . . . but the pall had lifted. Only yesterday, she'd awoken to the world around her, had found the bruise on her arm where a purple-black haze formed a perfect handprint. Standing before the oval Cheval mirror that had arrived days or weeks ago into her private room, she stared at her naked reflection between the ornately etched border. Awake, fully, she surveyed the visible signs of her physical ruin and through a gray curtain, she remembered every punch or pinch, or wicked grab to create those marks.

How the hell had he done it? How the hell had he manipulated her into his control to such extent?

Only one explanation existed and added anger to outrage.

Drugs. The heaviness in her mind, the dull ache and the lethargy in her body . . . both could only result from a constant dose of barbiturates. And she knew how easily he'd accomplished that. Too well, she remembered the maids delivering a morning tray and just as often, Hugh stood over her, commanding her to eat, sneering as she obeyed until she'd launched from the settee chair and fled into the bathroom to purge. Not only had he threatened her life—this evil bastard had threatened the life and health of her child . . . and for that, he would pay.

No other thought held dominion as she shifted her gaze to eye the white lace and silk reflected on the shiny glass over her shoulder. A wedding gown—her wedding gown—delivered by a half dozen maids only the day past. And she wore his ring, now. The immense diamond shot prisms into the dim atmosphere, refracting the dull lamplight as if bathed in neon. Tomorrow. Tomorrow, she would become Mrs. Hubert von Hendricks, heiress to a fortune, a princess.

Remembering the photography session through a fog, her blue eyes darkened several shades. The bastard had shown her the pictures in several magazines and tabloids, carefully posed pictures where she linked her arm through his and smiled on command. Posed. Sitting or standing inside the winery, inside the ancient parlor, in front of the Homestead . . .

Before or after she'd snuck from the house the second—or third time? She remembered Reichley and Miller had accompanied her reluctantly, agreeing to escort her to the homestead to visit with Emma and learn more of the family history. Midday should have been safe. Hugh had been away—attending business in the city he'd confided in one of his more arrogant tones if only to boast his importance. The bastard never missed an opportunity to flaunt his superiority, as if Jenna couldn't possibly grasp the complexities of business despite several college degrees.

Before, she remembered abruptly—before the photography session. Hugh had scheduled that photography session, enlisted an entire camera crew shortly after the evening of his alleged proposal. She'd been stoned out of her mind, she knew now, recalling only vague impressions of makeup artists and wardrobe artists rearranging her at Hugh's command.

She'd meant to use the homestead phone again. If she'd ditched her escorts, she might have slipped from the tour and used the house phone, intending to call her parents. Whatever the FBI had confided to them after her first attempt to escape had countered her distress call. No one had come to her rescue. That much she recalled if not much else about that evening and on the second attempt . . . They'd never reached the homestead.

Jenna remembered the dirty snow mounded on either side of the slushy lane . . . and Reichley weaving the winery's SUV through the tunnel of snowy tree limbs. Neither agent had trusted her, although she couldn't exactly recall what she'd done to worry them. They'd taken turns looking back at her, Miller over his shoulders; Reichley in the rearview mirror. Abruptly, the Land Rover had swerved, pitching her halfway across the seat as Reichley steered into the slide. For only an instant, Jenna had believed they'd struck a deer. In the next, she'd spotted the tawny fur sprawled half on the mound, half in the slush. Despite the agents' command to stay inside, she'd followed them out, stepping through the slush to judge for herself.

The animal was dead. Likely killed during the night, with the brown bloodstains trailing off the dirty mound from beneath its twisted, torn neck and scattered legs.

She'd seen enough deer slaughtered on the back roads surrounding Pittsburgh to know the animal hadn't collided with a vehicle on this narrow lane . . . and the spooked shine in the agents' eyes confirmed her belief.

Hugh had been furious that afternoon, and even in memory, her skin prickled. Not his first tirade. Hazy, she recalled dozens of evenings when his fury had shifted to a physical assault, but that evening was among the first and worst. Fear, genuine fear had blazed in his crazy eyes as he'd berated the agents for taking a chance with her safety. They'd found him in the solarium, apparently planning a quiet dinner—just the two of them—among the long draping leaves and immense summer blooms. The solarium had been warm enough for a summer dress—a new dress delivered that very afternoon. That once, the agents had taken the brunt of Hugh's hostility and even in her fog, Jenna wondered why they hadn't arrested him on the spot. When was it legal to strike a federal agent? Or call them idiots?

Only after releasing his wrath on Reichley, Hugh had settled down enough to mention wolves and rogue bear sometimes migrating down from Canada . . .

His warnings were enough. Jenna hadn't considered walking the lane again, not to visit the homestead or Emma . . . and Hugh's fists were the least of her concerns.

Again, her focus shifted to the wedding dress as she turned from the mirror. Meandering, she reached the side of the bed, settling near the nightstand. Mechanically, she began donning the flimsy blue lace thong and brassiere.

Thoughts adrift, she remembered the interviews, an endless stream of interviews that Hugh had offered throughout those photography sessions. Apparently, the threat of Lisa Blythe had passed. Any half intelligent reporter could have tracked down Hugh von Hendricks and his lousy winery. Hazy, she recalled him boasting about their whirlwind romance, about how they'd fallen in love at first sight . . . And when he'd shown her those tabloid-worthy articles, he'd laughed bitterly at how easily he'd dupe the public. In every interview, he'd portrayed her as a pauper's daughter and portrayed himself as the magnanimous lover, so smitten with her that he accepted her humble beginnings . . . and in private, he'd sneered. 'As long as we both know what you are, that's all that counts. And we do know that, don't we, my dearest little hussy . . .?'

You may not know who I am, dearest Hugh, but I do. She spoke only in her mind, letting the dull smile linger on her lips as she looked at this latest study in debauchery . . . a mere swath of cloth capping her nipples and slicing her bronze fur in half. Rather than the swatch of dark blue cloth draped on the drab brown quilt, she leaned over and scooped the sheer beige robe from the end of the bed.

Whether she felt more or less naked with the thong and lace glowing on full display under the sheer cloth, Jenna couldn't decide. She'd worked out the location of the cameras inside her rooms . . . and like all other encounters, she remembered the fuzzy moments when she'd confronted Hugh. She'd accused him of voyeurism and called him several choice names from . . . pervert to sleaze. And clearly, she recalled the wicked, glee shining in his crazy eyes when he'd frozen, waking to her enhanced sensitivity while squeezing her breast . . . 'How else will I keep these safe if I don't—' He halted his words, merely squeezing harder and drawing a gasp off her lips as he verified his effect.

Like a fish in a bowl, she lived in these four rooms, now, aware of the cameras strategically placed to watch her every move. And in odd moments, aware of Hugh watching the film, she caught herself taunting him through the lenses. Performing naked aerobics and calisthenics had incensed him at the onset and likely accounted for many of the bruises decorating her arms and legs. The bastard liked it rough, and even dosed, she'd gained a warped sense of accomplishment when igniting his passion toward fury. Better a bruise or welt, than a kiss or intimate embrace.

As if a clock counted down in her head, Jenna shifted her gaze to the digital clock on her nightstand. All the amenities of home from a bedside lamp and clock radio to a notepad with a von Hendricks letterhead strategically placed for easy access if she should decide to jot a letter to friends or family. She hadn't bothered, not since that first week around Christmas when she'd given Agent Miller several letters to forward via his home office. She'd still believed then that her safety, hence her family's safety, depended on her secrecy. She knew better now, although even with her senses clearing, she couldn't fathom a reason for her captivity.

Despite what Hugh had boasted for the reporters, neither love nor even fondness had developed between them. Behind closed doors, he preferred dressing her as a whore and treated her no better . . . but by the grace of God, he hadn't attempted to act on his twisted passions. Halfheartedly, in her fully woke state, she wondered if he might be impotent, might lack even the ability to rise his pecker to the occasion when his blood fired . . . and she might have mentioned that possibility.

For the cameras, she held her dull pose, but behind her dull gaze and lax smile, lurked the mind of a madwoman, too clearly recalling the pain of his bruising grip as he seethed down at her.

'We'll just save that little surprise for our wedding day,' he'd promised, and with that memory, Jenna nearly smiled.

The surprise would be on him.

Not only did she intend to take his name, she intended to take his life. Granted, she might end up in prison or the electric chair, but her child would reap the reward. Her child would be safe from ever meeting this monster, would never know anything more than the illusion Hugh had painted for the press. If she worked this right, her child would never know his mother was a murderess and if something went wrong, at least she could write her memoirs in prison to explain, if only to her offspring, what had driven her to madness.

Madness. It was madness.

But the moments were ticking down. At the fringes of her mind, she heard the countdown, sensing an end—Hugh's end, if she had it her way.

Killing Hugh von Hendricks might be a fitting justice and a benefit to the human race . . . but could she truly take a man's life? Forfeit her life . . . or saddle her child with that wretch's name, his legacy . . .

When she still loved the father of her child?

Maybe she should just walk up the aisle, turn around and address the crowd to announce the wedding was off.

Accusing Hugh of drugging her would be futile. She had no proof, and a house full of witnesses would stand against her. She'd end up in a padded cell where he might still hold the financial means to marry her and take her child—not unlike his grandmother consigned to an insane asylum.

Presently, her mind clearing, she wondered if that posed as salvation or curse, and either way, the thought annoyed her on a deeper plane. Was he so sure of his intimidation, his methods of persuasion, that he assumed she wouldn't dare rise against him? Or was this awareness a mere reprieve? Did he intend to drug her for the ceremony to keep her from causing any chaos? She could imagine him weaning her off the drugs merely to torment her; after all, she remained a prisoner in this room until the final moments now according to one maid who'd sounded sickeningly awed. Hugh had mentioned her family's arrival over breakfast. Allegedly, he'd welcomed them late last evening and opened the guesthouse for them . . . of course, mocking them to suggest they couldn't possibly acclimate comfortably to his overwhelming wealth. But something in his admission, in his presentation, niggled at her mind. A lie. She sensed the lie, and she suffered an internal shiver with a thought of that lie. She'd spoken with her mother, had mentioned her engagement . . . and dare not think about how hurt they might be with the slant of those news releases. A Cinderella story. A Fairytale, the tabloids had boasted . . . but suggested a late spring wedding.

'A private ceremony,' one article had quoted Hugh. 'A few close friends and family . . .'

Killing him was the only answer, she decided. Her family hadn't arrived: Hugh would never stoop to welcoming paupers into his home—not even his guesthouse, which didn't likely exist. The only attendees, if any, would be von Hendricks relatives, and in fleeting distant memory, she recalled meeting a California branch of the von Hendricks family. Arrogant, entitled, and condescending—and drug addicts, the lot of them. A mere prelude to Hubert von Hendricks and she suffered no illusions of their attendance at this farce. For proper etiquette, others might be dragged from New York, but Jenna couldn't recall hearing of any others on the east coast.

No outsiders would attend this affair. No one would stand in witness. At a base level, she knew she was on her own. If he planned an official ceremony at all, he wanted her wide awake for it and likely anticipated a scene. Probably looked forward to a scene. Any excuse would be better than none for what he planned for their wedding night.

Well, she had plans of her own and as her gaze listed toward the window, she just wished the day would pass faster. The sooner she became Mrs. Hugh von Hendricks, the sooner she could end this menace.

Someone had told her once, or possibly she'd learned it from the world's best teacher—the television—that any household item could become a weapon.

Listlessly she glanced at the nightstand as if judging the time, but in her mind's eye, she saw it there. A fine, #2 lead pencil sharpened to a wicked point. What would it feel like to drive a stake through this fellow's heart? Providing he had a heart. If he dripped green slime and turned into some evil alien from outer space, she wouldn't be surprised. A little alarmed, but not surprised. Thinking of him as something otherworldly and entirely evil helped. Taking his life was a favor to the human race, not merely a personal act of madness. Doubtful she would receive a medal for this act of heroism, but she could take comfort in her knowledge, and she would need all the comfort she could get with the life she was about to lay before her.

If only . . . if only things could have been different, she considered absently, her thoughts turning toward the image that remained so lifelike and real in her mind. Where other images from the past few months faded, this one had become only more clear . . . his dark eyes haunted, a sad smile curving his dark mustache, he'd stood as still as a granite sculpt, braced against the wind atop Mt Washington, scanning the city of Pittsburgh. He'd appeared so far away, already drifting away from her as if whisked on the chilly wind.

Where . . . where was he? Was he listening to the press releases, reading the magazines, hating her for the lies Hugh had woven? Was that why he hadn't called or come to her aid? Had Hugh controlled even that circumstance, feeding Darius even more lies than he'd fed the press? Listlessly, Jenna recalled Hugh spinning lies and twisting half-truths to paint Darius in the worst possible light. She could imagine it, the bastard embellishing on every fact. Weaving truths into lies. Nothing could she consider too low for Hugh von Hendricks. He'd known from the onset how deeply she loved Darius and he'd attempted every wicked wile imaginable to poison her love. If nothing else, she knew Darius or the brother Amad had phoned

Hugh to verify her safety, after all, unless Hugh had lied about that too, the brother and Darius had arranged for her stay in this madness. She should hate them—one or the other, either one, both of them—but somehow she believed at least the first words Hugh had spoken. They'd acted with her safety in mind. The threat of a killer had hovered over her . . . hovered still, she fully believed. Belying all of Hugh's deceit, that basic premise had enabled him to manipulate even the FBI toward his own devices. Why her, though? Why had this maniac—Hugh von Hendricks—fixated on her? And in her question, her thoughts turned full circle.

Darius. Somehow Darius was involved in Hugh's deception . . . and not for the first time, she heard the deep voice telling her the FBI suspected the killer was inside the von Hendricks Corporation. 'Trust no one . . .'

Lisa Blythe . . . Lisa might have been involved . . . but she wasn't the monster behind those killings. The monster who sought Darius's death, his destruction . . .

Her thoughts halted suddenly; her attention riveted on the window as the words slid through her still sluggish mind. 'My nemesis has power and influence,' Darius had said on that drive from Canton, referring to the probability of the FBI agents or the chauffeur working for the psycho.

Was it possible? Was . . . yes. It was possible. Hugh von Hendricks held the power, the influence.

On the receiving end of that power, Jenna knew the extent of Hugh's power, his resources, but did Darius know? Did he suspect even before sending her here?

In a gripped moment, a paradox, Jenna hoped that he did and prayed that he didn't. If Darius suspected, if he came here to confront Hugh . . . if he came . . .

A trap.

A private ceremony. The promise of friends and family. Her family hadn't arrived and at this moment, Jenna knew they hadn't been invited. No one had been invited.

And the trap wasn't just for Darius, Jenna knew in a moment of crystal clarity. Hugh wanted it all. Not just the winery. Hugh wanted the entire von Hendricks fortune from the title his older brother wore, to the hotel chains, to the distribution centers. Hugh had laid a trap for his brother . . . a trap which might have been laid as much as two years ago. This wedding . . . it was nothing more than bait to bring Amadeus von Hendricks into Hugh's domain, nothing more than an illusion to mask his brother's assassination. A cult . . . if a cult even existed, it would be blamed. Jenna could imagine it all pre-planned, the killers waiting in the wings, Hugh laying the groundwork to profess a crack in his security . . . and as her thoughts continued to turn over the details, she shivered internally. Hugh might marry her, but she suddenly doubted that very much. In fact, she was nearly certain that she might already be slated as the first victim. Hugh von Hendricks had no intention of marrying 'an ill-bred slut' who carried another man's child. She was beneath his station, or so he professed to her in private entreaty.

A slaughter . . . it was coming, and the prickles lifting at the nape of her neck only confirmed her belief. Like a lamb trussed and slated for an unholy altar, she rested in this room, and she likely headed the list of sacrificial lambs.

How soon would it start? How long before Hugh decided she was no longer any use to him? How far would he carry the wedding farce? Would she even gain an opportunity to use her weapon?

The answer erupted in a blinding epiphany. He wouldn't kill her before fulfilling at least one of his vile promises. Too many evenings, he'd spent restraining himself and psyching her for that main event to deny himself that final act of wicked dominance. His arrogance, his inflated ego, his wickedness would demand her ultimate submission. Before or after speaking vows remained the only question, and either way, she would get only one chance at him. If she failed . . .? If she failed, her life and the life of her child would be forfeit.

How much time, she wondered again and suddenly, she wasn't eager for the evening. A wicked chill sailed over the flimsy cloth, penetrating her nerve endings with an overwhelming sense of dread. The rehearsal dinner scheduled for this evening was yet another farce. Tonight, Hugh would spring his big surprise. Tonight, he would enter this room and attempt to fulfill his promise.

'You will beg for me, my darling,' he'd sneered only a few days earlier. 'You'll beg for me to take my fill before I'm through . . .'

And suddenly, the pencil seemed about as effective as a toothpick against that monster.

CHAPTER 24

S leep never came, not fully. Lying within the pitch-black compartment inside the Baron's immense black aircraft, Darius awoke fully into his curse on that long, troubling flight across the Atlantic. His body never moved, not to twitch or turn, not to rise or fall in bouts of snoring. As if the light bearing down on the sleek thick walls pinned him to the plush mattress, his body had fallen into a quietus which left his mind to wander. Beside him, curled up like a cat, Raphael rested in a similar dead sleep, and for a time, Darius sensed the child's restless thoughts, his fear of flying and the sunlight outside, an echo of his own discomfort.

By what method or technique the child drifted into a near natural sleep, Darius couldn't begin to guess, not then, not now. The Baron had admitted the child defied the unnatural laws that governed them, and Darius sensed the truth in those words. For all intents and purposes, the lad simply drifted off to sleep, resigned like any normal youngster to the demands on his little body. With his own thoughts in constant motion, Darius found the lad's ability a distraction and a nuisance. If he could, he would shake the lad into awareness for the sake of it then cursed the mere thought. Better the little devil sleep. In those first moments aboard the craft, even with the darkness to protect them, the lad had suffered a wild hysteria that hadn't ended until the Baron's annoyance level outweighed his amusement. In his father's arms, the lad had settled down to a quiet sobbing—and that hadn't ebbed until the lad had felt the sunrise. Darius had felt it as well, and even with his body fully under the power of the sun, he remained keenly aware and mildly anxious with the effects. Paralyzed. Or simply dead.

Either way, the reality had sunk fully into his consciousness. He was no longer a living, breathing member of society. He could no more rise with the sun than he could walk on the moon. In total conflict, his mind rejected the stasis of sleep. Instead, he listened to his cousins chatting quietly and dozing in the main part of the craft . . . and found a strangeness to visit their thoughts as they began to doze. He'd never met Kevin's wife, but he knew her the moment she awoke in the man's mind, a lovely woman who welcomed him with a smile and offered him comfort where no other things could. The Baron had never touched her, Darius knew, if only by the images inside his mind. For a time, Darius merely watched as the scenes scrolled inside the man's head . . . and in slow stages, he awoke to the chap's restlessness. On some level, Kevin sensed him there, an alien presence, an invader. If only in curiosity, Darius found his younger cousins' sleeping minds, and realized the same effect on them, though in Teddy, he found a welcoming embrace, as if the lad meant to comfort him even in sleep. Brian was far less hospitable. Uttering and grumbling, he repositioned and stirred, trying to wake and banish the usurper who only enhanced his already nightmarish images.

Splayed on the wide bed which could pass for a normal wealthy man's accommodation, the Baron rested . . . and Darius sensed the fellow was as awake as himself. Nothing of thoughts or images appeared, but in the stillness of his own mind, Darius identified the subtle probing, an almost curious nudge. By what method, Darius erected the wall around his thoughts, he couldn't fathom, but he sensed the slight surprise and appreciation in the other as the mental tentacles withdrew. The Baron wasn't asleep. Never slept.

And Darius wondered what plots might be conceived inside that dark active mind in these daylight hours, but in an odd moment, he found only indifference in himself. Presently, he'd welcome even a fraction of the Baron's control, his talent, his experience. That Jenna's life depended on the grandmaster of this wicked game, Darius harbored no doubts and the revelation offered no quiet comfort or relief. The Baron wasn't a man, not governed by laws of morality or decency. Arrogance and anger defined Amad's participation in this endeavor. He wanted an heir, a living, untainted heir . . . and only that desire weighed against the Baron's natural desire to take pride in Hugh's scheme. If the fellow had intended to marry Jenna, by whatever means or manipulations, the Baron would be riding the other side of this battle, and Darius doubted he would fare well on his own. He was not fool enough to believe himself a match for this elder beast, not with four hundred years of experience to strengthen the old man's talents.

Man? Old man?

The growl slipping off his lips woke Darius to his rise more effectively than the child stirring at his hip. Why the Baron had dragged the child aboard wasn't a great mystery. Rebecca wasn't a threat, but not even the Baron knew where his nemesis' power began and ended. As Amad had pointed out, this monstrosity could be more devious than its human counterparts could fathom. The Baroness and Hugh might believe the monster daft, but they had no idea what tricks the beast might have played with them. Revenge, the Baron had commented after dinner, revenge was the simplest of all motives for one beast, human or otherwise, to destroy another. Joseph Chauncy had motive. And what a grand coup to use the Baron's heirs in a plot to destroy him. Bringing Raphael along for safekeeping had offered the only solution. Amad hadn't said it aloud, but Darius had reached the same conclusion. Raphael's blood would be the ultimate prize in this game.

As if shot from a cannon, the child scrambled from his curled posture and sighed as if yawning from a long restful nap. Far slower, Darius stretched his frozen muscles, waking more to the ebbing pressure on his physical being. The sun was setting in the west . . . they were landing in the east. Barely, that thought surfaced when Darius reacted instantly to catch the child lunging into his arms. The small arms wrapped in a strangle-hold and shudders quaked through the slight body. The lad truly hated to fly . . . and before Darius could find the humor in his thought, he knew the reason belying the child's fright. The lad had flown once . . . without the aid of wings. And for two years, the child had lived within the wreck of his immortal limbs in the wake of his landing. For two years, Alanon Brock had tortured and tormented the lad as the Baron's curse had spiraled from the Carpathian Mountains to circle the globe. Finding heart, Darius spoke in a low tone. "We'll come aground soon enough, lad."

"I wannt doown now!" the muffled voice heaved.

"A pity," the Baron sighed. "We've at least two hours remaining. Do take the lad to the foredeck, will you? Show him the moon rise. It's coming up full."

Obviously, the Baron wasn't ready to rise. A dull lamp, no brighter than a candle watt ignited above the bed. Amad had moved only to stretch and drop an arm under his head in a more natural pose. Even in the dull light, his eyes glittered with an unnatural glow, but Darius needed little more than his enhanced night vision to see the smirk, to read the expression and grasp the intentions behind that mask. Nodding absently, Darius started toward the door, wondering which of the four privately employed flight attendants the Baron would summon.

"Send Teddy in, will you, Darius? I do believe I have a kink in my neck and the lad's a fantastic masseuse."

Whether he should be grateful or dismayed, Darius couldn't decide, but as he stepped through the door into the main cabin, he caught his cousin's pale blue eyes and read the subtle disappointment. Well, it had to happen sooner or later. "Your master beckons, Teddy," Darius said simply, and several pair of eyes pivoted toward him as Teddy's eyes brightened in quick delight. The lad was no fool. A half second later, his entire expression paled with fright. Darius smiled slightly and tipped his head to signal the boy into motion. "Wouldn't keep him waiting if I were you, lad."

Cheeks flushing, eyes darting, the boy climbed afoot clumsily and dropped his gaze away as if ashamed. As Darius sidestepped to let his cousin pass, the blue eyes lifted with a more desperate fear, a natural fright and reluctance.

"Best foot forward, lad," Darius said smoothly and added, "Keep a stiff upper lip."

"I-I . . . I."

Feeling the boy's confusion, Darius suffered a conflict of annoyance and dark amusement. "The choice was never yours, lad. Now, do get a move on it before he decides to torment you for another ten years, and I deem to let him."

Dismissing Teddy from his thought as the boy hurried past, Darius ran his gaze over his two other fully human cousins. Why they were both along, Darius hadn't quite decided. The Baron had plans, only the basics of which he'd outlined when ordering all three untainted Brocks to pack. True to form, Brian sent a scathing glance toward the closing door, then lifted a purely hateful gaze toward Darius. Kevin appeared only grim, and slightly worried as he tried to read Darius's dead calm gaze. Squatted in a chair apart from both others, still belted into the seat, Halbrook stared at his folded hands, but his face had paled the instant Darius had spoken. They were all afraid of him, he realized as he settled into the chair across from Kevin. The moon had not arisen. Even with the blinds drawn and locked into place over the few portal windows, Darius sensed the after light of day. Keeping the child against him, he looked over into Kevin's more concerned eyes, caught the flash toward the closed compartment. "You do realize, you can't help him, Kevin. Realize now, nor could I."

Brian grumbled, "You helped him all right. Helped him from the pan into the fire."

"Lad, you're tempting fate," Darius commented offhandedly and heard an echo of the Baron's words in his own voice. Brian apparently recognized the term; he dropped his gaze swiftly and clamped his tongue. Watching him, Darius felt his dark thoughts turning to realize, this lad could be a problem . . . a very serious problem considering the Baroness's influence. If he betrayed his oath, his word, he could bring the Baron's wrath upon the whole blasted Brock clan—*again.*

Without another thought, or even a first, Darius rose, and the change swelled over him, blasted through him, too fast to grasp. In a heartbeat, the primal force ascended, taking control. By reflex, in a single motion, he clasped the hand the boy lifted to thwart him and clamped his teeth on the palm. As Brian yelped, Darius locked his gaze on the wide brown eyes, tasting the mildly bittersweet elixir on his tongue. *Now, you're mine,* he said silently and heard the cry inside his mind.

To Raphael's uttered gasp at his collar, Darius snapped awake and withdrew his bite, rising and looking down into the tranced eyes. Uttering a breath, a curse, he turned his gaze to find Raphael studying him with a quiet accusation. "You don't understand, lad—"

"Oh, there's a few things I understand, my friend," Raphael said in a quiet tone. He nodded sagely and skimmed his glance toward Brian, then back. "You'll do what you need to do, Darius. Tis no way around that, now. You're more like pappa than you care to know."

"Lad, with his nature he would have destroyed the detente my clan's won with your father—"

"He's your father, too, Darius," the boy said quietly. "And there's more the reason you took Brian," he added carefully. "Was the . . . the way he looked at you, the way he felt about you to light your fire."

"I do believe I resent that implication, lad," Darius said, but his attention lingered on the internal cries and confusion.

"Aye, you will," Raphael said drearily, his blue eyes haunted. "You are like pappa, Darius . . . and me," he said sadly. "We weren't—noone of us—bad people upoon a time. I . . . I think aboot that sometimes. I woonder what I did to be caught up inside this wee body for so loong, always to be at odds with what I think is right and wrong. I-I wanted to do good by taking your life, Darius. Aye, I murdered you because I wanted to keep my promise and give you peace." His eyes moistened in remorse. "Instead, I've doone you worse harm . . . and it doesn't help to know that pappa let me, any more than it will make you feel better to know pappa brought Brian along for you."

"I doubt—"

"He knows us, Darius," Raphael interrupted gently, his eyes full. "He told me once I was like a fine wine to be savored. Aye, and you're no different. Even changed, you are full of human flavors. No matter the tricks your new nature played to justify the end in your mind, you took your cousin for spite and in arrogance, and you'll feel bad when you look at him."

"He would have betrayed us, lad," Darius said without a thought to the plural pronoun. On a separate plane, he listened to his cousin's confusion and fear. Brian had lived too long in the Baron's realm not to know what had been done to him . . . and the lad's thoughts spiraled around the physical pain. The boy feared physical pain . . . more than the loss of his human rights.

Looking deeper, sifting through the boy's thoughts, Darius found the source of that fear hinged on the Baroness. At seventeen, Brian had moved into the castle permanently, slated as manservant to the Baroness and the shrew had tormented him no differently than a vampire, taunting him and honing her techniques in reflection of the Baron. Brian's weakness was pain, and she'd hurt him, promising he could be hurt, would be hurt much worse when the Baron took him. To be fed upon daily . . . the boy had lived in terror of what Darius had endured over these past two months. No thoughts of betrayal in the boy's head or heart. Only fear of pain and confusion to know his cousin had taken from him . . . hurt him.

When Darius released his mental hold, Brian's eyes flooded, his face ducked, his hands sprang together as if on hinges and he drew a gasped breath as he cradled his injured hand. Shudders ran through him, quaking him and Darius suffered the burning pain lingering in the boy's wrist and palm, his arm.

Uttering another curse, waking more fully to the regret that Raphael had prognosticated, Darius noted his cousin's cringe and cower, heard the silent cry of fright. For all this cousin's bold and bullying remarks, he was little more than a frightened child at his core. He wouldn't have betrayed the Baron and risked the elder's wrath. Well, and it was too late to reverse the process . . . Darius leaned and caught the chin on his fingertips, lifting the pale, frightened face until he met the wide brown eyes. "Don't annoy me further, Brian, and those will be the only marks you ever suffer from me."

"Ah . . . ah, yes . . . yes, sir," Brian stammered.

Looking into the pale brown depths, Darius drank in the memories of what the Baroness had done to the boy, the horrors he'd survived . . . and before he quite understood his talent, he shifted and sorted, sending the memories back into the boy's mind in a different order. Not everything could be adjusted or molded, manipulated into dream form. But the worst of the wretched woman's acts were sent into the deeper realms and the boy's brow troubled with a tad more confusion. He knew something had been done, something had changed, and he understood nothing of what had just transpired. Well, and that made two of them, Darius might have mentioned as he looked at the less angry, more worried handsome face.

Withdrawing his hand, he noted the boy still looking up at him and realized in a lame moment, in his way, Brian had idolized him behind those sneers and angry glances. Admiration had become adoration.

Human nature was a fickle thing, Darius decided and turned from his cousin, colliding with Kevin's more dreading gaze. Without a need for mentalism, Darius read the expression, knowing the man believed he would be next, and last of the twelve to fall. "You're safe from me, cousin," Darius said offhandedly and returned to the chair across from Kevin. "You are his, and I think he'd probably kill me for touching you."

Kevin nodded, a simple agreement, understanding, but nothing of relief registered in his face or eyes. His time would come, he was sure of it. "What's it like for you now, Darius? I've watched you . . . I know you're not happy with what you just did. Was it truly beyond your control or was there a moment when you wanted to stop? An instant of hesitation?"

"Even if I thought I could answer you, doubtful I'd try," Darius said and held his cousin's gaze. "I will tell you, although you're safe, your proximity is a misery. You're too human and I'm too not, to be this close and confined in such a small space for so long." His gaze darted to the closed door; his perceptions blocked. Whether the Baron would follow through or merely removed the lad to keep him safe a while longer remained a mystery. Returning to Kevin with a faint smile, he commented, "Consider a time when you were most hungry, Kevin, and you'll have tipped the iceberg where I am now. That's my reward for being worthy of damnation. Eternal starvation and an uncontrollable desire to be sated. Does that help?"

"If I could change this for you—"

"Don't dwell on it, cousin," Darius warned in a quiet tempo, his gaze steady. "The only change would be mortal death, and I'm almost sad to admit, it would be yours before mine. For me, that option's gone. I would— and probably will—kill to survive. For my sake, if you still hate me just a tad, don't put your death on my immortal soul. I'd want to grieve, and I doubt I could. I'd have to fake it of course, for my own peace of mind, and I'd be double damned. Spare me that. I'd prefer to suffer the sound of your ticking heart and the smell of what I've lost."

"I still see a man when I look at you," Kevin said kindly. "And I still hear the man I've come to know." *And love*, he added only silently. "I couldn't take your life now any more than I could have months or years ago. We are cousins but I've thought of you more as the little brother I never had. That hasn't changed, Darius. Regardless of who or what you've become, that won't change. I'm here for you, as always, however benign that promise has always been between us."

"If . . . if my damnation is short lived, Kevin," Darius said with a thought of where they were destined and the probability of his own end. "If you survive me—"

"You're a survivor," Kevin said with a slight smile.

"I'm a . . . fledgling even in my own mind," Darius countered, not smiling. "And I don't have the luxury of illusions. If you survive me, honor the oath you've taken and see that our clan reaps the rewards of my passing. You've never met them or walked among them as I have, but they do exist. They're not just names or numbers in Halbrook's books. They're carpenters and artists, politicians and reverends—though it behooves me to wonder why," he said with a disgusted note. "I've met so many," he said absently, his gaze drifting and his hand shifting unconsciously to scuff the head resting on his shoulder. With a humph, he looked back to Kevin, "A paradox, cousin. I've loved them and hated them, envied and admired them, from the least to the most among them. What I would have given to be one of them, I've given now for them. Does that make me cursed or blessed? Or merely bitter? I can't decide," he said honestly.

"I would have destroyed them," he added, his gaze clearing and focusing on Kevin directly. "If given the chance, I would have destroyed the covenant and let the curse run its course. Only my word held that pact firm but the weight of what I was forced to do to them was wearing on me. Amad knew it. Out of compassion, I'd have betrayed him, and you. I couldn't keep doing what he asked of me much longer, not without feeling as if I were betraying each and every one of our clan by my actions. To propagate a race as fodder for a vampire . . .

"I truly couldn't continue. I'd have rather been dead, and that, too, Amad grasped. He had only two choices and I wasn't even aware of the corner I'd backed him into. Kill me which would have been too quick an end for the anger I incited in him. Or do what he did and let the chips fall where they may. The curse is broken. You're bound, as is your son Allen. The twelve remain his by their own vows." He glanced to Brian and smiled faintly, shaking his head and returning his gaze to Kevin. "Even Brian remains bound to him. By my own new vices, I've made the lad the very thing I bit him to prevent. Should I ever give him an order to break his word, it would be the third and final betrayal of a Brock against a von Hendricks. We'd have a bloody war the likes of which would make our present circumstance a mere fracas.

"I've wondered a time or two, Kevin, why us? Why our family? I've reached a conclusion and not one to offer comfort. The beast which fed upon Amad, the monster in that forest of four centuries past . . . how did our family know it existed? Who was that lad who accepted the young Amad von Hendricks like a bloody sacrifice? Uh, and the conclusion I've reached, truly lends no comfort. Our family, our clan, Kevin, consorted with the devil himself on that mount. Greed, lust for power, those were our ancestor's vices, and they bowed to the master of all darkness. Our own clan summoned the curse that's held us bound, and only by taking that curse into one of us, could we truly make amends for the evil our clan called forth. I have it fully inside me now. If I don't last long with it, don't mourn for me, but be glad and consider it a blessing."

"I don't think I could, Darius," Kevin commented sadly but already Darius's thoughts had taken flight.

How long could he truly live with this plague inside of him? How long could he perpetuate the evil? Jenna, his child . . . how long would he leave them untainted? How long would the Baron abide by his apparent decision to keep his clan free of the taint? Darius need only glance at Brian to realize the danger he posed to their clan. Was this lad an omen? A glimmer into the future? The chill inside of him was no longer a physical thing. His internal shudder remained an illusion to be shoved away, and he did so without a conscious thought.

To the passing of daylight into dusk, Darius reacted smoothly, shifting his hand and hitting the controls to raise the blinds to view the platinum sky spread before him. Too early for stars, too late for even a glimmer of sunlight melting colors on the horizon. As gray as his thoughts, the world offered nothing of promise beyond the thick tinted pane.

Was he rushing to save his pure love . . . or to slay an enemy in pure hatred? That he could no longer even decide, troubled him slightly more and by no surprise, he found the cobalt blue eyes watching him beneath a fan of thick black lashes. Even this weird connection remained a mystery in his mind. As a man, he'd come to love this little monster . . . in place of his own son, the child he'd never really known.

Oh, he'd shared a flat with the mother of his children, had come home every evening or in the early hours of the morning at the least. A dim little three-room flat with filthy windows to dull the view of an alley floor. For the first time in years, Darius allowed himself the memories, recalling the desperate conditions . . . and thought of the last time he'd seen his former wife. Thrilled . . . the woman had been only thrilled with the alimony settlement that set her and her infant daughter up for life. They lived well, the two of them . . . and fleetingly, he recalled his daughter's name—Shelly. Nicknamed after her mother. Shellene.

He hadn't seen that child in eight years, barely recalled she wore dishwater blond hair like her mother. If ever fodder existed for scandal, that child was it. She was no more a Brock than he was a von Hendricks, and if only with himself, he could admit his disinterest in the little beast at the onset. As he recalled, the Baron had done him a favor by nipping Shellene and eventually forcing her to wed the bartender who'd fathered the child. The bitch had signed over his son before ever receiving the taint and barely shed a single loose tear when leaving the barrister's office . . . . and Darius hated her as much now as he had then.

Too readily . . . too readily and clearly for the first time in eight years, he recalled suffering an unnatural urgency to return to that wretched flat at a reasonable hour. Most nights, he'd preferred visiting his own favorite pub and staying well into the evening. Not that evening. The strangeness to haunt him throughout his life, an unnatural sixth sense that had steered him clear of calamity and kept him out of the slammer, had driven him early from his latest lover's arms. A sense of something amiss, something dark and foreboding just over his horizon. Oh, and that sense hadn't failed him. He'd found his wife of nearly five years sitting at their chipped, wooden kitchen table, feeding the toddler in its highchair. By sense alone, he'd gone to the lad's bedroom, a small room he shared with his toddler sister. His animal-print quilt lay in shambles, a sure sign of another nightmare. And the nightmare had only begun.

'If you're looking for Dylan, you won't find him,' Shellene had called after him. 'A friend of your pap's stopped by this morning . . . He left a letter for you . . .' Short, simple and direct, that first letter from Halbrook, unsigned, introducing a nameless entity and suggesting if Darius ever wanted to see his son alive again, he shouldn't involve the authorities. '. . . A friend of your father. All will be explained soon . . .'

Even in reflection, Darius experienced the rage. Tenfold, his hostility rose in his present state, shooting red darks through his eyes, reflected on the portal glass. He'd come close to killing the mother of his son, if not in those first moments raging at her stupidity to allow a stranger to take his son. Then later, as that first day had dragged into two weeks of pure hell before the letter and train fare had arrived . . . and that had merely been a prelude of things to come.

Damned . . . he truly was damned, and no amusement came with the parallel's forming in his mind. Women and children. His curse. Had the mother of his first child cared enough to keep that lad safe, Dylan would never have been taken. Halbrook would have crumbled in the face of a tigress protecting her young. The man had merely waved his wealth and sophistication in Shellene's face, and the woman had believed an inheritance forthcoming.

Oh, and she'd struck gold on that score.

Parallels, Darius considered, as his gaze pierced the night sky, dismissing the first faint stars on the horizon.

Jenna Windrow . . . she carried his child, now. Did she love him or hate him for that detail? How much of the Baron's influence held her trapped in Hugh's domain? Perhaps the lure of Hugh's wealth and social status had attracted her, no differently than Shellene. Perhaps the Baron's influence had held her, but how to be certain? The pictures scrolling through his mind—from her kissing Hugh to her battling against him—appeared as real and tangible as his vivid memories of his time with her. Could the Baron have manipulated her—and him in those first few days? With his new perspective, he grasped the possibility, but what he'd felt for her—what he felt for her now, was real. More real with the effect of his present condition.

A vampire. He'd become the abomination he'd most feared from the onset.

Would she love him, still? Had she loved him at all?

And what of this child she carried? Would she offer it up as easily as Shellene had forfeited Dylan? Was it merely a meal ticket in her eyes even now?

His love might have been powerful enough to break the curse upon his clan . . . but if she betrayed him as a Brock lass had betrayed the Baron long ago, Darius would vow a vengeance as powerful as any Amad von Hendricks had invoked upon the Brocks of old.

And he wouldn't wait four hundred years to mete justice.

CHAPTER 25

Seated in front of the vanity mirror in her dressing room, Jenna concentrated on appearing as dull witted as the maid flitting around behind her. In hazy memories, she recalled this same, dull-eyed maid providing this service daily . . . after one of the first battles with Hugh over a new dress. With single-minded purpose, the stout young woman twirled and lifted, pinned Jenna's bronze mane into a classic Victorian style that Jenna might have appreciated at another time, in another place. The woman could probably make a fortune in any pricy salon with her eye for fashion, but glimpsing her face in the mirror, Jenna shivered internally. Glazed, the brown eyes never lifted from the task; her mouth remained curved as if poured in a manakin's mold. If Jenna had ever heard the woman's name, the memory was lost and no words passed between them now. Silently, the maid whipped up a fashion that offered a glimmer of hope.

Surely, Hugh wouldn't demand this elaborate style to compliment the dark blue evening gown unless he intended to follow through with some portion of this evening's events. There was always a chance, a slim chance, that she'd buckled to her rising paranoia as her mental fog had lifted. Maintaining her own dull-eyed interest, she glimpsed the shimmery material reflected at the edge of the mirror. The gown had arrived earlier, delivered by another pasty-faced maid who'd sounded oddly snide when announcing, 'Mr. von Hendricks sent this for you to wear this evening.'

Undoubtedly, the dress would dip low or rise high . . . unless he truly expected company.

Even in reflection, in dreamscape glimpses, Jenna knew Hugh's clothes fetish remained confined to their intimate dinners, either in his dining room, the solarium, or in her sitting room.

"There, now," the maid said in a wistful tone that suggested she floated on cloud nine as surely as her murky eyes indicated. Smiling, animated, she touched Jenna's shoulder while looking into the mirror as if to judge her accomplishment. "I'll help you with your dress, now, miss."

Biting her tongue from the string of curses on her lips, Jenna pushed from the stool, agreeing with a nod and her fixed, animated smile. Pretenses. Cameras. She wouldn't tip her hand anytime soon, and this damning daily service was another haunting memory. If not this hairstylist-cum-personal maid, then the other plump elder woman who lacked even the ambition to smile, had invaded her privacy and assisted dressing her more than once, which provided another good reason to unleash her wrath on Hubert von Hendricks. Timing, she coaxed silently as she slipped off the skimpy housecoat. Inhibition bedamned. She should probably be grateful this monster had allowed her to bathe herself.

Bungling through her efforts, Jenna assisted only slightly with the ordeal to manipulate the long dress over her coifed hair. A private dinner. The low dipped bustline barely covered her plump breasts and the blue cloth offered another illusion. The material draped from thin shoulder straps, slanting over her pregnancy swollen breasts, snugging to offer winks of black lace—the size of a stripper's pasty over her nipples—and clinging to her ribs and hips. Barely, the shimmery cloth dropped a respectable length to cover the sheer-top pantyhose, and if she moved wrong, that pencil thin thong would likely glow neon. The sleeves, by extension, clung to her arms from the wrists to her elbows where the material billowed and draped, connected to the shoulder straps by dainty jeweled buttons. Oh, he was dressing her for a private party all right, and the surprise would be on him, she decided as she glimpsed her own reflection. Almost amused, she noted the cat-like black outline of her own eyes, enhanced by the strips of eyeliner which the maid had applied, undoubtedly at the master's request. If memory served at all, she'd worn more makeup, in greater quantities in the past several months than she'd worn combined over the past several years.

A high classed hooker stood in the Cheval mirror staring back at her.

Concealing her ascending rage behind a plastic smile, Jenna stepped into the high heels the maid held for her and considered the alternative weapon in those spikes as she turned and allowed the maid to preen a few moments. A hooker. Even to her own eyes, she looked like a high-priced hooker, and she suffered no illusions to believe the very slight—highly visible—bulge at her abdomen was an accident. He hadn't missed an opportunity to flaunt her growing condition and taunt her, tsking on occasion, as if expecting her to feel self-conscious or ashamed, neither of which was even remotely possible. Even drugged, she knew she'd never buckled under his belittling tactics. Regardless of the circumstances, she'd conceived this child in love, and nothing Hugh could ever say would make her change her attitude toward this infant.

Hugh had to go. If for no other reason than to protect her child, she'd follow through with her plan.

"Now, you wait right here," the maid said as if Jenna had a choice, smiling her dim-witted smile as she patted Jenna's arm. "The mister will be along soon."

She would be ready, she might have answered, but merely nodded and returned the dumb smile as if she could hardly wait. The instant the maid passed into the hall, Jenna moved to the bed and made an elaborate show of fidgeting with the diamond tennis bracelet Hugh had given her. A dual motive, she considered as she deliberately broke the clasp and feigned a ghastly, terrified expression—as if fearing Hugh's reaction to the damaged jewels. A dual purpose, breaking that hasp. She wasn't wearing von Hendricks's diamonds. The absence—which he would notice—would likely tip the crazy man's scales. Anxiously, she fumbled with the nightstand drawer, and for the cameras, she made an elaborate production of shoving the bracelet toward the back of the drawer. Simultaneously, she collected the lead pencil and slid it up the conveniently tight sleeve. She couldn't have designed this dress more beautifully if she'd tried . . . and hazily, she recalled honing her acting skills, playing on Hugh's over-inflated ego. Even in her dullest moments, she'd laid the foundation of a plan, allowing the bastard to believe that his conditioning had rendered her compliant. At whim and whimsy, she'd portrayed the submissive, terrified if he even raised his voice, while at other times, becoming the vamp, to stroke his ego and feign a willingness to please.

Whatever remained of his willpower and restraint had drawn thin. She could push him over the edge, one way or another.

And she was armed.

Sitting back primly, folding her hands in her lap, she wondered how long she would wait . . . and she sensed the wait was over.

As if he carried an oily scent, she knew he stood outside the door before the key touched the lock.

The time had come to strip this maniac's gears. Without a first, or second thought, she slid one long leg over the other, crossing her knee and opening the high slit to her hip. She'd never needed to practice to boast an uncommon grace. Tilting her head slightly, coquettishly, she shifted her dull glaze toward the door as the shined dark panel opened and without a clear thought, she adopted a pose she'd seen in one of his filthy magazines, one he'd thrust in her face to compare her to the naked model in the centerfold. Despite his effort to appear disgusted by the 'smut' and the 'whore' spreading her legs for all the world, Jenna had recognized his fevered shine.

The same high shine ignited in his eyes as he sidled into the room, panning his gaze over her to feel like hot slime prickling her flesh.

She wanted the game over. Wanted this ordeal ended one way or another, and posing as a centerfold had already reaped a measure of success.

Slowing his step, letting the door close behind him, he darted manic glances over her and not for the first time, Jenna considered the probability of cocaine in Hugh's regard. Too bright, those dark blue eyes. Too manic.

Donning a feigned puzzled expression, Jenna watched him hesitate, likely savoring her confusion, and the touch of intimidation in her eyes. With an ample view of her breasts, his focus slid and held on her heaving mounds. No sense even attempting to control her racing heartbeat or sipped breaths; by the tight smile twitching his thin mustache, he judged her reaction as either fear or anticipation, and either way, he accurately predicted himself the cause.

The epitome of male charisma—or so he believed—he adopted a pose of nonchalance, tucking his hands in his hip pockets to hold back his jacket. As always, he wore a crisp black suit, looking as if he'd just stepped out of a Chinese laundry, and his black hair shined with a wet look that enhanced the new-wave style. Unfortunately, rather than portraying him as a hip, sophisticate, the shaved sides and style only portrayed him as a mid-aged man striving to remain a teenager. He was, Jenna decided, gross, from his glass-shined shoes to his grease-shined roof.

"My, my, don't you just look lovely, dearest," he said in a silky, low voice, his speeding eyes stabilizing. The smile slithered deeper into his thin mustache, kinking a corner of his lips and lighting a more feral shine. Even in the dim lamplight, his eyes appeared more black than blue. Dilated. Without a doubt, he'd bolstered his courage and primed himself for whatever his plan for this evening. Cocaine. Or Amphetamines. "All dolled up just for me."

She tilted her head deeper, lighting a more befuddled expression. "Of course," she said in a quavering voice. Her heart hammered a quicker beat, sounding like a tin drum clapping in her ears. Control. If she harbored any hope of surviving whatever this monster planned, she needed every ounce of control . . . and suddenly, she truly just wanted this game ended. If she needed to reverse these tables, force his hand, so be it. Not again would she sit down to a meal with this snake. Not a bite of a meal or sip of wine would she risk in his presence now. He meant to kill her. The brighter shine in his eyes as he skimmed an oily glance over her thigh only enhanced her belief. No dinner rehearsal, no wedding. He'd dressed her as a fantasy, and his slow attempted suave approach was a prelude. The idiot looked like a bad actor attempting to play a Cary Grant role for which he was sorely ill-equipped. She smiled more, rising a flicker of inner thoughts. He hated it when she smiled just so, undoubtedly, sensing her disdain and silent mockery.

He tried to enhance his smile, appearing slightly more apprehensive as he crossed the center of the room. "Now, what are you thinking, I wonder," he said as if teasing, adopting one of his pouting, lip-thrusting expressions.

"Oh, about you, Hubert," she said softly, honestly, as her eyes sparked with the dark, musing hint of her internal thoughts. The slime! Jenna watched his brow darken, knew at this moment he neither trusted her smile nor appreciated her honesty.

"Do you remember what today is, dearest? What we have planned?" he asked, trying hard to maintain his teasing pout while advancing the last steps to look down at her. His hands remained tucked in his hip pockets, maintaining his air of nonchalance.

"I . . ." she started, and the sound lingered. As if struggling with a thought, she tilted her head more, consciously offering him an eyeful of her cleavage. "Oh . . . yes. A rehearsal dinner. My family . . . They're waiting?" she said, feigning to sound hopeful even as her mouth dried. He was dangerous. Regardless of how she attempted to bolster her courage by silently slicing his ego to ribbons, she remembered too many of those moments with his hands clamping her arms or slamming her about. Even now, the bruises throbbed under the sheer cloth. Physically, she was no match for him, not in arm wrestling.

Breaking one hand free of a pocket, he offered an open palm, smiling serenely. "Our rehearsal dinner," he said sweetly. "We wouldn't want to keep everyone waiting too long," he said and clasped her fingers in a painful clamp.

She rose in front of him, stifling the curse she might have emitted in place of a gasp, wincing only slightly and donning a hurt shine as she looked up at him. He liked that. The bastard smiled more, enjoying the injured flash and confusion in her eyes. "Hugh, y-you're hurting me," she said softly, feigning the slight intimidation which came too readily to her mind. How would he play this now? "We h-have guests."

"They wouldn't expect us to come down too soon, dearest," he said, and his eyes sparked with that tiny light that appeared too often in prelude to his rages. His lips puckered, and he canted his head, still clamping her fingers on the brink of pain. "They think we're lovers already, after all, dearest," he said in a lower octave, a near whispery voice with his lips closing in. A black shine affected his wider pupils as he added, "And once they see you, they'll know why we're not wasting any time."

"Hugh," she huffed and backed off a breath, turning her head slightly and looking up at him with a tight rein on her rising anger. Hurt. He wanted her hurt. And she wasn't drugged, not drifting in that other world. All the reasons why she should hate him flowed toward the surface of her eyes, darkening the shade several degrees and apparently startling him enough to fade the pucker from his lips. "We're not lovers," she said in a quiet, far more calm tone that startled him a little more. "We're never going to be lovers, Hubert," she said and felt the tighter grip on her fingers as his eyes sparked. "Oh, you could force your way, I'm sure, dearest," she spoke with a lowering cadence. "But you'll never be Darius. Not in my mind. Not in my heart. He and I were lovers, Hubert. You couldn't compare to him—"

"You slut," he hissed softly, still looking into her eyes although his darted in the sockets like a pinball at full speed.

"Your slut, Hugh," she said with a slightly mocking tone, unleashing the rein on her temper. "That's right. Your slut, Hugh. I was his lover, but all I'll ever be is a slut in your arms because you're slime."

In a half second, his arm moved. Game over. Without a single clear thought, Jenna sprung her knee upward with the force and skill of a trained demolition expert, landing the blow as his hand locked on her arm. His eyes widened. He lurched with his gasped breath. Too late, she realized the full measure of his insanity unleashed. As if the kick fueled rather than destroyed, he rammed her backward, slammed her onto the mattress and growled his pain while scrambling over her. She kicked again, hitting his thigh and knee, hurting her own as he slammed his weight, pouncing like a beast from the fires of hell. His eyes flared blue-black, wide and more insane than ever before. His hands locked on her elbow joints, bruising on impact, but her hands remained free. One clawed and grabbed at his jacket, intent on raking his chest; the other struggled to free the pencil wedged against her arm. Words issued off his curled lips, assuring her in chiding tones, he'd have his due, promising her a good time even as his gape-mouth descended. Struggling and writhing, Jenna barely glimpsed his thin lips, understood his intentions. Not again would she suffer her lips mashed under his vile kisses! Snarling and heaving, she lunged, teeth snapping, and might have scraped his pouting lip. He dodged, lurching his head away and through her fury, she read his outrage and revelation. Neither drugged nor caught off-guard, no longer deceived by his lofty charade or pretenses toward sophistication . . . no holds barred.

He laughed, a weird, delighted laugh even as his weight shifted and he flashed a more vivid shine, a blazing madness of wicked delight.

Jenna suffered the knee landing on her wedged arm and glimpsed his palm lifting, lining up a shot on her cheek. In the next instant, the pencil eraser jabbed her forearm, driven down with his weight driving the lead point into his knee. With his yelp, his palm shifted, and she dodged. The clumsy strike barely grazed her ear. Whether more startled than hurt, he lurched, and suddenly, all motion became. Him, flying off her, his hands releasing, his eyes bulging with unnatural surprise

As if he were a rag doll of ghastly construct, he rose, and Jenna gained a shallow sense of someone else inside the room before Hugh twisted in midair. His gasped breath silenced under the wicked crack of a human fist slamming his gaping jaw. Heaving, scrambling, she cleared the edge of the bed before Hugh flailed and sailed, slamming the floor beyond the varnished footboard, shuddering the floor with his resounding thud.

Rescued! Someone! A male . . . Evan! Evan Trevane! His blond hair caught the light, his bearded face swung toward her and his hands reached, catching her before she hit the floor. Without a conscious thought, she clasped his hands, rising and reeling as he drew her under his arm, holding her in a quick, firm embrace. No time to waste! "We have to get out of here!" Jenna heaved and tugged to break free.

"Jenna! What's happened! What's this about!"

Across the room, Hugh lay in a crumble of black limbs, unconscious. But for how long?

Flashing a glance at the splayed tycoon, Jenna spun her gaze to find Evan's intense, pale eyes. "We ha-ave to get out of here!"

"I know," he said smoothly, likewise glancing at Hugh, wearing a puzzled frown on his brow, on his lips. His gaze lowered, haunted with as much confusion as concern, "I knew something was wrong here. Are you alright? Did he hurt you?"

"Fine!" she huffed, tugging free, her mind catching up to her rapid breath and racing heart. "Cameras!" she huffed and looked up into Evan again. "They'll know! They'll come here, Evan! We have to get out! It's like a prison! Guards! Security!" *The window!* "A car! We need a car! He's crazy, Evan!" she huffed.

"Slow down, Jen," he huffed, clasping her arm.

"You don't understand!" she snapped, recovering enough to recognize the doubt in his tense eyes. "He's the killer, Evan! The psycho! It's all been a trick! He's kept me drugged! A prisoner! We have to get out of here! These people are all crazy! We have to do something! I think it's a trap! I think Hugh's luring his brother here to kill him! We have to get out of here and warn him! We have to stop this! Are there really people downstairs?"

"Only the staff," he said, and appeared to catch on, at least enough to grasp her fear.

"Trust me, Evan! We have to get out of here!" she demanded and fleeted a thought to the door. Hugh hadn't locked it. Even at this moment, the security guards might be flying up the steps. She needed to think! Plan! She needed to know what Hugh had truly planned for this evening!! She needed to find a phone and reach the head of the von Hendricks company! The brother! Only Hugh's brother could stop this madness! Somehow, she would need to convince him of his brother's madness! Warn him! Riveting her gaze on Evan, she snapped, "Now! Evan! We have to find a phone!"

"All right," he huffed and shot his gaze down, up. "I have a rental car. We'll take the back steps. You'll need a coat."

"They'll have the exits blocked," she huffed as she started them both toward the closet. "It's crazy, Evan," she stated, waking to her hobbling, one shoe missing. Kicking off the other shoe, she yanked at the closet doors, grateful to find a pair of her own flats, sliding into them while tugging her coat from the corner of the closet. "I don't even know how to explain this," she heaved, welcoming his hands to help her with the coat, catching his troubled expression, confused eyes. Never had she been more grateful for a familiar face. "I'll explain. I will. Just as soon as we're out of here."

"I knew something wasn't right here, Jen. That's why I came early," he said with an attempt to smile his reassurance. "I had to see you. I had to talk to you, find out what this was all about," he stopped and cocked his head, glancing toward the door as if he heard someone coming. "We better get moving," he said more firmly and clasped her arm, starting them both to the door, looking down at her with a tense shine. "If you're right about the cameras, I don't know how much time we'll have. There's a stairway at the end of the hall. I saw a maid come through earlier. We'll go out that way, but once we step into the hall, they'll know something's wrong. We may need to run for it."

The cameras were in her room, she might have said, if not for a sudden thought. No one had come barging into this room yet. Sending a scathing glance toward the splayed, motionless body across the room, she knew why abruptly. The bastard had probably ordered the cameras turned off, or at least turned off the visual monitors so he could do his bidding. She should kill him! The thin stream of blood trailing off the corner of his lips into the oriental carpet offered shallow satisfaction.

If she killed him now, it would be cold-blooded murder.

Shaking the thought from her mind, she looked up at Evan, deciding, "Ready when you are."

To the sound of the compartment door opening, Darius fleeted a glance and thought, needed only a breath to know his flush-cheeked cousin hadn't changed even slightly. Behind him, the Baron emerged, clasping the lad's elbow and escorting him out with a push. In a glance, Darius read the annoyance as well as the tinge of anger in the dark blue eyes. No more capable of reading Amad's thoughts now than any time passed, Darius suffered his rising annoyance, miming the indifference and smirk. On his lap, Raphael had scooted to rest on his knees to look out the window, but with the intrusion, he turned his head, too.

With an angry tug on Teddy's arm, Amad shoved the worried boy to stand alongside Darius's chair and flashed a heated glance down into the startled eyes. "Down," he snapped.

Teddy wasted no time, ducking his head and lowering smoothly to his knees, fleeting a more frightened shine toward Darius.

Looking down at Darius with a peculiar spark of dark amusement, Amad commented, "Maybe you'd like to nip this cousin as well, eh, lad? You've not known this taste. Bent on feeding only on corruption. Mayhap, you need a taste of purity to warm your chilly blood."

Refusing either to rise to the taunt or the bait, Darius glanced off the bowed blond head and up to the Baron, letting his amusement surface. "The taste of true love doesn't appeal to you, then?"

"Ahh, my lad," Amad said and leaned, clasping Teddy's head and canting it to stretch the boy's neck for the taking. With his thumb, he traced a path over the carotid artery.

Despite his effort, Darius watched the vein becoming more visible against the milky white flesh, heard Teddy's gulping breath and sensed the fear belying the shivering posture. The fragrances enhanced tenfold, a scent of flowers and fresh breezes, an awakening to the natural world in all its allure. His blood heating, Darius lifted his darker shine toward the Baron, reining his unnatural impulses with an effort of will he hadn't exercised since holding Jenna for the first time . . . and the mere thought nearly boiled his blood. "If there's a point to this, possibly you'll get to it sometime soon?"

"You're right, of course," Amad said and tilted Teddy's head into a more natural bow, scuffing the waves and rising to his full height. A flicker of a smile twitching his black mustache, he commented, "If the lad's scent disturbs you, take it from him. For myself, I enjoy waking to the fragrances. Somewhat like having a fresh bouquet gracing my breakfast tray." With a humph, he flashed a downward glance to Raphael and offered his hands. "Come to pappa," he mused, and Raphael scrambled willingly, launching off Darius's thigh to land on the Baron's hip.

Looking at his still bowed, shivering cousin, two thoughts spiraled. He was no more eager to engage this lad and spoil him than Amad. And taking his blood wouldn't repay the kindness the young chap had offered more than once. Damn ungrateful means to reward him, in fact. "Go buckle into your seat, Ted," Darius idled in a low voice. "Maybe we'll find another means to corrupt you."

"Ahh," Amad said in feigned appreciation. "There's a reassurance that's bound to offer the lad hours of comfort."

"Maybe a subscription to a few magazines," Darius said dryly and glimpsed the wary, soft blue eyes as his cousin hustled off his knees and sidled hurriedly past the Baron.

Dramatically, the Baron dipped his head to draw a breath off the passing head, his eyes more amused as he likewise leaned and sniffed at the child in his arms. "My two favorite flavors. Corrupt innocence. Pure innocence," he mused and sidestepped to drop into the flight chair nearest Darius. Settling the youngster on his lap, he scuffed the tumble of black curls. "Possibly we should buy you a magazine subscription, eh, elf?"

"I already have lots of them," Raphael said. "I like the science ones."

Amad sighed and turned a disgusted gaze toward Darius. "Were I you, lad, I wouldn't bother attempting to corrupt your cousin. If my lil lad's any indication, you'll have the poor boy scoring through women's fashion magazines as avidly as you have my elf pouring through all manner of science digests. Corruption may not be your forte."

Halfheartedly recalling his stint as the child's governor, and his very real attempt to enlighten the child about the natural realm, Darius flashed a bemused shine and shrugged, "If the little lad begins ordering substances you've never heard mentioned before, I'd take interest, were I you. In fact, I'd be inclined toward worry if he began taking too great an interest in kitchen supplies. Corruption comes in many forms, not the least of what recent history dictates to be scientific inventions."

"Oh, and now, you've a thought to teach me something I don't already know?" the Baron huffed a laugh. "Lad, I nearly returned to Europe merely to see the results of the atom bomb. Lucky for me, you've festered the lad's interest in stars."

"It's like us, Pappa," Raphael said and drew the Baron's and Darius's gaze to see his quiet conviction, bright blue eyes shining. "Orion's always been Orion. Aye, and he just dances aboot in anoother place up in the sky. He dinnae change. And Hailey's Comet, too, Pappa. He's cooming back. Sooch the magazines saying. 'Member when we saw him?" he said while looking up at the Baron, who studied him more like an interesting lab specimen. "Joost like us, he keeps going and coming aboot. He doesnae change. They're like us. We're like them. You're Taurus, father," he said with a musing note.

"I should be glad you've not likened me to Scorpio, eh?"

"Oh, no. You're no spidery thing, Pappa. You're the bull," he said gravely.

"Who do you see yourself as, then, I'd wonder."

"I'm Gemini!" he said happily, his soft lips quivering. "Aye, two in the same thing."

The Baron harrumphed a sound and glanced at Darius. "What of your brother?"

"Oh, he's Orion," Raphael said offhandedly and danced a glance off Darius up to his father. "But maybe its joost me own wishful thinking. I sure wid like to go camping again."

"Orion," the Baron pondered and looked at Darius with a darker amusement. "The hunter, are you, lad? And a lucky thing, so it might be," he added. "I've a thought, we've lost track of our lass."

All humor gone, Darius studied the dark shine and noted the sparks of red, genuine anger. Jenna. Allegedly, she was reasonably safe and contained in Hugh's presence. The wedding was two days away. By the Baron's influence, Hubert wasn't expecting any visitors until the following evening, and he wouldn't dare risk harming her too early. According to Amad, their enemy sought a great deal of information and worked most of his manipulations through Hugh and others within the winery. Joseph wasn't about to tip his hand too soon or make a move before he knew the baron had arrived within his physical realm.

Something had gone wrong, Darius knew as he looked into the empty blue eyes. "What's happened?"

"Well, I mentioned this minx has given me a time, and now, you need only thank yourself for the present circumstance," Amad said, mocking indifference. "Had you not broken the bloody curse, I'd have slightly more dominion. The fact is, son, when you ascended, several residual effects spiraled outward. One, predominantly, affected the lass from what I can gather. She is, after all, carrying a Brock in her womb. A Brock, my lad. Having said as much, possibly you can work out the details."

The curse on the Brock clan had lifted . . . Amad von Hendricks no longer held a grudge nor any dominion. By extension, the Baron could no longer meddle in Jenna's mind without possibly affecting the fate of the Brock. Oh, and this wasn't an irony that Darius wanted to consider in great depth. After four hundred years, to have this curse broken, the lines severed . . . at the precise moment when that blasted connection could have done some good. "Damnation," Darius uttered, his gaze heated. "So, what exactly happened?" he growled. "Do you even know?"

"Suppose to an extent," he said smoothly. "Though I'm suffering a communication breakdown," he said. "Our lass apparently decided to take matters into her own hands. I'm sure the name Evan Trevane rings a bell in your mind, eh?"

"PR man in the Pittsburgh offices," Darius agreed, slightly more curious. "What has he to do with any of this?"

"Grand question," Amad said dryly. "One I should like to ask him, the moment I see him."

"The chap's name didn't just pop out of the woodwork, Amad," Darius growled. "Is Jenna with him?"

"I'd have to say, that's a possibility," the Baron said, enjoying his game. "Appears, Hugh received that 'chap' as unexpected company this evening.

As I understand, this lad suggested to my dear brother, that his dear brother—moi—enlisted his—this chap's services. He was rather convincing, even to my ears, so stating that I'd sent him ahead to manage the press corps, which could likely arrive at the winery gates starting early tomorrow morning. My thought is this . . . Our lass snuck about and made a phone call or two, one of which must have beckoned this savior, who has henceforth snatched the dear lass from my dear brother's clutches. There, lad, is the situation in all its critical mass."

"The bloody hell it is," Darius stated. "After all your blasted boasting of security, you're telling me Jenna and Evan merely walked out of the damned house, and you didn't enlist a single soul to bloody stop them?"

"Lad, there's where the bulk of a second critical mass comes into play. This chap landed a serious blow to both of my key security personnel. Took them out, silent and wily as a ghost. And that presents several more questions."

"Joseph . . . Evan?" Darius asked while fleeting a thought of Evan Trevane, doubting it. "I don't see that as a possibility, Amad. I know, Evan. I spent a bit of time with him over the course of those few days at the hotel. If he were in league with Joseph, I should have at least suspected."

"Lad, no offense to you, but you were mortal when you spent time with that chap," Amad said smoothly.

"I'd have at least suspected," Darius stated.

"Ever see him in full sunlight?"

"I haven't walked in full sunlight for longer than I can remember, Amad, save for that single day in Pittsburgh, and even then, I preferred the shade."

The Baron studied him a moment, then reached over with an open palm, stating, "Give me your right hand a moment."

Considering momentarily, Darius obliged and offered his hand in a similar open palm fashion, watching as the Baron clasped his hand from beneath, and looked as if he might engage in a twisted rendition of thumb wrestling. Instead, the Baron skimmed his thumb over Darius's thumb, drawing his attention to the scar. Lifting his gaze sharply, Darius ran into the cobalt eyes, doubting the implication.

"Do you by chance, recall the evening I found you in Halbrook's crypt?"

The memory came in an eye-blink . . . his hands trembling with a need to wrap around that squat neck, his anger rising.

"Think about it," Amad said simply and withdrew his hand, his gaze unmoving.

Darius remembered the hand locking on his biceps, yanking him back with a quick angry force. He'd landed, jammed in a corner of book-laden shelves, and . . . and he could see the Baron looking into him, holding him against that corner. In memory reflex, he remembered his heart hammering a quicker beat with that dead cobalt stare . . . and his own hand lifting, caught by the wrist until his fist hovered directly in front of him. He had felt the quick pain, a sliver of needle sparks as a sharp nail had slid across the scab over that thin line. Pain, quicksilver pain flashed again as the baron squeezed his thumb beneath the joint. In front of him, the blood raised in a flood from that freshly opened cut . . . and the baron had slashed a tongue across that cut to snatch the blood away. Clearing his more immediate focus, Darius glared into the cobalt eyes. "Should I be surprised by more lies, I wonder?"

"Hmm, you're referring to my admission that I've never tainted you, eh?"

"My entire clan—"

"I didn't lie to you, lad," Amad said smoothly. "Oh, I made a connection. I won't deny that. Looking into your eyes that eve, I knew I'd need to watch you more closely. You had no more or less of my corruption after than before I established that connection, nor, I'll add, have I ever controlled your will or your thoughts by any other than external grasp. I have listened to you, though, and had I ever sensed a need, I might have made demands, but you would never have known my invasion. Therein lies a lesson and a glimpse into the power I've bestowed on you, son," he said in a musing voice. "Now, ask yourself again. Is it possible this Evan Trevane could have been corrupted? Is it impossible to assume he's answering to a master, rather than the drumming of his heartbeat for a woman who stirs his purely human blood? Are you still so damned certain he's not in league with Joseph?"

"Obviously, my certainty isn't important. You're the master in this bloody game and you aren't uncertain enough to offer relief," Darius growled. "I believe it's time you tell me whatever game plan you have in mind."

"A rather simple plan, really, lad," Amad said with a wiry smirk. "When we reach the winery, if we encounter anyone without my scent, we'll consider them free game, whether they wear human or otherworldly fragrances. I am guessing, but I believe we may have quite a reception committee awaiting our arrival, but not as many as we might have had if we'd intended to arrive tomorrow."

"What if Joseph anticipated our early arrival?"

"Hmm, do I detect a wavering of trust? A touch of doubt that I would play this game with anything other than perfect strategy?"

"I wouldn't trust you to follow a schedule, even if you drew the plans in blood. Assuming this chap's not entirely daft, he should likewise anticipate such dereliction," Darius said bluntly. "And your cryptic style of outlining your strategy doesn't improve my frame of mind, nor engender trust."

"Lad, you've come into the game rather late in the play," Amad mused, and his dark eyes conveyed a more cryptic shine.

"And?"

"I have every faith in your ability to analyze details and reach sound conclusions, lad. I'm sure you'll work this out with no help from me."

The wedding, Darius realized in a flashing instant. This plotted wedding? Somehow this entire ordeal configured into the strategy, and Amad had just lied to him again! This wretched monster might have known as much as two years ago . . . or eight . . . where they would be at this moment.

Where the Baron's influence and genuine coincidence parted remained a mystery.

"Buckle up, lads," Amad said with a glance at their predominantly human companions. "I believe we're going aground, and it's likely to be a bit of a rocky ride."

Darius needed only another half second to realize they weren't putting down on a landing strip and the craft had already dipped into a rapid descent. Through the window, he glimpsed only darkness below and purple black sky to either side. No landing strip. His gaze slid toward Amad, who dropped a hand over the child's middle and clasped another over the boy's head, covering his wide blue eyes. Only amusement shined in the cobalt orbs. "Don't tell me," Darius mused. "We're landing in their backyard?"

"For shame, Darius. Do you believe for an instant, I'd enter my home through a backdoor?"

"How much time will we have?" Darius asked, not doubting for a moment,

"To avoid the ground troops awaiting us at the airport?" Amad shrugged, smirking. "More than enough to immobilize those around the house, I'd imagine. About now, our friends in the FBI . . . Hmm, yes. They're in place. Should be interesting to see."

Considering, Darius asked, "And to find Joseph?"

"Joseph's never been lost," he answered with a black shine.

CHAPTER 26

"If you're right about Hugh, we'll never make it to the main road," Evan stated as he slammed the gas, and the car skidded from the parking space alongside the house. "You said a phone . . . I think I know where we could find one."

"The homestead," Jenna acknowledged, half turned in the seat and watching, expecting to see a dozen bodies giving chase through the backdoors or across the snow-scaped lawns. No one flooded through arches or raced through the neon spotlights. Not a single soul had they encountered since dashing through the halls and stairwell. She'd heard the activity in the kitchen as she and Evan had hurried into the connecting hall, natural sounds of pans clanging, spoons and dishes scraping. No shouted anxious voices or orders.

Only after they sped past the last dwelling, Jenna settled sideways in the passenger seat, looking at Evan. "There's security around the homestead, too, Evan."

"Let me worry about that, dear," he said tensely. "Unless I'm mistaken, there's a way to get to the homestead from this lane—" He barely paused a beat to swing the small car into the back lane then flashed her a worried glance. "It's been a few years since I was up here," he said. "If I remember right, there's a lot of turns between Hugh's place and the main house. If you know a direct route, it could save some time."

A niggling thought threatened the edges of her mind, then clamored like a brass bell. 'Trust no one.' Darius's deep baritone voice echoed once more through her mind, and a cold gripping fear nearly froze the air in her lungs. Evan was here. His face turned forward toward the lane, his worried expression illuminated in the gauge lights from the dashboard. He wore a pullover sweater and corduroys, hadn't even stopped to grab a coat before making a mad dash through the house to this car. No security guards. No FBI agents with a private agenda, stationed in the hall where they'd usually lingered in Jenna faded memories. No one affiliated with the von Hendricks Corporation . . . but Hugh was the killer, the psycho. Likely the inside man that the FBI had believed inside the corporation. And Evan had been invited to the wedding? A wedding intended as a trap to remove the elder brother? Wrong! Something was wrong with her savior's presence, his timely arrival . . .

And thinking back in rapid sequence, Jenna remembered. Evan had attended the PR bash at the Chateau Suites. She'd met him only moments before meeting Darius in that banquet hall.

Not a sound, not a warning, not a raging curse had Evan uttered before he'd ripped Hugh off her and hammered his jaw with a force to knock the man cold.

'Darius the Great . . .' Those were the first words Evan had spoken to her . . . and she remembered the subtle antagonism in those first moments, in his offhanded comments. Evan had imparted the first mention of Darius's past . . . had mentioned the rise from alleged poverty to his current station. Evan had backed off . . . had withdrawn his initial intention to flirt with her, had seemed only to be waiting in the wings, she realized with a thought of him greeting her on that first morning after Darius's departure. Now, here he was again . . . cold-cocking a man who could undoubtedly ruin him, racing her away from a madhouse based exclusively on her word and hysteria?

Trust no one.

But did she have a choice? It wasn't as if she could dive from the car and find refuge around a corner! Unless she wanted to return to Hugh's house of horrors, his madness and promise of pain, she had no choice other than to trust Evan Trevane's offer for rescue and hope to God she could reach a telephone.

Reaching that single conclusion, she turned her attention to the headlight beams, searching for a landmark. Hazy, she remembered those first walks on this lane. On foot, the walk took nearly a half hour. By car, less than five minutes. Already, they traveled around one of the last bends before the lane split and branched, either to reach the homestead or spiral deeper into the winery. Mounds of snow remained heaped along the edges of the lane, but the barren limbs had shed the white mantel of recent snowfalls. A spiderweb tangle of black vines blotched the platinum sky overheard.

"Keep to the right," Jenna stated as Evan sped out of the bend. Stout trees, the trunks nearly buried in mounds, formed the fork in the road. Instinctively, Jenna grabbed the dashboard as the car skidded and Evan uttered a curse, bringing the car under control before careening off the mound of snow in their path.

"Christ, there's a lot of snow up here," he huffed, sounding as naturally annoyed as he was relieved to have avoided the collision. His gaze flashed to her; his brow notched in worry. "Do you know how much further?"

"A few caretaker huts are right up here. We'll need to leave the car," she answered. "Better slow down."

"Damn, I forgot about those cabins. It was like a village or something. Me and Lisa . . ." His voice trailed absently, then, "We can't leave the car. I'll slow down, but I don't think we can afford to waste any time," he decided. "I don't know what the hell's going on here, but I knew something wasn't right. Hugh was acting a little strange . . . What's this all about? Do you have any idea?" his eyes flashed over, tense, worried. "You said he's . . . Hugh's the killer? You mean in Pittsburgh?"

"Yes," she said, refusing to acknowledge any hint of doubt. When all else fails, stick to the original scenario, regardless of how badly another thought threatened to reach the foreground. "I think he's trying to take over the von Hendricks fortunes! I think he's using me—this wedding—to lure his brother here, and I think he intends to kill him. I know Hugh doesn't plan to marry me," she said in rushed words. "We need to warn his brother. Hugh's crazy, Evan."

He flashed another glance while slowing the car. "Somehow, I don't doubt that in the least," he said and turned his attention to the lane ahead, passing the first cottage at a safe, reasonable speed.

Hugh, she feared, wasn't the only crazy one. She tamped the thought with fierce determination. As long as she clung to that belief, there was a chance she could reach a phone, make those calls, alert the authorities. Still holding onto the dashboard, she watched the last cabin pass, not entirely relieved. If only she could run to Emma for help. No one. Not one single person in this winter wilderness would help her.

The car skidded stopped; the headlights extinguished.

Through the trees, the floodlights of the small parking lot glowed neon, but Jenna remembered the wooded entrance, the gardens. "There's a path through the trees," she stated. "If we can get to the backdoor, I should be able to shut off the alarms." Unless Hugh had changed the code.

"That'll be the first place they look for us," he stated. "When I was up here last, the main house wasn't entirely open, but they'd already opened the brewery for tourism. We'd probably have an easier time getting in there," he said while yanking his door. "Surely, we'll find a phone there. Even if it's just for security purposes."

With a hazy memory of attempting to make a call once before, Jenna realized Evan's accuracy. Hugh would check the homestead first. Was there a phone in the winery, though? In a hazy memory, she recalled visiting the winery, seeing the immense wooden vats and tremendous oak rafters. Evan was probably right. There would be a phone, but she couldn't recall seeing one. The homestead would be easier, quicker. Except, she hadn't grabbed the blasted keys. The house would explode like a lighthouse beacon.

Sliding from the car as Evan slid from the other side, Jenna listened for the sounds of anxious voices or car engines. By now, Hugh would be awake, and he probably had every state and local lawman, not to mention federal agents on her trail. Not a sound, though. She heard nothing beyond a distant, distinctive sound of an airplane muffled through the mantel of heavy clouds overhead. Catching up to Evan at the front of the car, she clasped his offered hand, feeling the chill of his fingers as he huffed, "We better hurry."

Surrealistic, the neon glow from the parking lot sprinkled through the trees, casting long, twisted shadows ahead. They couldn't leave the lane. Not as meticulously, the snow mounded, high and undoubtedly deep within the wild tangle to either side. Silence. Preternatural, the silence lingered, enhancing the scrape of her soles on the gravel, the huff of her breath as she broke into a trot with Evan's hand keeping a firm hold. Only a single carriage light glowed at the entrance to the winery, despite the wide plowed path to the entrances.

As they ran the last dozen strides to the door, Jenna barely fleeted a thought of how they might break through the heavy oak panels when she saw one begin to move. A trap . . . someone waiting! In a split second, she reversed her pull, skidding and pivoting, but Evan was faster, spinning with her, sweeping his arm about her waist and hoisting her off her feet. "Evannn!"

"It's alright, Jenna," he said in a low, empty tone. "They're friends."

Not a landing strip. As the wheels touched down, Darius felt the drag and bump, heard the human gasps of fright as he spied the distant glow of neon light marking Hugh's domain.

"Raphael," the Baron spoke conversationally. "You'll stay with Darius. For safety sake, Kevin, you and Teddy will enter the cockpit and lockup tight. Sadly, Brian, you and George will need remain in this section of the craft along with the pilot and stewards. If things should go badly, Kevin, you may need to fend off an attack from these lads. That said, lest you prefer becoming thralls to Joseph, you'll do well to await the sunlight before opening the hatches to make good your escape."

"I'd prefer to join this battle," Kevin said smoothly.

"Lad, as much as I've always appreciated your courage, you're not fairly equipped to be effective. Remain with the craft and await the sunlight unless one of us returns before the dawn. No others should you trust."

Rising off his seat as the craft bounced to a halt, Darius reached the door a half step behind Amad, Raphael between them.

While disengaging the door, Amad looked over his shoulder. "Time to hunt, Orion. You know the lass's scent. I assume you won't waste time catching it. Protect what's ours. I'll deal with Joseph."

"If he's hurt her, he's mine," Darius said bluntly.

Amad smiled as he looked down at Raphael, "Ready for a jaunt, lad?"

They were out the door, already flying across the snowy landscape before hitting the lane ahead of the aircraft. On a dozen planes, Darius drew in the scents and flavors, drawing in the sensations on every level to know even when Raphael's panic ascended in his wake. The child was no match for this race and with a whisp of thought, Darius pivoted and caught the boy, lifting him, pivoting and voicing a low, "Hold on, lad."

"Aye, soound advice," the boy huffed and flung his arms about Darius's neck.

Several lengths ahead, the Baron maintained a steady pace, speaking as if they were merely walking the lane at a leisurely pace. "I should have paid this winery a visit long before now," he commented. "It's rather interesting to note, all those in my thrall are more accurately in Joseph's control now. Credit where it's due, the lad's been clever."

"What does that mean in reference to our current assault?" Darius wondered as he poured on speed, picking up the rancid scent that he'd first identified in the Chateau Suites. A fetid scent, like something long dead, tinged the more natural crisp scents. He caught another scent though, enhanced a hundredfold in his mind. Jenna. Her aroma.

"Currently, lad, we've few allies in the reception party ahead," the Baron said in a musing tone. "Even our dear friends in the Federal Bureau have been turned and their loyalties now rest with Joseph. Ahhh, but there's a touch of humanity here," he mused as they raced closer to the grove where the lights softened and splashed through the trees. "Vanity. Joseph's adopted something of my nature to protect his living heirs." The Baron drew in a deep breath and sighed, "Emma Chauncy," he said smoothly. "He's left her pure and what a rage she must inspire."

"Emma, the curator of your house?"

"Aye, and I'm a man of my word," the Baron mused. "As I once promised him, I've never taken another nip from his bloodlines, but there's his pity. The lass was born of a thrall in my keep and tis a fact, she's still loyal to the von Hendricks."

"You're following Joseph's scent," Darius stated.

"Yes."

"I'm following Jenna's scent," he stated.

"Hopefully, yes," the Baron commented.

"And we're still traveling in the same direction."

"Hurrry," Raphael growled.

Kicking and struggling, Jenna gained only a fleeting glimpse of the others stepping out, circling and closing in behind her as Evan carried her through the open door. What the hell was going on here! What! "Evan! Put me down!" she heaved angrily as dull watt bulbs ignited around them.

"It's pointless to struggle, Jenna," he said in a lower pitch as he eased her down onto her feet, clasping her hands.

Gathering her footing, she looked up at him and her thoughts halted. This was, and wasn't, the man she;d met at Christmas. Caught, trapped within the unnatural shine of his pale blue eyes, she stared up at him, too clearly seeing the more prominent brows, the longer cut of his jaw and twist in his bearded lips. He seemed to smile, but no comfort came in that revelation. His blond hair mussed, barely fell over the length of his forehead . . . and he seemed taller, or hulking. In a fleeting instant, Jenna remembered . . . Lisa Blythe. A nightmare fight within her apartment, a crazy nightmare where Blythe had appeared more the monster than human. Here, now, stood Evan Trevane in the same metamorphose, and she wondered absently if she were suffering a hallucination—if she'd lost her mind entirely in Hugh von Hendrick's presence. Slowly, she looked around at the others, recognizing the faces of Hugh's staff, from the gardener to the security men who traipsed through the neon lights around Hugh's house. A half dozen, maybe more. Her gaze spiraled as she swayed and looked again up into Evan's tinted eyes. "Wha-at is this, Evan . . .?"

"There's someone you need to meet, darling," he said and began tugging her as he turned. "Someone who's been waiting to meet you."

Only for a second, she thought to bulk, but in the next instant, his eyes locked and held. She felt herself moving, turning with him, walking toward the deeper shadows of the winery. As if sleepwalking, she had no control of her legs, but in absent glances, she identified the immense wooden vats, and oak barrels stacked on either side. Behind her, footsteps plodded and shuffled on the stone floor, and at the edges of her mind, struggled to break free of Evan's grip, to reverse this course. Drugged . . . as if drugged again, she answered to another call. Madness! This was madness . . . She needed to run!

Snarling a sound, she tried tugging her hand away, but again, Trevane lanced her with a glance. Clearly, she saw his troubled brow, his thin curled lips within the soft brown beard. Walking as if through quicksand now, the images murky in the dull yellow glow, she retained neither sense to grasp direction nor intention. Moving. She was moving. Descending through shadows, one foot after another on wooden steps. Scents of wet stone and stagnant air touched her tongue and mind. Somewhere far away, barely a flicker of thought, she heard a clink of iron, as if chains rattled. And the light dimmed more, bulbs barely sending off a glow and yet blinding in the tunnel opening ahead.

"You shouldn't have fallen for Darius," the deep, low voice nearly whispered, strained unnaturally. "I could have protected you . . . would have protected you, darling. If you'd have come to me, I could have kept you safe. He couldn't help you then. He can't help you now. And too late for us . . ."

Even in stasis, she understood the words, and her mind fastened, fixated. *Darius.* Nothing else would she allow herself to think or feel, to see. *Darius.*

"We have company in the grove," Amad said lightly. "Do remember your lessons, son. These ones are human by half. You won't kill them, but they'll break."

"Can we recruit them?" Darius asked as his gaze riveted on the darkness, piercing the night to recognize the living shapes gathering. Low, like wolves, the bodies raced through the bush, sounding like a herd of deer to his sensitive ears.

"We could. But we'd waste time," the Baron answered smoothly.

Once standing in their shoes, however briefly, Darius gained insight to know they felt his advance, his presence. Already he moved too fast for the naked human eye, even tainted. As if the order and sequence of time had slowed—or sped up to feel natural in his mind—he watched them moving in slow motion. In fleeting instants, he located them, each and every one, despite how quickly he advanced on the grove. Vertigo. He was still too new to the changes inside of him. Moving outside the natural realm, he heard the anxious whispers of two men who sensed his advance. His shadow slipped across the snowy landscape as insubstantial as air. Five men, he counted, and in a split second, he countered the Baron's suggestion to stop and engage in combat. Jenna. Somewhere ahead, Jenna's life hovered in a precarious balance. He needed to reach her!

As Darius swept past the first men, the Baron idled a soft laugh, not slowing his pace as he commented, "You do learn swiftly, lad. A son to make a pappa proud."

"First line of defense," Darius considered. "The weakest. Mere foot soldiers. He'll have his lieutenants closer. Or did you lie to me about those ranks?"

"Almost too honest, so I was," Amad idled. "And you're right. He'll have his strongest line of defense around his lair. Unfortunately, they may be nearly as capable as ourselves. If the other I encountered—that dear Blythe—was any indication, we'll have our hands full. Bear in mind, they're nearly mature."

"Jolly good to tell me now," Darius commented as they sped onto the lane, cutting between the occupied cottages. In a blur, the lighted windows passed, and yet he took in the details of curtains and sensed the abandon within the walls. Others were afoot. Footfalls echoed, racing on some distant lane. Somewhere, possibly a mile away, an engine vibrated, idling. Against him, Raphael trembled, but not in fright. The little devil was more than amply equipped and prepared to battle for his life, despite his slight size. Unfortunately, his size made him vulnerable. "Keep yourself clear when this battle begins, lad," Darius stated firmly as he spotted the abandoned car a short distance ahead.

Jenna. Far more clearly, enhanced, he drew her scent from the car, but the vampire taint lingered just as strong. Evan Trevane. In league with Joseph. A lieutenant, and Darius had never guessed. Human. Fully human, he'd encountered Evan, never imagining the man could be anything more than what he appeared. "You didn't know about Trevane?" Darius wondered.

"He never crossed my mind nor path, lad, and he wasn't exactly key personnel in the Chateau. I assumed we'd dealt with the problem in Pittsburgh when I dispatched Blythe."

On equal wavelengths, Darius slowed at the sight and sense of light ahead, falling into a more natural step at the Baron's side as they moved through the last shadows near the winery entrance. On the surface, all appeared natural, but he sensed the presence behind the closed doors, felt the others stationed not far ahead and tasted their agitation. A half-dozen men on the outside—armed men, he realized, spotting a shotgun barrel laid across a fallen log at the far side of the barn-sized structure.

"We'll need be quick," the Baron commented quietly. "And this might be a good time to part company."

"The toonels below the house, pappa?" Raphael whispered as he settled more naturally on Darius's hip, his feral eyes sprinting to Amad.

"Aye, the very same," Amad said quietly. "If you and your brother take this entrance, I'll come in from the rear."

"I assume Joseph knows both entrances," Darius considered. "Just a thought here, Amad, but wouldn't he expect us to divide?"

"Lad, he may expect me and Raphael, but you'll come as a surprise to him."

"The Baroness would have informed him—" He barely started before realizing Amad's accuracy. Even if the Baroness had informed Joseph of Darius's status as a thrall, she hadn't divulged his newest status. Joseph was expecting only one adult and one child of his own ilk. Ergo, the natural weapons that would certainly prove effective if he was a tad human. That he could avoid a shotgun blast, he had no doubts. "Go then. We'll meet you below," Darius stated as Raphael slipped off his hip within the shadows.

"Steer clear of the lieutenants, elf," Amad stated. "And mind your brother."

"Aye, pappa," Raphael said grimly. "I'll be dealing with the lesser ones, you can be sure."

They were out of time, Darius knew at the same instant as the baron, waking fully to the rapid advance to sound like a deer sprinting through the darkness. A branch jutted from the lead assailant's hand; others rushed from their hiding places with intent to form a gauntlet. Pivoting in motion, coming in low and quick, Darius halted the branch as it swung, slammed his fist to the furry jaw as he yanked the branch away. Not a lieutenant. The huffed breath and grunt, the surprise registered a half second before the man fell under a crack of the wooden staff. Raphael had vanished. There and gone. The Baron had taken flight, and the grunt and crunch of a man falling echoed within the woods toward the lighted parking pavilion. In splitting seconds, Darius wheeled and sprinted a dozen steps, rounding another man who staggered and halted, apparently searching for a victim. With the club still in hand, Darius landed a quick blow, cracking the stout branch with a thud, felling the man in his tracks. In a split second, he heard the huffed breath, the clatter of iron, knowing where Raphael had gone even before he glimpsed the dark sprite-like figure dancing over the fallen log, collecting the rifle at the far end of the building. Whether the lad could fire the weapon, or intended to use it as a club, Darius lent not a moment to guess. Another armed man stood at the nearest corner of the building, poised and ready, his head pivoting in wild jerks to guard the lighted entrance. Further away—at the old homestead, Darius knew—another grunted sound and snarl echoed, marking an another soldier's demise. How many? How many others had Joseph turned? Fleetingly, he wondered as he sped over and under branches, not slowing again until he came behind the armed man. At the last second, the half-man realized his danger and spun. Catching the gun in one hand, the man's neck in the other, Darius drove the man hard against the wall and felt the bones snap under his grip, his senses reeling suddenly with the revelation as he looked into the bulging orbs.

A lieutenant. This one had been a lieutenant in the ranks, as near to a vampire as any living man could attain, but nothing of that revelation salved his instant of dread as he released the dead man. He had killed a man. Without ever a first or second thought of his supernatural strength, he'd just snapped the man's neck. A monster. He was a monster now.

Barely the body slumped within the shadows, sinking, when the arms came up and the feet scrambled. Not dead! Not a man, Darius realized in a fleeting instant. The body tried climbing, the head dangling like a melon to bob at the chest on a broken vine. Not a living man. Not this fellow. His neck unhinged, blood trailing off his parted lips, he grunted sounds while trying to push off the wall, to rise and swing blind. Without a clear thought, Darius pivoted the rifle in his hand and engaged the trigger. The blast shattered the stillness as efficiently as the bullet shattering whatever remained of the man's heart.

Almost at the same instant, Raphael appeared at his side, skidding stop with the shotgun held under his arm. "Well, and he's a goner, now."

"Stay behind me when we pass through the door, lad," Darius said in a voice as alien to him as the sensations quickening through his limbs. Changing. He was changing now, fully. The scent of blood, even tainted, quickened his senses, filling him and overriding whatever remained of his human nature. Joseph. The enemy. Enemies inside. An essence of smoke began spiraling around him, spilling off his lips, swelling rapidly and billowing.

"Blimey," Raphael uttered in an awed whisper. "Yooo've the knack nae different than pappa already, Darius! A fine talent, that!"

Tenfold, he understood his nature fully, but he lent no other thought to the changes, merely accepting, adapting. In the camouflage of his own design, he strode around the corner, walking within fog to the doors, the rifle held loose near his hip. He was no more a man than the beast who might even now be hurting Jenna. The illusion of humanity had fully shattered, a distant memory. Son by blood to a vampire, he tugged open the door letting the mist spiral inside and clasping Raphael's hand, darting through the opening with a speed to defy the semi-human men who hunched in the shadows. Without a second, or even a first thought, he fired the rifle a split second before another weapon could engage.

CHAPTER 27

Trapped in a nightmare from which no escape existed, Jenna stared vacantly at the monstrous image within her line of sight. Clearly, she identified the shadow of human dominion, from the shape of its head and shoulders, to the size of its trunk, but little else resembled a man. Long and gaunt, its face lowered and rose, held aloft by a thick chain at its neck which seemed to hold it in a sitting position against the wall. Round, devoid of eyelids, the red glowing orbs bulged from the sockets above wide, flared nostrils. Logically, it was not a living creature despite how its near human mouth opened and closed and a tongue lashed out, licking over long incisors and thin lips. No. Not a real thing. A nightmare image created by too many drugs. If she ever survived Hugh's torment, she would kill him for making her see monsters. No arms or legs. The beast rocked fore and aft, its rotting stench touching her nostrils despite the dreamscape.

A night haunt to beat all others. She would wake fighting and screaming, bashing herself in the head while fending off this monster in the quick of night.

Rational thought existed in this other world of nightmares.

"Commme closer," the voice spoke only in her mind.

With an iron resolve, paralyzed by instinct, if not rational thought, she stood firm. Whatever this abomination's dominion, she wanted no part of it, not in the physical nor dream realm. On dual planes, she grasped its agitation, its press against her mind, and felt her soles melded to the stone floor.

"Brinnng herrr to mmmeee!" the hissing voice snarled inside her mind and Evan Trevane's hands firmed on her biceps from behind, rekindling the bruises of Hugh's latest assault. More firmly, she molded her feet to the floor and braced against the push, but her flats skidded on the stone. Inside her, her heartbeat raced, hammering, and deeper, a second, quicker beat resounded as something moved within her waist. Her child! Darius's child! Whether this was a wicked nightmare or hallucination, that single thought firmed. Their child! If she allowed this monstrosity to touch her, it would touch her child, taint her child! That revelation blasted the haze and mist from her mind. Pivoting, she took a single step forward, throwing Evan off balance to stumble and in a single move, broke his hold as she spun away from him.

A wine cellar. Racks, wooden racks of dust-laden bottles rose from floor to ceiling on either side of doorway, well away from the beast's reach. Without a clear thought, Jenna dodged another hand meant to grab her, caught the neck of a bottle and whipped it from the rack. Pivoting, she slammed the bottle high. Glass shattered, wine blasted as Evan gasped a startled breath and stepped back. Others, others crowded the doorway, their heads pivoting, eyes glowing. In front of her, Evan growled as he swept the grape from his face and eyes. Not wasting an instant, Jenna pivoted and grabbed two more bottles, ever conscious of the chains rattling, the beast growling and hissing against the deeper wall. The room wasn't large. A single lantern offered a candle watt glow to illuminate the stone walls and ceiling. A wine cellar, she understood, but little else remained clear as she prepared to slam Evan a second time. Real or imagined, a nightmare or a hallucination, she would protect the tiny life swimming and rolling inside of her. Glaring at Evan as he started a forward step, she rejected the strangeness elongating his handsome face, snarling his lips in a grizzly mask. A nightmare image. "Stay the fuck awaaay from me, Evan!" she hissed.

"Put that down, Jenna," he growled through gnarled bearded lips, his eyes heating, glowing.

His eyes! Something about his eyes! She focused on the bearded lips, on the wine dripping and pouring, mixing with a flow of blood from his temple. By instinct, by reason, she held her focus dipped below his red eyes, watching his hands, prepared to swing another bottle, both bottles. "Don't you come a step closer, Evan," she heaved softly. "Not one step—"

"You will do as the master commands," Evan barely finished and started another step.

At the same instant, a shotgun blast resounded, echoing and shattering the silence. She'd heard that sound moments ago . . . at least once, she realized. At the wall, the beast emitted a raging sound and hiss, almost human. Evan froze. The three men at the door pivoted and started moving, but all three rose as if lifted and blown off their feet. In a split second, Jenna knew her mistake to have glimpsed toward those sailing bodies. Even as they landed, slamming the floor, Evan clasped one of her wrists. Wild, she swung her free arm, bringing the bottle down on his shoulder, missing his head. The ancient glass shattered, leaving a more lethal tube of spiked glass in her fist. Her life . . . her child's life! Slammed against the rack at her back, she gained an instant to rake toward Evan's head and kick at his shin, hearing his gasp and growl.

"Enough," a low seething voice commanded, and Jenna reacted as all others, halting in that half second to see the stranger animating over Evan's shoulder. The Baron Amadeus von Hendricks. As vivid as the painted image in the homestead dining room, the Baron Amad von Hendricks stood poised, a ghost fully animated , prepared to rip Evan away from her. Another facet of her nightmare, a ghost animating . . .

In dumbfound, Jenna watched Even ripped away, flung like a string puppet to slam into the deeper shadows at the far wall. Gasping, he crumbled into a heap alongside the abomination, and in slow motion, Jenna lifted her stricken gaze to find the strangely distorted face of the Baron. And he too, had undergone a change.

Feral red, rather than piercing blue, he looked down at her from an incredible height, then turned slightly, standing like a human shield in front of her. "Hello, Joseph," the deep voice resounded in a baritone pitch to silence even the men scrambling across the stone floor. Others advanced. Jenna heard the scrape and thudding footfalls, but nothing could she see beyond the tremendous black image.

Only a step behind Amad, Darius swept into the small room, breathing in the purely human essence of Jenna, darting his gaze to know she stood behind Amad only a few steps away. His attention riveted. His unnatural essence locked onto the ghastly image strung against the stone wall, dangling by a single chain about its neck. Joseph Chauncy, or what remained of him, was little more than a stump of ribs and bones. At Darius's back, Raphael skidded, stopped, and drew a quick gasp. Instinctively, Darius clasped the boy's shoulder in reflection of another moment, in the castle dungeon not long ago. Compared to Joseph, Thaddeus von Hendricks was handsome and lived in splendor. The years hadn't been kind to this beast, and in a heartbeat flash, Darius understood the full breadth of this beast's plot and hatred.

Two hundred years, he considered as he turned his gaze to see the Baron studying the beast, to see Joseph glaring up at him. For two hundred years, this beast had hung from that chain, its arms and legs undoubtedly ripped from the sockets at the onset.

"I can't say it's good to see you," the Baron said conversationally. "Honestly, I'd thought you gone to dust long before now."

"I'll haaave my duuue," the monstrosity snarled.

"Well, suppose you will, lad, but what you may feel is your due and what you receive, may be two different things," Amad said simply.

The monstrosity turned its bulging eyes, its head bobbing as it turned to lance Raphael. "Commme here lllitttle friend."

"Ohhh, Jooseph," Raphael uttered grimly. "Whoot's become of you."

The sadness in the young voice touched Darius to look down, confounded by the bright tears glistening on the round pale cheeks. At nearly the same instant, he sensed the presence and glimpsed motion at their back. Pivoting, he knew an instant of surprise as he rammed the arm skyward to send the gun barrel sailing and Hugh staggering. No lieutenant, but a pawn to that monster's bidding just the same. Blue-black, Hugh's eyes bulged as Darius drove him backward into the narrow tunnel. Parted, Hugh's thin lips emitted a hiss and humph as he slammed the stone, and Darius ripped the gun from his grip, clasping the wrists to slam both hands to the chest. "Nice to see you, Hubert," Darius growled.

"You're going tooo die, Darrrius," Hugh hissed.

With a mere memory flash of all the times he'd fantasized about killing Hugh, his temper rose, and he watched as Hugh's eyes widened more in shock and sudden fear. "You were saying . . ?"

"Y-y-youuu—"

"Darrrius!"

Incisors growing, his rage boiling, he heard the name in stereo, but the rage flowed through him now, and looking down into the stopped, frozen eyes, he watched the images flashing—his own memory glimpses flashing, merging with the dual images of Hugh's memories. In lightening flashes, Darius glimpsed Jenna's fear and felt Hugh's euphoria each time he struck her, belittled her, intimidated her. The growl came from the pit of his stomach as his head tipped of its own accord, his focus drawn to the scrawny neck, the pulsing vein.

"Darius! Nooo!" Raphael cried more desperately.

Beyond reason, beyond control, his focus intent upon the single act of destruction, he had no clear thought of his rage.

Darius! Here! No other thought held firm. He was here, Jenna had glimpsed him if only for an instant before the shadow had sailed through the door, and toward that image she was drawn. Dropping the second of her weapons, Jenna spun off the wall, lunging toward the door and reeled in the entrance to see the hulking image before her. Darius. This was Darius, she knew, if only by the long flowing walnut waves over the black collar of his cashmere coat. His back to her, she gained only a sense of him holding something—someone risen against the wall. Fear! And her own need wrenched the cry from her throat.

"Darius!"

The sound, a snarl—sounded so much like Evan's growl—her heart wrenched and breath halted in her chest. A nightmare! This surely was a nightmare! A wicked hallucination . . . but the towering image halted. Frozen now for an instant with the dark head tilted at an angle.

"Darius!" she heaved softly, uncertainly. In confusion, she felt a small chilly hand clasping hers, halting her, and her attention dropped to the ghostly pale image of the child, Raphael, looking as if he'd stepped from the shadowy portrait in the main house. Time, it seemed, then, slowed. Her senses reeled with a fringe of darkness threatening the edges of her sight. Too much, this was suddenly too much. Ghosts and monsters . . . the drugs. Shaking her head, she swayed her vision toward the hulking image in time to see him turning, and it seemed in slow motion, his profile changed in the dim light. Distorted, she glimpsed red eyes turning to her, like the eyes of a wild animal caught in a headlight beam . . .

Growling deep in his chest, Darius scored Hugh's cheek with his tooth, heard the man's scream of fury and fright, then pivoted, tossing the man aside like a rag as he glimpsed Jenna's started collapse, saw Raphael attempt to catch her. In a lightning swift move, he swept her into her arms, his too feral eyes flashing to find Amad merely looking at him. Across the shadowy room, the beast snarled and rattled its chains, its glowing orbs flashing toward its lieutenant still cowering at the wall.

"Geeettt uuuppp!" the beast snarled toward Trevane.

Merely sighing, Amad looked toward the half-man against the wall, and Trevane growled a more worried sound even as he tried to rise to his master's bid. As Evan collected and lunged, Amad sidestepped and caught the fellow's neck, wrenching him backwards against his chest and slashing his head down.

Darius heard Evan's cry only in the ether. He knew that sound, recognized the fading cry of a dying breath. His own anger defused by the warm, human flesh in his arms, Darius had heart and head to feel a pang of sorrow for Evan, knowing the Baron had no choice.

Amad let the limp body slide and crumble at his feet and turned his gaze to the raging beast against the wall. "Suppose I should have finished you years ago, Joseph," he said in a civil tone, sighing. "But alas, your time has come now."

"III'lll havvve yourrr heeead," the monstrous being snarled.

Amad shook his head almost grimly and strode forward his hand lashing above the beast's head and clasping the chain near the ring even as the bulbous head tried to lunge, and teeth snapped toward his wrist. With a single, seemingly effortless tug, Amad wrenched the ring from the wall, and the bloated trunk jostled like a fish on a hook, its snarl of rage echoing through the tunnels. Yanking the chain up, Amad drove his fist down and slammed the jaw with a crack to mash bone, effectively silencing the beast. Turning with the beast still dangling, jangling and writhing from the chain, Amad glanced to Raphael, then Darius even as he moved toward the wooden wine racks. "Do take my lad out into the tunnel, will you? A bit of unsightly business at hand."

Darius heard the wood splinter even as he insinuated himself in front of the child, turning with him from the shadowed crypt. The scream came only in his mind, and he heard Raphael's silent desperate cry, heard the boy's sorrow for the beast that had once been his friend. Far more clearly, more intensely, he felt Jenna's shudder within his arms, and cradled her closer, catching the scents, drinking in the flavors abounding from her wondrous form. As deeply now as the moment he'd seen her, his insides gripped.

Damned . . . he truly was damned; he knew at this moment. As much as he loved her, he could never again hold her or share the intimacies he'd known so briefly in her arms. Even to kiss her now could taint her.

Forcing Raphael ahead of him, his senses keening to the soles of the damned scraping on the tunnel floor, bodies animated to stumble about, Darius followed the child's black on black shadow within the tunnel. They were nearing the main house, the old homestead, Darius knew, recalling his brief visits to the winery. Once, only once, he'd satisfied his curiosity and taken the tour, stood in awe of the portrait still hanging above the mantel.

Immortality.

His own immortality.

And it struck a mean blow to realize today would have been his thirtieth birthday.

He would be twenty-nine forever.

How? How the bloody hell would he live the next six months, let alone six or sixty years without ever sharing another moment with his love?

His thoughts turning in wicked circles, he carried Jenna through the blackness, only vaguely aware of his unnatural vision eliminating the need for light. Even as they passed through the ancient door into the homestead's stone basement, he lent little thought to his direction.

As if stepping through time, Darius followed Raphael, aware of the boy's hesitation when encountering the red-velvet ropes cordoning off the parlor where he'd undoubtedly dwelt more than a hundred and fifty years ago. Even to his own senses, the soft neon glow casting shadows over the ancient décor remained disorienting. But not enough to halt him stepping over the barrier, lying Jenna on the daybed resting before the drawn velvet drapes. Chilled heart in his hands, fearing even the slight contact with his arms could taint her, he forfeited the warmth and settled to stoop alongside the velvet couch . . . and his attention riveted on the slight bulge at her center. His child. His creation. A natural born child free of curses and condemnation. Enthralled, as if he'd never seen the signs of creation in another woman, he watched the slight ripple of motion, too visible with the sheer blue cloth clinging to the mound.

Distractedly, he glanced to see Raphael arriving at his side, aware of the child nipping his nail with a smile quivering in his lips while at the same time, presenting a paisley-print pillow. As if touching precious glass, Darius lifted Jenna's head and sent signal for Raphael to do the honors. With the utmost care and reverence, suffering only to appear awed, the boy slid the pillow under the bronze hair and stole a second to fleet his slender fingers over a loose lock of silk at Jenna's neck. Like quicksilver, his pale fingers slipped over her cheek and his livid blue eyes lifted to Darius as bright with the thrill as any natural child receiving a rare privilege.

In a hushed voice, Raphael whispered, "Sh-she's beautiful, Darius! Every bit as beautiful as yee remembered in yee dreams." Appearing even more wide-eyed, he flashed his gaze to Jenna and back. "And she's me own long lost cousin, too!"

At the edges of his mind, Darius sensed her waking and for a split second, he considered keeping her asleep, tranced, if only to look upon her . . . and in the next instant, he knew the danger. For her, for his child . . .

All things at once, he knew what he need do, and his heart ached as he watched her long lashes begin to flutter. In one motion, he clasped Raphael's hand and pivoted, intending to whisk them both away.

"Darius?" the soft voice uttered.

To the uncertainty, the hushed fear, Darius halted and in slow motion, turned about to find her stark blue eyes staring up at him. If ever he felt less worthy of a thing, never more than at this moment . . . but he was a man, no longer chained to a monster . . . and he chose not to dwell on his own dominion. In slow motion, he lowered and captured the hand lifting toward him. "Jenna. . ."

Brow furrowed, eyes twitching widening with her waking thoughts, she focused on him exclusively, and in the next moment, she launched into his arms.

Uncontrollably, he gathered her as he'd held her a moment ago, lifting her and landing them on the couch, her cradled on his lap as she buried her face against him. She clung to his neck, holding on for dear lift as the sobs broke against his neck. Whether she believed him real, or a dream, she lent no first or second thought, but took no chances to release him.

Heart wrenching, he tipped his face into her hair, drawing the familiar human scents that had driven him wild even in life. She was his . . . and he knew abruptly, the wicked power of the vampire in him that would never let her go. He would protect her, from now until hell froze, he would protect her and the life she carried in her womb. Ultra sensitive, he heard the tiny heartbeat racing between them, and the paternal instincts that had carried him racing across several countries to save his first born, rose within him now, enhanced a hundredfold. God pity the soul to ever lift a hand against either one of them.

"Y-you're here . . . you're really here," Jenna sobbed, holding tighter.

"I am, luv," he attested, torn between his love for her and his fear of the same. Too new. Far too new to the changes inside of him, he suffered the paradox of his mental and physical desire. He could never lay with her again

. . . but he wanted her more desperately than he'd ever wanted another in his life.

The bouncing motion, soft thudding on carpet, drew Darius from his internal thoughts to find Raphael nibbling his index finger nail and bouncing on his heels in anticipation. Excitement danced in his livid blue eyes and his lips quivered on the verge of laughter. The lad hadn't ventured beyond the castle lands, not once in the last eight years that Darius knew, and his association with the outside world and humans hadn't boded well on him before that. Still, his manner and expression nearly screamed for an introduction.

"In a minute, lad," Darius managed as he absorbed the tremors and shudders wracking the body in his arms. She wasn't calming down, not on her own, not with the muffled words spurting off her lips, citing monsters, and Hugh, and Evan Trevane as a killer. Fearing for her, her sanity, her safety, Darius drew her carefully from her burrowed pose and tilted her head enough to see the shock and fear in her magnificent blue eyes . . . and it was done without a first or second thought. She was asleep, lulling against his shoulder and drawing a soft sighing breath. Finding Raphael's suddenly dismayed gaze, Darius whispered, "We need to get her out of here, lad. I'll introduce you, I promise. But we need to get her to the main house and away from this madness—"

As if timing his entrance, Amad strode into the room, stepping smoothly over the velvet cord and taking in the scene in a glance while lighting his hand on Raphael's shoulder. His expression grim, he commented, "I've sent for the limo. Why don't you and Raphael take our lass up to the house while I tie up the loose ends here and collect your cousins."

"We might need a doctor, Amad," Darius considered, oddly disoriented with the thought. "I'm not sure what all she believes, but she'll probably need something to calm down when she wakes."

"Well now, aren't we the practical ones," Amad mused. "Considering the lass has just suffered the mother of all nightmares, you might want to rearrange a few wires."

"I can't—"

"You don't have to nip her like you did your cousin, son, but you do seem to have a knack for twisting memories into dreams. If I might suggest . . .? Leave Hugh as the monster and I'll have the lad committed."

"I'm keeping my child," Darius stated. "He'll wear the Brock name."

"Humph," the Baron harrumphed and idled. "So, we'll see. Right now, we have a bit of a mess to clean up.

"Humph. Don't we just."

CHAPTER 28

To the sound of deep, lyrical voices, Jenna awoke slowly. Her muscles gripped, on the brink of cramping and an odd hysteria fringed her awareness as her fingers clamped, clinging to a chilly palm. Doubting, she cleared her focus to find the handsome face tipped above her, the dark eyes looking into her with an intensity to match her sudden terror.

"Shhh, luv. You're alright now."

"You . . . you're here. Truly?"

"I am," he said simply and his mustache twitched but the smile never touched his eyes as he continued to study her. "You're safe, now, luv. If nothing else at the moment, believe that, sweetheart. I'm here and I'm not going anywhere."

"But . . ." In wicked flashes, she saw Hugh above her, slamming her to a bed . . . the bed she occupied on the second floor of this monstrosity. In a rapid scan, she identified Hugh's living room, the epitome of class from a grandfather's clock and thick swag curtains, to a sprawling collection of handcrafted couches and chairs of an early American design. They were not alone, and the soft low voices had silenced with her awakening. Momentarily, she wondered if she'd imagine the sounds, then spotted the strangers . . . a half dozen oddly familiar men—and she drew a quick breath at the sight of the fellow in the nearest chair. A phantom image—an apparition stepped from a painting . . . with the younger ghost floating into her line of sight past Darius's shoulder. Her breath stuck looking into the livid blue eyes—laughing, sparkling eyes—beneath a swamp of thick black lashes to lend the child a near feminine appearance.

Full lips turned in a quivering smile, he spoke simply, "Hellow, lass."

"Uhhh." She was speaking to a ghost. Her mind had snapped.

Here was Darius, sitting on a stool alongside the flowered couch cushion, holding her hand, quivering a smile. "Jenna, this is Raphael von Hendricks."

"Of course he is," she said on a breath, accepting the madness spiraling in her mind. "Your picture doesn't do you justice, dear." She managed.

Darius quivered a smile. "I probably should have warned you, luv. The lad looks so much like his namesake, it's downright scary, but I assure you, he's not a ghost. I uhm . . . should also mention, he and his adopted father posed for the painting in the homestead. It's uh . . . I know it's a little off-putting at first."

Real? This child was real.

"I think I'm handsomer," Raphael said as he extended his smooth pale hand into her reach. He appeared real enough, and he dressed in modern garb from crisp blue jeans to a thick blue sweater. With his dark curls shimmering in the lamplight and blue eyes dancing with mischief, Jenna agreed, "You are handsomer, dear, and it's nice to meet you."

"Darius has told me loads about you, lass," the boy spoke with a hint of an accent. "I'm very happy to meet you," he offered while squeezing her hand gently.

Darius lifted a brow toward the boy, appearing slightly amused as he looked down at her. "I might have mentioned that you're the most stunning woman I've ever met."

"What . . . what's going on here, hon?" she asked hesitantly, not at all certain of the reality. "How . . . How are you here? What . . . what's happened."

He sobered on the instant, his mahogany eyes darkened several shades in a few ticks. "You've had a wicked experience, luv. I . . . I don't even know where to begin. We have a doctor—"

"Hugh . . . he meant to kill his brother," she remembered as the panic threatened to rise with the crawlies under her scalp. "He held me . . . I've been a prisoner here."

"That, luv, I learned only yesterday," he said in his dark, compelling voice. "I . . . well, there's no easy way to explain this, but I had an accident. I'm so sorry, Jenna. I would have been here sooner if I'd known—"

Another body stepped into her line of sight, hovering well over the child and Darius's head, and again, Jenna's senses floated with the disorientation. She needed no introduction. Amad von Hencricks. In the flesh.

"I'll accept the blame for his ignorance, Miss Windrow," he said while leaning over to offer his immense palm, his blue eyes glittered in reflection of the child. "Amadeus von Hendricks, at your service." As he clasped her hand, he continued, "In an attempt to keep him clear of the madness in Pittsburgh, I unwittingly put him in greater harms' way. When he nearly fell to his doom, I didn't have the heart to enlighten him of the news—or rather, the lies my brother was spewing. I only recently learned of your plight and for that I apologize."

"He . . . He . . . what's happened to him? Your brother?"

"He won't be bothering you again, madam. At the moment, he's in Federal custody. Eventually, he'll likely be transferred to a mental facility nearer my home in Romania."

"The . . . the mental institution where your grandmother . . .?"

"Likely so," he said grimly and danced his focus over her face. "Are you alright, Miss? I know he brutalized you," he spoke carefully. "We have a doctor coming."

"I don't need—"

"Luv," Darius intervened quietly. "Don't argue, please. For your sake, for our child's sake, please, when the doctor comes, accept her ministrations."

"I . . . I want to go home, Darius," she decided on the instant. "I don't care if Lisa's still . . ." Evan Trevane. Flashing, she saw his face, remembered him dragging her into the winery.

Darius gripped her hand, drawing her from the visions. "Lisa's no longer a threat. Nor uhm . . . nor any others."

"She . . . she was found? She's in custody."

"We think she was another victim, luv," Darius said quietly, carefully, appearing to judge how much to say. "Do you remember Evan coming here, Jenna?"

She held her breath, nodding. "He . . . I thought he meant to rescue me," she admitted, while tears threatened the edge of her eyes. "I-I want to go home, Darius—I'll see a doctor."

"Will you marry me, Jenna?"

A stillness swept through the room, a quietus dropped in her mind. She would have hocked her soul to marry this man just a few short months ago, but now . . . now, was not the time.

"I'm sorry, luv. I shouldn't have said right now. Not tonight. But that's all I could think about since I learned of your condition—even before coming here," he said quietly, sincerely. "I've lived in my own hellish misery for these several months and all I could think about was you. You don't need to answer now. But think about it, luv, and . . . and if you truly want to return home, I'm going with you. Tonight though, you need to rest—"

A throat cleared across the room and Darius flashed a smirk. "Right after I introduce you to a few of my cousins."

"M-more cousins?"

"I think I mentioned I hail from a pretty large clan, luv."

The introductions came in rapid fire, from the oldest, a handsome mid-aged fellow with a New York accent, to a young blond fellow with a French accent, and another young man who appeared slightly timid. Kevin, Teddy and Brian Brock, respectively, and each as handsome as the next. They'd arrived via the company jet, Jenna learned, and landed in the winery rather than the airport. According to Amad, it was either land in the fields or lend Darius a parachute . . . which was how he'd allegedly landed on his death bed. Had she called the headquarters, she wouldn't have heard about his accident. The von Hendricks Corporations was a company to value its privacy, especially with the threat of a killer in the ranks.

In the course of the introductions, Jenna discovered the silk robe and nightgown she wore, and by Darius's expression, realized he'd taken care of that detail, personally.

The nightmare was over. Truly over, and looking into his dark, fathomless brown eyes, she realized her fate was sealed. She loved him and she'd marry him when the time came.

EPILOGUE

Standing in the solarium, watching the moonlight dance on the snowy landscape, Darius sensed the presence arriving without a sound. In front of him, he watched the Baron's reflection animate on the glass, no more than two inches taller than him now, although he couldn't imagine when he'd grown the extra height.

"Likely when you were reborn with my blood," Amad said lightly.

Annoyed instantly with the mentalism, Darius growled. "I'll thank you to steer clear of my thoughts."

"You'll learn to shield in time, my lad. But at the moment, you're shouting."

With an effort, Darius closed his thoughts, erecting a wall and sensing the Baron's appreciation.

"Have you a thought how you'll manage this marriage proposal once she accepts?"

"Suppose it'll depend on where she'd like to live."

"Technically, you still hold a position in my company."

Darius focused on the eyes in the glass. "I won't be traveling the world over."

"Your lass might like to travel," the Baron mused. "Seems to me, she wasn't planted firmly in that apartment of hers. A stopping point or a waystation if you ask me."

"I'll keep my options open, but you know well enough, I've never had a home. It might be nice."

"I know where there's a winery in need of an occupant," the Baron idled, sounding distant suddenly. "Did I ever mention Rosemary?"

"Hm, no. But I recall a painting in the homestead bearing that name."

"Aye, the love of my life," he said listlessly. "I might have remained in America had things worked out differently," he continued of his own accord.

"She said no?"

"She said yes," the Baron commented. "And she's the reason I hung Joseph on that wall and sealed his tomb. After ripping off his arms and legs of course."

Darius tilted his head and eyed the Baron directly. The nobility of yesteryear shined through on his patrician features and stately posture. "Bloody hell," Darius uttered. "That idiot drained her."

"His first attempt to ruin me for giving him my gift of eternal life," Amad said and looked over. "Death was too good for him . . . and I couldn't fathom living here without her. She . . . she knew me for who I am and loved me still. Loved Raphael as well, though the lad fairly put her at wits end. Sometimes," he spoke while looking out at the silvery panorama. "I still hear her exasperation before she'd burst out laughing over one or another of his antics."

"He's never mentioned her."

"He never will," the Baron stated. "Nor will I again," he added and clasped Darius's shoulder. "Your choice, lad, tell her who and what you are, or not. You'll discover the key to aging and it's possible to live in this world despite being an anomaly."

"I won't ever make love to her."

"Lad," the Baron sighed and looked into him with a musing shine. "You have a virile, taint-free cousin in the next room, and I'd likely bring him for a visit should you want another child. Elsewise, you have a knack for mentalism and it's perhaps, not the same, but you know well enough, I've joined you a time or two on your quest these many years." He shrugged. "Up to you, lad, but it's an option."

"You've truly lifted the Brock curse."

"Aye, lad. Your clan's safe unless they cross me—or you—for that matter," he said darkly and shrugged. "I protect what's mine. And you are still that."

Long after the Baron returned to the main house, Darius stood contemplating the words. A normal life. A natural life might be beyond his reach. But a life still existed, and he loved her still, if not all the more.

Perhaps, he hadn't died in that study. Or life after death truly existed.

COMING SOON

MOURNING CHILD

Turn the page for a sneak peek at the next

Paranormal Mystery

by

J. K. Grueber!

Mourning Child

Chapter One

Standing at the head of the gathering, accepting and resenting that honor, Kip Patterson listened to the unfamiliar voice, chanting all too familiar words. A tribute to death, a testament to life. The words flowed over the physical remains of a woman Kip had respected, if not admired, from a distance. Behind him, cloth rustled, soles shuffled on the marble floor, an occasional muffled cough or sniff spread contagiously to create a constant background static. Those sounds, too, were familiar. The crunch of a solemn crowd packed into a comparably small room, a familiar room, a room from his past.

Déjà vu in reverse, Kip considered. Absently, his gaze listed past mounds of flowers. He'd stood inside this mausoleum once, if not a hundred times in the past. In brass wall sconces, electric candles glowed somberly against the marbleized squares, illuminating brass plaques inscribed with generations of family names. He might have read all the names carved on the plaques. Might have stood, committing the legends to memory for as familiar as the sights appeared to him. Overhead, the cathedral ceiling, a masterpiece of narrow tongue-and-groove strips in the pre-turn of the century design, shined to the patina of glass. Original, perhaps, but not authentic. The mausoleum was barely twenty years old, built in the early sixties. By design, the building remained symmetrical with the ancient headstones and Gothic black pillars at the entrance.

Misty Haven Cemetery—Whistlebrook Nursing Home. By style, by essence, the landmarks coexisted as Kip's childhood haunt.

The twitch in his mustache evoked nothing of humor as his abstract gaze returned to the everlasting vessel prostrate before him. His attention caught, held on the gold ribbon scrolled across a spread of red poinsettias. *Beloved Mother.* Even to his inner ear, those words sounded hollow and foreign, as if he'd finally found a language for which he possessed no quick grasp. Ironic, the words scrolled in English and basic cursive script. He certainly should understand those words. Simple, basic words.

Beloved Mother.

Had she arranged for that spread personally? Or had Bill Bickerman, her righthand man, or the *good doctor* Frances ordered the flowers? Marilyn had certainly left nothing to chance. From what Kip recalled of the past three days, his mother had arranged every detail, as much a stickler in death as in life.

Well, why not? She'd been alive when planning this auspicious occasion. It wouldn't surprise him to learn she'd posted an ad in the Randall Trib seeking a stand-in son to replace him in case he had business elsewhere. Clearly, he pictured her sitting primly in her winged-back-office chair, conducting auditions as efficiently as she ran interviews.

Another twitch affected his mustached lips, but nothing of genuine amusement touched his gray eyes or busy mind. Undecided between annoyance and anger, or simple admiration for the lady's countenance, Kip stood in regimental balance. Uncontrollably, his stomach protested the cloying floral perfumes as he stared at the crimson petals in perfect contrast to the emerald casket. She must have planned the Christmas décor, anticipating the season of her departure.

His attention snagged on the glistening brass and an almost overwhelming urge to throw the latches and yank open the casket gripped him. He hadn't seen her, not once laid eyes upon her since his arrival, and that thought bothered him more than he cared to consider. How dare she deny him that honor and right? To see her one last time?

She'd known she was dying. Eight months ago, she'd known she wouldn't last another full year, but apparently, that detail had slipped her mind four months ago when they'd met at the airport. Or had she truly believed it wouldn't matter to him one way or another? Damn it, he should have known. He should have seen...

With an iron resolve, Kip halted that thought, steeling his nerve and concentrating in time to hear Fr. Jordan's words.

"In the name of the Father and of the Son and of the Holy Spirit. Amen."

"Amen," Kip mouthed silently, if only to justify his single contribution to this ordeal. Whether adding the Catholic service represented a blessing or a final mockery of their relationship, Kip neither knew nor cared. Enlisting a priest seemed appropriate, and on that decision, he'd stood resolute.

"This concludes our interment services," a deep, hauntingly familiar voice intruded on the moment of silence. "Mr. Patterson has asked me to invite all of you to attend a luncheon being held at Whistlebrook in Marilyn's honor . . ."

"Mr. Patterson?"

Jolting at the hand touching his elbow, Kip glanced at the intent brown eyes. Fr. Jordan. But for an instant, the face belonged to a younger man, a bearded fellow with a spark of mischief to enthrall one lonely child.

'New hat?' the young priest asked, tapping the brim of the Brook's Bros. with just enough force to knock the crown to Kip's nose.

Automated, Kip tipped his abstracted gaze, catching briefly on the gold inscription 'Beloved Mother.' *His Mother.*

"You have my deepest sympathies," Fr. Jordan spoke in a gentle cadence inherent to his profession.

"Thank you," Kip answered and released one hand from his hat brim, clasping the proffered hand firmly. "Beautiful service," he managed awkwardly, uncertain of the protocol. Fifteen years—fifteen years had passed since he'd last attended a funeral and some memories were better left buried. "Thank you, sir."

Bodies shifted around them, voices subdued, sniffing. Before Jordan could offer further solace, another hand landed on Kip's shoulder. Fitzpatrick, the younger Fitzpatrick. Déjà vu in reverse.

Robert, eldest son and heir apparent to Fitzpatrick's Funeral Home, wore a grim smile, undoubtedly perfected in some elective mortician's class. Grim Smile 101. But he appeared sincere, eliciting only sorrow as he enlisted body language to steer Kip from the casket. "We'll drive you to Whistlebrook," the mortician spoke in are served tone while insinuating himself between Kip and the brass poles. "My father and I plan to attend the reception."

In an odd instant, Kip froze, his attention riveted past Fitzpatrick's lean shoulder, landing on the emerald casing. This was it—the last time he would see that ominous box. Gripped in wicked tension, Kip suffered an unbearable urge to snap the clasps and yank open the lid. Pandora's box . .
.

Marilyn's box!

An internal shudder sailed from his curly blond head to his shined-black heels, but as Kip turn toward the coffin, an arm slid about his elbow, tugging his shoulder. Abstracted, his attention dropped and snagged on the little woman shuffling against him. Rounded and flushed, almost glossier red than the crimson lipstick on her quivering lips, the woman's upturned face appeared wrecked. Blood-streaked brown eyes lifted, searching him . . . and Kip braced as if doused in a tumbler of ice water as the revelation slammed him. Edna Feeney . . . Nan Feeney.

He'd known this little woman his entire life, but her appearance had thrown him. He'd never seen her outside the Home, outside her element.

Rather than the usual food-stained white apron and black hairnet, a sheer black scarf covered her mound of puffy auburn hair, and at close range, Kip spotted the silver strands in the curl above her creased brow. The Yin to Marilyn's Yang, Edna had never embraced a fad, neither brow-plucking nor hairstyle, and the fashion industry had never made a nickel on her wardrobe. Even on this most auspicious occasion, she wore a sensible, teal-colored wool coat over a simple black skirt and blazer. Costume pearl clip-on earrings and a colorful beaded necklace accented her ensemble of black flats and practical brown handbag.

Disoriented, Kip's attention flashed past the scarf, landing, locking on the emerald vessel. Already, Fitzpatrick's assistants had begun removing the bouquets and flower arrangements from the pedestals around the casket. The service and rituals had ended. A 3'x8' foot hole awaited—*impossible!* Marilyn Patterson could not rest inside that blasted box! Four months ago, she'd joined him at a restaurant near the airport, late as usual, but her colors . . . *damn it!*

She was gone. Her remains rested inside that casket.

According to the elder John Fitzpatrick, Marilyn had demanded a closed casket, refusing even to consider allowing a troop of strangers to ogle her remains. Despite the elder mortician's reassurance and a sense of Marilyn's vanity; however, Kip knew she'd considered only one stranger when arranging her final ride and the revelation struck a wicked blow.

As much anger as pain flashed through his mind as he accepted the press of bodies turning him, directing him toward the entrance. Slipping his arm free of Edna's grasp, he glimpsed her pained eyes as he rested his arm more comfortably about her shoulder. At his shoulder blade, another hand rode, nudging him, keeping him moving as if sensing his need to pivot. Vaguely familiar and unfamiliar faces swam around him. A few of his mother's closet friends and associates, like Edna, hovered close to him, forming a gauntlet. Déjà vu in reverse. He'd seen these same listless glazed eyes, the tragic solemn expressions, the sorrowful shine of tears as if choreographed for a stage production. A tragedy. He'd seen all this before, had experienced the same detachment as a spectator.

Readily, the memories assaulted, more wicked than the wind whipping over the hillside and spiraling white powder across the salted stone walk. All the tiny details swept through Kip's mind, from hand gestures to his mother's arm, lifting, embracing a bereaved relative's shoulder, steering the sobbing loved one to a waiting limousine. Fitzpatrick, or another of his ilk, paced the stricken survivors through the rituals from the first viewing to the internment. A priest, pastor, or reverend always hovered close at hand with soft consoling words and reassurances of life everlasting.

Vacantly, Kip accepted dozens of murmured words, arm squeezes and fleeting touches on his black sleeves. Donning his hat, a memento from the past, he tipped the brim low to offset the wind, recalling a time when a slight breeze on the crest of this hill had sent him chasing after his hat. The hat fit him, now. Only a hearty gust of wind would render his head bare.

So many funerals. So damned many deaths. Uncontrollably, Kip shuddered, cursing his thought as he assisted Edna into the rear compartment of the first limousine in the longline. Momentarily, he stood, fanning his shaded gaze over the hillside, collecting impressions, remembering . . . orienting. Snow swirled around tall stone monuments, the wind undaunted. Tall pines and snow-capped hedges lent the oldest cemetery of Randall the aesthetic attraction of a golf course.

Across the lane on the snow swept rise against a backdrop of pines, two suited men stood in a position to survey the entire procession. Despite the hedge and tall emerald pines at their backs, they remained conspicuous, and Kip's attention snagged with a sudden thought of officials. By instinct, his senses keened, watching. One, sporting a pale gray coat, lifted a camera and panned the bodies hustling toward cars along the lane. Officials posing as paparazzi? For an instant, Kip fully doubted the probability of genuine photographers and reporters.

Reality.

Marilyn Patterson had reached celebrity status in Randall. A woman of means, a lady ahead of her time with the foresight and fortitude to preempt the woman's lib movement of the 60s. Somehow, however, her status didn't justify the photographers capturing this event for posterity or the reporters trailing after the State Senator and a half dozen other familiar, famous faces in the dispersing crowd.

In his annoyance, Kip rousted from his ambivalence, suddenly closer to his true nature than at any time in the past two days. Catching Fitzpatrick's sleeve, Kip dipped his head in time to avoid the panning camera and met the slightly older man's mourning gaze. His pale eyes direct, and chilly, shaded beneath the hat brim, Kip stated, "Get rid of the photographers, sir, as well as the reporters if you can. This is a private reception."

Fitzpatrick's gaze darted and anger flashed across his thin lips as he spotted the twosome on the hillside. The father, not the son, this aging mortician had dealt with his share of difficult circumstances. As if chiseled in steel, his jaw stiffened, and his voice lowered an octave. "I'll take care of it, young sir. Rest assured."

Satisfied, Kip started into the car but froze as his attention snagged. Too swiftly that face had pivoted, too smoothly ducked below a wide swooping black hat brim! His heart slammed a nasty beat as the woman turned, flowing into the procession filing toward the line of cars. She was lost—lost in the swarm of dark clad bodies—*the lady in black!*

Lifelike, the image slammed Kip . . . the mists swirling between headstones, as unsettling in memory as in life, fifteen years earlier. He'd only imagined her, then, surely. But how his imagination had run wild in those crazy seconds. Impatient and listless, he'd stood outside the crowd, awaiting his mother, anxious for the drive home. Then he'd seen her. The lady in black. She stood within the mist beyond the crypt, an apparition with a black veil swaying from the brim of a hat, concealing her facial features entirely. He shuddered, now, as he had then. She'd stared at him from behind that veil. He'd felt it. A vision of ill-omen . . . *and death had followed*.

Under his breath, Kip uttered a curse at his probable insanity and ducked into the shadowed compartment. The woman he'd just seen was neither an apparition nor an ill-omen. With his flashing glimpse, he'd identified a fine, slender build and classy style. A New-York-style. She probably worked for the National Enquirer.

Barely restraining a second curse, Kip settled into the seat alongside Edna.

Still sniffing, she wiped her cheeks and eyes with an embroidered handkerchief. And that, too, remained familiar. At a base level, Kip grasped her grief, understood the deep hollow pain she'd suffer in the days or weeks to come. He had no idea how to console her, any more than he knew how to handle the turmoil wrecking his equilibrium. This once, he truly had no control over the events or circumstances around him, and that wasn't a condition he intended to embrace.

The sooner he concluded this affair and boarded a plane to a far more agreeable climate, the better.

His thoughts drifting, Kip gazed through the tinted glass, preferring not to watch the crowd scattering. A mantel of angry gray clouds suspended above the towering pines—the promise of more snow too blasted obvious. And as much as he'd once loved a decent snowfall, the mere thought tipped his precarious balance toward anger.

He should have stayed in California. If he'd been thinking clearly three mornings past, he might have hired a stand-in son to attend this event. God knows, few people would have noticed or known the difference. An imposter—an intruder. He was an intruder here, little more than excess cargo occupying space in a limo reserved for friends and family.

That revelation appealed to him no more now than fifteen or twenty years earlier. Oliver Twist had held nothing over Kippen James Patterson, he considered with a rueful smile.

Without a glance, Kip knew when Bill Bickerman and Dr. Mark Frances entered the shadowy compartment, their presence only confirming and qualifying his dark thoughts. He truly didn't belong here, not in this limo, not in their company. They belonged. Edna Feeney—second in command at Whistlebrook despite what titles any others wore—had lived in the Home forever, a friend and ally, as close as a sister to Marilyn. And Mark Frances, physician, friend . . . hell, probably, her lover, to stand through thick and thin throughout the years. Bickerman had arrived later, but if the past few days were any indication, the man had gained Marilyn's favor and reciprocated in full. They belonged—

"Kip?" the deep strained voice intruded.

Jolted slightly, Kip found Mark Frances studying him grimly and wondered if he were truly as transparent as he felt.

"How are you holding up?"

Once, a very long time ago, the 'good doctor' Frances had been intimidating, if not outright terrifying. With a physique befitting a lumberjack standing well over six feet, the good doctor had always commanded attention. The years hadn't changed him tremendously. He still wore a beard and mustache, and his stark blue eyes possessed a tendency to see far more than one intended. A few errant strands of gray highlighted his beard and temples, sweeping through the neat walnut waves and lending creed to his sophistication. Presently, shadows lingered under his eyes, contradicting the hint of laugh lines webbed at the corners.

As if time stood still at Whistlebrook, the faces, Mark, Edna—a handful of others—remained unchanged.

"Are you alright?" Frances asked more carefully.

"Fine," Kip answered evenly and fleeted an odd distant memory. "Kipper," he said absently. The *good doctor* had called him 'Kipper,' . . . "Like a herring," Kip recalled the doctor professing, and remembered despising that nickname. Although he'd never mustered the courage to admit that detail. He was neither shy, nor a man easily intimidated any longer. "I hated that moniker," he commented, likely verifying his mental capacity . . . or incapacity, as Mark's faint grin and glance at Edna suggested.

"Suppose it's too late to apologize if it offended you," Dr. Frances said lightly, sinking more comfortably into the opposite seat as the limousine rolled forward.

"Suppose it is," Kip agreed and turned his focus through the tinted glass. Tombstones stood like dominos, awaiting a good wind to fall. Passing around the edge of the hill on the ridge road that overlooked a forest valley, the oldest section of Misty Haven came into view. At least two Gothic stone crypts clung to the hillside, braced against the ever-present wind that channeled off the river through ravines and slopes. Some of the smaller slabs and simple masonry crosses listed precariously, as if defying gravity to remain upright. Halfway down the slope, a small court surrounded by short, clipped hedges paid homage to a grand statue of St. John who stood erect, arms spread, palms dropped open, bestowing a blessing. Weathered stone steps descended the hill to reach the sanctuary, where masonry benches offered a quiet retreat and welcome respite from the steep hillside . . . *And someday, he would venture down those steps.*

Barely, Kip suffered the sway of nostalgia when he spotted the mini excavator balanced on the hillside. Only two slight rows of headstones separated the lane from a mound of over turned dirt. A gaping black wound in the snowy landscape designated Marilyn Patterson's final resting place.

His gaze held on the construction site as it passed, but his thoughts veered, recalling more involved projects, the smell of diesel fumes and hot oil, the crunch and grind of gears and explosions of stone. Religiously, Kip visited his new acquisition sat least once in the early stages, despite his firm adherence to anonymity. One more pair of dusty blue jeans, dirty t-shirt and hard hat generally went unnoticed with the size of the crews that Morning Sun Enterprises employed. More than once, Kip had satisfied his dark amusement to spend a day taking orders from a harried foreman of

Neanderthal build and disposition. Demolition sites had always stood high on his list of entertainment. Far more exhilarating than a night at the opera. Only slightly less satisfying than sex, although he wouldn't likely admit that to his latest roommate. Morgan, like dozens of others—long, blond and athletic—believed that her performance rated as the eighth natural wonder. Unfortunately, she couldn't hold a candle to a dozen carefully placed explosives shattering tons of iron, metal, glass and steel into a heap of smoking debris.

Acknowledgments

When I mentioned my next series tipping a little further left of center with the introduction of vampires in our midst, I met with a wide variety of reactions from serious doubt to, '*Ewww, why would you want to do that?*' And my reply, 'Why not?'

Generally, the characters in my novels come alive with full-blown personalities, natural trials, tribulations, and believable obstacles. The Vampire Tales isn't the exception; however, remember, this is a work of fiction. But who's to say that otherworldly entities don't walk among us? Maybe in the coming months, I'll offset this dark tale with the appearance of an angel in the visage of a man or woman.

If you don't believe in demons and angels, then you've never met a few of my friends or looked closely at a few of yours.

So saying, I'd like to mention some of the latter who've shared this journey and welcomed me into their midst beginning with my first novel, COLORS OF ENVY: A Paranormal Romance Mystery. From the organizers, vendors and visitors to several of the holistic health/psychic fairs in Ohio, I've learned a great deal about psychic phenomenon, astrology and the effects of the stars on our daily lives, and the healing power in crystals and stones. The most important take-away that I've gathered from these groups—don't assume the world is black and white. Whether it's a ghost in your closet or an apparition walking down a hall, one's as real as the other.

Thank you, Vanessa Fabec, Event Coordinator, (HHPF, LLC, dba Holistic Health and Psychic Fair,) Rev. Carol Borkoski (Angel Gift Center, LLC, Dillonvale, OH,) Christopher Dennis, Psychic Intuitive Medium, (Akron, OH,) Venette LaRocca, Astrologer, (Your Cosmic Rx,) Rev. Michael Black, Rev. Bryan Peters and Rev. Shane Miklos (The Healing Brew, LLC, Akron, OH.) To Anne, Janet, and countless others who are gifted with talents beyond our immediate grasp and an abstract understanding of our questionable reality, thank you. We all follow our own path to enlightenment, and you are all responsible for shedding light on the quest.

As in the first Vampire Tales novel with the help of Bruce Sanderson and his amazing photography skills, we've created a cover depicting an existing castle in Ohio, USA. Although we've taken liberties with the location and style of the Historical Loveland Castle and Museum, we've maintained the integrity of this historical masterpiece sprawled on the banks of the Little Miami River in Loveland, Ohio. The photograph on the cover of Damned By Death: A Vampire's Hammer offers only a sample of Chateau Laroche's grandeur. Whether you want to explore history via a self-guided tour, picnic on the riverside or participate in one of their special events, a visit to this amazing castle will surely satisfy the adventuring spirit in you.

You won't meet the Baron Amadeus von Hendricks, but you might encounter other interesting entities if you choose to visit.

For the latest news and updates from

J. K. Grueber visit:

Jkgrueber.com

"Thank you for reading!" J. K. Grueber